A True Friend
A Novel

By

Adeline Sergeant

A True Friend
A Novel
by Adeline Sergeant

Copyright © 2024

All Rights reserved.

ISBN: 978-93-62767-51-6

Published by

DOUBLE 9 BOOKS

2/13-B, Ansari Road
Daryaganj, New Delhi – 110002
info@double9books.com
www.double9books.com
Tel. 011-40042856

ABOUT THE AUTHOR

Adeline Sergeant was an English writer. Emily Frances Adeline Sergeant, the second daughter of Richard Sergeant and Jane (Hall), was born in Ashbourne, Derbyshire. She was homeschooled until the age of thirteen, when she began attending school in Weston-super-Mare. Emily's mother wrote children's books under the pen name 'Adeline', which she eventually used for her own writings. At the age of fifteen, Emily's poetry were published in a compilation that garnered favorable reviews in Weslayan periodicals. She got a scholarship to Queen's College, London. Her father died in 1870, and she spent several years as a governess in Riverhead, Kent. Her novel Jacobi's wife earned her a tiny £100 award in 1882, and it was serialized in London. Her writings were serialized in the Dundee newspaper for several years, during which time she resided from 1885 to 1887. Adeline then relocated to Bloomsbury, London, where she made enough money to sustain herself through her writing. In the late 1880s, she became interested in Fabianism and the condition of the impoverished in London. Over her literary career, she wrote over ninety novels, some of which had a religious tone. Her religious beliefs changed throughout time, and she briefly became agnostic in the 1880s. She finally converted to Catholicism at the end of the century.

CONTENTS

CHAPTER I
AN UNSUITABLE FRIENDSHIP 9

CHAPTER II
LADY CAROLINE'S TACTICS 18

CHAPTER III
AT HELMSLEY COURT 25

CHAPTER IV
ON THE ROAD 34

CHAPTER V
WYVIS BRAND 42

CHAPTER VI
JANETTA AT HOME 49

CHAPTER VII
NORA'S NEW ACQUAINTANCE 57

CHAPTER VIII
FATHER AND CHILD 65

CHAPTER IX
CONSULTATION 74

CHAPTER X
MARGARET 81

CHAPTER XI
JANETTA'S PROMISES 89

CHAPTER XII
JANETTA REMONSTRATES 97

CHAPTER XIII
SHADOWS 106

CHAPTER XIV
JANETTA'S FAILURE......112

CHAPTER XV
A BONE OF CONTENTION......119

CHAPTER XVI
SIR PHILIP'S OPINION......126

CHAPTER XVII
MARGARET'S FRIENDSHIP......133

CHAPTER XVIII
A NEW FRIEND......140

CHAPTER XIX
NORA'S PROCEEDINGS......146

CHAPTER XX
AN ELDER BROTHER......153

CHAPTER XXI
CUTHBERT'S ROMANCE......160

CHAPTER XXII
WYVIS BRAND'S IDEAL......167

CHAPTER XXIII
FORGET-ME-NOTS......173

CHAPTER XXIV
LADY ASHLEY'S GARDEN PARTY......180

CHAPTER XXV
SIR PHILIP'S DECISION......185

CHAPTER XXVI
"FREE!"......191

CHAPTER XXVII
A BIG BRIBE......197

CHAPTER XXVIII
"CHANGES MUST COME"......203

CHAPTER XXIX
MARGARET'S CONFESSION......210

CHAPTER XXX
IN REBELLION......217

CHAPTER XXXI
THE PLOUGHMAN'S SON...225

CHAPTER XXXII
THE FAILURE OF MARGARET 232

CHAPTER XXXIII
RETROSPECT..239

CHAPTER XXXIV
FROM DISTANT LANDS..246

CHAPTER XXXV
JULIET..253

CHAPTER XXXVI
THE FRUITS OF A LIE 259

CHAPTER XXXVII
NIGHT...266

CHAPTER XXXVIII
THE LAST SCENE...272

CHAPTER XXXIX
MAKING AMENDS...279

CHAPTER XL
MY FAITHFUL JANET 285

CHAPTER I
AN UNSUITABLE FRIENDSHIP

Janetta was the music governess—a brown little thing of no particular importance, and Margaret Adair was a beauty and an heiress, and the only daughter of people who thought themselves very distinguished indeed; so that the two had not, you might think, very much in common, and were not likely to be attracted one to the other. Yet, in spite of differing circumstances, they were close friends and allies; and had been such ever since they were together at the same fashionable school where Miss Adair was the petted favorite of all, and Janetta Colwyn was the pupil-teacher in the shabbiest of frocks, who got all the snubbing and did most of the hard work. And great offence was given in several directions by Miss Adair's attachment to poor little Janetta.

"It is an unsuitable friendship," Miss Polehampton, the principal of the school, observed on more than one occasion, "and I am sure I do not know how Lady Caroline will like it."

Lady Caroline was, of course, Margaret Adair's mamma.

Miss Polehampton felt her responsibility so keenly in the matter that at last she resolved to speak "very seriously" to her dear Margaret. She always talked of "her dear Margaret," Janetta used to say, when she was going to make herself particularly disagreeable. For "her dear Margaret" was the pet pupil, the show pupil of the establishment: her air of perfect breeding gave distinction, Miss Polehampton thought, to the whole school; and her refinement, her exemplary behavior, her industry, and her talent formed the theme of many a lecture to less accomplished and less decorous pupils. For, contrary to all conventional expectations, Margaret Adair was not stupid, although she was beautiful and well-behaved. She was an exceedingly intelligent girl; she had an aptitude for several arts and accomplishments, and she was remarkable for the delicacy of her taste and the exquisite discrimination of which she sometimes showed herself capable. At the same time she was not as clever—("not as *glaringly* clever," a friend of hers once expressed it)—as little Janetta Colwyn, whose nimble wits gathered knowledge as a bee collects honey under the most unfavorable circumstances. Janetta had to learn her lessons when the other girls had gone to bed, in a little room under the roof; a room which was like an ice-house in winter and an oven in summer; she was never able to be in time for her classes, and she often missed them altogether; but, in spite of these disadvantages, she generally proved herself the most advanced pupil in her division, and if pupil-teachers had been allowed to take prizes, would have carried off every first prize in the school. This, to be sure, was not allowed. It would not have been "the thing" for the little governess-pupil to take away the prizes from the girls whose parents paid between two and three hundred a year for their tuition (the fees were high, because Miss Polehampton's school was so exceedingly fashionable); therefore, Janetta's marks were not counted, and her exercises were put aside and did not come into competition with those of the other girls, and it was generally understood amongst the teachers that, if you wished to stand well with Miss Polehampton, it would be better not to praise Miss Colwyn, but rather to put forward the merits of some charming Lady Mary or Honorable Adeliza, and leave Janetta in the obscurity from which (according to Miss Polehampton) she was fated never to emerge.

Unfortunately for the purposes of the mistress of the school, Janetta was rather a favorite with the girls. She was not adored, like Margaret; she was not looked up to and respected, as was the Honorable Edith Gore; she was nobody's pet, as the little Ladies Blanche and Rose Amberley had been ever since they set foot in the school; but she was everybody's friend and comrade, the recipient of everybody's confidences, the sharer in everybody's joys or woes. The fact was that Janetta had the inestimable gift of sympathy; she understood the difficulties of people around her better than many women of twice her age would have done; and she was so bright and sunny-tempered and quick-witted that her very presence in a room was enough to dispel gloom and ill-temper. She was, therefore, deservedly popular, and did more to keep up the character of Miss Polehampton's school for comfort and cheerfulness than Miss Polehampton herself was ever likely to be aware. And the girl most devoted to Janetta was Margaret Adair.

"Remain for a few moments, Margaret; I wish to speak to you," said Miss Polehampton, majestically, when one evening, directly after prayers, the show pupil advanced to bid her teachers good-night.

The girls all sat round the room on wooden chairs, and Miss Polehampton occupied a high-backed, cushioned seat at a centre table while she read the portion of Scripture with which the day's work concluded. Near her sat the governesses, English, French and German, with little Janetta bringing up the rear in the draughtiest place and the most uncomfortable chair. After prayers, Miss Polehampton and the teachers rose, and their pupils came to bid them good-night, offering hand and cheek to each in turn. There was always a great deal of kissing to be got through on these occasions. Miss Polehampton blandly insisted on kissing all her thirty pupils every evening; it made them feel more as if they were at home, she used to say; and her example was, of course, followed by the teachers and the girls.

Margaret Adair, as one of the oldest and tallest girls in the school, generally came forward first for that evening salute. When Miss Polehampton made the observation just recorded, she stepped back to a position beside her teacher's chair in the demure attitude of a well-behaved schoolgirl—hands crossed over the wrists, feet in position, head and shoulders carefully erect, and eyes gently lowered towards the carpet. Thus standing, she was yet perfectly well aware that Janetta Colwyn gave her an odd, impish little look of mingled fun and anxiety behind Miss Polehampton's back; for it was generally known that a lecture was impending when one of the girls was detained after prayers, and it was very unusual for Margaret to be lectured! Miss Adair did not, however, look discomposed. A momentary smile flitted across her face at Janetta's tiny grimace, but it was instantly succeeded by the look of simple gravity becoming to the occasion.

When the last of the pupils and the last also of the teachers had filed out of the room, Miss Polehampton turned and surveyed the waiting girl with some uncertainty. She was really fond of Margaret Adair. Not only did she bring credit to the school, but she was a good, nice, lady-like girl (such were Miss Polehampton's epithets), and very fair to look upon. Margaret was tall, slender, and exceedingly graceful in her movements; she was delicately fair, and had hair of the silkiest texture and palest gold; her eyes, however, were not blue, as one would have expected them to be; they were hazel brown, and veiled by long brown lashes—eyes of melting softness and dreaminess, peculiarly sweet in expression. Her features were a very little too long and thin for perfect beauty; but they gave her a Madonna-like look of peace and calm which many were ready enthusiastically to admire. And there was no want of expression in her face; its faint rose bloom varied almost at a word, and the thin curved lips were as sensitive to feeling as could be desired. What was wanting in the face was what gave it its peculiar maidenly charm—a lack of passion, a little lack, perhaps, of strength. But at seventeen we look less for these characteristics than for the sweetness and docility which Margaret certainly possessed. Her dress of soft, white muslin was quite simple—the ideal dress for a young girl—and yet it was so beautifully made, so perfectly finished in every detail, that Miss Polehampton never looked at it without an uneasy feeling that she was *too* well-dressed for a schoolgirl. Others wore muslin dresses of apparently the same cut and texture; but what the casual eye might fail to observe, the schoolmistress was perfectly well aware of, namely, that the tiny frills at neck and wrists were of the costliest Mechlin lace, that the hem of the dress was bordered with the same material, as if it had been the commonest of things; that the embroidered white ribbons with which it was trimmed had been woven in France especially for Miss Adair, and that the little silver buckles at her waist and on her shoes were so ancient and beautiful as to be of almost historic importance. The effect was that of simplicity; but it was the costly simplicity of absolute perfection. Margaret's mother was never content unless her child was clothed from head to foot in materials of the softest, finest and best. It was a sort of outward symbol of what she desired for the girl in all relations of life.

This it was that disturbed Miss Polehampton's mind as she stood and looked uneasily for a moment at Margaret Adair. Then she took the girl by the hand.

"Sit down, my dear," she said, in a kind voice, "and let me talk to you for a few moments. I hope you are not tired with standing so long."

"Oh, no, thank you; not at all," Margaret answered, blushing slightly as she took a seat at Miss Polehampton's left hand. She was more intimidated by this unwonted kindness of address than by any imaginable severity. The schoolmistress was tall and imposing in appearance: her manner was usually a little pompous, and it did not seem quite natural to Margaret that she should speak so gently.

"My dear," said Miss Polehampton, "when your dear mamma gave you into my charge, I am sure she considered me responsible for the influences under which you were brought, and the friendships that you made under my roof."

"Mamma knew that I could not be hurt by any friendship that I made *here*," said Margaret, with the softest flattery. She was quite sincere: it was natural to her to say "pretty things" to people.

"Quite so," the schoolmistress admitted. "Quite so, dear Margaret, if you keep within your own grade in society. There is no pupil in this establishment, I am thankful to say, who is not of suitable family and prospects to become your friend. You are young yet, and do not understand the complications in which people sometimes involve themselves by making friendships out of their own sphere. But *I* understand, and I wish to caution you."

"I am not aware that I have made any unsuitable friendships," said Margaret, with a rather proud look in her hazel eyes.

"Well—no, I hope not," said Miss Polehampton with a hesitating little cough. "You understand, my dear, that in an establishment like mine, persons must be employed to do certain work who are not quite equal in position to—to—ourselves. Persons of inferior birth and station, I mean, to whom the care of the younger girls, and certain menial duties, must be committed. These persons, my dear, with whom you must necessarily be brought in contact, and whom I hope you will always treat with perfect courtesy and consideration, need not, at the same time, be made your intimate friends."

"I have never made friends with any of the servants," said Margaret, quietly. Miss Polehampton was somewhat irritated by this remark.

"I do not allude to the servants," she said with momentary sharpness. "I do not consider Miss Colwyn a servant, or I should not, of course, allow her to sit at the same table with you. But there is a sort of familiarity of which I do not altogether approve——"

She paused, and Margaret drew up her head and spoke with unusual decision.

"Miss Colwyn is my greatest friend."

"Yes, my dear, that is what I complain of. Could you not find a friend in your own rank of life without making one of Miss Colwyn?"

"She is quite as good as I am," cried Margaret, indignantly. "Quite as good, far more so, and a great deal cleverer!"

"She has capabilities," said the schoolmistress, with the air of one making a concession; "and I hope that they will be useful to her in her calling. She will probably become a nursery governess, or companion to some lady of superior position. But I cannot believe, my dear that dear Lady Caroline would approve of your singling her out as your especial and particular friend."

"I am sure mamma always likes people who are good and clever," said Margaret. She did not fly into a rage as some girls would have done, but her face flushed, and her breath came more quickly than usual—signs of great excitement on her part, which Miss Polehampton was not slow to observe.

"She likes them in their proper station, my dear. This friendship is not improving for you, nor for Miss Colwyn. Your positions in life are so different that your notice of her can but cause discontent and ill-feeling in her mind. It is exceedingly injudicious, and I cannot think that your dear mamma would approve of it if she knew the circumstances."

"But Janetta's family is not at all badly connected," said Margaret, with some eagerness. "There are cousins of hers living close to us—the next property belongs to them——"

"Do you know them, my dear?"

"I know *about* them," answered Margaret, suddenly coloring very deeply, and looking uncomfortable, "but I don't think I have ever seen them, they are so much away from home——"

"I know *about* them, too," said Miss Polehampton, grimly; "and I do not think that you will ever advance Miss Colwyn's interests by mentioning her connection with that family. I have heard Lady Caroline speak of Mrs. Brand and her children. They are not people, my dear Margaret, whom it is desirable for you to know."

"But Janetta's own people live quite near us," said Margaret, reduced to a very pleading tone. "I know them at home; they live at Beaminster—not three miles off."

"And may I ask if Lady Caroline visits them, my dear?" asked Miss Polehampton, with mild sarcasm, which brought the color again to Margaret's fair face. The girl could not answer; she knew well enough that Janetta's stepmother was not at all the sort of person whom Lady Caroline Adair would willingly speak to, and yet she did not like to say that her acquaintance with Janetta had only been made at a Beaminster dancing class. Probably Miss Polehampton divined the fact. "Under the circumstances," she said, "I think I should be justified in writing to Lady Caroline and asking her to remonstrate a little with you, my dear Margaret. Probably she would be better able to make you understand the impropriety of your behavior than I can do."

The tears rose to Margaret's eyes. She was not used to being rebuked in this manner.

"But—I don't know, Miss Polehampton, what you want me to do," she said, more nervously than usual. "I can't give up Janetta; I can't possibly avoid speaking to her, you know, even if I wanted to——"

"I desire nothing of the sort, Margaret. Be kind and polite to her, as usual. But let me suggest that you do not make a companion of her in the garden so constantly—that you do not try to sit beside her in class or look over the same book. I will speak to Miss Colwyn herself about it. I think I can make *her* understand."

"Oh, please do not speak to Janetta! I quite understand already," said Margaret, growing pale with distress. "You do not know how kind and good she has always been to me——"

Sobs choked her utterance, rather to Miss Polehampton's alarm. She did not like to see her girls cry—least of all, Margaret Adair.

"My dear, you have no need to excite yourself. Janetta Colwyn has always been treated, I hope, with justice and kindness in this house. If you will endeavor only to make her position in life less instead of more difficult, you will be doing her the greatest favor in your power. I do not at all mean that I wish you to be unkind to her. A little more reserve, a little more caution, in your demeanor, and you will be all that I have ever wished you to be—a credit to your parents and to the school which has educated you!"

This sentiment was so effusive that it stopped Margaret's tears out of sheer amazement; and when she had said good-night and gone to bed, Miss Polehampton stood for a moment or two quite still, as if to recover from the unwonted exertion of expressing an affectionate emotion. It was perhaps a reaction against it that caused her almost immediately to ring the bell a trifle sharply, and to say—still sharply—to the maid who appeared in answer.

"Send Miss Colwyn to me."

Five minutes elapsed before Miss Colwyn came, however, and the schoolmistress had had time to grow impatient.

"Why did you not come at once when I sent for you?" she said, severely, as soon as Janetta presented herself.

"I was going to bed," said the girl, quickly; "and I had to dress myself again."

The short, decided accents grated on Miss Polehampton's ear. Miss Colwyn did not speak half so "nicely," she said to herself, as did dear Margaret Adair.

"I have been talking to Miss Adair about you," said the schoolmistress, coldly. "I have been telling her, as I now tell you, that the difference in your positions makes your present intimacy very undesirable. I wish you to understand, henceforward, that Miss Adair is not to walk with you in the garden, not to sit beside you in class, not to associate with you, as she has hitherto done, on equal terms."

"Why should we not associate on equal terms?" said Janetta. She was a black-browed girl, with a clear olive skin, and her eyes flashed and her cheeks glowed with indignation as she spoke.

"You are not equals," said Miss Polehampton, with icy displeasure in her tone—she had spoken very differently to Margaret. "You have to work for your bread: there is no disgrace in that, but it puts you on a different level from that of Miss Margaret Adair, an earl's grand-daughter, and the only child of one of the richest commoners in England. I have never before reminded you of the difference in position between yourself and the young ladies with whom you have hitherto been allowed to associate; and I really think I shall have to adopt another method—unless you conduct yourself, Miss Colwyn, with a little more modesty and propriety."

"May I ask what your other method would be?" asked Miss Colwyn, with perfect self-possession.

Miss Polehampton looked at her for a moment in silence.

"To begin with," she said, "I could order the meals differently, and request you to take yours with the younger children, and in other ways cut you off from the society of the young ladies. And if this failed, I could signify to your father that our arrangement was not satisfactory, and that it had better end at the close of this term."

Janetta's eyes fell and her color faded as she heard this threat. It meant a good deal to her. She answered quickly, but with some nervousness of tone.

"Of course, that must be as you please, Miss Polehampton. If I do not satisfy you, I must go."

"You satisfy me very well except in that one respect. However, I do not ask for any promise from you now. I shall observe your conduct during the next few days, and be guided by what I see. I have already spoken to Miss Adair."

Janetta bit her lips. After a pause, she said—

"Is that all? May I go now?"

"You may go," said Miss Polehampton, with majesty; and Janetta softly and slowly retired.

But as soon as she was outside the door her demeanor changed. She burst into tears as she sped swiftly up the broad staircase, and her eyes were so blinded that she did not even see a white figure hovering on the landing until she found herself suddenly in Margaret's arms. In defiance of all rules—disobedient for nearly the first time in her life—Margaret had waited and watched for Janetta's coming; and now, clasped as closely together as sisters, the two friends held a whispered colloquy on the stairs.

"Darling," said Margaret, "was she very unkind?"

"She was very horrid, but I suppose she couldn't help it," said Janetta, with a little laugh mixing itself with her sobs. "We mustn't be friends any more, Margaret."

"But we will be friends—always, Janetta."

"We must not sit together or walk together——"

"Janetta, I shall behave to you exactly as I have always done." The gentle Margaret was in revolt.

"She will write to your mother, Margaret, and to my father."

"I shall write to mine, too, and explain," said Margaret with dignity. And Janetta had not the heart to whisper to her friend that the tone in which Miss Polehampton would write to Lady Caroline would differ very widely from the one that she would adopt to Mr. Colwyn.

CHAPTER II
LADY CAROLINE'S TACTICS

Helmsley Court was generally considered one of the prettiest houses about Beaminster; a place which was rich in pretty houses, being a Cathedral town situated in one of the most beautiful southern counties of England. The village of Helmsley was a picturesque little group of black and white cottages, with gardens full of old-fashioned flowers before them and meadows and woods behind. Helmsley Court was on slightly higher ground than the village, and its windows commanded an extensive view of lovely country bounded in the distance by a long low range of blue hills, beyond which, in clear days, it was said, keen eyes could catch a glimpse of the shining sea. The house itself was a very fine old building, with a long terrace stretching before its lower windows, and flower gardens which were the admiration of half the county. It had a picture gallery and a magnificent hall with polished floor and stained windows, and all the accessories of an antique and celebrated mansion; and it had also all the comfort and luxury that modern civilization could procure.

It was this latter characteristic that made "the Court," as it was commonly called, so popular. Picturesque old houses are sometimes draughty and inconvenient, but no such defects were ever allowed to exist at the Court. Every thing went smoothly: the servants were perfectly trained: the latest improvements possible were always introduced: the house was ideally luxurious. There never seemed to be any jar or discord: no domestic worry was ever allowed to reach the ears of the mistress of the household, no cares or troubles seemed able to exist in that serene atmosphere. You could not even say of it that it was dull. For the master of the Court was a hospitable man, with many tastes and whims which he liked to indulge by having down from London the numerous friends whose fancies matched his own, and his wife was a little bit of a fine lady who had London friends too, as well as neighbors, whom she liked to entertain. The house was seldom free from visitors; and it was partly for that very reason that Lady Caroline Adair, being in her own way a wise woman, had arranged that two or three years of her daughter's life should be spent at Miss Polehampton's very select boarding-school at Brighton. It would be a great drawback to Margaret, she reflected, if her beauty were familiar to all the world before she came out;

and really, when Mr. Adair would insist on inviting his friends constantly to the house, it was impossible to keep the girl so mewed up in the schoolroom that she would not be seen and talked of; and therefore it was better that she should go away for a time. Mr. Adair did not like the arrangement; he was very fond of Margaret, and objected to her leaving home; but Lady Caroline was gently inexorable and got her own way—as she generally did.

She does not look much like the mother of the tall girl whom we saw at Brighton, as she sits at the head of her breakfast-table in the daintiest of morning gowns—a marvelous combination of silk, muslin and lace and pale pink ribbons—with a tiny white dog reposing in her lap. She is a much smaller woman than Margaret, and darker in complexion: it is from her, however, that Margaret inherits the large, appealing hazel eyes, which look at you with an infinite sweetness, while their owner is perhaps thinking of the *menu* or her milliner's bill. Lady Caroline's face is thin and pointed, but her complexion is still clear, and her soft brown hair is very prettily arranged. As she sits with her back to the light, with a rose-colored curtain behind her, just tinting her delicate cheek (for Lady Caroline is always careful of appearance), she looks quite a young woman still.

It is Mr. Adair whom Margaret most resembles. He is a tall and exceedingly handsome man, whose hair and moustache and pointed beard were as golden once as Margaret's soft tresses, but are now toned down by a little grey. He has the alert blue eyes that generally go with his fair complexion, and his long limbs are never still for many minutes together. His daughter's tranquillity seems to have come from her mother; certainly it cannot be inherited from the restless Reginald Adair.

The third person present at the breakfast-table—and, for the time being, the only visitor in the house—is a young man of seven or eight-and-twenty, tall, dark, and very spare, with a coal-black beard trimmed to a point, earnest dark eyes, and a remarkably pleasant and intelligent expression. He is not exactly handsome, but he has a face that attracts one; it is the face of a man who has quick perceptions, great kindliness of heart, and a refined and cultured mind. Nobody is more popular in that county than young Sir Philip Ashley, although his neighbors grumble sometimes at his absorption in scientific and philanthropic objects, and think that it would be more creditable to them if he went out with the hounds a little oftener or were a rather better shot. For, being shortsighted, he was never particularly fond either of sport or of games of skill, and his interest had always centred on intellectual pursuits to a degree that amazed the more countrified squires of the neighborhood.

The post-bag was brought in while breakfast was proceeding, and two or three letters were laid before Lady Caroline, who, with a careless word of apology, opened and read them in turn. She smiled as she put them down and looked at her husband.

"This is a novel experience," she said. "For the first time in our lives, Reginald, here is a formal complaint of our Margaret."

Sir Philip looked up somewhat eagerly, and Mr. Adair elevated his eyebrows, stirred his coffee, and laughed aloud.

"Wonders will never cease," he said. "It is rather refreshing to hear that our immaculate Margaret has done something naughty. What is it, Caroline? Is she habitually late for breakfast? A touch of unpunctuality is the only fault I ever heard of, and that, I believe, she inherits from me."

"I should be sorry to think that she was immaculate," said Lady Caroline, calmly, "it has such an uncomfortable sound. But Margaret is generally, I must say, a very tractable child."

"Do you mean that her schoolmistress does not find her tractable?" said Mr. Adair, with amusement. "What has she been doing?"

"Nothing very bad. Making friends with a governess-pupil, or something of, that sort— —"

"Just what a generous-hearted girl would be likely to do!" exclaimed Sir Philip, with a sudden warm lighting of his dark eyes.

Lady Caroline smiled at him. "The schoolmistress thinks this girl an unsuitable friend for Margaret, and wants me to interfere," she said.

"Pray do nothing of the sort," said Mr. Adair. "I would trust my Pearl's instinct anywhere. She would never make an unsuitable friend!"

"Margaret has written to me herself," said Lady Caroline. "She seems unusually excited about the matter. 'Dear mother,' she writes, 'pray interpose to prevent Miss Polehampton from doing an unjust and ungenerous thing. She disapproves of my friendship with dear Janetta Colwyn, simply because Janetta is poor; and she threatens to punish Janetta—not me—by sending her home in disgrace. Janetta is a governess-pupil here, and it would be a great trouble to her if she were sent away. I hope that you would rather take *me* away than let such an injustice be done.'"

"My Pearl hits the nail on the head exactly," said Mr. Adair, with complacency. He rose as he spoke, and began to walk about the room. "She is quite old enough to come home, Caroline. It is June now, and the term ends in July. Fetch her home, and invite the little governess too, and you will soon see whether or no she is the right sort of friend for Margaret." He laughed in his mellow, genial way, and leaned against the mantel-piece, stroking his yellow moustache and glancing at his wife.

"I am not sure that that would be advisable," said Lady Caroline, with her pretty smile. "Janetta Colwyn: Colwyn? Did not Margaret know her before she went to school? Are there not some Colwyns at Beaminster? The doctor—yes, I remember him; don't you, Reginald?"

Mr. Adair shook his head, but Sir Philip looked up hastily.

"I know him—a struggling man with a large family. His first wife was rather well-connected, I believe: at any rate she was related to the Brands of Brand Hall. He married a second time after her death."

"Do you call that being well-connected, Philip?" said Lady Caroline, with gentle reproach; while Mr. Adair laughed and whistled, but caught himself up immediately and apologized.

"I beg pardon—I forgot where I was: the less any of us have to do with the Brands of Brand Hall the better, Phil."

"I know nothing of them," said Sir Philip, rather gravely.

"Nor anybody else"—hastily—"they never live at home, you know. So this girl is a connection of theirs?"

"Perhaps not a very suitable friend: Miss Polehampton may be right," said Lady Caroline. "I suppose I must go over to Brighton and see Margaret."

"Bring her back with you," said Mr. Adair, recklessly. "She has had quite enough of school by this time: she is nearly eighteen, isn't she?"

But Lady Caroline smilingly refused to decide anything until she had herself interviewed Miss Polehampton. She asked her husband to order the carriage for her at once, and retired to summon her maid and array herself for the journey.

"You won't go to-day, will you, Philip?" said Mr. Adair, almost appealingly. "I shall be all alone, and my wife will not perhaps return until to-morrow—there's no saying."

"Thank you, I shall be most pleased to stay," answered Sir Philip, cordially. After a moment's pause, he added, with something very like a touch of shyness—"I have not seen—your daughter since she was twelve years old."

"Haven't you?" said Mr. Adair, with ready interest. "You don't say so! Pretty little girl she was then! Didn't you think so?"

"I thought her the loveliest child I had ever seen in all my life," said Sir Philip, with curious devoutness of manner.

He saw Lady Caroline just as she was starting for the train, with man and maid in attendance, and Mr. Adair handing her into the carriage and gallantly offering to accompany her if she liked. "Not at all necessary," said Lady Caroline, with an indulgent smile. "I shall be home to dinner. Take care of my husband, Philip, and don't let him be dull."

"If they are making Margaret unhappy, be sure you bring her back with you," were Mr. Adair's last words. Lady Caroline gave him a kind but inscrutable little smile and nod as she was whirled away. Sir Philip thought to himself that she looked like a woman who would take her own course in spite of advice or recommendation from her husband or anybody else.

He smiled once or twice as the day passed on at her parting injunction to him not to let her husband be dull. He had known the Adairs for many years, and had never known Reginald Adair dull under any circumstances. He was too full of interests, of "fads," some people called them, ever to be dull. He took Sir Philip round the picture-gallery, round the stables, to the kennels, to the flower-garden, to his own studio (where he painted in oils when he had nothing else to do) with never-flagging energy and animation. Sir Philip's interests lay in different grooves, but he was quite capable of sympathizing with Mr. Adair's interests, too. The day passed pleasantly, and seemed rather short for all that the two men wanted to pack into it; although from time to time Mr. Adair would say, half-impatiently, "I wonder how Caroline is getting on!" or "I hope she'll bring Margaret back with her! But I don't expect it, you know. Carry was always a great one for education and that sort of thing."

"Is Miss Adair intellectual—too?" asked Sir Philip, with respect.

Mr. Adair broke into a sudden laugh. "Intellectual? Our Daisy?—our Pearl?" he said. "Wait until you see her, then ask the question if you like."

"I am afraid I don't quite understand."

"Of course you don't. It is the partiality of a fond father that speaks, my dear fellow. I only meant that these young, fresh, pretty girls put such questions out of one's head."

"She must be very pretty then," said Sir Philip, with a smile.

He had seen a great many beautiful women, and told himself that he did not care for beauty. Fashionable, talkative women were his abomination. He had no sisters, but he loved his mother very dearly; and upon her he had founded a very high ideal of womanhood. He had begun to think vaguely, of late, that he ought to marry: duty demanded it of him, and Sir Philip was always attentive, if not obedient, to the voice of duty. But he was not inclined to marry a girl out of the schoolroom, or a girl who was accustomed to the enervating luxury (as he considered it) of Helmsley Court: he wanted an energetic, sensible, large-hearted, and large-minded woman who would be his right hand, his first minister of state. Sir Philip was fairly wealthy, but by no means enormously so; and he had other uses for his wealth than the buying of pictures and keeping up stables and kennels at an alarming expense. If Miss Adair were so pretty, he mused, it was just as well that she was not at home, for, of course, it was possible that he might find a lovely face an attraction: and much as he liked Lady Caroline, he did not want particularly to marry Lady Caroline's daughter. That she treated him with great consideration, and that he had once overheard her speak of him as "the most eligible *parti* of the neighborhood," had already put him a little on his guard. Lady Caroline was no vulgar, match-making mother, he knew that well enough; but she was in some respects a thoroughly worldly woman, and Philip Ashley was an essentially unworldly man.

As he went upstairs to dress for dinner that evening, he was struck by the fact that a door stood open that he had never seen opened before: a door into a pretty, well-lighted, pink and white room, the ideal apartment for a young girl. The evening was chilly, and rain had begun to fall, so a bright little fire was burning in the steel grate, and casting a cheerful glow over white sheepskin rugs and rose-colored curtains. A maid seemed to be busying herself with some white material—all gauze and lace it looked—and another servant was, as Sir Philip passed, entering with a great white vase filled with red roses.

"Do they expect visitors to-night?" thought the young man, who knew enough of the house to be aware that the room was not one in general use. "Adair said nothing about it, but perhaps some people are coming from town."

A budget of letters was brought to him at that moment, and in reading and answering them he did not note the sound of carriage-wheels on the drive, nor the bustle of an arrival in the house. Indeed, he left himself so little time that he had to dress in extraordinary haste, and went downstairs at last in the conviction that he was unpardonably late.

But apparently he was wrong.

For the drawing-room was tenanted by one figure only—that of a young lady in evening dress. Neither Lady Caroline nor Mr. Adair had appeared upon the scene; but on the hearthrug, by the small crackling fire—which, in deference to the chilliness of an English June evening, had been lighted—stood a tall, fair, slender girl, with pale complexion, and soft, loosely-coiled masses of golden hair. She was dressed in pure white, a soft loose gown of Indian silk, trimmed with the most delicate lace: it was high to the milk-white throat, but showed the rounded curves of the finely-moulded arm to the elbow. She wore no ornaments, but a white rose was fastened into the lace frill of her dress at her neck. As she turned her face towards the new comer, Sir Philip suddenly felt himself abashed. It was not that she was so beautiful—in those first few moments he scarcely thought her beautiful at all—but that she produced on him an impression of serious, virginal grace and innocence which was almost disconcerting. Her pure complexion, her grave, serene eyes, her graceful way of moving as she advanced a little to receive him stirred him to more than admiration—to something not unlike awe. She looked young; but it was youth in perfection: there was some marvelous finish, delicacy, polish, which one does not usually associate with extreme youth.

"You are Sir Philip Ashley, I think?" she said, offering him her slim cool hand without embarrassment.

"You do not remember me, perhaps, but I remember you perfectly well, I am Margaret Adair."

CHAPTER III
AT HELMSLEY COURT

"Lady Caroline has brought you back, then?" said Sir Philip, after his first pause of astonishment.

"Yes," said Margaret, serenely. "I have been expelled."

"Expelled! *You?*"

"Yes, indeed, I have," said the girl, with a faintly amused little smile. "And so has my great friend, Janetta Colwyn. Here she is: Janetta, I am telling Sir Philip Ashley that we have been expelled, and he will not believe me."

Sir Philip turned in some curiosity to see the girl of whom he had heard for the first time that morning. He had not noticed before that she was present. He saw a brown little creature, with eyes that had been swollen with crying until they were well-nigh invisible, small, unremarkable features, and a mouth that was inclined to quiver. Margaret might afford to be serene, but to this girl expulsion from school had evidently been a sad trouble. He threw all the more kindness and gentleness into his voice and look as he spoke to her.

Janetta might have felt a little awkward if she had not been so entirely absorbed by her own woes. She had never set foot before in half so grand a house as this of Helmsley Court, nor had she ever dined late or spoken to a gentleman in an evening coat in all her previous life. The size and the magnificence of the room would perhaps have oppressed her if she had been fully aware of them. But she was for the moment very much wrapped up in her own affairs, and scarcely stopped to think of the novel situation in which she found herself. The only thing that had startled her was the attention paid to her dress by Margaret and Margaret's maid. Janetta would have put on her afternoon black cashmere and little silver brooch, and would have felt herself perfectly well dressed; but Margaret, after a little consultation with the very grand young person who condescended to brush Miss Colwyn's hair, had herself brought to Janetta's room a dress of black lace over cherry-colored silk, and had begged her to put it on.

"You will feel so hot downstairs if you don't put on something cool," Margaret had said. "There is a fire in the drawing-room: papa likes the rooms warm. My dresses would not have fitted you, I am so much taller than you; but mamma is just your height, and although you are thinner perhaps— —But I don't know: the dress fits you perfectly. Look in the glass, Janet; you are quite splendid."

Janetta looked and blushed a little—not because she thought herself at all splendid, but because the dress showed her neck and arms in a way no dress had ever done before. "Ought it to be—open—like this?" she said, vaguely. "Do you wear your dresses like this when you are at home?"

"Mine are high," said Margaret. "I am not 'out,' you know. But you are older than I, and you used to teach— —I think we may consider that you *are* 'out,'" she added, with a little laugh. "You look very nice, Janetta: you have such pretty arms! Now I must go and dress, and I will call for you when I am ready to go down."

Janetta felt decidedly doubtful as to whether she were not a great deal too grand for the occasion; but she altered her mind when she saw Margaret's dainty silk and lace, and Lady Caroline's exquisite brocade; and she felt herself quite unworthy to take Mr. Adair's offered arm when dinner was announced and her host politely convoyed her to the dining-room. She wondered whether he knew that she was only a little governess-pupil, and whether he was not angry with her for being the cause of his daughter's abrupt departure from school. As a matter of fact, Mr. Adair knew her position exactly, and was very much amused by the whole affair; also, as it had procured him the pleasure of his daughter's return home, he had an illogical inclination to be pleased also with Janetta. "As Margaret is so fond of her, there must be something in her," he said to himself, with a critical glance at the girl's delicate features and big dark eyes. "I'll draw her out at dinner."

He tried his best, and made himself so agreeable and amusing that Janetta lost a good deal of her shyness, and forgot her troubles. She had a quick tongue of her own, as everybody at Miss Polehampton's was aware; and she soon found that she had not lost it. She was a good deal surprised to find that not a word was said at the dinner table about the cause of Margaret's return: in her own home it would have been the subject of the evening; it would have been discussed from every point of view, and she would probably have been reduced to tears before the first hour was over. But here it was evident that the matter was not considered of great importance. Margaret looked serene as ever, and joined quietly in talk which was alarmingly unlike Miss

Polehampton's improving conversation: talk about county gaieties and county magnates: gossip about neighbors—gossip of a harmless although frivolous type, for Lady Caroline never allowed any talk at her table that was anything but harmless, about fashions, about old china, about music and art. Mr. Adair was passionately fond of music, and when he found that Miss Colwyn really knew something of it he was in his element. They discoursed of fugues, sonatas, concertos, quartettes, and trios, until even Lady Caroline raised her eyebrows a little at the very technical nature of the conversation; and Sir Philip exchanged a congratulatory smile with Margaret over her friend's success. For the delight of finding a congenial spirit had brought the crimson into Janetta's olive cheeks and the brilliance to her dark eyes: she had looked insignificant when she went in to dinner; she was splendidly handsome at dessert. Mr. Adair noticed her flashing, transitory beauty, and said to himself that Margaret's taste was unimpeachable; it was just like his own; he had complete confidence in Margaret.

When the ladies went back to the drawing-room, Sir Philip turned with a look of only half-disguised curiosity to his host. "Lady Caroline brought her back then?" he said, longing to ask questions, yet hardly knowing how to frame them aright.

Mr. Adair gave a great laugh. "It's been the oddest thing I ever heard of," he said, in a tone of enjoyment. "Margaret takes a fancy to that little black-eyed girl—a nice little thing, too, don't you think?—and nothing must serve but that her favorite must walk with her, sit by her, and so on—you know the romantic way girls have? The schoolmistress interfered, said it was not proper, and so on; forbade it. Miss Colwyn would have obeyed, it seems, but Margaret took the bit in a quiet way between her teeth. Miss Colwyn was ordered to take her meals at a side table: Margaret insisted on taking her meals there too. The school was thrown into confusion. At last Miss Polehampton decided that the best way out of the difficulty was first to complain to us, and then to send Miss Colwyn home, straight away. She would not send *Margaret* home, you know!"

"That was very hard on Miss Colwyn," said Sir Philip, gravely.

"Yes, horribly hard. So Margaret, as you heard, appealed to her mother, and when Lady Caroline arrived, she found that not only were Miss Colwyn's boxes packed, but Margaret's as well; and that Margaret had declared that if her friend was sent away for what was after all *her* fault, she would not stay an hour in the house. Miss Polehampton was weeping: the girls were in revolt, the teachers in despair, so my wife thought the best way out of the difficulty was to bring both girls away at once, and settle it with

Miss Colwyn's relations afterwards. The joke is that Margaret insists on it that she has been 'expelled.'"

"So she told me."

"The schoolmistress said something of that kind, you know. Caroline says the woman entirely lost her temper and made an exhibition of herself. Caroline was glad to get our girl away. But, of course, it's all nonsense about being 'expelled' as a punishment; she was leaving of her own accord."

"One could hardly imagine punishment in connection with her," said Sir Philip, warmly.

"No, she's a nice-looking girl, isn't she? and her little friend is a good foil, poor little thing."

"This affair may prove of some serious inconvenience to Miss Colwyn, I suppose?"

"Oh, you may depend upon it, she won't be the loser," said Mr. Adair, hastily. "We'll see about that. Of course she will not suffer any injury through my daughter's friendship for her."

Sir Philip was not so sure about it. In spite of his intense admiration for Margaret's beauty, it occurred to him that the romantic partisanship of the girl with beauty, position, and wealth for her less fortunate sister had not been attended with very brilliant results. No doubt Miss Adair, reared in luxury and indulgence, did not in the least realize the harm done to the poor governess-pupil's future by her summary dismissal from Miss Polehampton's boarding-school. To Margaret, anything that the schoolmistress chose to say or do mattered little; to Janetta Colwyn, it might some day mean prosperity or adversity of a very serious kind. Sir Philip did not quite believe in the compensation so easily promised by Mr. Adair. He made a mental note of Miss Colwyn's condition and prospects, and said to himself that he would not forget her. And this meant a good deal from a busy man like Sir Philip Ashley.

Meanwhile there had been another conversation going on in the drawing-room between the three ladies. Margaret put her arm affectionately round Janetta's waist as they stood by the hearthrug, and looked at her mother with a smile. Lady Caroline sank into an easy-chair on the other side of the fireplace, and contemplated the two girls.

"This is better than Claremont House, is it not, Janet?" said Margaret.

"Indeed it is," Janetta answered, gratefully.

"You found the way to papa's heart by your talk about music—did she not, mamma? And does not this dress suit her beautifully?"

"It wants a little alteration in the sleeve," said Lady Caroline, with the placidity which Janetta had always attributed to Margaret as a special virtue, but which she now found was merely characteristic of the house and family in general, "but Markham can do that to-morrow. There are some people coming in the evening, and the sleeve will look better shortened."

The remark sounded a little inconsequent in Janetta's ear, but Margaret understood and assented. It meant that Lady Caroline was on the whole pleased with Janetta, and did not object to introducing her to her friends. Margaret gave her mother a little smile over Janetta's head, while that young person was gathering up her courage in two hands, so to speak, before addressing Lady Caroline.

"I am very much obliged to you," she said at last, with a thrill of gratitude in her sweet voice which was very pleasant to the ear. "But—I was thinking—what time would be the most convenient for me to go home to-morrow?"

"Home? To Beaminster?" said Margaret. "But you need not go, dear; you can write a note and tell them that you are staying here."

"Yes, my dear; I am sure Margaret cannot part with you yet," said Lady Caroline, amiably.

"Thank you; it is most kind of you," Janetta answered, her voice shaking. "But I must ask my father whether I can stay—and hear what he says; Miss Polehampton will have written to him, and——"

"And he will be very glad that we have rescued you from her clutches," said Margaret, with a soft triumphant little laugh. "My poor Janetta! What we suffered at her hands!"

Lady Caroline lying back in her easy chair, with the candle light gleaming upon her silvery grey and white brocade with its touches of soft pink, and the diamonds flashing on her white hands, so calmly crossed upon the handle of her ivory fan, did not feel quite so tranquil as she looked. It crossed her mind that Margaret was acting inconsiderately. This little Miss Colwyn had her living to earn; it would be no kindness to unfit her for her profession. So, when she spoke it was with a shade more decision than usual in her tones.

"We will drive you over to Beaminster to-morrow, my dear Miss Colwyn, and you can then see your family, and ask your father if you may spend a few days with Margaret. I do not think that Mr. Colwyn will refuse us," she said, graciously. "I wonder when those men are coming, Margaret. Suppose you open the piano and let us have a little music. You sing, do you not?"

"Yes, a little," said Janetta.

"A little!" exclaimed Margaret, with contempt. "She has a delightful voice, mamma. Come and sing at once, Janetta, darling, and astonish mamma."

Lady Caroline smiled. She had heard a great many singers in her day, and did not expect to be astonished. A little governess-pupil, an under-teacher in a boarding-school! Dear Margaret's enthusiasm certainly carried her away.

But when Janetta sang, Lady Caroline was, after all, rather surprised. The girl had a remarkably sweet and rich contralto voice, and it had been well trained; and, moreover, she sang with feeling and passion which were somewhat unusual in one so young. It seemed as if some hidden power, some latent characteristic came out in her singing because it found no other way of expressing itself. Neither Lady Caroline nor Margaret understood why Janetta's voice moved them so much; Sir Philip, who came in with his host while the music was going on, heard and was charmed also without quite knowing why; it was Mr. Adair alone whose musical knowledge and experience of the world enabled him, feather-headed as in some respects he was, to lay his finger directly on the salient features of Janetta's singing.

"It's not her voice altogether, you know," he said afterwards to Philip Ashley, in a moment of confidence; "it's soul. She's got more of that commodity than is good for a woman. It makes her singing lovely, you know—brings tears into one's eyes, and all that sort of thing—but upon my honor I'm thankful that Margaret hasn't got a voice like that! It's women of that kind that are either heroines of virtue—or go to the devil. They are always in extremes."

"Then we may promise ourselves some excitement in watching Miss Colwyn's career," said Sir Philip, dryly.

After Janetta, Margaret sang; she had a sweet mezzo-soprano voice, of no great strength or compass, but perfectly trained and very pleasing to the ear. The sort of voice, Sir Philip thought, that would be soothing to the nerves of a tired man in his own house. Whereas, Janetta's singing had something impassioned in it which disturbed and excited instead of soothing. But he was quite ready to admire when Margaret called on him for admiration. They were sitting together on a sofa, and Janetta, who had just finished one of her songs, was talking to, or being talked to, by Mr. Adair. Lady Caroline had taken up a review.

"Is not Miss Colwyn's voice perfectly lovely?" Margaret asked, with shining eyes.

"It is very sweet."

"Don't you think she looks very nice?"—Margaret was hungering for admiration of her friend.

"She is a very pretty girl. You are very fond of each other?"

"Oh, yes, devoted. I am so glad I succeeded!" said the girl, with a great sigh.

"In getting her away from the school?"

"Yes."

"You think it was for her good?"

Margaret opened her lovely eyes.

"For her good?—to come here instead of staying in that close uncomfortable house to give music lessons, and bear Miss Polehampton's snubs?——" It had evidently never occurred to her that the change could be anything but beneficial to Janetta.

"It is very pleasant for her, no doubt," said Sir Philip, smiling in spite of his disapproval. "I only wondered whether it was a good preparation for the life of hard work which probably lies before her."

He saw that Margaret colored, and wondered whether she would be offended by his suggestion. After a moment's pause, she answered, gravely, but quite gently—

"I never thought of it in that way before, exactly. I want to keep her here, so that she should never have to work hard at all."

"Would she consent to that?"

"Why not?" said Margaret.

Sir Philip smiled and said no more. It was curious, he said to himself, to see how little conception Margaret had of lives unlike and outside her own. And Janetta's brave but sensitive little face, with its resolute brows and lips and brilliant eyes, gave promise of a determination and an originality which, he felt convinced, would never allow her to become a mere plaything or appendage of a wealthy household, as Margaret Adair seemed to expect. But his words had made an impression. At night, when Lady Caroline and her daughter were standing in the charming little room which had always been appropriated to Margaret's use, she spoke, with the unconscious habit of saying frankly anything that had occurred to her, of Sir Philip's remarks.

"It was so odd," she said; "Sir Philip seemed to think that it would be bad for Janetta to stay here, mamma. Why should it be bad for her, mamma, dear?"

"I don't think it will be at all bad for her to spend a day or two with us, darling," said Lady Caroline, keeping somewhat careful watch on Margaret's face as she spoke. "But perhaps it had better be by-and-bye. You know she wants to go home to-morrow, and we must not keep her away from her duties or her own sphere of life."

"No," Margaret answered, "but her duties will not always keep her at home, you know, mamma, dear."

"I suppose not, my dearest," said Lady Caroline, vaguely, but in the caressing tone to which Margaret was accustomed. "Go to bed, my sweetest one, and we will talk of all these things to-morrow."

Meanwhile Janetta was wondering at the luxury of the room which had been allotted to her, and thinking over the events of the past day. When a tap at the door announced Margaret's appearance to say good-night, Janetta was standing before the long looking-glass, apparently inspecting herself by the light of the rose-tinted wax candles in silver sconces which were fixed on either side of the mirror. She was in her dressing-gown, and her long and abundant hair fell over her shoulder in a great curly mass.

"Oh, Miss Vanity!" cried Margaret, with more gaiety of tone than was usual with her, "are you admiring your pretty hair?"

"I was thinking," said Janetta, with the intensity which often characterized her speech, "that *now* I understood you—now I know why you were so different from other girls, so sweet, so calm and beautiful! You have lived in this lovely place all your life! It is like a fairy palace—a dream-house—to me; and you are the queen of it, Margaret—a princess of dreams!"

"I hope I shall have something more than dreams to reign over some day," said Margaret, putting her arms round her friend's neck. "And whatever I am queen over, you must share my queendom, Janet. You know how fond I am of you—how I want you to stay with me always and be my friend."

"I shall always be your friend—always, to the last day of my life!" said Janetta, with fervor. The two made a pretty picture, reflected in the long mirror; the tall, fair Margaret, still in her soft white silk frock, with her arm round the smaller figure of the dark girl whose curly masses of hair half covered her pink cotton dressing-gown, and whose brown face was upturned so lovingly to her friend's.

"And I am sure it will be good for you to stay with me," said Margaret, answering an unspoken objection in her mind.

"Good for me? It is delicious—it is lovely!" cried Janetta, rapturously. "I have never had anything so nice in my whole life. Dear Margaret, you are so good and so kind—if there were only anything that I could do for you in return! Perhaps some day I shall have the chance, and if ever I have—*then* you shall see whether I am true to my friend or not!"

Margaret kissed her, with a little smile at Janetta's enthusiasm, which was so far different from the modes of expression customary at Helmsley Court, as to be almost amusing.

CHAPTER IV
ON THE ROAD

Miss Polehampton had, of course, written to Mr. and Mrs. Colwyn when she made up her mind that Janetta was to be removed from school; and two or three letters had been interchanged before that eventful day on which Margaret declared that if Janetta went she should go too. Margaret had been purposely kept in the dark until almost the last moment, for Miss Polehampton did not in the least wish to make a scandal, and annoyed as she was by Miss Adair's avowed preference for Janetta, she had arranged a neat little plan by which Miss Colwyn was to go away "for change of air," and be transferred to a school at Worthing kept by a relation of her own at the beginning of the following term. These plans had been upset by a foolish and ill-judged letter from Mrs. Colwyn to her stepdaughter, which Janetta had not been able to keep from Margaret's eyes. This letter was full of reproaches to Janetta for giving so much trouble to her friends; "for, of course," Mrs. Colwyn wrote, "Miss Polehampton's concern for your health is all a blind in order to get you away: and if it hadn't been for Miss Adair taking you up, she would have been only too glad to keep you. But knowing Miss Adair's position, she sees very clearly that it isn't fit for you to be friends with her, and so she wants to send you away."

This was in the main true, but Janetta, in the blithe confidence of youth, would never have discovered it but for that letter. Together she and Margaret consulted over it, for when Margaret saw Janetta crying, she almost forced the letter from her hand; and then it was that Miss Adair vindicated her claim to social superiority. She went straight to Miss Polehampton and demanded that Janetta should remain; and when the schoolmistress refused to alter her decision, she calmly replied that in that case *she* should go home too. Miss Polehampton was an obstinate woman, and would not concede the point; and Lady Caroline, on learning the state of affairs, at once perceived that it was impossible to leave Margaret at the school where open warfare had been declared. She accordingly brought both girls away with her, arranging to send Janetta to her own home next morning.

"You will stay to luncheon, dear, and I will drive you over to Beaminster at three o'clock," she said to Janetta at breakfast. "No doubt you are anxious to see your own people."

Janetta looked as if she might find it difficult to reply, but Margaret interposed a remark—as usual at the right moment.

"We will practice our duets this morning—if Janetta likes, that is; and we can have a walk in the garden too. Shall we have the landau, mamma?"

"The victoria, I think, dear," said Lady Caroline, placidly. "Your father wants you to ride with him this afternoon, so I shall have the pleasure of Miss Colwyn's society in my drive."

Margaret assented; but Janetta became suddenly aware, by a flash of keen feminine intuition, that Lady Caroline had some reason for wishing to go with her alone, and that she had purposely made the arrangement that she spoke of. However, there was nothing to displease her in this, for Lady Caroline had been most kind and considerate to her, so far, and she was innocently disposed to believe in the cordiality and sincerity of every one who behaved with common civility.

So she spent a pleasant morning, singing with Margaret, loitering about the garden with Mr. Adair, while Margaret and Sir Philip gathered roses, and enjoying to the full all the sweet influences of peace, refinement, and prosperity by which she was surrounded.

Margaret left her in the afternoon with rather a hasty kiss, and an assurance that she would see her again at dinner. Janetta tried to remind her that by that time she would have left the Court, but Margaret did not or would not hear. The tears came into the girl's eyes as her friend disappeared.

"Never mind, dear," said Lady Caroline, who was observing her closely, "Margaret has forgotten at what hour you were going and I would not remind her—it would spoil her pleasure in her ride. We will arrange for you to come to us another day when you have seen your friends at home."

"Thank you," said Janetta. "It was only that she did not seem to remember that I was going—I had meant to say good-bye."

"Exactly. She thinks that I am going to bring you back this afternoon. We will talk about it as we go, dear. Suppose you were to put on your hat now. The carriage will be here in ten minutes."

Janetta prepared for her departure in a somewhat bewildered spirit. She did not know precisely what Lady Caroline meant. She even felt a little nervous as she took her place in the victoria and cast a last look at the stately house in which she had spent some nineteen or twenty pleasant hours. It was Lady Caroline who spoke first.

"We shall miss your singing to-night," she said, amiably. "Mr. Adair was looking forward to some more duets. Another time, perhaps— —"

"I am always pleased to sing," said Janetta, brightening at this address.

"Yes—ye—es," said Lady Caroline, with a doubtful little drawl. "No doubt: one always likes to do what one can do so well; but—I confess I am not so musical as my husband or my daughter. I must explain why dear Margaret did not say good bye to you, Miss Colwyn. I allowed her to remain in the belief that she was to see you again to-night, in order that she might not be depressed during her ride by the thought of parting with you. It is always my principle to make the lives of those dear to me as happy as possible," said Margaret's mother, piously.

"And if Margaret had been depressed during her ride, Mr. Adair and Sir Philip might have suffered some depression also, and that would be a great pity."

"Oh, yes," said Janetta. But she felt chilled, without knowing why.

"I must take you into my confidence," said Lady Caroline, in her softest voice. "Mr. Adair has plans for our dear Margaret. Sir Philip Ashley's property adjoins our own: he is of good principles, kind-hearted, and intellectual: he is well off, nice-looking, and of a suitable age—he admires Margaret very much. I need say no more, I am sure."

Again she looked keenly at Janetta's face, but she read there nothing but interest and surprise.

"Oh—does Margaret know?" she asked.

"She feels more than she knows," said Lady Caroline, discreetly. "She is in the first stage of—of—emotion. I did not want the afternoon's arrangements to be interfered with."

"Oh, no! especially on *my* account," said Janetta, sincerely.

"When I go home I shall talk quietly to Margaret," pursued Lady Caroline, "and tell her that you will come back another day, that your duties called you home—they do, I am sure, dear Miss Colwyn—and that you could not return with me when you were so much wanted."

"I'm afraid I am not much wanted," said Janetta, with a sigh; "but I daresay it is my duty to go home— —"

"I am sure it is," Lady Caroline declared; "and duty is so high and holy a thing, dear, that you will never regret the performance of it."

It occurred dimly to Janetta at that point that Lady Caroline's views of duty might possibly differ from her own; but she did not venture to say so.

"And, of course, you will never repeat to Margaret——"

Lady Caroline did not complete her sentence. The coachman suddenly checked the horses' speed: for some unknown reason he actually stopped short in the very middle of the country road between Helmsley Court and Beaminster. His mistress uttered a little cry of alarm.

"What is the matter, Steel?"

The footman dismounted and touched his hat.

"I'm afraid there has been an accident, my lady," he said, as apologetically, as if he were responsible for the accident.

"Oh! Nothing horrible, I hope!" said Lady Caroline, drawing out her smelling-bottle.

"It's a carriage accident, my lady. Leastways, a cab. The 'orse is lying right across the road, my lady."

"Speak to the people, Steel," said her ladyship, with great dignity. "They must not be allowed to block up the road in this way."

"May I get out?" said Janetta, eagerly. "There is a lady lying on the path, and some people bathing her face. Now they are lifting her up—I am sure they ought not to lift her up in that way—oh, please, I must go just for one minute!" And, without waiting for a reply, she stepped, out of the victoria and sped to the side of the woman who had been hurt.

"Very impulsive and undisciplined," said Lady Caroline to herself, as she leaned back and held the smelling-bottle to her own delicate nose. "I am glad I have got her out of the house so soon. Those men were wild about her singing. Sir Philip disapproved of her presence, but he was charmed by her voice, I could see that; and poor, dear Reginald was positively absurd about her voice. And dear Margaret does *not* sing so well—it is no use pretending that she does—and Sir Philip is trembling on the verge—oh, yes, I am sure that I have been very wise. What is that girl doing now?"

The victoria moved forward a little, so that Lady Caroline could obtain a clearer view of what was going on. The vehicle which caused the obstruction—evidently a hired fly from an inn—was uninjured, but the horse had fallen between the shafts and would never rise again. The occupants of the fly—a lady, and a much younger man, perhaps her son—

had got out, and the lady had then turned faint, Lady Caroline heard, but was not in any way hurt. Janetta was kneeling by the side of the lady — kneeling in the dust, without any regard to the freshness of her cotton frock, by the way — and had already placed her in the right position, and was ordering the half-dozen people who had collected to stand back and give her air. Lady Caroline watched her movements and gestures with placid amusement, and went so far as to send Steel with the offer of her smelling salts; but as this offer was rejected she felt that nothing else could be done. So she sat and looked on critically.

The woman — Lady Caroline was hardly inclined to call her a lady, although she did not exactly know why — was at present of a ghastly paleness, but her features were finely cut, and showed traces of former beauty. Her hair was grey, with rebellious waves in it, but her eyebrows were still dark. She was dressed in black, with a good deal of lace about her; and on her ungloved hand Lady Caroline's keen sight enabled her to distinguish some very handsome diamond rings. The effect of the costume was a little spoiled by a large gaudy fan, of violent rainbow hues, which hung at her side; and perhaps it was this article of adornment which decided Lady Caroline in her opinion of the woman's social status. But about the man she was equally positive in a different way. He *was* a gentleman: there could be no doubt of that. She put up her eye-glass and gazed at him with interest. She almost thought that she had seen him somewhere before.

A handsome man, indeed, and a gentleman; but, oh, what an ill-tempered one, apparently! He was dark, with fine features, and black hair with a slight inclination to wave or curl (as far at least as could be judged when the extremely well-cropped state of his head was taken into consideration); and from these indications Lady Caroline judged him to be "the woman's" son. He was tall, muscular, and active looking: it was the way in which his black eyebrows were bent above his eyes which made the observer think him ill-tempered, for his manner and his words expressed anxiety, not anger. But that frown, which must have been habitual, gave him a distinctly ill-humored look.

At last the lady opened her eyes, and drank a little water, and sat up. Janetta rose from her knees, and turned to the young man with a smile. "She will soon be better now," she said. "I am afraid there is nothing else that I can do — and I think I must go on."

"I am very much obliged to you for your kind assistance," said the gentleman, but without any abatement of the gloom of his expression. He gave Janetta a keen look — almost a bold look — Lady Caroline thought, and then smiled a little, not very pleasantly. "Allow me to take you to your carriage."

Janetta blushed, as if she were minded to say that it was not her carriage; but returned to the victoria, and was handed to her seat by the young man, who then raised his hat with an elaborate flourish which was not exactly English. Indeed, it occurred to Lady Caroline at once that there was something French about both the travelers. The lady with the frizzled grey hair, the black lace dress and mantel, the gaudy blue and scarlet fan, was quite foreign in appearance; the young man with the perfectly fitting frock-coat, the tall hat, the flower in his button-hole, was—in spite of his perfectly English accent—foreign too. Lady Caroline was cosmopolitan enough to feel an access of greater interest in the pair in consequence.

"They have sent to the nearest inn for a horse," said Janetta, as the carriage moved on; "and I dare say they will not have long to wait."

"Was the lady hurt?"

"No, only shaken. She is subject to fainting fits, and the accident quite upset her nerves, her son said."

"Her son?"

"The gentleman called her mother."

"Oh! You did not hear their name, I suppose?"

"No. There was a big B on their traveling bag."

"B—B—?" said Lady Caroline, thoughtfully. "I don't know any one in this neighborhood whose name begins with B, except the Bevans. They must have been merely passing through; and yet the young man's face seemed familiar to me."

Janetta shook her head. "I never saw them before," she said.

"He has a very bold and unpleasant expression," Lady Caroline remarked, decidedly. "It spoils him entirely: otherwise he is a handsome man."

The girl made no answer. She knew, as well as Lady Caroline, that she had been stared at in a manner that was not quite agreeable to her, and yet she did not like to endorse that lady's condemnation of the stranger. For he was certainly very nice-looking—and he had been so kind to his mother that he could not be entirely bad—and to her also his face was vaguely familiar. Could he belong to Beaminster?

As she sat and meditated, the tall spires of Beaminster Cathedral came into sight, and a few minutes brought the carriage across the grey stone bridge and down the principal street of the quaint old place which called itself a city, but was really neither more nor less than a quiet country town. Here Lady Caroline turned to her young guest with a question—"You live in Gwynne Street, I believe, my dear?"

"Yes, at number ten, Gwynne Street," said Janetta, suddenly starting and feeling a little uncomfortable. The coachman evidently knew the address already, for at that moment he turned the horse's heads to the left, and the carriage rolled down a narrow side-street, where the tall red brick houses had a mean and shabby aspect, and seemed as if constructed to keep out sun and air as much as possible.

Janetta always felt the closeness and the shabbiness a little when she first came home, even from school, but when she came from Helmsley Court they struck her with redoubled force. She had never thought before how dull the street was, nor noticed that the railings were broken down in front of the door with the brass-plate that bore her father's name, nor that the window-curtains were torn and the windows sadly in need of washing. The little flight of stone steps that led from the iron gate to the door was also very dirty; and the servant girl, whose head appeared against the area railings as the carriage drove up, was more untidy, more unkempt, in appearance than ever Janetta could have expected. "We can't be rich, but we might be *clean*!" she said to herself in a subdued frenzy of impatience, as she fancied (quite unjustly) that she saw a faint smile pass over Lady Caroline's delicate, impassive face. "No wonder she thinks me an unfit friend for dear Margaret. But—oh, there is my dear, darling father! Well, nobody can say anything against him at any rate!" And Janetta's face beamed with sudden joy as she saw Mr. Colwyn coming down the dirty steps to the ricketty little iron gate, and Lady Caroline, who knew the surgeon by sight, nodded to him with friendly condescension.

"How are you, Mr. Colwyn?" she said, graciously. "I have brought your daughter home, you see, and I hope you will not scold her for what has been *my* daughter's fault—not your's."

"I am very glad to see Janetta, under any circumstances," said Mr. Colwyn, gravely, as he raised his hat. He was a tall spare man, in a shabby coat, with a careworn aspect, and kindly, melancholy eyes. Janetta noticed with a pang that his hair was greyer than it had been when last she went back to school.

"We shall be glad to see her again at Helmsley Court," said Lady Caroline. "No, I won't get out, thank you. I have to get back to tea. Your daughter's box is in front. I was to tell you from Miss Polehampton, Mr. Colwyn, that her friend at Worthing would be glad of Miss Colwyn's services after the holidays."

"I am much obliged to your ladyship," said Mr. Colwyn, with grave formality. "I am not sure that I shall let my daughter go."

"Won't you? Oh, but she ought to have all possible advantages! And can you tell me, Mr. Colwyn, by any chance, *who* are the people whom we passed on the road to Beaminster—an oldish lady in black and a young man with very dark hair and eyes? They had B on their luggage, I believe."

Mr. Colwyn looked surprised.

"I think I can tell you," he said, quietly. "They were on their way from Beaminster to Brand Hall. The young man was a cousin of my wife's: his name is Wyvis Brand, and the lady in black was his mother. They have come home after an absence of nearly four-and-twenty years."

Lady Caroline was too polite to say what she really felt—that she was sorry to hear it.

CHAPTER V
WYVIS BRAND

On the evening of the day on which Lady Caroline drove with Janetta Colwyn to Beaminster, the lady who had fainted by the wayside was sitting in a rather gloomy-looking room at Brand Hall—a room known in the household as the Blue Drawing-room. It had not the look of a drawing-room exactly: it was paneled in oak, which had grown black with age, as had also the great oak beams that crossed the ceiling and the polished floor. The furniture also was of oak, and the hangings of dark but faded blue, while the blue velvet of the chairs and the square of Oriental carpet, in which blue tints also preponderated, did not add cheerfulness to the scene. One or two great blue vases set on the carved oak mantel-piece, and some smaller blue ornaments on a sideboard, matched the furniture in tint; but it was remarkable that on a day when country gardens were overflowing with blossom, there was not a single flower or green leaf in any of the vases. No smaller and lighter ornaments, no scrap of woman's handiwork—lace or embroidery—enlivened the place: no books were set upon the table. A fire would not have been out of season, for the evenings were chilly, and it would have had a cheery look; but there was no attempt at cheeriness. The woman who sat in one of the high-backed chairs was pale and sad: her folded hands lay listlessly clasped together on her lap, and the sombre garb that she wore was as unrelieved by any gleam of brightness as the room itself. In the gathering gloom of a chilly summer evening, even the rings upon her fingers could not flash. Her white face, in its setting of rough, wavy grey hair, over which she wore a covering of black lace, looked almost statuesque in its profound tranquillity. But it was not the tranquillity of comfort and prosperity that had settled on that pale, worn, high-featured face—it was rather the tranquillity that comes of accepted sorrow and inextinguishable despair.

She had sat thus for fully half an hour when the door was roughly opened, and the young man whom Mr. Colwyn had named as Wyvis Brand came lounging into the room. He had been dining, but he was not in evening dress, and there was something unrestful and reckless in his way of moving round the room and throwing himself in the chair nearest his mother's, which roused Mrs. Brand's attention. She turned slightly towards him, and became conscious at once of the fumes of wine and strong tobacco with which her son had made her only too familiar. She looked at him for a moment, then clasped her hands tightly together and resumed her former position, with her sad face turned to the window. She may have breathed a sigh as she did so, but Wyvis Brand did not hear it, and if he had heard it, would not perhaps have very greatly cared.

"Why do you sit in the dark?" he said at last, in a vexed tone.

"I will ring for lights," Mrs. Brand answered quietly.

"Do as you like: I am not going to stay: I am going out," said the young man.

The hand that his mother had stretched out towards the bell fell to her side: she was a submissive woman, used to taking her son at his word.

"You are lonely here," she ventured to remark, after a short silence: "you will be glad when Cuthbert comes down."

"It's a beastly hole," said her son, gloomily. "I would advise Cuthbert to stay in Paris. What he will do with himself here, I can't imagine."

"He is happy anywhere," said the mother, with a stifled sigh.

Wyvis uttered a short, harsh laugh.

"That can't be said of us, can it?" he exclaimed, putting his hand on his mother's knee in a rough sort of caress. "We are generally in the shadow while Cuthbert is in the sunshine, eh? The influence of this old place makes me poetical, you see."

"*You* need not be in the shadow," said Mrs. Brand. But she said it with an effort.

"Needn't I?" said Wyvis. He thrust his hands into his pockets and leaned back in his chair with another laugh. "I have such a lot to make me cheerful, haven't I?"

His mother turned her eyes upon him with a look of yearning tenderness which, even if the room had been less dimly lighted, he would not have seen. He was not much in the habit of looking for sympathy in other people's faces.

"Is the place worse than you expected?" she asked, with a tremor in her voice.

"It is mouldier—and smaller," he replied, curtly. "One's childish impressions don't go for much. And it is in a miserable state—roof out of

A True Friend | 43

repair—fences falling down—drainage imperfect. It has been allowed to go to rack and ruin while we were away."

"Wyvis, Wyvis," said his mother, in a tone of pain, "I kept you away for your own sake. I thought you would be happier abroad."

"Oh—happier!" said the young man, rather scornfully. "Happiness isn't meant for me: it isn't in my line. It makes no difference to me whether I am here or in Paris. I should have been here long ago if I had had any idea that things were going wrong in this way."

"I suppose," said Mrs. Brand, carefully controlling her voice, "that you will not have the visitors you spoke of if the house is in so bad a state."

"Not have visitors? Of course I shall have visitors. What else is there for me to do with myself? We shall get the house put pretty straight by the 12th. Not that there will be any shooting worth speaking of on *my* place."

"If nobody comes before the 12th, I think we can make the house habitable. I will do my best, Wyvis."

Wyvis laughed again, but in a softer key. "You!" he said. "You can't do much, mother. It isn't the sort of thing you care about. You stay in your own rooms and do your needle-work; I'll see to the house. Some men are coming long before the 12th—the day after to-morrow, I believe."

"Who?"

"Oh, Dering and St. John and Ponsonby, I expect. I don't know whether they will bring any one else."

"The worst men of the worst set you know!" sighed his mother, under her breath. "Could not you have left them behind?"

She felt rather than saw how he frowned—how his hand twitched with impatience.

"What sort of friends am I likely to have?" he said. "Why not those that amuse me most?"

Then he rose and went over to the window, where he stood for some time looking out. Turning round at last, he perceived from a slight familiar movement of his mother's hand over her eyes that she was weeping, and it seemed as if his heart smote him at the sight.

"Come, mother," he said, kindly, "don't take what I say and do so much to heart. You know I'm no good, and never shall do anything in the world. You have Cuthbert to comfort you—"

"Cuthbert is nothing to me—*nothing*—compared with you, Wyvis."

The young man came to her side and put his hand on her shoulder. The passionate tone had touched him.

"Poor mother!" he said, softly. "You've suffered a good deal through me, haven't you? I wish I could make you forget all the past—but perhaps you wouldn't thank me if I could."

"No," she said, leaning forward so as to rest her forehead against his arm. "No. For there has been brightness in the past, but I see little brightness in the future either for you or for me."

"Well, that is my own fault," said Wyvis, lightly but bitterly. "If it had not been for my own youthful folly I shouldn't be burdened as I am now. I have no one but myself to thank."

"Yes, yes, it was my fault. I pressed you to do it—to tie yourself for life to the woman who has made you miserable!" said Mrs. Brand, in a tone of despairing self-accusation. "I fancied—then—that we were doing right."

"I suppose we were doing right," said Wyvis Brand sternly, but not as if the thought gave him any consolation. "It was better perhaps that I should marry the woman whom I thought I loved—instead of leaving her or wronging her—but I wish to God that I had never seen her face!"

"And to think that I persuaded you into marrying her," moaned the mother, rocking herself backward and forward in the extremity of her regretful anguish; "I—who ought to have been wiser—who might have interfered——"

"You couldn't have interfered to much purpose. I was mad about her at the time," said her son, beginning to walk about the room in a restless, aimless manner. "I wish, mother, that you would cease to talk about the past. It seems to me sometimes like a dream; if you would but let it lie still, I think that I could fancy it was a dream. Remember that I do not blame you. When I rage against the bond, I am perfectly well aware that it was one of my own making. No remonstrance, no command would have availed with me for a moment. I was determined to go my own way, and I went."

It was curious to remark that the roughness and harshness of his first manner had dropped away from him as it did drop now and then. He spoke with the polished utterance of an educated man. It was almost as though he at times put on a certain boorishness of demeanor, feeling it in some way demanded of him by circumstances—but not natural to him after all.

"I will try not to vex you, Wyvis," said his mother, wistfully.

"You do not vex me exactly," he answered, "but you stir my old memories too often. I want to forget the past. Why else did I come down here, where I have never been since I was a child? where Juliet never set foot, and where I have no association with that miserable passage in my life?"

"Then why do you bring those men down, Wyvis? For *they* know the past: *they* will recall old associations— —"

"They amuse me. I cannot be without companions. I do not pretend to cut myself off from the whole world."

As he spoke thus briefly and coldly, he stopped to strike a match, and then lighted the wax candles that stood on the black sideboard. By this act he meant perhaps to put a stop to the conversation of which he was heartily tired. But Mrs. Brand, in the half-bewildered condition of mind to which long anxiety and sorrow had reduced her, did not know the virtue of silence, and did not possess the magic quality of tact.

"You might find companions down here," she said, pertinaciously, "people suited to your position—old friends of your father's, perhaps— —"

"Will they be so willing to make friends with my father's son?" Wyvis burst out bitterly. Then, seeing from her white and stricken face that he had hurt her, he came to her side and kissed her penitently. "Forgive me, mother," he said, "if I say what you don't like. I've been hearing about my father ever since I came to Beaminster two days ago. I have heard nothing but what confirmed my previous idea about his character. Even poor old Colwyn couldn't say any good of him. He went to the devil as fast as ever he could go, and his son seems likely to follow in his footsteps. That's the general opinion, and, by George, I think I shall soon do something to justify it."

"You need not live as your father did, Wyvis," said his mother, whose tears were flowing fast.

"If I don't, nobody will believe it," said the young man, moodily. "There is no fighting against fate. The Brands are doomed, mother: we shall die out and be forgotten—all the better for the world, too. It is time we were done with: we are a bad lot."

"Cuthbert is not bad. And you—Wyvis, you have your child."

"Have I? A child that I have not seen since it was six months old! Brought up by its mother—a woman without heart or principle or anything that is good! Much comfort the child is likely to be to me when I get hold of it."

"When will that be?" said Mrs. Brand, as if speaking to herself rather than to him. But Wyvis replied:

"When she is tired of it—not before. I do not know where she is."

"Does she not draw her allowance?"

"Not regularly. And she refused her address when she last appeared at Kirby's. I suppose she wants to keep the child away from me. She need not trouble. The last thing I want is her brat to bring up."

"Wyvis!"

But to his mother's remonstrating exclamation Wyvis paid no attention in the least: his mood was fitful, and he was glad to step out of the ill-lighted room into the hall, and thence to the silence and solitude of the grounds about the house.

Brand Hall had been practically deserted for the last few years. A tenant or two had occupied it for a little time soon after its late master's withdrawal from the country; but the house was inconvenient and remote from towns, and it was said, moreover, to be damp and unhealthy. A caretaker and his wife had, therefore, been its only inhabitants of late, and a great deal of preparation had been required to make it fit for its owner when he at last wrote to his agents in Beaminster to intimate his intention of settling at the Hall.

The Brands had for many a long year been renowned as the most unlucky family in the neighborhood. They had once possessed a great property in the county; but gambling losses and speculation had greatly reduced their wealth, and even in the time of Wyvis Brand's grandfather the prestige of the family had sunk very low. In the days of Mark Brand, the father of Wyvis, it sank lower still. Mark Brand was not only "wild," but weak: not only weak, but wicked. His career was one of riotous dissipation, culminating in what was generally spoken of as "a low marriage"—with the barmaid of a Beaminster public-house. Mary Wyvis had never been at all like the typical barmaid of fiction or real life: she was always pale, quiet, and refined-looking, and it was not difficult to see how she had developed into the sorrowful, careworn woman whom Wyvis Brand called mother; but she came of a thoroughly bad stock, and was not untouched in reputation. The county people cut Mark Brand after his marriage, and never took any notice of his wife; and they were horrified when he insisted on naming his eldest son after his wife's family, as if he gloried in the lowliness of her origin. But when Wyvis was a small boy, his father resolved that neither he nor his children should be flouted and jeered at by county magnates any longer. He went abroad, and remained abroad until his death, when Wyvis was twenty years of age and Cuthbert, the younger son, was barely twelve. Some people said that the discovery of some particularly disgraceful deed was imminent when he left his native shores, and that it was for this reason that he had never returned to England; but Mark Brand himself always spoke as if his health were too weak, his nerves too delicate, to bear the rough breezes of his own country and the brusque manners of his compatriots. He had brought up his son according to his own ideas; and the result did not seem entirely satisfactory. Vague rumors occasionally reached Beaminster of scrapes and scandals in which the young Brands figured; it was said that Wyvis was a particularly black sheep, and that he did his best to corrupt his younger brother Cuthbert. The news that he was coming back to Brand Hall was not received with enthusiasm by those who heard it.

Wyvis' own story had been a sad one—perhaps more sad than scandalous; but it was a story that the Beaminster people were never to hear aright. Few knew it, and most of those who knew it had agreed to keep it secret. That his wife and child were living, many persons in Paris were aware; that they had separated was also known, but the reason of that separation was to most persons a secret. And Wyvis, who had a great dislike to chatterers, made up his mind when he came to Beaminster that he would tell to nobody the history of the past few years. Had it not been for his mother's sad face, he fancied that he could have put it out of his mind altogether. He half resented the pertinacity with which she seemed to brood upon it. The fact that she had forwarded—had almost insisted upon—the unfortunate marriage, weighed heavily upon her mind. There had been a point at which Wyvis would have given it up. But his mother had espoused the side of the girl, persuaded the young man to fulfill his promises to her—and repented it ever since. Mrs. Wyvis Brand had developed an uncontrollable love for strong drink, as well as a temper that made her at times more like a mad woman than an ordinary human being; and when she one day disappeared from her husband's home, carrying his child with her, and announcing in a subsequent letter that she did not mean to return, it could hardly be wondered at if Wyvis drew a long breath of relief, and hoped that she never would.

CHAPTER VI
JANETTA AT HOME

When Lady Caroline drove away from Gwynne Street, Janetta was left by the tumble-down iron gate with her father, in whose hand she had laid both her own. He looked at her interrogatively, smiled a little and said—"Well, my dear?" with a softening of his whole face which made him positively beautiful in Janetta's eyes.

"Dear, dearest father!" said the girl, with an irrepressible little sob. "I am so glad to see you again!"

"Come in, my dear," said Mr. Colwyn, who was not an emotional man, although a sympathetic one. "We have been expecting you all day. We did not think that they would keep you so long at the Court."

"I'll tell you all about it when I get in," said Janetta, trying to speak cheerily, with an instinctive remembrance of the demands usually made upon her fortitude in her own home. "Is mamma in?" She always spoke of the present Mrs. Colwyn, as "mamma," to distinguish her from her own mother. "I don't see any of the children."

"Frightened away by the grand carriage, I expect," said Mr. Colwyn, with a grim smile. "I see a head or two at the window. Here, Joey, Georgie, Tiny—where are you all? Come and help to carry your sister's things upstairs." He went to the front door and called again; whereupon a side door opened, and from it issued a slip-shod, untidy-looking woman in a shawl, while over her shoulder and under her arm appeared a little troop of children in various stages of growth and untidiness. Mrs. Colwyn had the peculiarity of never being ready for any engagement, much less for any emergency: she had been expecting Janetta all day, and with Janetta some of the Court party; but she was nevertheless in a state of semi-undress, which she tried to conceal underneath her shawl; and on the first intimation of the approach of Lady Caroline's carriage she had shut herself and the children into a back room, and declared her intention of fainting on the spot if Lady Caroline entered the front door.

"Well, Janetta," she said, as she advanced towards her stepdaughter and presented one faded cheek to be kissed, "so your grand friends have brought you home! Of course they wouldn't come in; I did not expect them, I am sure. Come into the front room—and children, don't crowd so; your sister will speak to you by-and-bye."

"Oh, no, let me kiss them now," said Janetta, who was receiving a series of affectionate hugs that went far to blind her eyes to the general deficiency of orderliness and beauty in the house to which she had come. "Oh, darlings, I am so glad to see you again! Joey, how you have grown! And Tiny isn't Tiny any longer! Georgie, you have been plaiting your hair! And here are Curly and Jinks! But where is Nora?"

"Upstairs, curling her hair," shouted the child who was known by the name of Jinks. While Georgie, a well-grown girl of thirteen, added in a lower tone,

"She would not come down until the Court people had gone. She said *she* didn't want to be patronized."

Janetta colored, and turned away. Meanwhile Mrs. Colwyn had dropped into the nearest arm-chair, and Mr. Colwyn strayed in and out of the room with the expression of a dog that has lost its master. Georgie hung upon Janetta's arm, and the younger children either clung to their elder sister, or stared at her with round eyes and their fingers in their mouths. Janetta felt uncomfortably conscious of being more than usually interesting to them all. Joe, the eldest boy, a dusty lad of fourteen, all legs and arms, favored her with a broad grin expressive of delight, which his sister did not understand. It was Tiny, the most gentle and delicate of the tribe, who let in a little light on the subject.

"Did they send you away from school for being naughty?" she asked, with a grave look into Janetta's face.

A chuckle from Joey, and a giggle from Georgie, were instantly repressed by Mr. Colwyn's frown and Mrs. Colwyn's acid remonstrance.

"What are you thinking of, children? Sister is never naughty. We do not yet quite understand why she has left Miss Polehampton's so suddenly, but of course she has some good reason. She'll explain it, no doubt, to her papa and me. Miss Polehampton has been a great deal put out about it all, and has written a long letter to your papa, Janetta; and, indeed, it seems to *me* as if it would have been more becoming if you had kept to your own place and not tried to make friends with those above you——"

"Who are those above her, I should like to know?" broke in the grey-haired surgeon with some heat. "My Janet's as good as the best of them any day. The Adairs are not such grand people as Miss Polehampton makes out—I never heard of such insulting distinctions!"

"Fancy Janetta being sent away—regularly expelled!" muttered Joey, with another chuckle.

"You are very unkind to talk in that way!" said Janetta, addressing him, because at that moment she could not bear to look at Mr. Colwyn. "It was not *that* that made Miss Polehampton angry. It was what she called insubordination. Miss Adair did not like to see me having meals at a side-table—though I didn't mind one single bit!—and she left her own place and sat by me—and then Miss Polehampton was vexed—and everything followed naturally. It was not just my being friends with Miss Adair that made her send me away."

"It seems to me," said Mr. Colwyn, "that Miss Adair was very inconsiderate."

"It was all her love and friendship, father," pleaded Janetta. "And she had always had her own way; and of course she did not think that Miss Polehampton really meant— —"

Her weak little excuses were cut short by a scornful laugh from her stepmother.

"It's easy to see that you have been made a cat's-paw of, Janetta," she said. "Miss Adair was tired of school, and took the opportunity of making a to-do about you, so as to provoke the schoolmistress and get sent away. It does not matter to her, of course: *she* hasn't got her living to earn. And if you lose your teaching, and Miss Polehampton's recommendations by it, it doesn't affect her. Oh, I understand these fine ladies and their ways."

"Indeed," said Janetta, in distress, "you quite misunderstand Miss Adair, mamma. Besides, it has not deprived me of my teaching: Miss Polehampton had told me that I might go to her sister's school at Worthing if I liked; and she only let me go yesterday because she became irritated at—at—some of the things that were said— —"

"Yes, but I shall not let you go to Worthing," said Mr. Colwyn, with sudden decisiveness. "You shall not be exposed to insolence of this kind any longer. Miss Polehampton had no right to treat you as she did, and I shall write and tell her so."

"And if Janetta stays at home," said his wife complainingly, "what is to become of her career as a music-teacher? She can't get lessons here, and there's the expense— —"

"I hope I can afford to keep my daughter as long as I am alive," said Mr. Colwyn with some vehemence. "There, don't be vexed, my dear child," and he laid his hand tenderly on Janetta's shoulder, "nobody blames you; and your friend erred perhaps from over-affection; but Miss Polehampton"— with energy—"is a vulgar, self-seeking, foolish old woman, and I won't have you enter into relations with her again."

And then he left the room, and Janetta, forcing back the tears in her eyes, did her best to smile when Georgie and Tiny hugged her simultaneously and Jinks beat a tattoo upon her knee.

"Well," said Mrs. Colwyn, lugubriously, "I hope everything will turn out for the best; but it is not at all nice, Janetta, to think that Miss Adair has been expelled for your sake, or that you are thrown out of work without a character, so to speak. I should think the Adairs would see that, and would make some compensation. If they don't offer to do so, your papa might suggest it— —"

"I'm sure father would never suggest anything of the kind," Janetta flashed out; but before Mrs. Colwyn could protest, a diversion was effected by the entrance of the missing Nora, and all discussion was postponed to a more fitting moment.

For to look at Nora was to forget discussion. She was the eldest of the second Mrs. Colwyn's children—a girl just seventeen, taller than Janetta and thinner, with the thinness of immature girlhood, but with a fair skin and a mop of golden-brown hair, which curled so naturally that her younger brother's statement concerning those fair locks must surely have been a libel. She had a vivacious, narrow, little face, with large eyes like a child's— that is to say, they had the transparent look that one sees in some children's eyes, as if the color had been laid on in a single wash without any shadows. They were very pretty eyes, and gave light and expression to a set of rather small features, which might have been insignificant if they had belonged to an insignificant person. But Nora Colwyn was anything but insignificant.

"Have your fine friends gone?" she said, peeping into the room in pretended alarm. "Then I may come in. How are you, Janetta, after your sojourn in the halls of dazzling light?"

"Don't be absurd, Nora," said her sister, with a sudden backward dart of remembrance to the tranquil beauty of the rooms at Helmsley Court and the silver accents of Lady Caroline. "Why didn't you come down before?"

"My dear, I thought the nobility and gentry were blocking the door," said Nora, kissing her. "But since they are gone, you might as well come upstairs with me and take off your things. Then we can have tea."

Obediently Janetta followed her sister to the little room which they always shared when Janetta was at home. It might have looked very bare and desolate to ordinary eyes, but the girl felt the thrill of pleasure that all young creatures feel to anything that bears the name of home, and became aware of a satisfaction such as she had not experienced in her luxurious bedroom at Helmsley Court. Nora helped her to take off her hat and cloak, and to unpack her box, insisting meanwhile on a detailed relation of all the events that had led to Janetta's return three weeks before the end of the term, and shrieking with laughter over what she called "Miss Poley's defeat."

"But, seriously, Nora, what shall I do with myself, if father will not let me go to Worthing?"

"Teach the children at home," said Nora, briskly; "and save me the trouble of looking after them. I should like that. Or get some pupils in the town. Surely the Adairs will recommend you!"

This constant reference to possible aid from the Adairs troubled Janetta not a little, and it was with some notion of combatting the idea that she repaired to the surgery after tea, in order to get a few words on the subject with her father. But his first remark was on quite a different matter.

"Here's a pretty kettle of fish, Janet! The Brands are back again!"

"So I heard you say to Lady Caroline."

"Mark Brand was a cousin of your mother's," said Mr. Colwyn, abruptly; "and a bad lot. As for these sons of his, I know nothing about them—absolutely nothing. But their mother——" he shook his head significantly.

"We saw them to day," said Janetta.

"Ah, an accident of that kind would be a shock to her: she does not look strong. They wrote to me from the 'Clown,' where they had stayed for the last two days; some question relative to the drainage of Brand Hall. I went to the 'Crown' and saw them. He's a fine-looking man."

"He has not altogether a pleasant expression," remarked Janetta, thinking of Lady Caroline's strictures; "but I—liked—his face."

"He looks ill-tempered," said her father. "And I can't say that he showed me much civility. He did not even know that your poor mother was dead. Never asked whether she had left any family or anything."

"Did you tell him?" asked Janetta, after a pause.

"No. I did not think it worth while. I am not anxious to cultivate his acquaintance."

"After all, what does it matter?" said the girl coaxingly, for she thought she saw a shadow of disappointment upon his face.

"No, what does it matter?" said her father, brightening up at once. "As long as we are happy with each other, these outside people need not disturb us, need they?"

"Not a bit," said Janetta. "And—you are not angry with me, are you, father, dear?"

"Why should I be, my Janet? You have done nothing wrong that I know of. If there is any blame it attaches to Miss Adair, not to you."

"But I do not want you to think so, father. Miss Adair is the greatest friend that I have in all the world."

And she found a good many opportunities of repeating; this conviction of hers during the next few days, for Mrs. Colwyn and Nora were not slow to repeat the sentiment with which they had greeted her—that the Adairs were "stuck-up" fine people, and that they did not mean to take any further notice of her now that they had got what they desired.

Janetta stood up gallantly for her friend, but she did feel it a little hard that Margaret had not written or come to see her since her return home. She conjectured—and in the conjecture she was nearly right—that Lady Caroline had sacrificed her a little in order to smooth over things with her daughter: that she had represented Janetta as resolved upon going, resolved upon neglecting Margaret and not complying with her requests; and that Margaret was a little offended with her in consequence. She wrote an affectionate note of excuse to her friend, but Margaret made no reply.

In the first ardor of a youthful friendship, Janetta's heart ached over this silence, and she meditated much as she lay nights upon her little white bed in Nora's attic (for she had not time to meditate during the day) upon the smoothness of life which seemed necessary to the Adairs and the means they took for securing it. On the whole, their life seemed to her too artificial, too much like the life of delicate hot-house flowers under glass; and she came to the conclusion that she preferred her own mode of existence—troublous and hurried and common as it might seem in the eyes of the world to be. After all, was it not pleasant to know that while she was at home, there was a little more comfort than usual for her over-worked, hardly-driven, careworn father; she could see that his meals were properly cooked and served when he came in from long and weary expeditions into the country or amongst the poor of Beaminster; she could help Joey and Georgie in the evenings with their respective lessons; she could teach and care for the younger children all day long. To her stepmother she did not feel that she was very useful; but she could at any rate make new caps for her, new lace fichus and bows, which caused Mrs. Colwyn occasionally to remark with some complacency that Janetta had been quite *wasted* at Miss Polehampton's school: her proper destiny was evidently to be a milliner.

Nora was the one person of the family who did not seem to want Janetta's help. Indirectly, however, the elder sister was more useful to her than she knew; for the two went out together and were companions. Hitherto Nora had walked alone, and had made one or two undesirable girl acquaintances. But these were dropped when she had Janetta to talk to, dropped quietly, without a word, much to their indignation, and without Janetta's knowing of their existence.

It became a common thing for the two girls to go out together in the long summer evenings, when the work of the day was over, and stroll along the country roads, or venture into the cool shadow of the Beaminster woods. Sometimes the children went with them: sometimes Janetta and Nora went alone. And it was when they were alone one evening that a somewhat unexpected incident came to pass.

The Beaminster woods ran for some distance in a northerly direction beyond Beaminster, and there was a point where only a wire fence divided them from the grounds of Brand Hall. Near this fence Janetta and her sister found themselves one evening—not that they had purposed to reach the boundary, but that they had strayed a little from the beaten path. As they neared the fence they looked at each other and laughed.

"I did not know that we were so near the lordly dwelling of your relations!" said Nora, who loved to tease, and knew that she could always rouse Janetta's indignation by a reference to her "fine friends."

"I did not know either," returned Janetta, good-humoredly. "We can see the house a little. Look at the great red chimneys."

"I have been over it," said Nora, contemptuously. "It's a poor little place, after all—saving your presence, Netta! I wonder if the Brands mean to acknowledge your existence? They——"

She stopped short, for her foot had caught on something, and she nearly stumbled. Janetta stopped also, and the two sisters uttered a sudden cry of surprise. For what Nora had stumbled over was a wooden horse—a child's broken toy—and deep in the bracken before them, with one hand beneath his flushed and dimpled cheek, there lay the loveliest of all objects—a sleeping child.

CHAPTER VII
NORA'S NEW ACQUAINTANCE

"He must have lost his way," said Janetta, bending over him. "Poor little fellow!"

"He's a pretty little boy," said Nora, carelessly. "His nurse or his mother or somebody will be near, I dare say—perhaps gone up to the house. Shall I look about?"

"Wait a minute—he is awake—he will tell us who he is."

The child, roused by the sound of voices, turned a little, stretched himself, then opened his great dark eyes, and fixed them full on Janetta's face. What he saw there must have reassured him, for a dreamy smile came to his lips, and he stretched out his little hands to her.

"You darling!" cried Janetta. "Where did you come from, dear? What is your name?"

The boy raised himself and looked about him. He looked about five years old, and was a remarkably fine and handsome child. It was in perfectly clear and distinct English—almost free from any trace of baby dialect—that he replied—

"Mammy brought me. She said I should find my father here. I don't want my father," he remarked, decidedly.

"Who is your father? What is your name?" Nora asked.

"My name is Julian Wyvis Brand," said the little fellow, sturdily; "and I want to know where my father lives, if you please, 'cause it'll soon be my bed-time, and I'm getting very hungry."

Janetta and her sister exchanged glances.

"Is your father's name Wyvis Brand, too?" asked Janetta.

"Yes, same as mine," said the boy, nodding. He stood erect now, and she noticed that his clothes, originally of fashionable cut and costly material, were torn and stained and shabby. He had a little bundle beside him, tied up in a gaudy shawl; and the broken toy-horse seemed to have fallen out of it.

"But where is your mother?"

"Mammy's gone away. She told me to go and find my father at the big red house there. I did go once; but they thought I was a beggar, and they sent me away. I don't know what to do, I don't. I wish mammy would come."

"Will she come soon?"

"She said no. Never, never, never. She's gone over the sea again," said the boy, with the abstracted, meditative look which children sometimes assume when they are concocting a romance, and which Janetta was quick to remark. "I think she's gone right off to America or London. But she said that I was to tell my father that she would never come back."

"What are we to do?" said Nora, in an under tone.

"We must take him to Brand Hall," Janetta answered, "and ask to see either Mrs. Brand or Mr. Wyvis Brand."

"Won't it be rather dreadful?"

Janetta turned hastily on her sister. "Yes," she said, with decision, "it is very awkward, indeed, and it may be much better that you should not be mixed up in the matter at all. You must stay here while I go up to the house."

"But, Janetta, wouldn't you rather have some one with you?"

"I think it will be easier alone," Janetta answered. "You see, I have seen Mrs. Brand and her son already, and I feel as if I knew what they would be like. Wait for me here: I daresay I shall not be ten minutes. Come, dear, will you go with me to see if we can find your father?"

"Yes," said the boy, promptly putting his hand in hers.

"Are these your things in the bundle?"

"Yes; mammy put them there. There's my Sunday suit, and my book of 'Jack, the Giantkiller,' you know. And my wooden horse; but it's broke. Will you carry the horse for me?—and I'll carry the bundle."

"Isn't it too heavy for you?"

"Not a bit," and the little fellow grasped it by both bands, and swung it about triumphantly.

"Come along, then," said Janetta, with a smile. "Wait for me here, Nora, dear: I shall then find you easily when I come back."

She marched off, the boy stumping after her with his burden. Nora noticed that after a few minutes' walk her sister gently relieved him of the load and carried it herself.

"Just like Janetta," she soliloquized, as the two figures disappeared behind a clump of tall trees; "she was afraid of spoiling the moral if she did not let him *try* at least to carry the bundle. She always is afraid of spoiling the moral: I never knew such a conscientious person in my life. I am sure, as mamma says, she sets an excellent example."

And then Nora balanced herself on the loose wire of the fence, which made an excellent swing, and poising herself upon it she took off her hat, and resigned herself to waiting for Janetta's return. Naturally, perhaps, her meditations turned upon Janetta's character.

"I wish I were like her," she said to herself. "Wherever she is she seems to find work to do, and makes herself necessary and useful. Now, I am of no use to anybody. I don't think I was ever meant to be of use. I was meant to be ornamental!" She struck the wire with the point of her little shoe, and looked at it regretfully. "I have no talent, mamma says. I can look nice, I believe, and that is all. If I were Margaret Adair I am sure I should be very much admired! But being only Nora Colwyn, the doctor's daughter, I must mend socks and make puddings, and eat cold mutton and wear old frocks to the end of the chapter! What a mercy I am taller than Janetta! My old dresses are cut down for her, but she can't leave me *her* cast-off ones. That little wretch, Georgie, will soon be as tall as I am, I believe. Thank goodness, she will never be as pretty." And Miss Nora, who was really excessively vain, drew out of her pocket a small looking-glass, and began studying her features as therein reflected: first her eyes, when she pulled out her eyelashes and stroked her eyebrows; then her nose, which she pinched a little to make longer; then her mouth, of which she bit the lips in order to increase the color and judge of the effect. Then she took some geranium petals from the flowers in her belt and rubbed them on her cheeks: the red stain became her mightily, she thought, and was almost as good as rouge.

Thus engaged, she did not hear steps on the pathway by which she and Janetta had come. A man, young and slim, with a stoop and a slight halt in his walk, with bright, curling hair, worn rather longer than Englishmen usually wear it, with thin but expressive features, and very brilliant blue eyes—this was the personage who now appeared upon the scene. He stopped short rather suddenly when he became aware of the presence of a young lady upon the fence—perhaps it was to him a somewhat startling one: then, when he noted how she was engaged, a smile broke gradually over his countenance. He once made a movement to advance, then restrained himself and waited; but some involuntary rustle of the branches above him or twigs under his feet revealed him. Nora gave a little involuntary cry, dropped her looking-glass, and colored crimson with vexation at finding that some one was watching her.

"What ought I to do, I wonder?" Such was the thought that flashed through the young man's mind. He was remarkably quick in receiving impressions and in drawing conclusions. "She is not a French girl, thank goodness, fresh from a convent, and afraid to open her lips! Neither is she the conventional young English lady, or she would not sit on a fence and look at herself in a pocket looking-glass. At least, I suppose she would not: how should I know what English girls would do? At any rate, here goes for addressing her."

All these ideas passed through his mind in the course of the second or two which elapsed while he courteously raised his hat, and advanced to pick up the fallen hand-glass. But Nora was too quick for him. She had slipped off the fence and secured her mirror before he could reach it; and then, with a look of quite unnecessary scorn and anger, she almost turned her back upon him, and stood looking at the one angle of the house which she could see.

The young man brushed his moustache to conceal a smile, and ventured on the remark that he had been waiting to make.

"I beg your pardon; I trust that I did not startle you."

"Not at all," said Nora, with dignity. But she did not turn round.

"If you are looking for the gate into the grounds," he resumed, with great considerateness of manner, "you will find it about twenty yards further to your left. Can I have the pleasure of showing you the way?"

"No, thank you," said Miss Nora, very ungraciously. "I am waiting for my sister." She felt that some explanation was necessary to account for the fact that she did not immediately walk away.

"Oh, I beg your pardon," said the young man once more, but this time in a rather disappointed tone. Then, brightening—"But if your sister has gone up to our house why won't you come in too?"

"*Your* house?" said Nora, unceremoniously, and facing him with an air of fearless incredulity, which amused him immensely. "But *you* are not Mr. Brand?"

"My name is Brand," said the young fellow, smiling the sunniest smile in the world, and again raising his hat, with what Nora now noticed to be a rather foreign kind of grace: "and if you know it, I feel that it is honored already."

Nora knitted her brows. "I don't know what you mean," she said, impatiently, "but you are not Mr. Brand of the Hall, are you?"

"I live at the Hall, certainly, and my name is Brand—Cuthbert Brand, at your service."

"Oh, I see. Not Wyvis Brand?" said Nora impulsively. "Not the father of the dear little boy that we found here just now?"

Cuthbert Brand's fair face colored. He looked excessively surprised.

"The father—a little boy? I am afraid," he said, with some embarrassment of manner, "that I do not exactly know what you mean——"

"It is just this," said Nora, losing her contemptuous manner and coming closer to the speaker; "when my sister and I were walking this way we saw a little boy lying here fast asleep. He woke up and told us that his name was Julian Wyvis Brand, and that his mother had left him here, and told him to find his father, who lived at that red house."

"Good heavens! And the woman—what became of her?"

"The boy said she had gone away and would not come back."

"I trust she may not," muttered Cuthbert angrily to himself. A red flush colored his brow as he went on. "My brother's wife," he said formally, "is not—at present—on very friendly terms with him; we did not know that she intended to bring the child home in this manner: we thought that she desired to keep it—where is the boy, by the way?"

"My sister has taken him up to the Hall. She said that she would see Mr. Brand."

Cuthbert raised his eyebrows. "See my brother?" he repeated as if involuntarily. "My brother!"

"She is his second cousin, you know: I suppose that gives her courage," said Nora smiling at the tone of horror which she fancied must be simulated for the occasion. But Cuthbert was in earnest—he knew Wyvis Brand's temper too well to anticipate anything but a rough reception for any one who seemed inclined to meddle with his private affairs. And if Nora's sister were like herself! For Nora did not look like a person who would bear roughness or rudeness from any one.

"Then are you my cousin, too?" he asked, suddenly struck by an idea that sent a gleam of pleasure to his eye.

"Oh, no," said Nora, demurely. "I'm no relation. It is only Janetta—her mother was Mr. Brand's father's cousin. But that was not my mother—Janetta and I are stepsisters."

"Surely that makes a relationship, however," said Cuthbert, courageously. "If your stepsister is my second cousin, you must be a sort of step-second-cousin to me. Will you not condescend to acknowledge the connection?"

"Isn't the condescension all on your side?" said Nora coolly. "It may be a connection, but it certainly isn't a relationship."

"I am only too glad to hear you call it a connection," said Cuthbert, with gravity. And then the two laughed—Nora rather against her will—Cuthbert out of amusement at the situation, and both out of sheer light-heartedness. And when they had laughed the ice seemed to be broken, and they felt as if they were old friends.

"I did not know that any of our relations were living in Beaminster," he resumed, after a moment's pause.

"I suppose you never even heard our name," said Nora, saucily.

"I don't—know——" he began, in some confusion.

"Of course you don't. Your father had a cousin and she married a doctor—a poor country surgeon, and so of course you forgot all about her existence. She was not *my* mother, so I can speak out, you know. Your father never spoke to her again after she married *my* father."

"More shame to him! I remember now. Your father is James Colwyn."

Nora nodded. "I think it was a very great shame," she said.

"And so do I," said Cuthbert, heartily.

"It was all the worse," Nora went on, quite forgetting in her eagerness whom she was talking to, "because Mr. Brand was not himself so very much thought of, you know—people did not think—oh, I forgot! I beg your pardon!" she suddenly ejaculated, turning crimson as she remembered that the man to whom she was speaking was the son of the much-abused Mr. Brand, who had been considered the black sheep of the county.

"Don't apologize, pray," said Cuthbert, lightly. "I'm quite accustomed to hearing my relations spoken ill of. What was it that people did not think?"

"Oh," said Nora, now covered with confusion, "of course I could not tell you."

"It was so very bad, was it?" said the young man, laughing. "You need not be afraid. Really and seriously, I have been told that my poor father was not very popular about here, and I don't much wonder at it, for although he was a good father to us he was rather short in manner, and, perhaps, I may add, in temper. Wyvis is like him exactly, I believe."

"And are you?" asked Nora.

Cuthbert raised his hat and gave it a tremendous flourish. "Mademoiselle, I have not that honor," he replied.

"I suppose I ought not to have asked," said Nora to herself, but this time she restrained herself and did not say it aloud. "I wonder where Janetta is?" she murmured after a moment's silence. "I did not think that she would be so long."

If Cuthbert thought the remark ungracious, as he might well have done, he made no sign of discomfiture. "Can I do anything?" he asked. "Shall I go to the house and find out whether she has seen my brother? But then I shall have to leave you."

"Oh, that doesn't matter," said Nora, innocently.

"Doesn't it? But I hardly like the idea of leaving you all alone. There might be tramps about. If you are like all the other young ladies I have known, you will have an objection to tramps."

"I am sure," said Nora, with confidence, "that I am not at all like the other young ladies you know; but at the same time I must confess that I don't like tramps."

"I knew it. And I saw a tramp—I am sure I did—a little while ago in this very wood. He was ragged and dirty, but picturesque. I sketched him, but I think he would not be a pleasant companion for you."

"Do you sketch?" said Nora quickly.

"Oh, yes, I sketch a little," he answered in a careless sort of way—for what was the use of telling this little girl that his pictures had been hung in the Salon and the Academy, or that he had hopes of one day rising to fame and fortune in his recently adopted profession? He was not given to boasting of his own success, and besides, this child—with her saucy face and guileless eyes—would not understand either his ambitions or his achievements.

But Nora's one talent was for drawing, and although the instruction she had received was by no means of the best, she had good taste and a great desire to improve her skill. So Cuthbert's admission excited her interest at once.

"Have you been sketching now?" she asked. "Oh, do let me see what you have done?"

Cuthbert's portfolio was under his arm. He laughed, hesitated, then dropped on one knee beside her and began to exhibit his sketches. It was thus—side by side, with heads very close together—that Janetta, much to her amazement, found them on her return.

CHAPTER VIII
FATHER AND CHILD

Janetta had set off on her expedition to Brand Hall out of an impulse of mingled pity and indignation—pity for the little boy, indignation against the mother who could desert him, perhaps against the father too. This feeling prevented her from realizing all at once the difficult position in which she was now placing herself; the awkwardness in which she would be involved if Mr. Brand declared that he knew nothing of the child, or would have nothing to do with it. "In that case," she said to herself, with an admiring glance at the lovely little boy, "I shall have to adopt him, I think! I wonder what poor mamma would say!"

She found her way without difficulty to the front-door of the long, low, rambling red house which was dignified by the name of Brand Hall. The place had a desolate look still, in spite of its being inhabited. Scarcely a window was open, and no white blinds or pretty curtains could be seen at the casements. The door was also shut; and as it was one of those wide oaken doors, mantled with creepers, and flanked with seats, which look as if they should always stand hospitably open, it gave the stranger a sense of coldness and aloofness to stand before it. And, also, there was neither bell nor a knocker—a fact which showed that few visitors ever made their appearance at Brand Hall. Janetta looked about her in dismay, and then tapped at the door with her fingers, while the child followed her every movement with his great wondering eyes, and finally said, gravely—

"I think they have all gone to sleep in this house, like the people in the 'Sleeping Beauty' story."

"Then you must be the Fairy Prince to wake them all up," said Janetta, laughingly.

The boy looked at her as if he understood; then, suddenly stooping, he picked up a fallen stick and proceeded to give the door several smart raps upon its oaken panels.

This summons procured a response. The door was opened, after a good deal of ineffectual fumbling at bolts and rattling of chains, by an old, white-haired serving man, who looked as if he had stepped out of the story to which

Julian had alluded. He was very deaf, and it was some time before Janetta could make him understand that she wanted to see Mrs. Brand. Evidently Mrs. Brand was not in the habit of receiving visitors. At last he conducted her to the dark little drawing-room where the mistress of the house usually sat, and here Janetta was received by the pale, grey-haired woman whom she had seen fainting on the Beaminster road. It was curious to notice the agitation of this elderly lady on Janetta's appearance. She stood up, crushed her handkerchief between her trembling fingers, took a step towards her visitor, and then stood still, looking at her with such extraordinary anxiety that Janetta was quite confused and puzzled by it. Seeing that her hostess could not in any way assist her out of her difficulty, she faced it boldly by introducing herself.

"My name is Janetta Colwyn," she began. "I believe that my mother was a relation of Mr. Brand's—a cousin——"

"Yes, a first cousin," said Mrs. Brand, nervously. "I often heard him speak of her—I never saw her——"

She paused, looked suspiciously at Janetta, and colored all over her thin face. Janetta paused also, being taken somewhat by surprise.

"No, I don't suppose you ever saw her," she said, "but then you went abroad, and my dear mother died soon after I was born. Otherwise, I daresay you would have known her."

Mrs. Brand gave her a strange look. "You think so?" she said. "But no—you are wrong: she always looked down on me. She never would have been friendly with me if she had lived."

"Indeed," said Janetta, very much astonished. "I always heard that it was the other way—that Mr. Brand was angry with *her* for marrying a poor country surgeon, and would not speak to her again."

"That is what they may have said to you. But you were too young to be told the truth," said the sad-faced woman, beginning to tremble all over as she spoke. "No, your mother would not have been friends with me. I was not her equal—and she knew I was not."

"Oh, indeed, you make a mistake: I am sure you do," cried Janetta, becoming genuinely distressed as this view of her mother's character and conduct was fixed upon her. "My mother was always gentle and kind, they tell me; I am sure she would have been your friend—as I will be, if you will let me." She held out her hands and drew those of the trembling woman into her warm young clasp. "I am a cousin too," she said, blushing a little as she asserted herself in this way, "and I hope you will let me come to see you sometimes and make you less lonely."

"I am always lonely, and I always shall be lonely to the end of time," said Mrs. Brand, slowly and bitterly. "However"—with an evident attempt to recover her self-possession—"I shall always be pleased to see you. Did—did—your father send you here to-night?"

"No," said Janetta, remembering her errand. "He does not know——"

"Does not know?" The pale woman again looked distressed. "Oh," she said, turning away with a sigh and biting her lip, "then I shall not see you again."

"Indeed you will," said Janetta, warmly. "My father would never keep me away from any one who wanted me—and one of my mother's relations too. But I came to-night because I found this dear little boy outside your grounds. He tells me that his name is Julian Wyvis Brand, and that he is your son's little boy."

For the first time Mrs. Brand turned her eyes upon the child. Hitherto she had not noticed him much, evidently thinking that he belonged to Janetta, and was also a visitor. But when she saw the boy's sweet little face and large dark eyes, she turned pale, and made a gesture as of warning or dislike.

"Take him away! take him away," she said. "Yes, I can see that it is *her* child—and his child too. She must be here too, and she has been the ruin of my boy's life!" And then she sank into a chair and burst into an agony of tears.

Janetta felt, with an inexpressible pang, that she had set foot in the midst of some domestic tragedy, the like of which had never come within her ken before. She was conscious of a little recoil from it, such as is natural to a young girl who has not learnt by experience the meaning of sorrow; but the recoil was followed by a rush of that sympathy for which she had always shown a great capacity. Her instinct led her instantly to comfort and console. She knelt down beside the weeping woman and put one arm round her, drawing the little boy forward with her left hand as she spoke.

"Oh, don't cry—don't cry!" she murmured. "He has come to be a joy and a comfort to you, and he wants you to love him too."

"Won't you love me, grandmamma?" said the sweet childish voice. And Julian laid his hand on the poor woman's shaking knee. "Don't cry, grandmamma."

It was this scene which met the eyes of Wyvis Brand when he turned the handle of the drawing-room door and walked into the room. His mother weeping, with a child before her, and a dark-haired girl on her knees with one arm round the weeping woman and one round the lovely child. It was a pretty picture, and Wyvis Brand was not insensible to its beauty.

He stood, looking prom one to another of the group.

"What does all this mean?" he asked, in somewhat harsh tones.

His mother cried aloud and caught the child to her breast.

"Oh, Wyvis, be kind—be merciful," she gasped. "This is your child— your child. You will not drive him away. She has left him at our door."

Wyvis walked into the room, shut the door behind him, and leaned against it.

"Upon my word," he said, sarcastically, "you will give this lady—whose name I haven't the pleasure of knowing—a very fine idea of our domestic relations. I am not such a brute, I hope, as to drive away my own child from my door; but I certainly should like to know first whether it is my child; and more particularly whether it is my son and heir, as I have no doubt that this young gentleman is endeavoring to persuade you. Did *you* bring the child here?" he said, turning sharply to Janetta.

"I brought him into the house, certainly," she said, rising from her knees and facing him. "I found him outside your fence; and he told me that his name was Julian Wyvis Brand."

"Pretty evidence," said Mr. Brand, very rudely, as Janetta thought. "Who can tell whether the child is not some beggar's brat that has nothing to do with me?"

"Don't you know your own little boy when you see him?" Janetta demanded, indignantly.

"Not I. I have not set eyes on him since he was a baby. Turn round, youngster, and let me have a look at you."

The child faced him instantly, much as Janetta herself had done. There was a fearless look in the baby face, an innocent, guileless courage in the large dark eyes, which must surely, thought Janetta, touch a father's heart. But Wyvis Brand looked as if it would take a great deal to move him.

"Where do you come from?" said Mr. Brand, sternly.

"From over the sea."

"That's no answer. Where from?—what place?"

68 | A True Friend

The boy looked at him without answering.

"Are you dumb?" said Wyvis Brand, harshly. "Or have you not been taught what to say to that question? Where do you come from, I say?"

Mrs. Brand murmured an inarticulate remonstrance; Janetta's eyes flashed an indignant protest. Both women thought that the boy would be dismayed and frightened. But he, standing steady and erect, did not flinch. His color rose and his hands clenched themselves at his side, but he did not take his eyes from his father's face as he replied.

"I come with mammy from Paris."

"And pray where is your mother?"

"Gone back again. She told me to find my father. Are you my father?" said the child, with the utmost fearlessness.

"What is your name?" asked Wyvis, utterly disregarding the question.

"Julian Wyvis Brand."

"He's got the name pat enough," said Wyvis, with a sardonic laugh. "Well, where did you live in Paris? What sort of a house had you?"

"It was near the church," said the little boy, gravely. "The church with the big pillars round it. There was a bonnet shop under our rooms, and the rooms were all pink and white and gold—prettier than this," he said, wistfully surveying the gloomy room in which he stood.

"And who took care of you when your mother was out?" asked Mr. Brand. Even Janetta could see, by the swift, subtle change that had passed over his face, that he recognized the description of the room.

"Susan. She was my nurse and mammy's maid as well. She was English."

The man nodded and set his lips. "He knows what to say," he remarked.

"Oh, Wyvis!" exclaimed his mother, as if she could repress her feelings no longer; "don't you see how like he is to you!—don't you *feel* that he is your own child?"

"I confess the paternal feelings are not very strong in me," said her son, dryly, "but I have a fancy the boy is mine for all that. Haven't you a letter or a remembrance of some sort to give me, young man?"

The boy shook his head.

"There may be something amongst his things—some book or trinket that you would remember," said Janetta, speaking with timidity. Mr.

Brand gave her a keen look, and Mrs. Brand accepted the suggestion with eagerness.

"Oh, yes, yes, let us look. Have you a box, my dear, or a bag?—oh, a bundle, only: give it me, and let me see what is inside."

"It is unnecessary, mother," said Wyvis, coldly. "I am as convinced as you can wish me to be that this is Juliet's child."

But Mrs. Brand, with trembling fingers and parted lips, was helping Janetta to unfasten the knots of the big handkerchief in which the child's worldly goods were wrapped up. Wyvis Brand stood silently beside the two women, while little Julian pressed closer and pointed out his various treasures as they were one by one disclosed.

"That's my book," he said; "and that's my best suit. And that's—oh, I don't know what *that* is. I don't know why mammy put it in."

"*I* know," said Wyvis Brand, half under his breath.

The object that called forth this remark was a small morocco box, loosely wrapped in tissue-paper. Wyvis took it out of his mother's hand, opened it, and stood silently gazing at its contents. It held a ring, as Janetta could easily see—a hoop of gold in which were three opals—not a very large or costly-looking trinket, but one which seemed to have memories or associations connected with it—to judge, at least, by the look on Wyvis Brand's dark face. The women involuntarily held their breath as they glanced at him.

At last with a short laugh, he slipped the little case into his pocket, and turned upon his heel.

"I suppose that this is evidence enough," he said. "It is a ring I once gave her—our engagement ring. Not one of much value, or you may be sure that she would never have sent it back."

"Then you are convinced—you are certain——" His mother did not finish the sentence, but her son knew what she meant.

"That he is my son? my wife's child? Oh, yes, I am pretty sure of that. He had better be put to bed," said Wyvis, carelessly. "You can find a room for him somewhere, I dare say."

"There is the old nursery," said Mrs. Brand, in breathless eagerness. "I looked into it yesterday; it is a nice, cheerful room—but it has not been used for a long time——"

"Do as you like; don't consult me," said her son. "I know nothing about the matter." And he turned to the door, without another look towards his son.

But little Julian was not minded to be treated in this way. His large eyes had been fixed upon his father with a puzzled and rather wistful expression. He now suddenly started from his position at Mrs. Brand's knee, and pursued his father to the door.

"Say good-night, please," he said, pulling at Mr. Brand's coat with a fearlessness which amused Janetta and startled Mrs. Brand.

Wyvis looked down at him with a curious and indescribable expression. "You're not shy, at any rate," he said, drily. "Well, good-night, young man. What?"—the boy had held up his face to be kissed.

The father hesitated. Then a better and softer feeling seemed to pass over his face. He stooped down and let the child put his arms round his neck, and press a warm kiss on his cheek. A short laugh then escaped his lips, as if he were half-ashamed of his own action. He went out of the room and shut the door behind him without looking round, and little Julian returned to his grandmother's knee, looking well satisfied with himself.

Janetta felt that she ought to go, and yet that she hardly liked trusting the child to the sole care of Mrs. Brand, who was evidently so much unnerved as to be of little use in deciding what was to be done with him. And at the first hint of departure grandmother and child both clung to her as if they felt her to be their sheet-anchor in storm. She was not allowed to go until she had inspected the nursery and pronounced it too damp for Julian's use, and seen a little bed made up for the child in Mrs. Brand's own room, where a fire was lighted, and everything looked cosey and bright. Poor little Julian was by this time half-dead with sleep; and Janetta could not after all make up her mind to leave him until she had seen him tucked up and fast asleep. Then she bethought herself of Nora, and turned to go. Mrs. Brand, melted out of her coldness and shy reserve, caught her by the hand.

"My dear," she said, "what should we have done without you?"

"I don't think that I have done very much," said Janetta, smiling.

"You have done more than I could ever do. If I had brought that child to my son he would never have acknowledged it."

"He does not look so hard," said the girl involuntarily.

"He *is* hard, my dear—hard in his way—but he is a good son for all that—and he has had sore trouble, which has made him seem harder and sterner than he is. I cannot thank you enough for all that you have done to-day."

"Oh, Mrs. Brand, I have done nothing," said Janetta, blushing at the elder woman's praise. "But may I come to see you and little Julian again? I should like so much to know how he gets on."

"You may come, dear, if your father will let you," said Mrs. Brand, with rather a troubled look. "It would be a blessing—a charity—to me: but I don't know whether it would be right to let you—your father must decide."

And then Janetta took her leave.

She was surprised to find that Mr. Brand was lounging about the hall as she came out, and that he not only opened the door for her but accompanied her to the garden gate. He did not speak for a minute or two, and Janetta, not seeing her way clear to any remarks of her own, wondered whether they were to walk side by side to the gate in utter silence. Presently, however, he said, abruptly.

"I have not yet heard to whom I am indebted for the appearance of that little boy in my house."

"I am not exactly responsible," said Janetta, "I only found him outside and brought him in to make inquiries. My name is Janetta Colwyn."

"Colwyn? What? the doctor's daughter?"

"Yes, the doctor's daughter," said Janetta, smiling frankly at him, "and your second cousin."

Wyvis Brand's hand went up to his hat, which he lifted ceremoniously.

"I wish I had had the introduction earlier," he said, in a much pleasanter tone.

Janetta could not exactly echo the sentiment, and therefore maintained a discreet silence.

"You must have thought me a great brute," said Wyvis, with some sensitiveness in his tone.

"Oh, no: I quite saw how difficult it was for you to understand who I was, and how it had all come about."

"You saw a great deal, then."

"Oh, I know that it sounds impertinent to say so," Janetta answered, blushing a little and walking a trifle faster, "but I did not mean it rudely, I assure you."

He seemed to take no notice. He was looking straight before him, with a somewhat sombre expression in his fine dark eyes.

"What you could not see," he said, perhaps more to himself than to her, "was what no one will ever guess. Nobody knows what the last few years have been to me. My mother has seen more of it than any one else, but even to her my life has been something of a mystery—a sealed book. You should remember this—remember all that I have passed through—before you blame me for the way in which I received that child to-day."

"I did not blame you," said Janetta, eagerly. "I only felt that there was a great deal which I could not understand."

He turned his gloomy eyes upon her. "Just so," he said. "You cannot understand. And it is useless for you to try."

"I am very sorry," Janetta faltered, scarcely knowing why she said so.

Wyvis laughed. "Don't trouble to be sorry over my affairs," he said. "They are not worth sorrow, I assure you. But—if I may make one request— will you kindly keep silence (except, of course, to your parents) about this episode? I do not want people to begin gossiping about that unhappy woman who has the right, unfortunately, to call herself my wife."

Janetta promised, and with her promise the garden gate was reached, and the interview came to an end.

CHAPTER IX
CONSULTATION

Janetta was rather surprised that Mr. Wyvis Brand did not offer to accompany her for at least part of her way homewards, but she set down his remissness to absorption in his own rather complicated affairs. In this she was not mistaken. Wyvis was far more depressed, and far more deeply buried in the contemplation of his difficulties, than anybody knew, and it completely escaped his memory until afterwards that he ought to have offered Miss Colwyn an escort. Janetta, however, was well used to going about the world alone, and she proceeded briskly to the spot where she had left Nora, and was much astonished to find that young person deep in conversation with a strange young man.

But the young man had such an attractive face, such pleasant eyes, so courteous a manner, that she melted towards him before he had got through his first sentence. Nora, of course, ought to have introduced him; but she was by no means well versed in the conventionalities of society, and therefore left him to do what he pleased, and to introduce himself.

"I find that I am richer than I thought," said Cuthbert Brand, "in possessing a relative whom I never heard of before! Miss Colwyn, are we not cousins? My name is Brand—Cuthbert Brand."

Janetta's face lighted up. "I have just seen Mrs. Brand and your brother," she said, offering him her hand.

"And, oh, Janetta!" cried Nora at once, "do tell us what happened. Have you left the little boy at Brand Hall? And is it really Mr. Brand's little boy?"

"Yes, it is, and I have left him with his father," said Janetta, gravely. "As it is getting late, Nora, we had better make the best of our way home."

"You will let me accompany you?" said Cuthbert, eagerly, while Nora looked a little bit inclined to pout at her sister's serious tone. "It is, as you say, rather late; and you have a long walk before you."

"Thank you, but I could not think of troubling you. My sister and I are quite accustomed to going about by ourselves. We escort each other," said Janetta, smiling, so that he should not set her down as utterly ungracious.

"I am a good walker," said Cuthbert, coloring a little. He was half afraid that they thought his lameness a disqualification for accompanying them. "I do my twenty miles a day quite easily."

"Thank you," Janetta said again. "But I could not think of troubling you. Besides, Nora and I are so well used to these woods, and to the road between them and Beaminster, that we really do not require an escort."

A compromise was finally effected. Cuthbert walked with them to the end of the wood, and the girls were to be allowed to pursue their way together along the Beaminster road. He made himself very agreeable in their walk through the wood, and did not leave them, without a hope that he might be allowed one day to call upon his newly-discovered cousins.

"He has adopted us, apparently, as well as yourself," said Nora, as the two girls tramped briskly along the Beaminster road. "He seems to forget that *we* are not his relations."

"He is very pleasant and friendly," said Janetta.

"But why did you say he might call?" pursued Nora. "I thought that you would say that we did not have visitors—or something of that sort."

"My dear Nora! But we do have visitors."

"Yes; but not of that kind."

"Don't you want him to come?" said Janetta, in some wonderment; for it had struck her that Nora had shown an unusual amount of friendliness to Mr. Cuthbert Brand.

"No, I don't," said Nora, almost passionately. "I *don't* want to see him down in our shabby, untidy little drawing-room, to hear mamma talk about her expenses and papa's difficulties—to see all that tribe of children in their old frocks—to see the muddle in which we live! I don't want him there at all."

"Dear Nora, I don't think that the Brands have been accustomed to live in any very grand way. I am sure the rooms I went into this evening were quite shabby—nearly as shabby as ours, and much gloomier. What does it matter?"

"It does not matter to you," said Nora; "because you are their relation. It is different for us. You belong to them and we don't."

"I think you are quite wrong to talk in that way. It is nothing so very great and grand to be related to the Brands."

"They are 'County' people," said Nora, with a scornful little emphasis on the word. "They are like your grand Adairs: they would look down on a country doctor and his family, except just now and then when they could make them useful."

"Look down on father? What are you thinking of?" cried Janetta, warmly. "Nobody looks down on father, because he does good, honest work in the world, and everybody respects him; but I am afraid that a good many people look down on the Brands. You know that as well as I do, Nora; for you have heard people talk about them. They are not at all well thought of in this neighborhood. I don't suppose there is much honor and glory to be gained by relationship to them."

In which Janetta was quite right, and showed her excellent sense. But Nora was not inclined to be influenced by her more sagacious sister.

"You may say what you like," she observed; "but I know very well that it is a great advantage to be related to 'the County.' Poor papa has no connections worth speaking of, and mamma's friends are either shopkeepers or farmers; but your mother was the Brands' cousin, and see how the Adairs took you up! They would never have made a fuss over *me*."

"What nonsense you talk, Nora!" said Janetta, in a disgusted tone.

"Nonsense or not, it is true," said Nora, doggedly; "and as long as people look down upon us, I don't want any of your fine friends and relations in Gwynne Street."

Janetta did not condescend to argue the point; she contented herself with telling her sister of Wyvis Brand's desire that the story of his wife's separation from him should not be known, and the two girls agreed that it would be better to mention their evening's adventure only to their father.

It was quite dark when they reached home, and they entered the house in much trepidation, fearing a volley of angry words from Mrs. Colwyn. But to their surprise and relief Mrs. Colwyn was not at home. The children explained that an invitation to supper had come to her from a neighbor, and that "after a great deal of fuss," as one of them expressed it, she had accepted it and gone, leaving word that she should not be back until eleven o'clock, and that the children were to go to bed at their usual hour. It was past the younger children's hour already, and they of course were jubilant.

The elder sisters set to work instantly to get the young ones into their beds, but this was a matter of some difficulty. A general inclination to uproariousness prevailed in Mrs. Colwyn's absence, and it must be confessed that neither Janetta nor Nora tried very hard to repress the little ones' noise. It was a comfort to be able, for once, to enjoy themselves without fear of Mrs. Colwyn's perpetual snarl and grumble. A most exciting pillow-fight was going on in the upstairs regions, and here Janetta was holding her own as boldly as the boldest, when the sound of an opening door made the combatants pause in their mad career.

"What's that? The front door? It's mamma!" cried Georgie, with conviction.

"Get into bed, Tiny!" shouted Joey. Tiny began to cry.

"Nonsense, children," said Nora, with an air of authority. "You know that it can't be mamma. It is papa, of course, coming in for his supper. And one of us must go down."

"I'll go," said Janetta, hurriedly. "I want a little talk with him, you know."

There was a general chorus of "Oh, don't go, Janetta!" "Do stay!" "It will be no fun when you are gone!" which stimulated Nora to a retort.

"Well, I must say you are all very polite," she said. "One would think that I was not here at all!"

"You are not half such good fun as Janetta," said Joey. "You don't throw yourself into everything as she does."

"I must throw myself into giving father his supper, I'm afraid," said Janetta, laughing, "so good-night, children, and do go to bed quietly now, for I don't think father will like such a dreadful noise."

She was nearly choked by the fervent embraces they all bestowed upon her before she went downstairs. Nora, who stood by, rolling up the ribbon that she had taken from Tiny's hair, felt a little pang of jealousy. Why was it that everyone loved Janetta and valued her so much? Not for what she did, because her share of household duty was not greater than that of Nora, but for the way in which she did it. It always seemed such a pleasure to her to do anything for any one—to serve another: never a toil, never a hardship, always a deep and lasting pleasure. To Nora it was often a troublesome matter to help her sister or her schoolboy brother, to attend on her mother, or to be thoughtful of her father's requirements; but it was never troublesome to Janetta. And as Nora thought of all this, the tears came involuntarily to her eyes. It seemed so *easy* to Janetta to be good, she thought! But perhaps it was no easier to Janetta than to other people.

Janetta ran down to the dining-room, where she found her father surveying with a rather dissatisfied air the cold and scanty repast which was spread out for him. Mr. Colwyn was so much out that his meals had to be irregular, and he ate them just when he had a spare half hour. On this occasion he had been out since two o'clock in the afternoon, and had not had time even for a cup of tea. He had been attending a hopeless case, moreover, and one about which he had been anxious for some weeks. Fagged, chilled, and dispirited, it was no wonder that he had returned home in not the best of tempers, and that he was a little disposed to find fault when Janetta made her appearance.

"Where is mamma?" he began. "Out, I suppose, or the children would not be making such a racket overhead."

"They are going to be quiet now, dear father," said his daughter, kissing him, "and mamma has gone out to supper at Mrs. Maitland's. I am going to have mine with you if you will let me."

"And is this what you are going to have for your supper?" said Mr. Colwyn, half ruefully, half jestingly, as he glanced again at the table, where some crusts of bread reposed peacefully on one dish, and a scrag of cold mutton on another. "After your sojourn at Miss Polehampton's and among the Adairs, I suppose you don't know how to cook, Jenny?"

"Indeed I do, father, and I'm going to scramble some eggs, and make some coffee this very minute. I am sorry the table is not better arranged, but I have been out, and was just having a little game with the children before they went to bed. If you will sit down by the fire, I shall be ready in a very few minutes, and then I can tell you about a wonderful adventure that Nora and I had this evening in the Beaminster wood."

"You should not roam about those woods so much by yourselves; they are too lonely," said Mr. Colwyn; but he said it very mildly, and dropped with an air of weariness into the arm-chair that Janetta had wheeled forward for him. "Well, well! don't hurry yourself, child. I shall be glad of a few minutes' rest before I begin my supper."

Janetta in a big white apron, Janetta flitting backwards and forwards between kitchen and dining-room, with flushed cheeks and brightly shining eyes, was a pretty sight—"a sight to make an old man young," thought Mr. Colwyn, as he watched her furtively from beneath his half-closed eyelids. She looked so trim, so neat, so happy in her work, that he would be hard to satisfy who did not admire her, even though she was not what the world calls strictly beautiful. She succeeded so well in her cooking operations, with which she would not allow the servant to intermeddle, that in a very short time a couple of dainty dishes and some coffee smoked upon the board; and

Janetta bidding her father come to the table, placed herself near him, and smilingly dispensed the savory concoction.

She would not enter upon any account of her evening's work until she felt sure that the wants of her father's inner man were satisfied; but when supper was over, and his evening pipe—the one luxury in the day he allowed himself—alight, she drew up a hassock beside his chair and prepared for what she called "a good long chat."

Opportunities for such a chat with her father were rather rare in that household, and Janetta meant to make the most of this one. Nora had good-naturedly volunteered to stay away from the dining-room, so as to give Janetta the chance that she wished for; and as it was now barely ten o'clock, Janetta knew that she might perhaps have an hour of her father's companionship—if, at least, he were not sent for before eleven o'clock. At eleven he would probably go to Mrs. Maitland's to fetch his wife home.

"Well, Janet, and what have you to tell me?" he said kindly, as he stretched out his slippered feet to the blaze, and took down his pipe from the mantel-piece. The lines had cleared away from his face as if by magic; there was a look of rest and peace upon his face that his daughter liked to see. She laid her hand on his knee and kept it there while she told him of her experiences that evening at Brand Hall.

Mr. Colwyn's eyebrows went up as he listened. His face expressed astonishment, and something very like perplexity. But he heard the whole story out before he said a word.

"Well, you have put your head into the lion's den!" he said at last, in a half-humorous tone.

"What I want to know is," said Janetta, "why it is thought to be a lion's den! I don't mean that I have heard the expression before, but I have gathered in different ways an impression that people avoid the house——"

"The family, not the house, Janet!"

"Of course I *mean* the family, father, dear. What have they done that they should be shunned?"

"There is a good deal against them in the eyes of the world. Your poor mother, Janetta, always stood up for them, and said that they were more sinned against than sinning."

"*They?* But these young men were not grown up then?"

"No; it was their father and——"

Mr. Colwyn stopped short and seemed as if he did not like to go on.

"Tell me, father," said Janetta, coaxingly.

"Well, child, I don't know that you ought to hear old scandals. But you are too wise to let them harm you. Brand, the father of these two young fellows, married a barmaid, the daughter of a low publican in the neighborhood."

"What! The Mrs. Brand that I saw to-day? *She* a barmaid—that quiet, pale, subdued-looking woman?"

"She has had trouble enough to make her look subdued, poor soul! She was a handsome girl then; and I daresay the world would have overlooked the marriage in time if her character had been untarnished. But stories which I need not repeat were afloat; and from what I have lately heard they are not yet forgotten."

"After all these years! Oh, that does seem hard," said Janetta, sympathetically.

"Well—there are some things that the world does not forgive, Janet. I have no doubt that the poor woman is much more worthy of respect and kindness than her wild sons; and yet the fact remains that if Wyvis Brand had come here with his brother alone, he would have been received everywhere, and entertained and visited and honored like any other young man of property and tolerable repute; but as he has brought his mother with him, I am very much afraid that many of the nicest people in the county mean to 'cut' him."

"It is very unfair, surely."

"Yes, it is unfair; but it is the way of the world, Janetta. If a woman's reputation is ever so slightly blackened, she can never get it fair and white again. Hence, my dear, I am a little doubtful as to whether you must go to Brand Hall again, as long as poor Mrs. Brand is there."

"Oh, father, and I promised to go!"

"You must not make rash promises another time, my child."

"But she wants me, father—she is so lonely and so sad?"

"I am sorry, my Janet, but I don't know——"

"Oh, do let me, father. I shall not be harmed; and I don't mind what the world says."

"But perhaps *I* mind," said Mr. Colwyn, quaintly.

CHAPTER X
MARGARET

Janetta looked so rueful at this remark that her father laughed a little and pulled her ear.

"I am not given to taking much notice of what the world says," he told her, "and if I thought it right for you to go to Brand Hall I should take no notice of town talk; but I think that I can't decide this matter without seeing Mrs. Brand for myself."

"I thought you had seen her, father?"

"For ten minutes or so, only. They wanted to ask me a question about the healthiness of Brand Hall, drains, and all that kind of thing. That young Brand struck me as a very sullen-looking fellow."

"His face lightens up when he talks," said Janetta, coloring and feeling hurt for a moment, she could not have told why.

"He did not talk to me," said her father, drily. "I am told that the other son has pleasanter manners."

"Cuthbert? Oh, yes," Janetta said, quickly. "He is much more amiable at first sight; he made himself very agreeable to Nora and me." And forthwith she related how the second son had made acquaintance with her sister and herself.

Mr. Colwyn did not look altogether pleased.

"H'm!—they seem very ready to cultivate us," he said, with a slight contraction of the brow. "Their father used not to know that I existed. Janet, I don't care for Nora to see much of them. You I can trust; but she is a bit of a featherbrain, and one never knows what may happen. Look to it."

"I will, father."

"And I will call on Mrs. Brand and have a chat with her. Poor soul! I daresay she has suffered. Still that does not make her a fit companion for my girls."

"If I could be of any use to her, father——"

"I know that's all you think of, Janet. You are a good child—always wanting to help others. But we must not let the spirit of self-sacrifice run away with you, you know."

He pinched her cheek softly as he spoke, and his daughter carried the long supple fingers of his hand to her lips and kissed them tenderly.

"Which reminds me," he went on rather inconsequently, "that I saw another of your friends to-day. A friend whom you have not mentioned for some time, Janetta."

"Who was that?" asked Janetta, a little puzzled by his tone.

"Another friend whom I don't quite approve of," said her father, in the same half-quizzical way, "though from a different reason. If poor Mrs. Brand is not respectable enough, this friend of yours, Janet, is more than respectable; ultra-respectable—aristocratic even— —"

"Margaret Adair!" cried Janetta, flushing to the very roots of her hair. "Did you see her, father? Has she quite forgotten me?" And the tears stood in her eyes.

"I did not see Miss Margaret Adair, my dear," said her father kindly. "I saw her mother, Lady Caroline."

"Did you speak to her, father?"

"She stopped her ponies and spoke to me in the High Street, Janet. She certainly has very winning manners."

"Oh, has she not, father!" Janetta's cheeks glowed. "She is perfectly charming, I think. I do not believe that she could do anything disagreeable or unkind."

Mr. Colwyn shook his head, with a little smile. "I am not so sure of that, Janetta. These fine ladies sometimes do very cold and cruel things with a perfectly gracious manner."

"But Lady Caroline would not," said Janetta, coaxingly. "She was quite kind and sweet to me all the time that I stayed at her house, although— —"

"Although afterwards," said Mr. Colwyn, shrewdly, "she could let you stay here for weeks without seeming to remember you, or coming near you for an hour!"

Janetta's cheeks crimsoned, but she did not reply. Loyal as she was to her friend, she felt that there was not much to be said for her at that moment.

"You are a good friend," said her father, in a half-teasing, half-affectionate tone. "You don't like me to say anything bad of her, do you?

Well, my dear, for your comfort I must tell you that she did her best to-day to make up for past omissions. She spoke very pleasantly about you."

"Did she say why—why——" Janetta could not complete the sentence.

"Why they had not written or called? Well, she gave some sort of an explanation. Miss Adair had been unwell—she had had a cold or something which looked as if it might turn to fever, and they did not like to write until she was better."

"I knew there was some good reason!" said Janetta fervently.

"It is well to take a charitable view of things," returned her father, rather drily; but, seeing her look of protest, he changed his tone. "Well, Lady Caroline spoke very kindly, my dear, I must acknowledge that. She wants you to go over to Helmsley Court to-morrow."

"Can I go, father?"

Mr. Colwyn made a grimace. "Between your disreputable friends and your aristocratic ones, I'm in a difficulty, Janet."

"Don't say so, father dear!"

"Well, I consented," said Mr. Colwyn, in rather a grudging tone. "She said that she would send her carriage for you to-morrow at noon, and that she would send you back again between six and seven. Her daughter was most anxious to see you, she said."

Janetta lifted up a happy face. "I knew that Margaret would be true to me. I never doubted her."

Mr. Colwyn watched her silently for a moment, then he put his hand upon her head, and began smoothing the thick black locks. "You have a very faithful nature, my Janet," he said, tenderly, "and I am afraid that it will suffer a great many shocks in this work-a-day world of ours. Don't let it lead you astray, my child. Remember there is a point at which faithfulness may degenerate into sheer obstinacy."

"I don't think it will ever do so with me."

"Well, perhaps not, for you have a clear head on those young shoulders of yours. But you must be careful."

"And I may go to Lady Caroline's, father?"

"Yes, my dear, you may. And now I must go: my time is up. I have had a very pleasant hour, my Janet."

As she raised herself to receive her father's kiss, she felt a glow of pleasure at his words. It was not often that he spoke so warmly. He was a man of little speech on ordinary occasions: only when he was alone with his best-loved daughter, Janetta, did he ever break forth into expressions of affection. His second marriage had been in some respects a failure; and it did not seem as if he regarded his younger children with anything approaching the tenderness which he bestowed upon Janetta. Good-humored tolerance was all that he gave to them: a deep and almost passionate love had descended from her mother to Janetta.

He went out to fetch his wife home from her supper-party; and Janetta hastened up to her room, not being anxious to meet her stepmother on her return, in the state of rampant vanity and over-excitement to which an assembly of her friends usually brought her. It could not be said that Mrs. Colwyn actually drank too much wine or beer or whisky; and yet there was often a sensation abroad that she had taken just a little more than she could bear; and her stepdaughter was sensitively aware of the fact. From Nora's slighting tone when she had lately spoken of her mother, Janetta conjectured that the sad truth of Mrs. Colwyn's danger had dawned upon the girl's mind also, and it certainly accounted for some new lines in Mr. Colwyn's face, and for some additional streaks of white in his silvering hair. Not a word had been said on the subject amongst the members of the family, but Janetta had an uneasy feeling that there were possibly rocks ahead.

At this moment, however, the prospect of seeing her dear Margaret again completely obliterated any thought of her stepmother from Janetta's mind; and when she was snugly ensconced in her own little, white bed, she could not help shedding a few tears of relief and joy. For Margaret's apparent fickleness had weighed heavily on Janetta's mind; and she now felt proud of the friend in whom she had believed in spite of appearances, and of whose faithfulness she had steadily refused to hear a doubt. These feelings enabled her to bear with cheerfulness some small unpleasantnesses next morning from her stepmother on the subject of her visit. "Of course you'll be too grand to do a hand's turn about the house when you come back again from Helmsley Court!" said Mrs. Colwyn, snappishly.

"Dear mamma, when I am only going for half a day!"

"Oh, I know the ways of girls. Because Miss Adair, your fine friend, does nothing but sit in a drawing-room all day, you'll be sure to think that you must needs follow her example!"

"I hope Margaret will do something beside sit in a drawing-room," said Janetta, with her cheery laugh; "because I am afraid that she might find that a little dull."

But in spite of her cheeriness her spirits were perceptibly lowered when she set foot in the victoria that was sent for her at noon. Her stepmother's way of begrudging her the friendship which school-life had bestowed upon Janetta was as distasteful to her as Miss Polehampton's conviction of its unsuitability had been. And for one moment the tears of vexation gathered in her brown eyes as she was driving away from the shabby little house in Gwynne Street; and she had resolutely to drive away unwelcome thoughts before she could resign herself to enjoyment of her visit.

The day was hot and close, and the narrow streets of old Beaminster were peculiarly oppressive. It was delightful to bowl swiftly along the smooth high road, and to enter the cool green shades of the park round Helmsley Court. "How pleasant for Margaret to live here always!" Janetta said to herself with generous satisfaction in her friend's good fortune. "I wonder what she would do in Gwynne Street!" And then Janetta laughed, and felt that what suited *her* would be very inappropriate to Margaret Adair.

Janetta's unselfish admiration for her friend was as simple as it was true, and it was never alloyed by envy or toadyism. She would have been just as pleased to see Margaret in a garret as in a palace, supposing that Margaret were pleased with the garret. And it was with almost passionate delight that she at length flung herself into her friend's arms, and felt Margaret's soft lips pressed to her brown flushed cheeks.

"Margaret! Oh, it is delightful to see you again!" she exclaimed.

"You poor darling: did you think that we were never going to meet?" said Margaret. "I have been so sorry, dear— —"

"I knew that you would come to see me, or send for me as soon as you could," said Janetta quickly. "I trusted you, Margaret."

"I have had such a bad cold," Margaret went on, still excusing herself a little, as it seemed to Janetta. "I have had to stay in two rooms for nearly a fortnight, and I went down to the drawing-room only last night."

"I wish I could have nursed you! Don't you remember how I nursed you through one of your bad colds at school?"

"Yes, indeed. I wish you could have nursed me now; but mamma was afraid that I had caught measles or scarlet fever or something, and she said it would not be right to send for you."

Janetta was almost pained by the accent of continued excuse.

"Of course, dear, I understand," she said, pressing her friend's arm caressingly. "I am so sorry you have been ill. You look quite pale, Margaret."

The two girls were standing in Margaret's sitting-room, adjoining her bedroom. Margaret was dressed completely in white, with long white ribbons floating amongst the dainty folds of her attire; but the white dress, exquisitely as it was fashioned, was less becoming to her than usual, for her face had lost a little of its shell-like bloom. She turned at Janetta's words and surveyed herself a little anxiously in a long glass at her side.

"I do look pale in this dress," she said. "Shall I change it, Janetta?"

"Oh, no, dear," Janetta answered, in some surprise. "It is a charming dress."

"But I do not like to look so pale," said Margaret, gravely. "I think I will ring for Villars."

"You could not look nicer—to me—in any dress!" exclaimed her ardent admirer.

"You dear—oh, yes; but there may be visitors at luncheon."

"I thought you would be alone," faltered Janetta, with a momentary glance at her own neat and clean, but plain, little cotton frock.

"Well, perhaps there will be only one person beside yourself," said Margaret, turning aside her long neck to catch a glimpse of the shining coils behind. "And I don't know that it matters—it is only Sir Philip Ashley."

"Oh, I remember him. He was here when we came back from Brighton."

"He is often here."

"What lovely flowers!" Janetta exclaimed, rather to break a pause that followed than because she had looked particularly at a bouquet that filled a large white vase on a table. But the flowers really were lovely, and Margaret's face expressed some satisfaction. "Did they come out of your garden?"

"No, Sir Philip sent them."

"Oh, how nice!" said Janetta. But she was a little surprised too. Had not the Adairs plenty of flowers without receiving contributions from Sir Philip's conservatories?

"And you have a dog, Margaret?"—as a pretty little white Esquimaux dog came trotting into the room. "What a darling! with a silver collar, too!"

"Yes, I like a white dog," said Margaret, tranquilly. "Mamma's poodle snaps at strangers, so Sir Philip thought that it would be better for me to have a dog of my own."

Sir Philip again! Janetta felt as if she must ask another question or two, especially when she saw that her friend's white eyelids had been lowered, and that a delicate flush was mantling the whiteness of her cheek; but she paused, scarcely knowing how to begin; and in the pause, the gong for luncheon sounded, and she was (somewhat hastily, she fancied) led downstairs.

Lady Caroline and Mr. Adair received their visitor with great civility. Sir Philip came forward to give her a very kindly greeting. Their behavior was so cordial that Janetta could hardly believe that she had doubted their liking for her. She was not experienced enough as yet to see that all this apparent friendliness did not mean anything but the world's way of making things pleasant all round. She accepted her host's attentions with simple pleasure, and responded to his airy talk so brightly that he lost no time in assuring his wife after luncheon that his daughter's friend was really "a very nice little girl."

After luncheon, Janetta thought at first that she was again going to be defrauded of a talk with her friend. Margaret was taken possession of by Sir Philip, and walked away with him into a conservatory to gather a flower; Mr. Adair disappeared, and Janetta was left for a few moments' conversation with Lady Caroline. Needless to remark, Lady Caroline had planned this little interview; she had one or two things that she wanted to say to Miss Colwyn. And she really did feel kindly towards the girl, because—after all—she was Margaret's friend, and the mother was ready to allow Margaret her own way to a very great extent.

"Dear Miss Colwyn," she began, "I have been so sorry that we could not see more of you while our poor Margaret was ill. *Now* I hope things will be different."

Janetta remarked that Lady Caroline was very kind.

"I have been thinking of a method by which I hoped to bring you together a little more—after the holidays. Of course we are going away very soon now—to Scotland; and we shall probably not return until October; but when that time comes—my dear Miss Colwyn, I am sure you will not be offended by the question I am going to ask?"

"Oh, no," said Janetta, hastily.

"Are you intending to give any singing or music lessons in the neighborhood?"

"If I can get any pupils, I shall be only too glad to do so."

"Then *will* you begin with dear Margaret?"

"Margaret?" said Janetta, in some astonishment. "But Margaret has had the same teaching that I have had, exactly!"

"She needs somebody to help her. She has not your talent or your perseverance. And she would so much enjoy singing with you. I trust that you will not refuse us, Miss Colwyn."

"I shall be very glad to do anything that I can for Margaret," said Janetta, flushing.

"Thank you so much. Once a week then—when we come back again. And about terms— —"

"Oh, Lady Caroline, I shall be only too glad to sing with Margaret at any time without— —"

"Without any talk about terms?" said Lady Caroline, with a charming smile of comprehension. "But that, my dear, I could not possibly allow. No, we must conduct the matter on strictly business-like principles, or Mr. Adair would be very much displeased with me. Suppose we say— —" And she went on to suggest terms which Janetta was too much confused to consider very attentively, and agreed to at once. It was only afterwards that she discovered that they were lower than any which she should ever have thought of suggesting for herself, and that she should have to blush for Lady Caroline's meanness in mentioning them to her father! But at present she saw nothing amiss.

Lady Caroline went on smoothly. "I want her to make the most of her time, because she may not be able to study up by-and-bye. She will come out this winter, and I shall take her to town in the spring. I do not suppose that I shall ever have another opportunity—if, at least, she marries as early as she seems likely to do."

"Margaret! Marry!" ejaculated Janetta. She had scarcely thought of such a possibility.

"It is exceedingly probable," said Lady Caroline, rather coldly, "that she will marry Sir Philip Ashley. It is a perfectly suitable alliance."

It sounded as if she spoke of a royal marriage!

CHAPTER XI
JANETTA'S PROMISES

"But please," Lady Caroline proceeded, "do not mention what I have said to anyone, least of all to Margaret. She is so sensitive that I should not like her to know what I have said."

"I will not say anything," said Janetta.

And then Lady Caroline's desire for conversation seemed to cease. She proposed that they should go in search of her daughter, and Janetta followed her to the conservatory in some trouble and perplexity of mind. It struck her that Margaret was not looking very well pleased when they arrived—perhaps, she thought, because of their appearance—and that Sir Philip had a very lover-like air. He was bending forward a little to take a white flower from Margaret's hand, and Janetta could not help a momentary smile when she saw the expression of his face. The earnest dark eyes were full of tenderness, which possibly he did not wish to conceal. Janetta could never doubt but that he loved her "rare pale Margaret" from the very bottom of his heart.

The two moved apart as Lady Caroline and Janetta came in. Lady Caroline advanced to Sir Philip and walked away with him, while Margaret laid her hand on Janetta's arm and led her off to her own sitting-room. She scarcely spoke until they were safely ensconced there together and then, with a half-pouting, mutinous expression on her softly flushed face—

"Janetta," she began, "there is something I must tell you."

"Yes, dear?"

"You saw Sir Philip in the conservatory?"

"Yes."

"I can't think why he is so foolish," said Margaret; "but actually, Janetta—he wants to marry me."

"Am I to call him foolish for that?"

"Yes, certainly. I am too young. I want to see a little more of the world. He is not at all the sort of man that I want to marry."

"Why not?" said Janetta, after waiting a little while.

"Oh," said Margaret, with an intonation that—for her—was almost petulant; "he is so absurdly suitable!"

"*Absurdly* suitable, dear Margaret?"

"Yes. Everything is so neatly arranged for us. He is the right age, he has the right income, the right views, the right character—he is even"— said Margaret, with increasing indignation—"even the right *height*! It is absurd. I am not to have any will of my own in the matter, because it is all so beautifully suitable. I am to be disposed of like a slave!"

Here was indeed a new note of rebellion.

"Your father and mother would never make you marry a man whom you did not like," said Janetta, a little doubtfully.

"I don't know. Papa would not; but mamma!—--I am afraid mamma will try. And it is very hard to do what mamma does not like."

"But you could explain to her——"

"I have nothing to explain," said Margaret, arching her delicate brows. "I like Sir Philip very well. I respect him very much. I think his house and his position would suit me exceedingly well; and yet I do not want to marry him. It is so unreasonable of me, mamma says. And I feel that it is; and yet—what can I do?"

"There is—nobody—else?" hazarded Janetta.

Margaret opened her lovely eyes to their fullest extent.

"Dearest Janetta, who else could there be? Who else have I seen? I have been kept in the schoolroom until now—when I am to be married to this most suitable man! Now, confess, Janetta, would you like it? Do your people want to marry you to anybody?"

"No, indeed," said Janetta, smiling. "Nobody has expressed any desire that way. But really I don't know what to say, Margaret; because Sir Philip does seem so perfectly suitable—and you say you like him?"

"Yes, but I only like him; I don't love him." Margaret leaned back in her chair, crossed her hands behind her golden head, and looked dreamily at the opposite wall. "You know I think one ought to love the man one marries—don't you think so? I have always thought of loving once and once only—like Paul and Virginia, you know, or even Romeo and Juliet—and of giving *all* for love! That would be beautiful!"

"Yes, it would. But it would be very hard too," said Janetta, thinking how lovely Margaret looked, and what a heroine of romance—what a princess of dreams—she would surely be some day. And she, poor, plain, brown, little Janetta! There was probably no romance in store for her at all.

But Life holds many secrets in her hand; and perhaps it was Janetta and not Margaret for whom a romance was yet in store.

"Hard? Do you call it hard?" Margaret asked, with a curiously exalted expression, like that of a saint absorbed in mystic joys. "It would be most easy, Janetta, to give up everything for love."

"I don't know," said Janetta—for once unsympathetic. "Giving up everything means a great deal. Would you like to go away from Helmsley Court, for instance, and live in a dingy street with no lady's maid—only a servant of all-work—on three hundred a year?"

"I think I could do anything for a man whom I loved," sighed Margaret; "but I cannot feel as if I should ever care enough for Sir Philip Ashley to do it for him."

"What sort of a man would you prefer for a husband, then?" asked Janetta.

"Oh, a man with a history. A man about whom there hung a melancholy interest—a man like Rochester in 'Jane Eyre'——"

"Not a very good-tempered person, I'm afraid!"

"Oh, who cares about good temper?"

"I do, for one. Really, Margaret, you draw a picture which is just like my cousin, Wyvis Brand."

Janetta was sorry when she had said the words. Margaret's arms came down from behind her head, and her eyes were turned to her friend's face with an immediate awakening of interest.

"Mr. Brand, of Brand Hall, you mean? I remember you told me that he was your cousin. So you have met him? And he is like Rochester?"

"I did not say that exactly," said Janetta, becoming provoked with herself. "I only said that you spoke of a rather melancholy sort of man, with a bad temper, and I thought that the description applied very well to Mr. Brand."

"What is he like? Dark?"

"Yes."

"Handsome?"

"I suppose so. I do not like any face, however handsome, that is disfigured by a scowl."

"Oh, Janetta, how charming! Tell me some more about him; I am so much interested."

"Margaret, don't be silly! Wyvis Brand is a very disagreeable man—not a good man either, I believe—and I hope you will never know him."

"On the contrary," said Margaret, with a new wilful light in her eyes, "I intend mamma to call."

"Lady Caroline will be too wise."

"Why should people not call upon the Brands? I hear the same story everywhere—'Oh, no, we do not intend to call.' Is there really anything wrong about them?"

Janetta felt some embarrassment. Had not she put nearly the same question to her own father the night before? But she could not tell Margaret Adair what her father had said to her.

"If there were—and I do not know that there is—you could hardly expect me to talk about it, Margaret," she said, with some dignity.

Margaret's good breeding came to her aid at once. "I beg your pardon, dear Janetta. I was talking carelessly. I will say no more about the Brands. But I must remark that it was *you* who piqued my curiosity. Otherwise there is nothing extraordinary in the fact of two young men settling down with their mother in a country house, is there?"

"Nothing at all."

"And I am not likely to see anything of them. But, Janetta," said Margaret, reverting to her own affairs, "you do not sympathize with me as I thought you would. Would not you think it wrong to marry where you did not love? Seriously, Janetta?"

"Yes, seriously, I should," said Janetta, her face growing graver, and her eyes lighting up. "It is a profanation of marriage to take for your husband a man whom you don't love with your whole heart. Oh, yes, Margaret, you are quite, quite right in that—but I am sorry too, because Sir Philip seems so nice."

"And, Janetta, dear, you will help me, will you not?"

"Whenever I can, Margaret? But what can I do for you?"

"You can help me in many ways, Janetta. You don't know how hard it is sometimes"—and Margaret's face resumed a wistful, troubled look. "Mamma is so kind; but she wants me sometimes to do things that I do not like, and she is so *surprised* when I do not wish to do them."

"You will make her understand in time," said Janetta, almost reverentially. Her ardent soul was thrilled with the conception of the true state of things as she imagined it; of Margaret's pure, sweet nature being dragged down to Lady Caroline's level of artificial worldliness. For, notwithstanding all Lady Caroline's gentleness of manner, Janetta was beginning to find her out. She began to see that this extreme softness and suavity covered a very persistent will, and that it was Lady Caroline who ruled the house and the family with an iron hand in a velvet glove.

"I am afraid not," said Margaret, submissively. "She is so much more determined than I am. Neither papa nor I could ever do anything against her. And in most things I like her to manage for me. But not my marriage!"

"No, indeed."

"Will you stand by me, Janetta, dear?"

"Always, Margaret."

"You will always be my friend?"

"Always dear."

"You make me feel strong when you say 'always' so earnestly, Janetta."

"Because I believe," said Janetta, quickly, "that friendship is as strong a tie as any in the world. I don't think it ought to be any less binding than the tie between sisters, between parents and child, even"—and her voice dropped a little—"even between husband and wife. I have heard it suggested that there should be a ceremony—a sort of form—for the making of a friendship as there is for other relations in life; a vow of truth and fidelity which two friends could promise to observe. Don't you think that it would be rather a useless thing, even if the thought is a pretty one? Because we make and keep or break our vows in our own heart, and no promise would bind us more than our own hearts can do."

"I hope yours binds you to me, Janetta?" said Margaret, half playfully, half sadly.

"It does, indeed."

And then the two girls kissed each other after the manner of impulsive and affectionate girls, and Margaret wiped away a tear that had gathered in the corner of her eye. Her face soon became as tranquil as ever; but Janetta's brow remained grave, her lips firmly pressed together long after Margaret seemed to have forgotten what had been said.

Things went deeper with Janetta than with Margaret. Girlish and unpractical as some of their speeches may appear, they were spoken or listened to by Janetta with the utmost seriousness. She was not of a nature to take things lightly. And during the pause that followed the conversation about friendship, she was mentally registering a very serious and earnest resolution, worthy indeed of being ranked as the promise or the vow of which she spoke, that she would always remain Margaret's true and faithful friend, in spite of all the chances and changes of this transitory world. A youthful foolish thing to do, perhaps; but the world is so constituted that the things done or said by very young and even very foolish persons sometimes dominate the whole lives of much older and wiser persons. And more came out of that silent vow of Janetta's than even she anticipated.

The rest of the day was very delightful to her. She and Margaret were left almost entirely to themselves, and they formed a dozen plans for the winter when Margaret should be back again and could resume her musical studies. Janetta tried to express her natural reluctance at the thought of giving lessons to her old school-companion, but Margaret laughed her to scorn. "As if you could not teach me?" she said. "Why, I know nothing about the theory of music—nothing at all. And you were far ahead of anybody at Miss Polehampton's! You will soon have dozens of pupils, Janetta. I expect all Beaminster to be flocking to you before long."

She did not say, but it crossed her mind that the fact of *her* taking lessons from Janetta would probably serve as a very good advertisement. For Miss Adair was herself fairly proficient in the worldly wisdom which did not at all gratify her when exhibited by her mother.

Janetta was sent home in the gathering twilight with a delightfully satisfied feeling. She was sure that Margaret's friendship was as faithful as her own. And why should there not be two women as faithful to each other in friendship as ever Damon and Pythias, David and Jonathan, had been of old? "Margaret will always be her own sweet, high-souled self," Janetta mused. "It is I who may perhaps fall away from my ideal—I hope not; oh, I hope not! I hope that I shall always be faithful and true!"

There was a very tender look upon her face as she sat in Lady Caroline's victoria, her hands clasped together upon her lap, her mouth firmly closed, her eyes wistful. The expression was so lovely that it beautified the whole of her face, which was not in itself strictly handsome, but capable of as many changes as an April day. She was so deeply absorbed in thought that she did not see a gentleman lift his hat to her in passing. It was Cuthbert Brand, and when the carriage had passed him he stood still for a moment and looked back at it.

"I should like to paint that girl's face," he said to himself. "There is soul in it—character—passion. Her sister is prettier by far; but I doubt whether she is capable of so much."

But the exalted beauty had faded away by the time Janetta reached her home, and when she entered the house she was again the bright, sensible, energetic, and affectionate sister and daughter that they all knew and loved: no great beauty, no genius, no saint, but a generous-hearted English girl, who tried to do her duty and to love her neighbor as herself.

Her father met her in the hall.

"Here you are," he said. "I hardly expected you home as yet. Everybody is out, so you must tell *me* your experiences and adventures if you have any to tell."

"I have not many," said Janetta, brightly. "Only everybody has been very, very kind."

"I'm glad to hear of it; but I should be surprised if people were not kind to my Janet."

"Nobody is half so kind as you are," said Janetta, fondly. "Have you been very busy to-day, father?"

"Very, dear. And I have been to Brand Hall."

He drew her inside his consulting-room as he spoke. It was a little room near the hall-door, opposite the dining-room. Janetta did not often go there, and felt as if some rather serious communication were to be made.

"Did you see the little boy, father?"

"Yes—and his grandmother."

"And may I go to see Mrs. Brand?"

Mr. Colwyn paused for a moment, and when he spoke his voice was broken by some emotion. "If you can do anything to help and comfort that poor woman, my Janet," he said at length, "God forbid that I should ever hinder you! I will not heed what the world says in face of sorrow such as she has known. Do what you can for her."

"I will, father; I promise you I will."

"It is the second promise that I have made to-day," said Janetta, rather thoughtfully, as she was undressing herself that night; "and each of them turns on the same subject—on being a friend to some one who needs friendship. The vocation of some women is to be a loving daughter, a true wife, or a good mother; mine, perhaps, is to be above everything else a true friend. I don't think my promises will be hard to keep!"

But even Janetta, in her wisdom, could not foresee what was yet to come.

CHAPTER XII
JANETTA REMONSTRATES

It was with a beating heart that Janetta, a few days later, crossed once more the threshold of her cousin's house. Her father's words about Mrs. Brand had impressed her rather painfully, and she felt some shyness and constraint at the thought of the reason which he had given her for coming. How she was to set about helping or comforting Mrs. Brand she had not the least idea.

These thoughts were, however, put to flight by an un-looked-for scene, which broke upon her sight as she entered the hall. This hall had to be crossed before any of the other rooms could be reached; it was low-ceiled, paneled in oak, and lighted by rather small windows, with stained glass in the lower panes. Like most rooms in the house it had a gloomy look, which was not relieved by the square of faded Turkey carpet in the centre of the black polished boards of the floor, or by the half-dozen dusky portraits in oak frames which garnished the walls. When Janetta was ushered in she found this ante-room or entrance chamber occupied by three persons and a child. These, as she speedily found, consisted of Wyvis Brand and his little boy, and two gentlemen, one of whom was laughing immoderately, while the other was leaning over the back of the chair and addressing little Julian.

Janetta halted for a moment, for the old servant who had admitted her seemed to think that his work was done when he had uttered her name, and had already retreated; and his voice being exceedingly feeble, the announcement had passed unnoticed by the majority of the persons present, if not by all. Wyvis Brand had perhaps seen her, for his eyes were keen, and the shadow in which she stood was not likely to veil her from his sight; but he gave no sign of being conscious of her presence. He was standing with his back to the mantel-piece, his arms crossed behind his head; there was a curious expression on his face, half-smile, half-sneer, but it was evident that he was merely looking and listening, not interfering with what was going on.

It needed only a glance to see that little Julian was in a state of extraordinary excitement. His face was crimson, his eyes were sparkling and yet full of tears; his legs were planted sturdily apart, and his hands were clenched. His head was drawn back, and his whole body also seemed as if it wanted to recoil, but placed as he was against a strong oaken table he could evidently go back no further. The gentleman on the chair was offering him something—Janetta could not at first see what—and the boy was vehemently resisting.

"I won't have it! I won't have it!" he was crying, with the whole force of his lungs. "I won't touch it! Take the nasty stuff away!"

Janetta wondered whether it were medicine he was refusing, and why his father did not insist upon obedience. But Wyvis Brand, still standing by the mantel-piece, only laughed aloud.

"No shirking! Drink it up!" said the strange gentleman, in what Janetta thought a curiously unpleasant voice. "Come, come, it will make a man of you——"

"I don't want to be made a man of! I won't touch it! I promised I never would! You can't make me!"

"You must be taught not to make rash promises," said the man, laughing. "Come now——"

But little Julian had suddenly caught sight of Janetta's figure at the door, and with a great bound he escaped from his tormentor and flung himself upon her, burying his face in her dress, and clutching its folds as if he would never let them go.

"It's the lady! the lady!" he gasped out. "Oh, please don't let them make me drink it! Indeed, I promised not."

Janetta came forward a little, and at her appearance every one looked more or less discomfited. The gentleman on the chair she recognized as a Mr. Strangways, a man of notoriously evil life, who had a house near Beaminster, and was generally shunned by respectable people in the neighborhood. He started up, and looked at her with what she felt to be a rather insolent gaze. Wyvis Brand stood erect, and looked sullen. The other gentleman, who was a stranger, rose from his chair in a civiller manner than his friend had done.

Janetta put her arms round the little fellow, and turned a rather bewildered face towards Mr. Brand. "Was it—was it—medicine?" she asked.

"Of a kind," said Wyvis, with a laugh.

"It was brandy—*eau-de-vie*—horrid hot stuff that *maman* used to drink," said little Julian, with a burst of angry sobs, "and I promised not—I promised old Susan that I never would!"

She took the mother's hand and held it gently between her own, uttering some few soothing sentences as she did so. Presently the poor woman's sobs grew quieter, and she returned the pressure of Janetta's hand.

"Thank you, my dear," she said at last. "You have a very kind heart. But it is no use telling me to be comforted. I understand my sons, as I understood my husband before them. They cannot help it. What is in the blood will come out."

"Surely," said Janetta, in a very low tone, "there is always the might and the mercy of God to fall back upon—to help us when we cannot help ourselves."

"Ah, my dear, if I could believe in that I should be a happier woman," said Mrs. Brand, sorrowfully.

Janetta stayed a little longer, and when she went the elder woman allowed herself to be kissed affectionately, and asked in a wistful tone, as Julian had done, when she would come again.

The girl was glad to find that the hall was empty when she crossed it again. She had no fancy for encountering the insolent looks (as she phrased it to herself) of Wyvis Brand and his hateful friends. But she had reckoned without her host. For when she reached the gate into the high-road, she found Mr. Brand leaning against it with his elbows resting on the topmost bar, and his eyes gloomily fixed on the distant landscape. He started when he saw her, raised his hat and opened the gate with punctilious politeness. Janetta bowed her thanks, but without any smile; she was not at all in charity with her cousin, Wyvis Brand.

He allowed her to pass him, but before she had gone half a dozen yards, he strode after her and caught her up. "Will you let me have a few words with you?" he said, rather hoarsely.

"Certainly, Mr. Brand." Janetta turned and faced him, still with the disapproving gravity upon her brow.

"Can't we walk on for a few paces?" said Wyvis, with evident embarrassment. "I can say what I want to say better while we are walking. Besides, they can see us from the house if we stand here."

Privately Janetta thought that this would be no drawback, but she did not care to make objections, so turned once more and walked on silently.

"I want to speak to you," said the man, presently, with something of a shamefaced air, "about the little scene you came upon this afternoon——"

"Yes," said Janetta. She did not know how contemptuously her lips curled as she said the word.

"You came at an unfortunate moment," he went on, awkwardly enough. "I was about to interpose; I should not have allowed Jack Strangways to go too far. Of course you thought that I did not care."

"Yes," said Janetta, straightforwardly. Wyvis bit his lip.

"I am not quite so thoughtless of my son's welfare," he said, in a firmer tone. "There was enough in that glass to madden a child—almost to kill him. You don't suppose I would have let him take that?"

"I don't know. You were offering no objection to it when I came in."

"Do you doubt my word?" said Wyvis, fiercely.

"No. I believe you, if you mean really to say that you were not going to allow your little boy to drink what Mr. Strangways offered him."

"I do mean to say it"—in a tone of hot anger.

Janetta was silent.

"Have you nothing to say, Miss Colwyn?"

"I have no right to express any opinion, Mr. Brand."

"But I wish for it!"

"I do not see why you should wish for it," said Janetta, coldly, "especially when it may not be very agreeable to you to hear."

"Will you kindly tell me what you mean?" The words were civil, but the tone was imperious in the extreme.

"I mean that whether you were going to make Julian drink that poisonous stuff or not, you were inflicting a horrible torture upon him," said Janetta, as hotly as Wyvis himself could have spoken. "And I cannot understand how you could allow your own child to be treated in that cruel way. I call it wicked to make a child suffer."

Had she looked at her companion, she would have seen that his face had grown a little whiter than usual, and that he had the pinched look about his nostrils which—as his mother would have known—betokened rage. But she did not look; and, although he paused for a moment before replying, his voice was quite calm when he spoke again.

"Torture? Suffering? These are very strong words when applied to a little harmless teasing."

"I do not call it harmless teasing when you are trying to make a child break a promise that he holds sacred."

"A very foolish promise!"

"I am not so sure of that."

"Do you mean to insult me?" said Wyvis, flushing to the roots of his hair.

"Insult you? No; certainly not. I don't know why you should say so!"

"Then I need not explain," he answered drily, though still with that flush of annoyance on his face. "Perhaps if you think over what you have heard of that boy's antecedents, you will know what I mean."

It was Janetta's turn to flush now. She remembered the stories current respecting old Mr. Brand's drinking habits, and the rumors about Mrs. Wyvis Brand's reasons for living away from her husband. She saw that her words had struck home in a manner which she had not intended.

"I beg your pardon," she said involuntarily; "I never meant—I never thought—anything—I ought not to have spoken as I did."

"You had much better say what you mean," was the answer, spoken with bitter brevity.

"Well, then, I will." Janetta raised her eyes and looked at him bravely. "After all, I am a kinswoman of yours, Mr. Brand, and little Julian is my cousin too; so I *have* some sort of a right to speak. I never thought of his antecedents, as you call them, and I do not know much about them; but if they were—if they had been not altogether what you wish them to be—don't you see that this very promise which you tried to make him break was one of his best safeguards?"

"The promise made by a child is no safeguard," said Wyvis, doggedly.

"Not if he is forced to break it!" exclaimed Janetta, with a touch of fire.

They walked on in silence for a minute or two, and then Wyvis said,

"Do you believe in a promise made by a child of that age?"

"Little Julian has made me believe in it. He was so thoroughly in earnest. Oh, Mr. Brand, do you think that it was right to force him to do a thing against his conscience in that way?"

"You use hard words for a very simple thing, Miss Colwyn," said Wyvis, in a rather angry tone. "The boy was not forced—I had no intention of letting him drink the brandy."

"No," said Janetta, indignantly. "You only let him think that he was to be forced to do it—you only made him lose faith in you as his natural protector, and believe that you wished him to do what he thought wrong! And you say there was no cruelty in that?"

Wyvis Brand kept silence for some minutes. He was impressed in spite of himself by Janetta's fervor.

"I suppose," he said, at last, "that the fact is—I don't know what to do with a child. I never had any teaching or training when I was a child, and I don't know how to give it. I know I'm a sort of heathen and savage, and the boy must grow up like me—that is all."

"It is often said to be a heathen virtue to keep one's word," said Janetta, with a half smile.

"Therefore one that I can practice, you mean? Do you always keep your word when you give it?"

"I try to."

"I wish I could get you to give your word to do one thing."

"What is that?"

Wyvis spoke slowly. "You see how unfit I am to bring up a child—I acknowledge the unfitness—and yet to send him away from us would almost break my mother's heart—you see that."

"Yes."

"Will not you sometimes look in on us and give us a word of advice or—or—rebuke? You are a cousin, as you reminded me, and you have the right. Will you help us a little now and then?"

"You would not like it if I did."

"Was I so very savage? I have an awful temper, I know. But I am not quite so black as I'm painted, Miss Colwyn. I do want to do the best for that boy—if I knew how——"

"Witness this afternoon," said Janetta, with good-humored satire.

"Well, that shows that I *don't* know how. Seriously, I am sorry—I can't say more. Won't you stand our friend, Cousin Janetta?"

It was the first time he had addressed her in that way.

"How often am I to be asked to be somebody's friend, I wonder!" said Janetta to herself, with a touch of humor. But she answered, quite gravely, "I should like to do what I can—but I'm afraid there is nothing that I can do, especially"—with a sudden flush—"if your friends—the people who come to your house—are men like Mr. Strangways."

Wyvis looked at her sideways, with a curious look upon his face.

"You object to Mr. Strangways?"

"He is a man whom most people object to."

"Well—if I give up Mr. Strangways and his kind——"

"Oh, *will* you, Cousin Wyvis?"

She turned an eager, sparkling face upon him. It occurred to him, almost for the first time, to admire her. With that light in her eye, that color in her cheek, Janetta was almost beautiful. He smiled.

"I shall be only too glad of an excuse," he said, with more simplicity and earnestness than she had as yet distinguished in his voice. "And then—you will come again?"

"I will—gladly."

"Shake hands on it after your English fashion," he said, stopping short, and holding out his own hand. "I have been so long abroad that I almost forget the way. But it is a sign of friendliness, is it not?"

Janetta turned and laid her hand in his with a look of bright and trustful confidence. Somehow it made Wyvis Brand feel himself unworthy. He said almost nothing more until they parted at Mr. Colwyn's door.

CHAPTER XIII
SHADOWS

But Janetta had not much chance of keeping her promise for some time to come. She was alarmed to find, on her return home that evening, that her father had come in sick and shivering, with all the symptoms of a violent cold, followed shortly by high fever. He had caught a chill during a long drive undertaken in order to see a motherless child who had been suddenly taken ill, and in whose case he took a great interest. The child rapidly recovered, but Mr. Colwyn's illness had a serious termination. Pleurisy came on, and made such rapid inroads upon his strength that in a very few days his recovery was pronounced impossible. Gradually growing weaker and weaker, he was not able even to give counsel or direction to his family, and could only whisper to Janetta, who was his devoted nurse, a few words about "taking care" of the rest.

"I will always do my very best for them, father; you may be sure of that," said Janetta, earnestly. The look of anxious pain in his eyes gave her the strength to speak firmly—she must set his mind at ease at any cost.

"My faithful Janet," she heard him whisper; and then he spoke no more. With his hand still clasped in hers he died in the early morning of a chill October day, and the world of Beaminster knew him no more.

The world seemed sadly changed for Janetta when her father had gone forth from it; and yet it was not she who made the greatest demonstration of mourning. Mrs. Colwyn passed from one hysterical fit into another, and Nora sobbed herself ill; but Janetta went about her duties with a calm and settled gravity, a sober tearlessness, which caused her stepmother to dub her cold and heartless half a dozen times a day. As a matter of fact the girl felt as if her heart were breaking, but there was no one but herself to bear any of the commonplace little burdens of daily life which are so hard to carry in the time of trouble; and but for her thoughtful presence of mind the whole house would have degenerated into a state of chaos. She wrote necessary letters, made arrangements for the sad offices which were all that could be rendered to her father now, interviewed the dressmaker, and ordered meals for the children. It was to her that the servants and tradespeople came for orders; it was she who kept her mother's room quiet, and nursed Nora, and provided necessary occupation for the awed and bewildered children.

"You don't seem to feel it a bit, Janetta," Mrs. Colwyn said to her on the day before the funeral. "And I'm sure you were always your father's favorite. He never cared half so much for any of the children as he did for you, and now you can't even give him a tributary tear."

Mrs. Colwyn was fond of stilted expressions, and the thought of "a tributary tear" seemed so incongruous to Janetta when compared with her own deep grief, that—much to Mrs. Colwyn's horror—she burst into an agitated little laugh, as nervous people sometimes do on the most solemn occasions.

"To laugh when your father is lying dead in the house!" ejaculated Mrs. Colwyn, with awful emphasis. "And you that he thought so loving and dutiful— —!"

Then poor Janetta collapsed. She was worn out with watching and working, and from nervous laughter she passed to tears so heart-broken and so exhausting that Mrs. Colwyn never again dared to accuse her openly of insensibility. And perhaps it was a good thing for Janetta that she did break down in this way. The doctor who had attended her father was growing very uneasy about her. He had not been deceived by her apparent calmness. Her white face and dark-ringed eyes had told him all that Janetta could not say. "A good thing too!" he muttered when, on a subsequent call, Tiny told him, with rather a look of consternation, that her sister "had been crying." "A good thing too! If she had not cried she would have had a nervous fever before long, and then what would become of you all?"

During these dark days Janetta was inexpressibly touched by the marks of sympathy that reached her from all sides. Country people trudged long distances into town that they might gaze once more on the worn face of the man who had often assuaged not only physical but mental pain, and had been as ready to help and comfort as to prescribe. Townsfolk sent flowers for the dead and dainties for the living; but better than all their gifts was the regret that they expressed for the death of a man whom everyone liked and respected. Mr. Colwyn's practice, though never very lucrative, had been an exceedingly large one; and only when he had passed away did his townsfolk seem to appreciate him at his true worth.

In the sad absorption of mind which followed upon his death, Janetta almost forgot her cousins, the Brands. But when the funeral took place, and she went with her brother Joe to the grave, as she insisted upon doing in spite of her stepmother's tearful remonstrances, it was a sort of relief and satisfaction to her to see that both Wyvis and Cuthbert Brand were present. They were her kinsmen, after all, and it was right for them to be there. It made her feel momentarily stronger to know of their presence in the church.

But at the grave she forgot them utterly. The beautiful and consoling words of the Burial Service fell almost unheeded on her ear. She could only think of the blank that was made in her life by the absence of that loving voice, that tender sympathy, which had never failed her once. "My faithful Janet!" he had called her. There was no one to call her "my faithful Janet" now.

She was shaken by a storm of silent sobs as these thoughts came over her. She made scarcely a sound, but her figure was swayed by the tempest as if it would have fallen. Joe, the young brother, who could as yet scarcely realize the magnitude of the loss which he had sustained, glanced at her uneasily; but it was not he, but Wyvis Brand, who suddenly made a step forward and gave her—just in time—the support of his strong arm. The movement checked her and recalled her to herself. Her weeping grew less violent, and although strong shudders still shook her frame, she was able to walk quietly from the grave to the carriage-door, and to shake hands with Wyvis Brand with some attempt at calmness of demeanor.

He came to the house a few days after the funeral, but Janetta happened to be out, and Mrs. Colwyn refused to see him. Possibly he thought that some slight lurked within this refusal, for he did not come again, and a visit at a later date from Mrs. Brand was so entirely embarrassing and unsatisfactory that Janetta could hardly wish for its repetition. Mrs. Colwyn, in the deepest of widow's weeds, with a white handkerchief in her hand, was yet not too much overcome by grief to show that she esteemed herself far more respectable than Mrs. Brand, and could "set her down," if necessary; while poor Mrs. Brand, evidently comprehending the reason of Mrs. Colwyn's bridlings and tossings, was nervous and flurried, sat on the edge of a chair, and looked—poor, helpless, elderly woman—as if she had never entered a drawing-room before.

The only comfort Janetta had out of the visit was a moment's conversation in the hall when Mrs. Brand took her leave.

"My dear—my dear," said Mrs. Brand, taking the girl's hand in hers, "I am so sorry, and I can't do anything to comfort you. Your father was very kind to me when I was in great trouble, years ago. I shall never forget his goodness. If there is anything I can ever do for you, you must let me do it for his sake."

Janetta put up her face and kissed the woman to whom her father had been "very kind." It comforted her to hear of his goodness once again. She loved Mrs. Brand for appreciating it.

That little sentence or two did her more good than the long letters which she was receiving every few days from Margaret, her chosen friend. Margaret was sincerely grieved for Janetta's loss, and said many consoling things in her sweet, tranquil, rather devotional way; but she had not known Mr. Colwyn, and she could not say the words that Janetta's heart was aching for—the words of praise and admiration of a nobly unselfish life which alone could do Janetta any good. Yes, Margaret's letters were distinctly unsatisfactory—not from want of feeling, but from want of experience of life.

Graver necessities soon arose, however, than those of consolation in grief. Mr. Colwyn had always been a poor man, and the sum for which he had insured his life was only sufficient to pay his debts and funeral expenses, and to leave a very small balance at his banker's. He had bought the house in Gwynne Street in which he lived, and there was no need, therefore, to seek for another home; and Mrs. Colwyn had fifty pounds a year of her own, but of course it was necessary that the two elder girls should do something for themselves. Nora obtained almost immediately a post as under-teacher in a school not far from Beaminster, and Georgie was taken in as a sort of governess-pupil, while Joe was offered—chiefly out of consideration for his father's memory—a clerkship in a mercantile house in the town, and was considered to be well provided for. Curly, one of the younger boys, obtained a nomination to a naval school in London. Thus only Mrs. Colwyn, Tiny, and "Jinks" remained at home—with Janetta.

With Janetta!—That was the difficulty. What was Janetta to do? She might probably with considerable ease have obtained a position as resident governess in a family, but then she would have to be absent from home altogether. And of late the Colwyns had found it best to dispense with the maid-servant who had hitherto done the work of the household—a fact which meant that Janetta, with the help of a charity orphan of thirteen, did it nearly all herself.

"I might send home enough money for you to keep an efficient servant, mamma," she said one day, "if I could go away and find a good situation."

It never occurred either to her or to her stepmother that any of her earnings were to belong to Janetta, or be used for her behoof.

"It would have to be a very good situation indeed, then," said Mrs. Colwyn, with sharpness. "I don't suppose you could get more than fifty pounds a year—if so much. And fifty pounds would not go far if we had a woman in the house to feed and pay wages to. No, you had better stay at home and get some daily teaching in the neighborhood. With your recommendations it ought to be easy enough for you to do so."

"I am afraid not," said Janetta, with a little sigh.

"Nonsense! You could get some if you tried—if you had any energy, any spirit: I suppose you would like to sit with your hands before you, doing nothing, while I slaved my fingers to the bone for you," said Mrs. Colwyn, who never got up till noon, or did anything but gossip and read novels when she was up; "but I would be ashamed to do that if I were a well-educated girl, whose father spent I don't know how much on her voice, and expected her to make a living for herself by the time she was one-and-twenty! I must say, Janetta, that I think it very wrong of you to be so slack in trying to earn a little money, when Nora and Georgie and Joey are all out in the world doing for themselves, and you sitting here at home doing nothing at all."

"I am sorry, mamma," said Janetta, meekly. "I will try to get something to do at once."

She did not think of reminding Mrs. Colwyn that she had been up since six o'clock that morning helping the charity orphan to scrub and scour, cooking, making beds, sewing, teaching Tiny between whiles, and scarcely getting five minutes' rest until dinner-time. She only began to wonder how she could manage to get all her tasks into the day if she had lessons to give as well. "I suppose I must sit up at night and get up earlier in the morning," she thought to herself. "It is a pity I am such a sleepy person. But use reconciles one to all things."

Mrs. Colwyn meanwhile went on lecturing.

"And above all things, Janetta, remember that you ask high terms and get the money always in advance. You are just like your poor father in the way you have about money; I never saw anyone so unpractical as he was. I'm sure half his bills are unpaid yet, and never will be paid. I hope you won't be like *him*, I'm sure——"

"I hope I shall be like him in every possible respect," said Janetta, with compressed lips. She rose as she spoke and caught up the basket of socks that she was mending. "I don't know how you can bear to speak of him in that slighting manner," she went on, almost passionately. "He was the best, the kindest of men, and I cannot bear to hear it." And then she hurriedly left the room and went into her father's little surgery—as it had once been called—to relieve her overcharged heart with a burst of weeping. It was not often that Janetta lost patience, but a word against her father was sufficient to upset her self-command nowadays. She rested her head against the well-worn arm-chair where he used to sit, and kissed the back of it, and bedewed it with her tears.

"Poor father! dear father!" she murmured. "Oh, if only you were here, I could bear anything! Or if she had loved you as you deserved, I could bear with her and work for her willingly—cheerfully. But when she speaks against you, father dear, how *can* I live with her? And yet he told me to take care of her, and I said I would. He called me 'his faithful Janet.' I do not want to be unfaithful, but—oh father, father, it is hard to live without you!"

The gathering shades of the wintry day began to gather round her; but Janetta, her face buried in the depths of the arm-chair, was oblivious of time. It was almost dark before little Tiny came running in with cries of terror to summon her sister to Mrs. Colwyn's help.

"Mamma's ill—I think she's dying. Come, Janet, come," cried the child. And Janetta hurried back to the dining-room.

She found Mrs. Colwyn on the sofa in a state of apparent stupor. For this at first Janetta saw no reason, and was on the point of sending for a doctor, when her eye fell upon a black object which had rolled from the sofa to the ground. Janetta looked at it and stood transfixed.

There was no need to send for a doctor. And Janetta saw at once that she could not be spared from home. The wretched woman had found a solace from her woes, real and imaginary, in the brandy bottle.

CHAPTER XIV
JANETTA'S FAILURE

The terrible certainty that Janetta had now acquired of Mrs. Colwyn's inability to control herself decided her in the choice of an occupation. She knew that she must, if possible, earn something; but it was equally impossible for her to leave home entirely, or even for many hours at a stretch; she was quite convinced that constant watching, and even gentle restraint, could alone prevail in checking the tendency which her stepmother evinced. She understood now better than she had ever done why her father's brow had been so early wrinkled and his hair grey before its time. Doubtless, he had discovered his wife's unfortunate tendency, and, while carefully concealing it or keeping it within bounds, had allowed it often to weigh heavily upon his mind. Janetta realized with a great shock that *she* could not hope to exert the influence or the authority of her father, that all her efforts might possibly be unavailing unless they were seconded by Mrs. Colwyn herself, and that public disgrace might yet be added to the troubles and anxieties of their lives.

There is something so particularly revolting in the spectacle of this kind of degradation in a woman, that Janetta felt as if the discovery that she had made turned her positively ill. She had much ado to behave to the children and the servant as if nothing were amiss; she got her stepmother to bed, and kept Tiny out of the room, but the effort was almost more than she knew how to bear. She passed a melancholy evening with the children—melancholy in spite of herself, for she did her best to be cheerful—and spent a sleepless night, rising in the morning with a bad headache and a conviction as of the worthlessness of all things which she did not very often experience.

She shrank sensitively from going to Mrs. Colwyn's room. Surely the poor woman would be overcome with pain and shame; surely she would understand how terrible the exposure of her disgrace had been to Janetta. But at last Mrs. Colwyn's bell sounded sharply, and continued to ring, and the girl was obliged to run upstairs and enter her stepmother's room.

Mrs. Colwyn was sitting up in bed, with the bell-rope in her hand, an aggrieved expression upon her face.

"Well, I'm sure! Nine o'clock and no breakfast ready for me! I suppose I may wait until everybody else in the house is served first; I must say, Janetta, that you are very thoughtless of my comfort."

Contrary to her usual custom Janetta offered no word of excuse or apology. She was too much taken aback to speak. She stood and looked at her stepmother with slightly dilated eyes, and neither moved nor spoke.

"What *are* you staring at?" said Mrs. Colwyn, sinking back on her pillows with a faint—very faint—touch of uneasiness in her tones. "If you are in a sulky mood, Janetta, I wish you would go away, and send my breakfast up by Ph[oe]be and Tiny. I have a wretched headache this morning and can't be bothered."

"What would you like?" said Janetta, with an effort.

"Oh, anything. Some coffee and toast, perhaps. I dare say you won't believe it—you are so unsympathetic—but I was frightfully ill last night. I don't know how I got to bed; I was quite insensible for a time—all from a narcotic that I had taken for neuralgia——"

"I'll go and get your breakfast ready," said Janetta abruptly. "I will send it up as soon as I can."

She left the room, unheeding some murmured grumbling at her selfishness, and shut the door behind her. On the landing it must be confessed that she struck her foot angrily on the floor and clenched her hands, while the color flushed into her mobile, sensitive little face. There was nothing that Janetta hated more than a lie. And her stepmother was lying to her now.

She sent up the breakfast tray, and did not re-enter the room for some time. When at last she came up, Mrs. Colwyn had had the fire lighted and was sitting beside it in a rocking-chair, with a novel on her lap. She looked up indolently as Janetta entered.

"Going out?" she said, noticing that the girl was in her out-door wraps. "You are always gadding."

"I came to speak to you before I went out," said Janetta, patiently. "I am going to the stationer's, and to the Beaminster *Argus* Office. I mean to make it well known in the town that I want to give music and singing-lessons. And, if possible, I shall give them here—at our own house."

"You'll do nothing of the sort!" said Mrs. Colwyn, shrilly. "I'll not have a pack of children about the house playing scales and singing their Do, Re,

Mi, till my head is fit to split. You'll remember, Miss, that this is *my* house, and that you are living on *my* money, and behave yourself."

"Mamma," said Janetta, steadily, advancing a step nearer, and turning a shade paler than she had been before, "please think what you are saying. I am willing to work as hard as I can, and earn as much as I can. But I dare not go away from home—at any rate for long—unless I can feel sure that—that what happened last night—will not occur again."

"What happened!—what happened last night?—I don't know what you mean."

"Don't say that, mamma: you know—you know quite well. And think what a grief it would have been to dear father—what a disgrace it will be to Joe and Nora and the little ones and all of us—if it ever became known! Think of yourself, and the shame and the sin of it!"

"I've not the least notion what you are talking about, Janetta, and I beg that you will not address me in that way," said Mrs. Colwyn, with an attempt at dignity. "It is very undutiful indeed, and I hope that I shall hear no more of it."

"I'll never speak of it again, mamma, unless you make it necessary. All I mean is that you must understand—I cannot feel safe now—I must be at home as much as possible to see that Tiny is safe, and that everything is going on well. You must please let me advertise for pupils in our own house."

Mrs. Colwyn burst into tears. "Oh, well, have your own way! I knew that you would tyrannize, you always do whenever you get the chance, and very foolish I have been to give you the opportunity. To speak in that way to your father's wife—and all because she had to take a little something for her nerves, and because of her neuralgia! But I am nobody now: nobody, even in my own house, where I'm sure I ought to be mistress if anybody is!"

Janetta could do or say nothing more. She gave her stepmother a dose of sal volatile, and went away. She had already searched every room and every cupboard in the house, except in Mrs. Colwyn's own domain, and had put every bottle that she could find under lock and key; but she left the house with a feeling of terrible insecurity upon her, as if the earth might open at any moment beneath her feet.

She put advertisements in the local papers and left notices at some of the Beaminster shops, and, when these attempts produced no results, she called systematically on all the people she knew, and did her best—very much against the grain—to ask for pupils. Thanks to her perseverance she soon got three or four children as music pupils, although at a very low rate of remuneration. Also, she gave two singing lessons weekly to the daughter of the grocer with whom the Colwyns dealt. But these were not paid for in money, but in kind. And then for a time she got no more pupils at all.

Janetta was somewhat puzzled by her failure. She had fully expected to succeed as a teacher in Beaminster. "When the Adairs come back it will be better," she said, hopefully, to herself. "They have not written for a long time, but I am sure that they will come home soon. Perhaps Margaret is going to be married and will not want any singing lessons. But I should think that they would recommend me: I should think that I might refer to Lady Caroline, and surely people would think more of my abilities then."

But it was not confidence in her abilities that was lacking so much as confidence in her amiability and discretion, she soon found. She called one day at the house of a schoolmistress, who was said to want assistance in the musical line, and was received with a stiffness which did not encourage her to make much of her qualifications.

"The fact is, Miss Colwyn," said the preceptress at length, "I have heard of you from Miss Polehampton."

Janetta was on her feet in a moment. "I know very well what that means," she said, rather defiantly.

"Exactly. I see that Miss Polehampton's opinion of you is justifiable. You will excuse my mentioning to you, as it is all for your own good, Miss Colwyn, that Miss Polehampton found in you some little weakness of temper, some want of the submissiveness and good sense which ought to characterize an under-teacher's demeanor. I have great confidence in Miss Polehampton's opinion."

"The circumstances under which I left Miss Polehampton's could be easily explained if you would allow me to refer you to Lady Caroline Adair," said Janetta, with mingled spirit and dignity.

"Lady Caroline Adair? Oh, yes, I have heard all about that," said the schoolmistress, in a tone of depreciation. "I do not need to hear any other version of the story. You must excuse my remarking, Miss Colwyn, that temper and sense are qualities as valuable in music-teaching as in any other; and that your dismissal from Miss Polehampton's will, in my opinion, be very much against you, in a place where Miss Polehampton's school is so well known, and she herself is so much respected."

"I am sorry to have troubled you," said Janetta, not without stateliness, although her lips trembled a little as she spoke. "I will wish you good-morning."

The schoolmistress bowed solemnly, and allowed the girl to depart. Janetta hastened out of the house—glad to get away before the tears that had gathered in her eyes could fall.

At an ordinary time she would have been equally careful that they did not fall when she was in the street; but on this occasion, dazed, wounded, and tormented by an anxiety about the future, which was beginning to take the spring out of her youth, she moved along the side-walk with perfect unconsciousness that her eyes were brimming over, and that two great tears were already on her cheeks.

It was a quiet road, and there was little likelihood of encountering any one whom she knew. Therefore Janetta was utterly abashed when a gentleman, who had met her, took off his hat, glanced at her curiously, and then turned back as if by a sudden impulse, and addressed her by name.

"Miss Colwyn, I think?"

She looked up at him through a blinding haze of tears, and recognized the tall, spare figure, the fine sensitive face, the kind, dark eyes and intellectual forehead. The coal-black beard and moustache nearly hid his mouth, but Janetta felt instinctively that this tell-tale feature would not belie the promise of the others.

"Sir Philip Ashley," she murmured, in her surprise.

"I beg your pardon," he said, with the courtesy that she so well remembered; "I stopped you on impulse, I fear, because I felt a great desire to express to you my deep sympathy with you in your loss. It may seem impertinent for me to speak, but I knew your father and respected and trusted him. We had some correspondence about sanitary matters, and I was greatly relying on his help in certain reforms that I wish to institute in Beaminster. He is a great loss to us all."

"Thank you," Janetta said unsteadily.

"Will you let me ask whether there is anything in which I can help you just now."

"Oh, no, nothing, thank you." She had brushed away the involuntary tear, and smiled bravely as she replied. "I did not think that I should meet anybody: it was simply that I was disappointed about—about—some lessons that I hoped to get. Quite a *little* disappointment, you see."

"Was it a little disappointment? Do you want to give lessons — singing lessons?"

"Yes; but nobody will have me to teach them," said Janetta, laughing nervously.

Sir Philip looked back at the house which they had just passed. "That is Miss Morrison's school: you came out of it, did you not? Does she not need your help?"

"I do not suit her."

"Why? Did she try your voice?"

"Oh, no. It was for other reasons. She was prejudiced against me," said Janetta, with a little gulp.

"Prejudiced? But why? — may I ask?"

"Oh, she had heard something she did not like. It does not matter: I shall get other pupils by-and-bye."

"Is it important to you to have pupils?" Sir Philip asked, as seriously and anxiously as if the fate of the empire depended on his reply.

"Oh, most important." Janetta's face and voice were more pathetic than she knew. Sir Philip was silent for a moment.

"I have heard you sing," he said at length, in his grave, earnest way. "I am sure that I should have no hesitation in recommending you — if my recommendation were of any use. My mother may perhaps hear of somebody who wants lessons, if you will allow me to mention the matter to her."

"I shall be very much obliged to you," said Janetta, feeling grateful and yet a little startled — it did not seem natural to her in her sweet humility that Sir Philip and his mother should interest themselves in her welfare. "Oh, *very* much obliged."

Sir Philip raised his hat and smiled down kindly upon her as he said good-bye. He had been interested from the very first in Margaret's friend. And he had always been vaguely conscious that Margaret's friendship was not likely to produce any very desirable results.

Janetta went on her way, feeling for the moment a little less desolate than she had felt before. Sir Philip turned homewards to seek his mother, who was a woman of whom many people stood in awe, but whose kindness of heart was never known to fail. To her Sir Philip at once poured out his story with the directness and Quixotic ardor which some of his friends found incomprehensible, not to say absurd. But Lady Ashley never thought so.

She smiled very kindly as her son finished his little tale.

"She is really a good singer, you say? Mr. Colwyn's daughter. I have seen him once or twice."

"He was a good fellow."

"Yes, I believe so. Miss Morrison's school, did you mention? Why, Mabel Hartley is there." Mabel Hartley was a distant cousin of the Ashleys. "I will call to-morrow, Philip, and find out what the objection is to Miss Colwyn. If it can be removed I don't see why she should not teach Mabel, who, I remember, has a voice."

Lady Ashley carried out her intention, and announced the result to her son the following evening.

"I have not succeeded, dear. Miss Morrison has been prejudiced by some report from Miss Polehampton, with whom Miss Colwyn and Margaret Adair were at school. She said that the two girls were expelled together."

Sir Philip was silent for a minute or two. His brows contracted. "I was afraid," he said, "that Miss Adair's championship of her friend had not been conducted in the wisest possible manner. She has done Miss Colwyn considerable harm."

Lady Ashley glanced at him inquiringly. She was particularly anxious that he should marry Margaret Adair.

"Is Lady Caroline at home?" her son asked, after another and a longer pause.

"Yes. She came home yesterday—with dear Margaret. I am sure, Philip, that Margaret does not know it if she has done harm."

"I don't suppose she does, mother. I am sure she would not willingly injure any one. But I think that she ought to know the circumstances of the case."

And then he opened a book and began to read.

Lady Ashley never remonstrated. But she raised her eyebrows a little over this expression of Sir Philip's opinion. If he were going to try to tutor Margaret Adair, whose slightest wish had never yet known contradiction, she thought it probable that the much-wished for marriage would never take place at all.

CHAPTER XV
A BONE OF CONTENTION

Poor Janetta, plodding away at her music lessons and doing the household work of her family, never guessed that she was about to become a bone of contention. But such she was fated to be, and that between persons no less distinguished than Lady Caroline Adair and Sir Philip Ashley—not to speak of Sir Philip and Margaret!

Two days after Janetta's unexpected meeting with Sir Philip, that gentleman betook himself to Helmsley Court in a somewhat warm and indignant mood. He had seen a good deal of Margaret during the autumn months. They had been members of the same house-party in more than one great Scottish mansion: they had boated together, fished together, driven and ridden and walked together, until more than one of Lady Caroline's acquaintances had asked, with a covert smile, "how soon she might be allowed to congratulate".... The sentence was never quite finished, and Lady Caroline never made any very direct reply. Margaret was too young to think of these things, she said. But other people were very ready to think of them for her.

The acquaintance had therefore progressed a long way since the day of Margaret's return from school. And yet it had not gone quite so far as onlookers surmised, or as Lady Caroline wished. Sir Philip was most friendly, most attentive, but he was also somewhat absurdly unconscious of remark. His character had a simplicity which occasionally set people wondering. He was perfectly frank and manly: he spoke without *arrière-pensée*, he meant what he said, and was ready to believe that other people meant it too. He had a pleasant and courteous manner in society, and liked to be on friendly terms with every one he met; but at the same time he was not at all like the ordinary society man, and had not the slightest idea that he differed from any such person—as indeed he did. He had very high aims and ideals, and he took it for granted, with a really charming simplicity, that other people had similar aims and similar (if not higher) ideals. Consequently he now and then ran his head against a wall, and was laughed at by commonplace persons; but those who knew him well loved him all the better for his impracticable schemes and expectations.

But to Margaret he seemed rather like a firebrand. He took interest in things of which she had never heard, or which she regarded with a little delicate disdain. A steam-laundry in Beaminster, for example—what had a man like Sir Philip Ashley to do with a steam-laundry? And yet he was establishing one in the old city, and actually assuring people that it would "pay." He had been exerting himself about the drainage of the place and the dwellings of the poor. Margaret was sorry in a vague way for the poor, and supposed that drainage had to be "seen to" from time to time, but she did not want to hear anything about it. She liked the pretty little cottages in the village of Helmsley, and she did not mind begging for a holiday for the school children (who adored her) now and then; and she had heard with pleasure of Lady Ashley's pattern alm-houses and dainty orphanage, where the old women wore red cloaks, and the children were exceedingly picturesque; but as a necessary consequence of her life-training, she did not want to know anything about disease or misery or sin. And Sir Philip could not entirely keep these subjects out of his conversation, although he tried to be very careful not to bring a look that he knew well—a look of shocked repulsion and dislike—to Margaret's tranquil face.

She welcomed him with her usual sweetness that afternoon. He thought that she looked lovelier than ever. The day was cold, and she wore a dark-green dress with a good deal of gold embroidery about it, which suited her perfectly. Lady Caroline, too, was graciousness itself. She received him in her own little sitting-room—a gem of a room into which only her intimate friends were admitted, and made him welcome with all the charm of manner for which she was distinguished. And to add to her virtues, she presently found that she had letters to write, and retired into an adjoining library, leaving the door open between the two rooms, so that Margaret might still be considered as under her chaperonage, although conversation could be conducted without any fear of her overhearing what was said. Lady Caroline knew so exactly what to do and what to leave undone!

As soon as she was gone, Sir Philip put down his tea-cup and turned with an eager movement to Margaret.

"I have been wanting to speak to you," he said. "I have something special—something important to say."

"Yes?" said Margaret, sweetly. She flushed a little and looked down. She was not quite ignorant of what every one was expecting Sir Philip Ashley to say.

"Can you listen to me for a minute or two?" he said, with the gentle eagerness of manner, the restrained ardor which he was capable— unfortunately for him—of putting into his most trivial requests. "You are sure you will not be impatient?"

Margaret smiled. Should she accept him? she was thinking. After all, he was very nice, in spite of his little eccentricities. And really—with his fine features, his tall stature, his dark eyes, and coal-black hair and beard—he was an exceedingly handsome man.

"I want you to help me," said Sir Philip, in almost a coaxing tone. "I want you to carry out a design that I have formed. Nobody can do it but you. Will you help me?"

"If I can," said Margaret, shyly.

"You are always good and kind," said Sir Philip, warmly. "Margaret— may I call you Margaret? I have known you so long."

This seemed a little irregular, from Miss Adair's point of view.

"I don't know whether mamma— —" she began, and stopped.

"Whether she would like it? I don't think she would mind: she suggested it the other day, in fact. She always calls me 'Philip,' you know: perhaps you would do the same?"

Again Margaret smiled; but there was a touch of inquiry in her eyes as she glanced at him. She did not know very much about proposals of marriage, but she fancied that Sir Philip's manner of making one was peculiar. And she had had it impressed upon her so often that he was about to make one that it could hardly be considered strange if his manner somewhat bewildered her.

"I want to speak to you," said the young man, lowering his earnest voice a little, "about your friend, Miss Colwyn."

Now, why did the girl flush scarlet? Why did her hand tremble a little as she put down her cup? Philip lost the thread of the conversation for a minute or two, and simply looked at her. Then Margaret quietly took down a screen from the mantel-piece and began to fan herself. "It is rather hot here, don't you think?" she said, serenely. "The fire makes one feel quite uncomfortable."

"It *is* a large one," said Sir Philip, with conviction. "Shall I take any of the coal off for you? No? Well, as I was saying, I wished to speak to you about your friend, Miss Colwyn."

"She has lost her father lately, poor thing," said Margaret, conversationally. "She has been very unhappy."

"Yes, and for more reasons than one. You have not seen her, I conclude, since his death?"

"No, he died in August or September, did he not? It is close upon December now—what a long time we have been away! Poor Janetta!—how glad she will be to see me!"

"I am sure she will. But it would be just as well for you to hear beforehand that her father's death has brought great distress upon the family. I have had some talk with friends of his, and I find that he left very little money behind."

"How sad for them! But—they have not removed?—they are still at their old house: I thought everything was going on as usual," said Margaret, in a slightly puzzled tone.

"The house belongs to them, so they might as well live in it. Two or three of the family have got situations of some kind—one child is in a charitable institution, I believe."

"Oh, how dreadful! Like Lady Ashley's Orphanage?" said Margaret, shrinking a little.

"No, no; nothing of that kind—an educational establishment, to which he has got a nomination. But the mother and the two or three children are still at home, and I believe that their income is not more than a hundred a year."

Sir Philip was considerably above the mark. But the mention of even a hundred a year, though not a large income, produced little impression upon Margaret.

"That is not very much, is it?" she said, gently.

"Much! I should think not," said Sir Philip, driven almost to discourtesy by the difficulty of making her understand. "Four or five people to live upon it and keep up a position! It is semi-starvation and misery."

"But, Sir Philip, does not Janetta give lessons? I should have thought she could make a perfect fortune by her music alone. Hasn't she tried to get something to do?"

"Yes, indeed, poor girl, she has. My mother has been making inquiries, and she finds that Miss Colwyn has advertised and done everything she could think of—with very little result. I myself met her three or four days ago, coming away from Miss Morrison's, with tears in her eyes. She had failed to get the post of music-teacher there."

"But why had she failed? She can sing and play beautifully!"

"Ah, I wanted you to ask me that! She failed—because Miss Morrison was a friend of Miss Polehampton's, and she had heard some garbled and distorted account of Miss Colwyn's dismissal from that school."

Sir Philip did not look at her as he spoke: he fancied that she would be at once struck with horror and even with shame, and he preferred to avert his eyes during the moment's silence that followed upon his account of Janetta's failure to get work. But, when Margaret spoke, a very slight tone of vexation was the only discoverable trace of any such emotion.

"Why did not Janetta explain?"

Sir Philip's lips moved, but he said nothing.

"That affair cannot be the reason why she has obtained so little work, of course?"

"I am afraid that to some extent it is."

"Janetta could so easily have explained it!"

"May I ask how she could explain it? Write a letter to the local paper, or pay a series of calls to declare that she had not been to blame? Do you think that any one would have believed her? Besides—you call her your friend: could she exculpate herself without blaming you; and do you think that she would do that?"

"Without blaming me?" repeated Margaret. She rose to her full height, letting the fan fall between her hands, and stood silently confronting him. "But," she said, slowly—"I—I was not to blame."

Sir Philip bowed.

"You think that I was to blame?"

"I think that you acted on impulse, without much consideration for Miss Colwyn's future. I think that you have done her an injury—which I am sure you will be only too willing to repair."

He began rather sternly, he ended almost tenderly—moved as he could not fail to be by the soft reproach of Margaret's eyes.

"I cannot see that I have done her any injury at all; and I really do not know how I can repair it," said the girl, with a cold stateliness which ought to have warned Sir Philip that he was in danger of offending. But Philip was rash and warm-hearted, and he had taken up Janetta's cause.

"Your best way of repairing it," he said, earnestly, "would be to call on Miss Morrison yourself and explain the matter to her, as Miss Colwyn cannot possibly do—unless she is a very different person from the one I take her for. And if that did not avail, go to Miss Polehampton and persuade her to write a letter——"

He stopped somewhat abruptly. The look of profound astonishment on Margaret's face recalled him to a sense of limitations. "Margaret!" he said, pleadingly, "won't you be generous? You can afford to do this thing for your friend!"

"Go to Miss Morrison and explain! *Persuade* Miss Polehampton!—after the way she treated us! But really it is too ridiculous, Sir Philip. You do not know my friend, Miss Colwyn. She would be the last person to wish me to humiliate myself to Miss Polehampton!"

"I do not see that what she wishes has much to do with it," said Sir Philip, very stiffly. "Miss Colwyn is suffering under an injustice. I ask you to repair that injustice. I really do not see how you can refuse."

Margaret looked as if she were about to make some mutinous reply; then she compressed her lips and lowered her eyes for a few seconds.

"I will ask mamma what she thinks," she said at last, in her usual even tones.

"Why should you ask her?" said Sir Philip, impetuously. "What consultation is needed, when I simply beg you to be your own true self—that noble, generous self that I am sure you are! Margaret, don't disappoint me!"

"I didn't know," said the girl, with proud deliberateness, "that you had any special interest in the matter, Sir Philip."

"I have this interest—that I love you with all my heart, Margaret, and hope that you will let me call you my wife one day. It is this love, this hope, which makes me long to think of you as perfect—always noble and self-sacrificing and just! Margaret, you will not forbid me to hope?"

He had chosen a bad time for his declaration of love. He saw this, and his accent grew more and more supplicating, for he perceived that the look of repulsion, which he knew and hated, was already stealing into Margaret's lovely eyes. She stood as if turned into stone, and did not answer a word. And it was on this scene that Lady Caroline broke at that moment—a scene which, at first sight, gave the mother keen pleasure, for it had all the orthodox appearance of love-making: the girl, silent, downcast, embarrassed; the man passionate and earnest, with head bent towards her fair face, and hands outstretched in entreaty.

But poor Lady Caroline was soon to be undeceived, and her castle in the air to come tumbling down about her ears.

CHAPTER XVI
SIR PHILIP'S OPINION

"Is anything the matter?" said Lady Caroline, suavely.

She had been undecided for a minute as to whether she had not better withdraw unseen, but the distressed expression on her-daughter's face decided her to speak. She might at least prevent Margaret from saying anything foolish.

Sir Philip drew back a little. Margaret went—almost hurriedly—up to her mother, and put her hand into Lady Caroline's.

"Will you tell him? will you explain to him, please?" she said. "I do not want to hear any more: I would rather not. We could never understand each other, and I should be very unhappy."

Sir Philip made an eager gesture, but Lady Caroline silenced him by an entreating glance and then looked straight into her daughter's eyes. Their limpid hazel depths were troubled now: tears were evidently very near, and Lady Caroline detested tears.

"My darling child," she said, "you must not agitate yourself. You shall hear nothing that you do not want to hear. Sir Philip would never say anything that would pain you."

"I have asked her to be my wife," said Sir Philip, very quietly, "and I hope that she will not refuse to hear me say that, at least."

"But that was not all," said Margaret, suddenly turning on him her grieving eyes—eyes that always looked so much more grieved than their owner felt—and her flushing, quivering face: "You told me first that I was wrong—selfish and unjust; and you want me to humiliate myself—to say that it was my fault——"

"My dearest Margaret!" exclaimed Lady Caroline, in amaze, "what can you mean? Philip, are we dreaming?—Darling child, come with me to your room: you had better lie down for a little time while I talk to Sir Philip. Excuse me a moment, Sir Philip—I will come back."

Margaret allowed herself to be led from the room. This outbreak of emotion was almost unprecedented in her history; but then Sir Philip had attacked her on her tenderest side—that of her personal dignity. Margaret Adair found it very hard to believe that she was as others are, and not made of a different clay from them.

Some little time elapsed before Lady Caroline's return. She had made Margaret lie down, administered sal volatile, covered her with an eiderdown quilt, and seen her maid bathing the girl's forehead with eau de Cologne and water before she came back again. And all this took time. She apologized very prettily for her delay, but Sir Philip did not seem to heed her excuses: he was standing beside the fire, meditatively tugging at his black beard, and Lady Caroline had some difficulty in thinking that she could read the expression of his face.

"I do not quite understand all this," she said, with her most amiable expression of countenance, as she seated herself on the other side of the soft white hearthrug. "Margaret mentioned Miss Colwyn's name: I am quite at a loss to imagine how Miss Colwyn comes to be mixed up in the matter."

"I am very sorry," said Sir Philip, ruefully. "I never thought that there would be any difficulty. I seem to have offended Margaret most thoroughly."

Lady Caroline smiled. "Girls soon forget a man's offences," she said, consolingly. "What did you say?"

And then Sir Philip, with some hesitation, told the story of his plea for Janetta Colwyn.

The smile was frozen on Lady Caroline's lips. She sat up straight, and stared at her visitor. When he had quite ended his explanation, she said, as icily as she knew how to speak—

"And you asked my daughter to justify Miss Colwyn at the cost of her own feelings—I might almost say, of her own social standing in the neighborhood!—-"

"Isn't that a little too strong, Lady Caroline? Your daughter's social standing would not be touched in the least by an act of common justice. No one who heard of it but would honor her for exculpating her friend!"

"Exculpating! My dear Philip, you are too Quixotic! Nobody accuses either of the girls of anything but a little thoughtlessness and defiance of authority——"

"Exactly," said Philip, with some heat, "and therefore while the report of it will not injure your daughter, it may do irreparable harm to a girl who has her own way to make in the world. The gossip of Beaminster tea-tables is not to be despised. The old ladies of Beaminster are all turning their backs on Miss Colwyn, because common report declares her to have been expelled—or dismissed—in disgrace from Miss Polehampton's school. The fact that nobody knows exactly *why* she was dismissed adds weight to the injury. It is so easy to say, 'They don't tell why she was sent away— something too dreadful to be talked about,' and so on. My mother tells me that there is a general feeling abroad that Miss Colwyn is not a person to be trusted with young girls. Now that is a terrible slur upon an innocent woman who has to earn her own living, Lady Caroline; and I really must beg that you and Margaret will set yourselves to remove it."

"Really, Philip! Quite a tirade!"

Lady Caroline laughed delicately as she spoke, and passed a lace handkerchief across her lips as though to brush away a smile. She was a little puzzled and rather vexed, but she did not wish to show her true opinion of Sir Philip and his views.

"And so," she went on, "you said all this to my poor child; harrowed her feelings and wounded her self-respect, and insisted on it that she should go round Beaminster explaining that it was her fault and not Janetta Colwyn's that Miss Polehampton acted in so absurdly arbitrary a manner!"

"You choose to put it in that way," said Sir Philip, drawing down his brows, "and I cannot very well contradict you; but I venture to think, Lady Caroline, that you know quite well what I mean."

"I should be glad if you would put it into plain words. You wish Margaret—to do—what?"

"I very much wish that she would go to Miss Morrison and explain to her why Miss Colwyn left school. There is no need that she should take any blame upon herself. You must confess that it was she who took the law into her own hands, Lady Caroline; Miss Colwyn was perfectly ready to submit. And I think that as this occurrence has been made the ground for refusing to give Miss Colwyn the work that she urgently needs, it is Miss Adair's plain duty to try at least to set the matter right. I do not see why she should refuse."

"You have no pride yourself, I suppose? Do you suppose that Mr. Adair would allow it?"

"Then you might do it for her, Lady Caroline," said Sir Philip, turning round on her, with his winning, persuasive manner, of which even at that moment she felt the charm. "It would be so easy for you to explain it quietly to Miss Morrison, and ask her to give that poor girl a place in her school!

Who else could do it better? If Margaret is not—not quite strong enough for the task, then will you not help us out of our difficulty, and do it for her?"

"Certainly not, Sir Philip. Your request seems to me exceedingly unreasonable. I do not in the least believe that Miss Morrison has refused to take her for that reason only. There is some other, you may depend upon it. I shall not interfere."

"You could at least give her a strong recommendation."

"I know nothing about the girl except that she sings fairly well," said Lady Caroline, in a hard, determined voice. "I do not want to know anything about her—she has done nothing but make mischief and cause contention ever since I heard her name. I begin to agree with Miss Polehampton—it was a most unsuitable friendship."

"It has been a disastrous friendship for Miss Colwyn, I fear. You must excuse me if I say that it is hardly generous—after having been the means of the loss of her first situation—to refuse to help her in obtaining another."

"I think I am the best judge of that. If you mean to insinuate, Sir Philip, that your proposal for Margaret's hand which we have talked over before, hinges on her compliance with your wishes in this instance, you had better withdraw it at once."

"You must be aware that I have no such meaning," said Sir Philip, in a tone that showed him to be much wounded.

"I am glad—for your own sake—to hear it. Neither Mr. Adair nor myself could permit Margaret to lower herself by going to explain her past conduct to a second-rate Beaminster schoolmistress."

Sir Philip stood silent, downcast, his eyebrows contracting over his eyes until—as Lady Caroline afterwards expressed it—he positively scowled.

"You disagree with me, I presume?" she inquired, with some irony in her tone.

"Yes, Lady Caroline, I do disagree with you. I thought that you—and Margaret—would be more generous towards a fatherless girl."

"You must excuse me if I say that your interest in 'a fatherless girl' is somewhat out of place, Sir Philip. You are a young man, and it is not quite seemly for you to make such a point of befriending a little music governess. I am sorry to have to speak so plainly, but I must say that I do not think such interest befits a gentleman, and especially one who has been asking us for our daughter."

"My love for Margaret," said Sir Philip, gravely, "cannot blind me to other duties."

"There are duties in the world," rejoined Lady Caroline, "between which we sometimes have to choose. It seems to me that you may have to choose between your love for Margaret and your 'interest' in Janetta Colwyn."

"I hardly think," said her guest, "that I deserve this language, Lady Caroline. However, since these are your opinions, I can but say that I deeply regret them—and take my leave. If you or Miss Adair should wish to recall me you have but to send me a word—a line: I shall be ready to come. Your daughter knows my love for her. I am not yet disposed to give up all hope of a recall."

And then he took his leave with a manner of punctilious politeness which, oddly enough, made Lady Caroline feel herself in the wrong more than anything that he had said. She was more ruffled than Margaret had ever seen her when at last she sought the girl's room shortly before the ringing of the dressing-bell.

She found Margaret looking pale and a little frightened, but perfectly composed. She came up to Lady Caroline and put her arms round her mother's neck with a caressing movement.

"Dear mamma," she said, "I am afraid I was not quite polite to Sir Philip."

"I think, dear, that Sir Philip was scarcely polite to you. I am not at all satisfied with his conduct. He is quite unreasonable."

Margaret slowly withdrew her arms from her mother's neck, looked at her uneasily, and looked down again.

"He thinks that I ought to do something for Janetta—to make people think well of her, I suppose."

"He is utterly preposterous," said Lady Caroline.

"Do you think I ought to go to Miss Morrison about Janetta, mamma?"

"No, indeed, my dearest. Your father would never hear of it."

"I should like to do all that I could for her. I am very fond of her, indeed I am, although Sir Philip thinks me so selfish." And Margaret's soft hazel eyes filled with tears, which fell gently over her delicate cheeks without distorting her features in the least.

"Don't cry, my darling; please don't cry," said her mother, anxiously. "Your eyelids will be red all the evening, and papa will ask what is the matter. Have you any rose water?—Of course you will do all you can for your poor little friend: you are only too fond of her—too generous!—Sir Philip does not understand you as I do; he has disappointed me very much this afternoon."

"He was very unkind," said Margaret, with the faintest possible touch of resentment in her soft tones.

"Think no more of him for the present, dear. I dare say he will be here to-morrow, penitent and abashed. There goes the dressing-bell. Are you ready for Markham now? Put on your pink dress."

She spoke pleasantly, and even playfully, but she gave Margaret a searching glance, as though she would have read the girl's heart if she could. But she was reassured. Margaret was smiling now; she was as calm as ever; she had brushed the tears from her eyes with a filmy handkerchief and looked perfectly serene. "I am rather glad that you have found Sir Philip unreasonable, mamma," she said, placidly; "I always thought so, but you did not quite agree with me."

"The child's fancy is untouched," said Lady Caroline to herself as she went back to her room, "and I am thankful for it. She is quite capable of a little romantic folly if nobody is near to put some common-sense into her sometimes. And Philip Ashley has no common-sense at all."

She was glad to see that at dinner Margaret's serenity was still unruffled. When Mr. Adair grumbled at the absence of Sir Philip, whom he had expected to see that evening, the girl only looked down at her plate without a blush or a word of explanation. Lady Caroline drew her daughter's arm through her own as they left the dining-room with a feeling that she was worthy of the race to which she belonged.

But she was not in the least prepared for the first remark made by Margaret when they reached the drawing-room.

"Mamma, I must go to see Janetta to-morrow."

"Indeed, dear? And why?"

"To find out whether the things that Sir Philip has been saying are true."

"No, Margaret, dear, you really must not do that, darling. It would not be wise. What Sir Philip says does not matter to us. I cannot have you interfering with Miss Colwyn's concerns in that way."

Margaret was very docile. She only said, after a moment's pause—

"May I not ask her to give me the singing lessons we arranged for me to take?"

Lady Caroline considered for a minute or two and then said—

"Yes, dear, you may ask her about the singing lessons. In doing that you will be benefiting her, and giving her a practical recommendation that ought to be very valuable to her."

"Shall I drive over to-morrow?"

"No, write and ask her to come here to lunch. Then we can arrange about hours. I have not the least objection to your taking lessons from her ... especially as they are so cheap," said Lady Caroline to herself, "but I do not wish you to talk to her about Miss Polehampton's conduct. There is no use in such discussions."

"No, mamma," said the dutiful Margaret.

"And Sir Philip will be pleased to hear that his favorite is being benefited," said her mother, with a slightly sarcastic smile.

Margaret held up her stately head. "It matters very little to me whether Sir Philip is pleased or not," she said with a somewhat lofty accent, not often heard from the gentle lips of Margaret Adair.

CHAPTER XVII
MARGARET'S FRIENDSHIP

Margaret wrote her note to Janetta, and put her friend into something of a dilemma. She always felt it difficult to leave Mrs. Colwyn alone for many hours at a time. She had done her best to prevent her from obtaining stimulants, but it was no easy thing to make it impossible; and it was always dangerous to remove a restraining influence. At last she induced an old friend, a Mrs. Maitland, to spend the day with her stepmother, while she went to Helmsley Court; and having thus provided against emergencies, she was prepared to spend some pleasant hours with Margaret.

The day was cold and frosty, with a blue sky overhead, and the ground hard as iron underfoot. A carriage was sent for Janetta, and the girl was almost sorry that she had to be driven to her destination, for a brisk walk would have been more to her taste on this brilliant December day. But she was of course bound to make use of the carriage that came for her, and so she drove off in state, while Tiny and Jinks danced wildly on the doorstep and waved their hands to her in hilarious farewells. Mrs. Colwyn was secluding herself upstairs in high indignation at Janetta's presumption—first, in going to Helmsley Court at all, and, secondly, in having invited Mrs. Maitland to come to dinner—but Janetta did her best to forget the vexations and anxieties of the day, and to prepare herself as best she might for the serene atmosphere of Helmsley Court.

It was more than three months since her father's death, and she had not seen Margaret for what seemed to her like a century. In those three months she had had some new and sad experiences, and she almost wondered whether Margaret would not think her changed beyond knowledge by the troubles of the past. But in this fancy Janetta only proved herself young at heart; in later years she found, as we all find, that the outer man is little changed by the most terrible and heart-rending calamities. It was almost a surprise to Janetta that Margaret did not remark on her altered appearance. But Margaret saw nothing very different in her friend. Her black mourning garments certainly made her look pale, but Margaret was not a sufficiently keen observer to note the additional depth of expression in Janetta's dark eyes, or the slightly pathetic look given to her features by the thinning of her cheeks and the droop of her finely curved mouth. Lady Caroline, however, noticed all these points, and was quite aware that these changes, slight though they were, gave force and refinement to the girl's face. Secretly, she was embittered against Janetta, and this new charm of hers only added to her dislike. But, outwardly, Lady Caroline was sweetness and sympathy personified.

"You poor darling," said Margaret, when she stood with Janetta in Miss Adair's own little sitting-room, awaiting the sound of the luncheon bell; "what you must have suffered! I have felt for you, Janetta—oh, more than I can tell! You are quite pale, dear; I do hope you are better and stronger than you were?"

"I am quite well, thank you," said Janetta.

"But you must have had so much to bear! If I lost my friends—my dear father or mother—I know I should be broken-hearted. You are so brave and good, Janetta, dear."

"I don't feel so," said Janetta, sorrowfully. "I wish I did. It would be rather a comfort sometimes."

"You have a great deal of trouble and care, I am afraid," said Margaret, softly. She was resolved to be staunch to her friend, although Sir Philip had been so disagreeable about Janetta. She was going to show him that she could take her own way of showing friendship.

"There have been a good many changes in the family, and changes always bring anxieties with them," said Janetta, firmly. She had particularly resolved that she would not complain of her troubles to the Adairs; it would seem like asking them to help her—"sponging upon them," as she disdainfully thought. Janetta had a very fair share of sturdy pride and independence with which to make her way through the world.

Margaret would have continued the subject, but at that moment the bell rang, and Janetta was glad to go downstairs.

It was curious, as she remembered afterwards, to find that the splendors of the house, the elaboration of service, now produced not the slightest impression upon her. She had grown out of her former girlish feeling of insignificance in the presence of powdered footmen and fashionable ladies' maids. The choice flowers, the silver plate, the dainty furniture and hangings, which had once excited and almost awed her imagination, were perceived by her with comparative indifference. She was a woman, not a child, and these things were but as toys to one who had stood so lately face to face with the larger issues of life and death. Mr. Adair and Lady Caroline talked pleasantly to her, utterly ignoring, of course, any change in her circumstances or recent source of trouble, and Janetta did her best to respond. It was by way of trying to introduce a pleasant subject of conversation that she said at length to her hostess—

"I met Sir Philip Ashley the other day. He is so kind as to say that he will try to find me some pupils."

"Indeed," said Lady Caroline, drily. She did not approve of the introduction of Sir Philip's name or of Janetta's professional employment. Margaret flushed a little, and turned aside to give her mother's poodle a sweet biscuit.

"Sir Philip is a kind, good fellow," said Mr. Adair, who had not been admitted behind the scenes; "and I am sure that he will do what he can. Do you know his mother yet? No? Ah, she's like an antique chatelaine: one of the stateliest, handsomest old ladies of the day. Is she not, Caroline?"

"She is very handsome," said Lady Caroline, quietly, "but difficult to get on with. She is the proudest woman I ever knew."

The servants were out of the room, or she would not have said so much. But it was just as well to let this presuming girl know what she might expect from Sir Philip's mother if she had any designs upon him. Unfortunately her intended warning fell unheeded upon Janetta's ear.

"Is she, indeed?" said Mr. Adair, with interest. He was the greatest gossip of the neighborhood. "She is one of the Beauchamps, and of course she has some pride of family. But otherwise—I never noticed much pride about her. Now, how does it manifest itself, do you think?"

"Really, Reginald," said Lady Caroline, with her little smile; "how can I tell you? You must surely have noticed it for yourself. With her equals she is exceedingly pleasant; but I never knew anyone who could repress insolence or presumption with a firmer hand."

"What a pleasant person!" said Mr. Adair, laughing and looking mirthfully at Margaret. "We shall have to be on our good behavior when we see her, shall we not, my Pearl?"

This turn of conversation seemed to Lady Caroline so unfortunate that she rose from the table as soon as possible, and adjourned further discussion of the Ashleys to another period. And it was after luncheon that she found occasion to say to Janetta, in her softiest, silkiest tones—

"Perhaps it would be better, dear Miss Colwyn, if you would be so very kind as not to mention Sir Philip Ashley to Margaret unless she speaks of him to you. There is some slight misunderstanding between them, and Sir Philip has not been here for a day or two; but that it will be all cleared up very shortly, I have not the slightest doubt."

"Oh, I am sure I hope so! I am very sorry."

"There is scarcely any occasion to be sorry; it is quite a temporary estrangement, I am sure."

Janetta looked at Margaret with some concern when she had an opportunity of seeing her closely and alone, but she could distinguish no shade upon the girl's fair brow, no sadness in her even tones. Margaret talked about Janetta's brothers and sisters, about music, about her recent visits, as calmly as if she had not a care in the world. It was almost a surprise to Janetta when, after a little pause, she asked with some hesitation—

"You said you saw Sir Philip Ashley the other day?"

"Yes," answered Janetta, blushing out of sympathy, and looking away, so that she did not see the momentary glance of keen inquiry which was leveled at her from Margaret's hazel eyes.

"What did he say to you, dear?" asked Miss Adair.

"He spoke of my father—he was very kind," said Janetta, unconscious that her answer sounded like a subterfuge in her friend's ears. "He asked me if I wanted pupils; and he said that he would recommend me."

"Oh," said Margaret. Then, after another little pause—"I daresay you have heard that we are not friends now?"

"Yes," Janetta replied, not liking to say more.

For a moment Margaret raised her beautiful eyebrows.

"So Sir Philip had told her *already*!" she said to herself, with a little surprise. And she was not pleased with this mark of confidence on Sir Philip's part. It did not occur to her that Lady Caroline had been Janetta's informant.

"I refused him," she said, quietly. "Mamma is vexed about it, but she does not wish to force me to marry against my will, of course."

"Oh, but surely, Margaret, dear, you will change your mind?" said Janetta.

"No, indeed," Margaret answered, slightly lifting her graceful head. "Sir Philip is not a man whom I would ever marry."

And then she changed the subject. "See what a dear little piano I have in my sitting-room. Papa gave it to me the other day, so that I need not practice in the drawing-room. And what about our singing lessons, Janetta? Could you begin them at once, or would you rather wait until after the Christmas holidays?"

Janetta reflected. "I should like to begin them at once, dear, if I can manage it."

"Have you so many pupils, then?" Margaret asked quickly.

"Not so very many; but I mean—I am afraid I cannot spare time to come to Helmsley Court to give them. Do you go to Beaminster? Would you very much mind coming to our house in Gwynne Street?"

"Not at all," said Margaret, ever courteous and mindful of her friend's feelings. "But I must speak to mamma. It may be a little difficult to have the horses out sometimes ... that will be the only objection, I think."

But it seemed as if there were other objections. For Lady Caroline received the proposition very coldly. It really took her aback.. It was one thing to have little Miss Colwyn to lunch once a week, and quite another to send Margaret to that shabby little house in Gywnne Street. "Who knows whether the drains are all right, and whether she may not get typhoid fever?" said Lady Caroline to herself, with a shudder. "There are children in the house—they may develop measles or chicken-pox at any moment—you never know when children of that class are free from infection. And I heard an odd report about Mrs. Colwyn's habits the other day. Oh, I think it is too great a risk."

But when she said as much after Janetta's departure, she found Margaret for once recalcitrant. Margaret had her own views of propriety, and these were quite as firmly grounded as those of Lady Caroline. She had treated Janetta, she considered, with the greatest magnanimity, and she meant to be magnanimous to the end. She had made the gardener cut Miss Colwyn a basket of his best flowers and his choicest forced fruit; she had herself directed the housekeeper to see that some game was placed under the coachman's box when Miss Colwyn was driven home; and she had sent a box of French sweets to Tiny, although she had never seen that young lady in her life, and had a vague objection to all Janetta's relations. She felt, therefore, perfectly sure that she had done her duty, and she was not to be turned aside from the path of right.

"I don't think that I shall run into any danger, mamma," she said, quietly. "The children are to be kept out of the way, and I shall see nobody but Janetta. She said so, very particularly. I daresay she thought of these things."

"I don't see why she should not come here."

"No, nor I. But she says that she has so much to do."

"Then it could not be true that she had no pupils, as she told Sir Philip," said Lady Caroline, looking at her daughter.

Margaret was silent for a little time. Then she said, very deliberately—

"I am almost afraid, mamma, that Janetta is not quite straightforward."

"That was always my own idea," said Lady Caroline, rather eagerly. "I never quite trusted her, darling."

"We always used to think her so truthful and courageous," said Margaret, with regret. "But I am afraid——You know, mamma, I asked her what Sir Philip said to her, and she did not say a single word about having talked to him of our leaving Miss Polehampton's. She said he had spoken of her father, and of getting pupils for her, and so on."

"Very double-faced!" commented Lady Caroline.

"And—mamma, she must have seen Sir Philip again, because he had told her that we—that I—that we had quarreled a little, you know." And Margaret really believed that she was speaking the truth.

"I think it is quite shocking," said Lady Caroline. "And I really do not understand, dearest, why you still persist in your infatuation for her. You could drop her easily now, on the excuse that you cannot go to Beaminster so often."

"Yes, I know I could, mamma," said Margaret, quietly. "But if you do not mind, I would rather not do so. You see, she is really in rather difficult circumstances. Her father has left them badly off, I suppose, and she has not many advanced pupils in Beaminster. We always promised that she should give me lessons; and if we draw back now, we may be doing her real harm; but if I take—say, a dozen lessons, we shall be giving her a recommendation, which, no doubt, will do her a great deal of good. And after that, when she is 'floated,' we can easily drop her if we wish. But it would be hardly kind to do it just now, do you think?"

"My darling, you are quite too sweet," said Lady Caroline, languidly. "Come and kiss me. You shall have your way—until Easter, at any rate."

"We should be giving Sir Philip no reason to blame us for want of generosity, either," said Margaret.

"Exactly, my pet."

There was again a silence, which Margaret broke at last by saying, with gentle pensiveness—

"Do you think that she will ask me to be her bridesmaid, mamma, if she marries Sir Philip? I almost fancy that I should decline."

"I should think that you would," said Lady Caroline.

CHAPTER XVIII
A NEW FRIEND

Margaret's presents of fruit, flowers, and game conciliated Mrs. Colwyn's good-will, and she made no objection when Janetta informed her a few days later that Miss Adair's singing lessons were about to begin. There was time for two lessons only before Christmas Day, but they were to be continued after the first week in the New Year until Margaret went to town. Janetta was obliged, out of sheer shame, to hide from Mrs. Colwyn the fact that Lady Caroline had tried to persuade her to lower the already very moderate terms of payment, on the ground that her daughter would have to visit Gwynne Street for her lessons.

However, the first lesson passed off well enough. Margaret brought more gifts of flowers and game, and submitted gracefully to Janetta's instructions. There was no time for conversation, for the carriage came punctually when an hour had elapsed, and Margaret, as she dutifully observed, did not like to keep the horses waiting. She embraced Janetta very affectionately at parting, and was able to assure Lady Caroline afterwards that she had not seen any other member of the family.

Just as Miss Adair's carriage drove away from Mrs. Colwyn's door, another—a brougham this time—was driven up. "The Colwyns must be having a party," said a rather censorious neighbor, who was sitting with a friend in the bow-window of the next house. "Or else they are having very fine pupils indeed." "That's not a pupil," said her companion, craning forward to get a better view of the visitor; "that's Lady Ashley, Sir Philip Ashley's mother. What's she come for, I wonder?"

Janetta wondered too.

She was greatly impressed by Lady Ashley's personality. The lofty forehead, the aquiline nose, the well-marked eyebrows, the decided chin, the fine dark eyes, all recalled Sir Philip to her mind, and she said to herself that when his hair became silvery too, the likeness between him and his mother would be more striking still. The old lady's dignified manner did not daunt her as Lady Caroline's caressing tones often did. There was a sincerity, a grave gentleness in Lady Ashley's way of speaking which Janetta thoroughly appreciated. "Lady Ashley is a true *grande dame*, while

Lady Caroline is only a fine lady," she said to herself, when analyzing her feelings afterwards. "And I know which I like best."

Lady Ashley, on her side, was pleased with Janetta's demeanor. She liked the plainness of her dress, the quiet independence of her manner, and the subdued fire of her great dark eyes. She opened proceedings in a very friendly way.

"My son has interested me in your career, Miss Colwyn," she said, "and I have taken the liberty of calling in order to ask what sort of teaching you are willing to undertake. I may hear of some that will suit you."

"You are very kind," Janetta answered. "I was music governess at Miss Polehampton's, and I think that music is my strong point; but I should be quite willing to teach other things—if I could get any pupils."

"And how is it that you do not get any pupils?"

Janetta hesitated, but a look into the old lady's benevolent face invited confidence. She answered steadily—

"I am afraid that my sudden departure from Miss Polehampton's school has prejudiced some people against me."

"And could not somebody write to Miss Polehampton and get her to give you a testimonial?"

"I am afraid she would refuse."

"And that is all Margaret Adair's fault, is it not?" said Lady Ashley, shrewdly but kindly.

She was amused to see the flush of indignation in Janetta's face. "Margaret's fault? Oh no, Lady Ashley. It was not *Margaret's* fault any more than mine. We were both not very—not very respectful, perhaps, but I was, if anything, much worse than Margaret. And she shared my fate with me; she left when I did."

"You are a staunch friend, I see. And are you friendly with her still?"

"Oh yes," said Janetta, with enthusiasm. "She is so good—so kind—so beautiful! She has been here to-day to have a singing lesson—perhaps you saw her drive away just as you came up? She brought me these lovely flowers this afternoon."

There was a kindly look in Lady Ashley's eyes.

"I am very glad to hear it," she said. "And now, my dear, would you mind singing me something? I shall be better able to speak of your qualifications when I have heard you."

"I shall be very pleased to sing to you," said Janetta, and she sat down to the piano with a readiness which charmed Lady Ashley as much as the song she sang, although she sang it delightfully.

"That is very nice—very nice indeed," murmured Lady Ashley. Then she deliberated for a moment, and nodded her head once or twice. "You have been well taught," she said, "and you have a very sympathetic voice. Would you mind singing at an evening party for me in the course of the winter? You will be seen and heard; and you may get pupils in that way."

Janetta could but falter out a word of thanks. An introduction of this sort was certainly not to be despised.

"I will let you know when it takes place," said Lady Ashley, "and give you a hint or two about the songs. Will two guineas an evening satisfy you as you are a beginner?—for two songs, I mean? Very well, then, I shall count upon you for my next evening party."

She was rising to go, when the door was suddenly thrown open, and a tall, untidy figure made its appearance in the aperture. The daylight had almost faded, and the fire gave a very uncertain light—perhaps it was for that reason that Mrs. Colwyn took no notice of Lady Ashley, and began to speak in a thick, broken voice.

"It's shameful, shameful!" she said. "Visitors all afternoon—never brought them—t'see me—once. Singing and squalling all the time—not able to get a wink—wink o' sleep——"

"Oh, please, come away," said Janetta, going hurriedly up to the swaying figure in the faded dressing-gown, and trying gently to force her backwards. "I will tell you all about it afterwards; please come away just now."

"I'll not come away," said Mrs. Colwyn, thickly. "I want some money—money—send Ph[oe]be for a drop o' gin——"

"I'll go, my dear Miss Colwyn," said Lady Ashley, kindly. She was touched by the despair in Janetta's face. "I can't do any good, I am afraid. You shall hear from me again. Don't come to the door. Shall I send my servants to you?"

"Who's that? Who's that?" screamed the half-maddened woman, beginning to fling herself wildly out of Janetta's restraining arms. "Let me get at her, you bad girl! letting people into my house——"

"Can you manage? Do you want help?" said Lady Ashley, quickly.

"No, no, nothing; I can manage if you will only please go," Janetta cried, in her desperation. And Lady Ashley, seeing that her departure was really wished for, hurried from the house. And Janetta, after some wrestling and coaxing and argument, at last succeeded in putting her stepmother to bed, and then sat down and wept heartily.

What would Lady Ashley think? And how could she now recommend pupils to go to a house where a drunken woman was liable at any moment to appear upon the scene?

As a matter of fact, this was just what Lady Ashley was saying at that moment to her son.

"She is a thorough little gentlewoman, Philip, and a good musician; but, with *such* a connection, how can I send any one to the house?"

"It was unlucky, certainly," said Sir Philip, "but you must remember that you came unexpectedly. Her pupils' hours will be guarded, most probably, from interruption."

"One could never be sure. I have been thinking of sending Miss Bevan to her. But suppose a *contretemps* of this kind occurred! Poor Mary Bevan would never get over it."

"It is her stepmother, not her own mother," said Sir Philip, after a little pause. "Not that that makes it much better for her, poor little thing!"

"I assure you, Philip, it went to my heart to see that fragile girl struggling with that big woman. I would have helped her, but she entreated me to go, and so I came away. What else could I do?"

"Nothing, I suppose. There may be murder committed in that house any day, if this state of things goes on."

Lady Ashley sighed. Sir Philip walked about the room, with his hands in his pockets and his head bent on his breast.

"Margaret Adair had been there to-day," said his mother, watching him.

Sir Philip looked up.

"Why?" he said, keenly.

"To take a singing lesson. She had brought flowers. Miss Colwyn spoke of her very warmly, and when I touched on the subject of Miss Polehampton's treatment, would not allow that Margaret had anything to do with it. She is a very faithful little person, I should think."

"Far more generous than Margaret," muttered her son. Then, sombrely, "I never told you what happened at Helmsley Court the other day. Margaret refused me."

"Refused you—entirely?"

"No appeal possible."

"On what grounds?"

"Chiefly, I think, because I wanted her to make reparation to Miss Colwyn."

"Then, Philip, she is not worthy of you."

"She has had a bad training," he said, slowly. "A fine nature ruined by indulgence and luxury. She has never been crossed in her life."

"She will find out what it is to be crossed some day. My poor Phil! I am very sorry."

"We need not talk about it, mother, dear. You will be all in all to me now."

He sat down beside her, and took her hand in his, then kissed it with a mingling of tenderness and respect which brought the tears to Lady Ashley's eyes.

"But I do not want to be all in all to you, you foolish boy," she assured him. "I want to see you with a wife, with children of your own, with family ties and interests and delights."

"Not yet, mother," he answered in a low tone. "Some day, perhaps."

And from the pained look in his dark eyes she saw that he suffered more than he would have liked to own for the loss of Margaret. She said no more, but her heart ached for her boy, and she was hardly able to comfort herself with the recollection that Time heals all wounds—even those that have been made by Love.

Sir Philip had accepted Margaret's refusal as final. He had no reason to hope that she would ever change her mind towards him. Perhaps if he had known how large a part of her thoughts he occupied, in spite of her declaration that she did not like him, he might have had some hope of a more favorable hearing in the future. But he had no conception of any under-current of feeling in Margaret Adair. She had always seemed to him so frank, with a sweet, maidenly frankness, so transparent—without shallowness, that he was thrown into despair when she dismissed him. He was singularly ignorant of the nature of women, and more especially of young girls. His mother's proud, upright, rather inflexible character, conjoined with great warmth of affection and rare nobility of mind, had given him a high standard by which to judge other women. He had never had a sister, and was not particularly observant of young girls. It was therefore a greater disappointment to him than it would have been to many men to find that Margaret could be a little bit obstinate, a little bit selfish, and not at all disposed to sacrifice herself for others. She lowered his whole conception of womankind.

At least, so he said to himself, as he sat that evening after dinner over his library fire, and fell into a mood of somewhat sombre hue. What poets and philosophers had said of the changeful, capricious, shallow, and selfish nature of women was then true? His mother was a grand exception to the rule, 'twas true; but there were no women like her now. These modern girls thought of nothing but luxury, comfort, self-indulgence. They had no high ideals, no thought of the seriousness of life.

But even as he made his hot accusation against women of the present day, his heart smote him a little for his injustice. He certainly did know one girl who was eminently faithful and true; who worked hard, and, as he had just found out, suffered greatly—a girl whose true nobility of mind and life was revealed to him as if by a lightning flash of intuition.

What a helpmate Janetta Colwyn would be to any man! Her bright intelligence, her gift of song, her piquante, transitory beauty, her honesty and faithfulness, made up an individuality of distinct attractiveness. And yet he was not very much attracted. He admired her, he respected her; but his pulses did not quicken at the thought of her as they quickened when he thought of Margaret. Why should they indeed? She was a country surgeon's daughter, of no particular family; she had very undesirable connections, and she was very poor—there was nothing in Janetta's outer circumstances to make her a fitting wife for him. And yet the attraction of *character* was very great. He wanted a wife who would be above all things able to help him in his work—work of reform and of philanthropy: a selfish, luxurious, indolent woman could be no mate for him. Janetta Colwyn was the woman that he had been seeking since first he thought of marriage; and yet—ah, there was nothing wrong with her except that she was not Margaret. But of Margaret he must think no more.

Lady Ashley would have been very much astonished if she had known how far her idolized son had gone that night along the road of a resolution to ask Janetta Colwyn to be his wife.

CHAPTER XIX
NORA'S PROCEEDINGS

Janetta scarcely expected to hear from Lady Ashley again, and was not surprised that days and weeks passed on in silence as regarded her engagement to sing at the evening party. She did not reflect that Christmas brought its own special duties and festivities, and that she was not likely to be wanted until these were over. In the meantime, the holidays began, and she had to prepare as best she could, though with a heavy heart, for the homecoming of her brothers and sisters. There was very little to "keep Christmas" upon; and she could not but be grateful when her scanty store was enlarged by gifts from the Adairs, and also (to her great astonishment) from Sir Philip Ashley and from Wyvis Brand.

"Game, of course!" said Nora, whom she told of these windfalls on the first night of the sisters' arrival from their school. "Well, I'm not sorry: we don't often have grouse and woodcock at the luxurious table of Miss Peacock & Co.; but from three people at once! it will surely be monotonous."

"Don't be ridiculous, Nora. Lady Caroline has sent me a turkey, and the Brands have presented us with fowls and a side of home-cured bacon—very acceptable too, I can tell you! It is only Sir Philip who has sent game."

"Ah, he is the fine gentleman of them all," said Nora, whose spirits were high in spite of the depression that occasionally overcast the whole family when they remembered that this Christmas would be spent without their father's loving presence in their home. "The others are commonplace! Have they been here lately?"

"Wyvis Brand called when I was out, and did not come in. Mrs. Brand has been."

"Not the other one—Cuthbert?" said Nora, with great carelessness.

"No. I think he has been in Paris."

"And haven't you been there at all?"

"I couldn't go, Nora. I have been too busy. Besides—there is something that I must tell you—I wish I could put it off, but I want you to help me."

The two girls were in their bedroom, and in the darkness and stillness of the night Janetta put her arms round Nora's neck and told her of her mother's besetting weakness. She was surprised and almost alarmed at the effect upon her stepsister. Nora shuddered two or three times and drew several painful breaths; but she did not cry, and Janetta had expected an agony of tears. It was in a low, strained voice that the girl said at last—

"You say you have tried to hide it. Even if you have succeeded, it is not a thing that can be hidden long. Everybody will soon know. And it will go on from bad to worse. And—oh, Janetta, she is not your own mother, but she is mine!"

And then she burst at last into the fit of weeping for which Janetta had been waiting. But it was more piteous than violent, and she seemed to listen while Janetta tried to comfort her, and passively endured rather than returned the elder sister's caresses. Finally the two girls fell asleep in each other's arms.

The effect upon Nora of this communication was very marked. She looked pale and miserable for the next few days, and was irritable when her depression was remarked. For the children's sakes, Janetta tried to make a few mild festivities possible: she had a tiny Christmas tree in the back dining-room, and a private entertainment of snapdragon on Christmas Eve; and on Christmas Day afternoon the younger ones roasted chestnuts in the kitchen and listened to the tales that nobody could tell half so well as "dear old Janet." But Mrs. Colwyn openly lamented the hard-heartedness thus displayed, and locked herself into her bedroom with (Janetta feared) some private stores of her own; and Nora refused to join the subdued joviality in the kitchen, and spent the afternoon over a novel in the front sitting-room. From the state of her eyes and her handkerchief at tea-time, however, Janetta conjectured that she had been crying for the greater part of the time.

It was useless to remonstrate with Mrs. Colwyn, but Janetta thought that something might be done with her daughter. When Nora's depression of spirits had lasted for some days, Janetta spoke out.

"Nora," she said, "I told you of our trouble, because I thought that you would help me to bear it; but you are making things worse instead of better."

"What do you mean?" asked Nora.

"It is no use fretting over what cannot be helped, dear. If we are careful we can do much to lessen the danger and the misery of it all. Mamma has been much better lately: there has been nothing—no outbreak—since Lady Ashley came. It is possible that things may be better. But we must keep home cheerful, dear Nora: it does nobody any good for you and me to look miserable."

"But I feel so miserable," said Nora, beginning to cry again.

"And is that the only thing we have to think of?" demanded Janetta, with severity.

"She is not *your* mother," murmured the girl.

"I know that, darling, but I have felt the trouble of it as much as I think you can do."

"That is impossible!" said Nora, sitting up, and pushing back the disheveled blonde curls from her flushed face—she had been lying on her bed when Janetta found her and remonstrated; "quite impossible. Because you are not of her blood, not of her kith and kin: and for me—for all of us— it is worse, because people can always point to us, and say, 'The taint is in their veins: their mother drank—they may drink, too, one day,' and we shall be always under a ban!"

Janetta was struck by the fact that Nora looked at the matter entirely from her own point of view—that very little affection for her mother was mingled with the shame and the disgrace that she felt. Mrs. Colwyn had never gained her children's respect; and when the days of babyhood were over she had not retained their love. Nora was hurt, indignant, ashamed; but she shrank from her mother more than she pitied her.

"What do you mean by 'under a ban?'" Janetta asked, after a little silence.

Nora colored hotly.

"I mean," she said, looking down and fingering her dress nervously; "I mean—that—if any of us wanted to get married——"

Janetta laughed a little. "Hadn't we better wait until the opportunity arises" she said, half-satirically, half affectionately.

"Oh, you don't know!" exclaimed Nora, giving her shoulders a little impatient twist. "I may have had the opportunity already, for all you know!"

Janetta's tone changed instantly. "Nora, dear, have you anything of that sort to tell me? Won't you trust me?"

"Oh, there's nothing to tell. It's only—Cuthbert."

"Cuthbert Brand! Nora! what do you know of him?"

"Didn't you know?" said Nora, demurely. "He teaches drawing at Mrs. Smith's school."

"Teaches—but, Nora, why does he teach?"

"He is an artist: I suppose he likes it."

"How long has he been teaching there?"

"Soon after I went first," said Nora, casting down her eyes. There was a little smile upon her face, as though she were not at all displeased at the confession. But a cold chill crept into Janetta's heart.

"Has it been a scheme—a plot, then? Did you suggest to him that he should come—and pretend that he was a stranger."

"Oh, Janetta, don't look so solemn! No, I did not suggest it. He met me one day when I was out with Georgie shopping, and he walked with us for a little way and found out where we lived, and all about us. And then I heard from Mrs. Smith that she had arranged with him to teach drawing to the girls. She did not know who he was, except that he had all sorts of medals and certificates and things, and that he had exhibited in the Royal Academy."

"And you did not say to her openly that he was a connection of yours?"

"He isn't," said Nora, petulantly. "He is *your* connection, not mine. There was no use in saying anything, only Georgie used to giggle so dreadfully when he came near her that I was always afraid we should be found out."

"You might at least have left Georgie out of your plot," said Janetta, who was very deeply grieved at Nora's revelations. "I always thought that *she* was straightforward."

"You needn't be so hard on us, Janetta," murmured Nora. "I'm sure we did not mean to be anything but straightforward."

"It was not straightforward to conceal your acquaintance with Mr. Cuthbert Brand from Mrs. Smith. Especially," said Janetta, looking steadily at her sister, "if you had any idea he came there to see you."

She seemed to wait for an answer, and Nora felt obliged to respond.

"He never said so. But, of course"—with a little pout—"Georgie and I knew quite well. He used to send me lovely flowers by post—he did not write to me, but I knew where they came from, for he would sometimes put his initials inside the lid; and he always looked at my drawings a great deal more than the others—and he—he looked at me too, Janetta, and you need not be so unbelieving."

There was such a curious little touch of Mrs. Colwyn's irritability in Nora's manner at that moment that Janetta stood and looked at her without replying, conscious only of a great sinking at the heart. Vain, affected, irresponsible, childish!—were all these qualities to appear in Nora, as they had already appeared in her mother, to lead her to destruction? Mr. Colwyn's word of warning with respect to Nora flashed into her mind. She brought herself to say at last, with dry lips—

"This must not go on."

Nora was up in arms in a moment. "What must not go on? There is nothing to stop. We have done nothing wrong!"

"Perhaps not," said Janetta, slowly. "Perhaps there is nothing worse than childish folly and deceit on *your* part, but I think that Mr. Cuthbert Brand is not acting in an honorable manner at all. Either you must put a stop to it, Nora, or I shall."

"What can I do, I should like to know?"

"You had better tell Mrs. Smith," said the elder sister, "that Mr. Brand is a second-cousin of mine. That the connection was so distant that you had not thought of mentioning it until I pointed out to you that you ought to do so, and that you hope she will pardon you for what will certainly seem to her very underhand conduct."

Nora shrank a little. "Oh, I can't do that, Janetta: I really can't. She would be so angry!"

"There is another way, then: you must tell Cuthbert Brand not to send you any more flowers, and ask him to give no more drawing lessons at that school."

"Oh, Janetta, I *can't*. He has never said that he came to see me, and it would look as if I thought——"

"What you do think in your heart," said Janetta. Then, thinking that she had been a little brutal, she added, more gently—"But there is perhaps no need to decide to-day or to-morrow what we are to do. We can think over it and see if there is a better way. All that I am determined upon is that your doings must be fair and open."

"And you won't speak to anybody else about it, will you?" said Nora, rather relieved by this respite, and hoping to elude Janetta's vigilance still.

"I shall promise nothing," Janetta answered. "I must think about it."

She turned to leave the room, but was arrested by a burst of sobbing and a piteous appeal.

"You are very unkind, Janetta. I thought that you would have sympathized."

Janetta stood still and sighed. "I don't know what to say, Nora," she said.

"You are very cold—very hard. You do not care one bit what I feel."

Perhaps, thought Janetta, the reproach had some truth in it. At any rate she went quietly out of the room and closed the door, leaving Nora to cry as long and as heartily as she pleased.

The elder sister went straight to Georgie. That young person, frank and boisterous by nature, was not given to deceit, and, although she was reluctant at first to betray Nora's confidence, she soon acknowledged that it was a relief to her to speak the truth and the whole truth to Janetta. Her account tallied in the main with the one given by Nora. There did not seem to have been more than a little concealment, a little flirting, a little folly; but Janetta was aghast to think of the extent to which Nora might have been compromised, and indignant at Cuthbert Brand's culpable thoughtlessness—if it was nothing worse.

"What people have said of the Brands is true," she declared vehemently to herself. "They work mischief wherever they go; they have no goodness, no pity, no feeling of right and wrong. I thought that Cuthbert looked good, but he is no better than the others, and there is nothing to be hoped from any of them. And father told me to take care of his children—and I promised. What can I do? His 'faithful Janetta' cannot leave them to take their own way—to go to ruin if they please! Oh, my poor Nora! You did not mean any harm, and perhaps I *was* hard on you!"

She relieved herself by a few quiet but bitter tears; and then she was forced to leave the consideration of the matter for the present, as there were many household duties to attend to which nobody could manage but herself.

When she was again able to consider the matter, however, she began to make up her mind that she must act boldly and promptly if she meant to act at all. Nora had no father, and practically no mother: Janetta must be both at once, if she would fulfil her ideal of duty. And by degrees a plan of action formed itself in her mind. She would go to the Brands' house, and ask for Cuthbert himself. Certainly she had heard that he was in Paris, but surely he would have returned by this time—for New Year's Day if not for Christmas Day! She would see him and ask him to forbear—ask him not to send flowers to her little sister, who was too young for such attentions—to herself Janetta added, "and too silly." He could be only amusing himself—and he should not amuse himself at Nora's expense. He had a nice face, too, she could not help reflecting, he did not look like a man who would do a wanton injury to a fatherless girl. Perhaps, after all, there was some mistake.

And if she could not see him, she would see Mrs. Brand. The mother would, no doubt, help her: she had been always kind. Of Wyvis Brand she scarcely thought. She hoped that she might not see him—she had never spoken to him, she remembered, since the day when he had asked her to be his friend.

CHAPTER XX
AN ELDER BROTHER

She did not say a word to Nora about her scheme. The next day—it was the third of January, as she afterwards remembered—was bright and clear, a good day for walking. She told her sisters that she had business abroad, and gave them the directions respecting the care of their house and their mother that she thought they needed; then set forth to walk briskly from Gwynne Street to the old Red House.

She purposely chose the morning for her expedition. She was not making a call—she was going on business. She did not mean to ask for Mrs. Brand even, first of all; she intended to ask for Mr. Cuthbert Brand. Wyvis would probably be out; but Cuthbert, with his sedentary habits and his slight lameness, was more likely to be at home painting in the brilliant morning light than out of doors.

It was nearly twelve o'clock when she reached her destination. She went through the leafless woods, for that was the shortest way and the pleasantest—although she had thought little of pleasantness when she came out, but still it was good to hear the brittle twigs snap under her feet, and note the slight coating of frost that made the rims of the dead leaves beautiful—and it was hardly a surprise to her to hear a child's laugh ring out on the air at the very spot where, months before, she and Nora had found little Julian Brand. A moment later the boy himself came leaping down the narrow woodland path towards her with a noisy greeting; and then—to Janetta's vexation and dismay—instead of nurse or grandmother, there emerged from among the trees the figure of the child's father, Wyvis Brand. He had a healthier and more cheerful look than when she saw him last: he was in shooting coat and knickerbockers, and he had a gun in his hand and a couple of dogs at his heels. He lifted his hat and smiled, as if suddenly pleased when he saw her, but his face grew grave as he held out his hand. Both thought instinctively of their last meeting at her father's grave, and both hastened into commonplace speech in order to forget it.

"I am glad to see you again. I hope you are coming to our place," he said. And she—

"I hope Mrs. Brand is well. Is she at home?"

"No, she's not," said little Julian, with the frank fearlessness of childhood. "She's gone out for the whole day with Uncle Cuthbert, and father and I are left all by ourselves; and father has let me come out with him; haven't you, father?" He looked proudly at his father, and then at Janetta, while he spoke.

"So it appears," said Wyvis, with a queer little smile.

"Grandmother said I was to take care of father, so I'm doing it," Julian announced. "Father thinks I'm a brave boy now—not a milksop. He said I was a milksop, you know, the last time you came here."

"Come, young man, don't you chatter so much," said his father, with a sort of rough affectionateness, which struck Janetta as something new. "You run on with the dogs, and tell the servants to get some wine or milk or something ready for Miss Colwyn. I'm sure you are tired," he said to her, in a lower tone, with a searching glance at her pale face.

It was hardly fatigue so much as disappointment that made Janetta pale. She had not expected to find both Mrs. Brand and Cuthbert out, and the failure of her plan daunted her a little, for she did not often find it an easy thing to absent herself from home for several hours.

"I am not tired," said Janetta, unsteadily, "but I thought I should find them in—Mrs. Brand, I mean——"

"Did you want to see them—my mother, I mean—particularly?" asked Wyvis, either by accident or intention seeming to parody her words.

"I have not seen her for a long time." Janetta evaded giving a direct answer. "I thought that I should have had a little talk with her. If she is out, I think that I had better turn back."

"You had better rest for a little while," he said. "It is a long walk, and in spite of what you may say, you do look tired. If you have business with my mother, perhaps I may do as well. She generally leaves all her business to me."

"No," said Janetta, with considerable embarrassment of manner. "It is nothing—I can come another time."

He looked at her for a moment as if she puzzled him.

"You have been teaching music in Beaminster, I believe?"

"Yes—and other things."

"May I ask what other things?"

Janetta smiled. "I have a little sister, Tiny," she said, "and I teach her everything she learns. Reading, writing, and arithmetic, you know. And a neighbor's little boy comes in and learns with her."

"I have been wondering," said Wyvis, "whether you would care to do anything with that boy of mine."

"That dear little Julian? Oh, I should be glad," said Janetta, more freely than she had yet spoken. "He is such a sweet little fellow."

"He has a spirit of his own, as you know," said the father, with rather an unwilling smile. "He is not a bad little chap; but he has lately attached himself a good deal to me, and I have to go into the stables and about the land a good deal, and I don't think it's altogether good for him. I found him"—apologetically—"using some very bad language the other day. Oh, you needn't be afraid; he won't do it again; I think I thrashed it out of him—"

"Oh, that's worse!" said Janetta, reproachfully.

"What do you mean?"

"To strike a little fellow like that, when he did not know that what he was saying was wrong! And why did you take him where he would hear language of that kind? Wasn't it more your fault than his?"

Wyvis bent his head and shrugged his shoulders. "If the truth were known, I dare say he heard me use it," he said dryly. "I'm not mealy-mouthed myself. However, I've taught him that he must not do it."

"Have you, indeed? And don't you think that example will prove stronger than precept, or even than thrashing?" said Janetta. "If you want to teach him not to use bad words, you had better not use them yourself, Mr. Brand."

"Mr. Brand?" said Wyvis; "I thought it was to be Cousin Wyvis. But I've disgusted you; no wonder. I told you long ago that I did not know how to bring up a child. I asked you to help us—and you have not been near the place for months."

"How could I help you, if you mean to train him by oaths and blows?" asked Janetta.

"That's plain speaking, at any rate," he said. "Well, I don't mind; in fact, I might say that I like you the better for it, if you'll allow me to go so far. I don't know whether you're right or not. Of course it won't do for him to talk as I do while he's a baby, but later on it won't signify; and a thrashing never did a boy any harm."

"Do you mean that you are in the habit of swearing?" said Janetta, with a direct simplicity, which made Wyvis smile and wince at the same time.

"No, I don't," he said. "I always disliked the habit, and I was determined that Julian shouldn't contract it. But I've lived in a set that was not over particular; and I suppose I fell into their ways now and then."

"Apart from the moral point of view, no *gentleman* ever does it!" said Janetta, hotly.

"Perhaps not. Perhaps I'm not a gentleman. My relations, the publicans of Roxby, certainly were not. The bad strain in us will out, you see."

"Oh, Cousin Wyvis, I did not mean that," said Janetta, now genuinely distressed. "It is only that—I do wish you would not talk in that way—use those words, I mean. Julian is sure to catch them up, and you see yourself that that would be a pity."

"I am to govern my tongue then for Julian's sake?"

"Yes, and for your own."

"Do you *care* whether I govern it or not, Janetta?"

How oddly soft and tender his voice had grown!

"Yes, I do care," she answered, not very willingly, but compelled to truthfulness by her own conscience and his constraining gaze.

"Then I swear I will," he exclaimed, impetuously. "It is something to find a woman caring whether one is good or bad, and I won't prove myself utterly unworthy of your care."

"There is your mother: *she* cares."

"Oh, yes, she cares, poor soul, but she cries over my sins instead of fighting them. Fighting is not her *métier*, you know. Now, you—you fight well."

"That is a compliment, I suppose?" said Janetta, laughing a little and coloring—not with displeasure—at his tone.

"Yes," he said; "I like the fighting spirit."

They had been walking slowly along the path, and now they had reached the gate that opened into the grounds. Here, as he opened it, Janetta hesitated, and then stopped short.

"I think I had better make the best of my way back," she said. "It is getting late."

"Not much after twelve. Are we not friends again?"

"Oh yes."

"And will you think over what I said about my boy?"

"Do you really mean it?"

"Most decidedly. You couldn't come here, I suppose—you wouldn't leave home?"

"No, I could not do that. How would he get to me every day?"

"I would bring him myself, or send him in the dog-cart. I or my brother would look after that." Then, seeing a sudden look of protest in Janetta's face, he added quickly—"You don't like that?"

"It is nothing," said Janetta, looking down.

"Is it to me or to my brother that you object?"

He smiled as he spoke, but, a little to his surprise, Janetta kept silence, and did not smile. Wyvis Brand was a man of very quick perceptions, and he saw at once that if she seemed troubled she had a reason for it.

"Has Cuthbert offended you?" he asked.

"I have only spoken to him once—four months ago."

"That is no answer. What has he been about? I have some idea, you know," said Wyvis, coolly, "because I came across some sketches of his which betrayed where his thoughts were straying. Your pretty sister quite captivated him, I believe. Has he been getting up a flirtation?"

"I suppose it is a joke to him and to you," said Janetta, almost passionately, "but it is no joke to us. Yes, I came to speak to him or to your mother about it. Either she must leave the school where she is teaching, or he must let her alone."

"You had better not speak to my mother; it will only worry her. Come in, and tell me about it," said Wyvis, opening the gate, and laying his hand gently on her arm.

She did not resent his tone of mastery. In spite of the many faults and errors that she discerned in him, it always seemed to her that a warmer and finer nature lay below the outside trappings of roughness and coldness than was generally perceptible. And when this better nature came to the front, it brought with it a remembrance of the tie of kinship, and Janetta's heart softened to him at once.

He took her into a room which she guessed to be his own private sanctum—a thoroughly untidy place, littered with books, papers, tools, weapons, gardening implements, pipes and tobacco jars, in fine confusion.

He had to clear away a pile of books from a chair before she could sit down. Then he planted himself on a corner of the solid, square oak table in the middle of the room, and prepared to listen to her story. Julian, who interrupted them once, was ordered out of the room again in such a peremptory tone that Janetta was somewhat startled. But really the boy did not seem to mind.

By dint of leading questions he drew from her an outline of the facts of the case, but she softened them, for Nora's sake, as much as possible. She looked at him anxiously when she had done, to see whether he was angry.

"You know," she said, "I don't want to sow dissension of any kind between you."

Wyvis smiled. "I know you don't. But I assure you Cuthbert and I never quarreled in our lives. That is not one of the sins you can lay to my charge. He is a whimsical fellow, and I suspect that this has been one of his freaks — not meaning to hurt anybody. If you leave him to me, I'll stop the drawing-lessons at any rate, and probably the flowers."

"Don't let him think that Nora cares," she said. "She is quite a child — if he had sent her bonbons she would have liked them even better than flowers."

"I understand. I will do my best — as you are so good as to trust me," he answered, lowering his voice.

A little silence fell between them. Something in the tone had made Janetta's heart beat fast. Then there rose up before her — she hardly knew why — the vision of a woman, an imaginary woman, one whom she had never seen — the woman with Julian's eyes, the woman who called herself the wife of Wyvis Brand. The thought had power to bring her to her feet.

"And now I must really go."

"Not yet," he said, smiling down at her with a very kindly look in his stern dark eyes. "Do you know you have given me a great deal of pleasure to-day? You have trusted me to do a commission for you — a delicate bit of work too — and that shows that you don't consider me altogether worthless."

"You may be sure that I do not."

"Yes, we are friends. I have some satisfaction in that thought. Do you know that you are the first woman who has ever made a *friend* of me? who has ever trusted me, and taught me — for a moment or two — to respect myself? It is the newest sensation I have had for years."

"Not the sensation of respecting yourself, I hope?"

"Yes, indeed. You don't know—you will never know—how I've been handicapped in life. Can you manage to be friendly with me even when I don't do exactly as you approve? You are at liberty to tell me with cousinly frankness what you dislike."

"On that condition we can be friends," said Janetta, smiling and tendering her hand. She meant to say good-bye, but he retained the little hand in his own and went on talking.

"How about the boy? You'll take him for a few hours every day?"

"You really mean it?"

"I do, indeed. Name your own terms."

She blushed a little, but was resolved to be business-like.

"You know I can't afford to do it for nothing," she said. "He can come from ten to one, if you like to give me——" and and then she mentioned a sum which Wyvis thought miserably inadequate.

"Absurd!" he cried. "Double that, and then take him! When can he come?"

"Next week, if you like. But I mean what I say——"

"So do I, and as my will is stronger than yours I shall have my own way."

Janetta shook her head, and, having by this time got her hand free, she managed to say good-bye, and left the house much more cheerfully than she had entered it. Strange to say, she had a curious feeling of trust in Wyvis Brand's promise to help her; it seemed to her that he was a man who would endeavor at all costs to keep his word.

CHAPTER XXI
CUTHBERT'S ROMANCE

Janetta was hardly surprised when, two days later, she was asked to give a private audience to Mr. Cuthbert Brand. She had not yet told Nora of the course that she had pursued, for she was indeed rather unnecessarily ashamed of it. "It was just like a worldly mamma asking a young man his intentions about her daughter," she said to herself, with a whimsical smile. "Probably nothing will come of it but a cessation of these silly little attentions to Nora." But she felt a little shy and constrained when she entered the drawing-room, and, while shaking hands with her cousin, she did not lift her eyes to his face.

When she had taken a seat, however, and managed to steal a glance at him, she was half-provoked, half-reassured. Cuthbert's mobile face was full of a merry, twinkling humor, and expressed no penitence at all. She was so much astonished that she forgot her shyness, and looked at him inquiringly without opening her lips.

Cuthbert laughed—an irrepressible little laugh, as if he could not help it. "Look here, Cousin Janetta," he said, "I'm awfully sorry, but I really can't help it. The idea of you as a duenna and of Wyvis as a heavy father has been tickling me ever since yesterday, and I shall have to have it out sooner or later. I assure you it's only a nervous affection. If I didn't laugh, I *might* cry or faint, and that would be worse, you know."

"I don't quite see the joke," said Janetta, gravely.

"The joke," said Cuthbert, "lies in the contrast between yourself and the role you have taken upon you."

"It is a role that I am obliged to take upon me," interposed Janetta; "because my sisters have no father, and a mother whose health makes it impossible for her to guard them as she would like to do."

"Now you're going to be severe," said Cuthbert; "and indeed I am guiltless of anything but a little harmless fooling. I can but tender my humblest apologies, and assure you that I have resigned my post in Mrs. Smith's educational establishment, and that I will keep my flowers in future to myself, unless I may send them with your consent and that of my authoritative elder brother."

Janetta was not mollified. "It is easy for you to talk of it so lightly," she said, "but you forget that you might have involved both my sisters in serious trouble."

"Don't you think I should have been able to get them out again?" said Cuthbert, with all the lightness to which she objected. "Don't you think that I could have pacified the schoolmistress? There is one thing that I must explain. My fancy for teaching was a fad, undertaken for its own sake, which led me accidentally at first to Mrs. Smith's school. I did not know that your sisters were there until I had made my preliminary arrangements."

Janetta flushed deeply, and did not reply. Nora's imagination had been more active than she expected. Cuthbert, who was watching her, saw the flush and the look of surprise, and easily guessed what had passed between the sisters.

"Did you ever read Sheridan's 'Rivals?'" he asked, quietly. "Don't you remember the romantic heroine who insisted on her romance? She would hardly consent to marry a man unless he had a history, and would help her to make one for herself?"

"I don't think that Nora is at all like Lydia Languish."

"Possibly not, in essentials. But she loves romance and mystery and excitement, as Lydia Languish did. It is a very harmless romance that consists in sending a few cut flowers by Parcel Post, Cousin Janetta."

"I know—it sounds very little," Janetta said, "but it may do harm for all that."

"Has it done harm to your sister, then?" Cuthbert inquired, with apparent-innocence, but with the slight twinkle of his eye, which told of inward mirth. Janetta was again growing indignant, and was about to answer rather sharply, when he once more changed his tone. "There," he said, "I have teased you quite enough, haven't I? I have been presuming on our relationship to be as provoking as I could, because—honestly—I thought that you might have trusted me a little more. Now, shall I be serious?"

"If you can," said Janetta.

"That's awfully severe. By nature, I must tell you, I am the most serious, not to say melancholy, person in creation. But on a fine day my spirits run away with me. Now, Janetta—I may call you Janetta, may not I?—I am going to be serious, deadly serious, as serious as if it were a wet day in town. And the communication that I wish to make to you as the head of the family, which you seem to be, is that I am head over ears in love with your sister Nora, and that I beg for the honor of her hand."

"You are joking," said his hearer, reproachfully.

"Never was joking further from my thoughts. Getting married is an exceedingly solemn business, I believe. I want to marry Nora and take her to Paris."

"Oh, this is ridiculous: you can't mean it," said Janetta.

"Why ridiculous? Did I not tell you that I admired Miss Lydia Languish? Her desire for a romance was quite praiseworthy: it is what every woman cherishes in her heart of hearts: only Nora, being more naive and frank and child-like than most women, let me see the desire more clearly than women mostly do. That's why I love her. She is natural and lovable and lovely. Don't tell me that I can't win her heart. I know I may have touched her fancy, but that is not enough. Let me have the chance, and I think that I can go deeper still."

"You said that you would be serious, but you don't know how serious this is to me," said Janetta, the tears rising to her eyes. "My father told me to take care of her: she is very young—and not very wise; and how am I to know whether you mean what you say?"

"I do mean it, indeed!" said Cuthbert, in a much graver tone. "I have got into the habit of talking as if I felt very little—a ridiculous habit, I acknowledge—but, in this matter, I mean it from the bottom of my heart."

"I suppose, then," said Janetta, tremulously, "that you must speak to mamma—and to Nora. I am not at all the head of the house, although you are pleased—in fun—to call me so. I am only Nora's half-sister, fond of her and anxious about her, and ready to do all that I can do for her good."

Cuthbert looked at her intently. Her face was pale, and the black dress that she wore was not altogether becoming to her dark eyes and complexion, but there was something pathetic to him in the weight of care which seemed to sit upon those young brows and bear down the slender shoulders of the girl. The new sensation thus given caused him to say, with sudden earnestness—

"Will you forgive me for having spoken and acted so thoughtlessly? I never meant to cause you so much anxiety. You see, I am not very well acquainted with English ways, and I may have made more mistakes than I knew. When Nora is my wife you shall not have to fear for her happiness."

"You speak very confidently of making her your wife," said Janetta, forgiving him in her heart, nevertheless. "But you have no house—no profession, have you?"

"No income, you mean?" said Cuthbert, with his merry smile. "Oh, yes, I have a profession. It does not pay me quite so well as it might do, but I think I shall do better by-and-bye. Then I have a couple of hundreds a year of my own. Is it too much of a pittance to begin upon?"

"Nora is quite too young to begin upon anything. If only you would leave her alone for a year or two!—till she is a little more staid and sensible!"

"But that's too late, don't you see? That's where my apologies have to come in. I have disturbed the peace already, haven't I?"

"Mr. Brand," said Janetta, gravely, in spite of an exclamation of protest from her cousin, "I don't think that we are going quite deeply enough into the matter. There are one or two things that I must say: there is no one else to say them. Nora is young and foolish, but she is affectionate and sensitive, and if she once cares for you, you may make the happiness or the misery of her life. Our dear father told me to take care of her. And I am not sure that he would have sanctioned her engagement to you."

"I'd better send Wyvis to talk to you," said Cuthbert, starting up and nearly upsetting a chair in his eagerness. "I knew he could manage and—and explain things better than I could. He's well up in the family affairs. Will you see him now?"

"Now?"

"He's outside waiting. He wouldn't come in. I'll go and send him to you. No, don't object: there are ever so many things that you two elders had better talk over together. I must say," said Cuthbert, beginning to laugh again in his light-hearted way, "that, when I think of Wyvis as a family man, bent on seeing his younger brother *se ranger*, and you as Nora's stern guardian, I am seized with an access of uncontrollable mirth."

He caught up his hat and left the room so quickly that Janetta, taken by surprise, could not stop him. She tried to follow, but she was too late: he had rushed off, leaving the hall-door open, and a draught of cold air was ascending the stairs and causing her stepmother peevishly to remark that Janetta's visitors were really intolerable. "Who *was* it, this time?" she asked of her second daughter Georgie, who was standing at the window—the mother and her girls being assembled in Mrs. Colwyn's bedroom, her favorite resort on cold afternoons.

A True Friend | 163

Georgie gave a little giggle—her manners were not perfect, in spite of a term at Mrs. Smith's superior seminary for young ladies—and answered, under her breath—

"It was Mr. Cuthbert Brand."

Nora's book fell from her knee. When she picked it up her cheeks were crimson and her eyes were flashing fire.

"Don't be absurd, Georgie. It was *not*."

"Indeed it was, Nora. I suppose he came to see Janetta, and Janetta has sent him away. Oh, how he's running, although he is a little lame! He has caught some one—his brother, I believe it is; and now the brother's walking back with him."

"I shall go down," said Mrs. Colwyn, with dignity. "It is not at all proper for a young person like Janetta to receive gentlemen alone. I shall go and sit in the drawing-room myself."

"Then Janetta will take her visitors into the dining-room," said Nora, abruptly. "She has only business with these people, mamma: they don't come to visit us because they like us—it is only when they want us to do something for them; so I would not put myself out for them if I were you. And as for Janetta's being young, she is the oldest person amongst us." And then Nora turned to her book, which she held upside down without being at all aware of it.

"I do not know what you mean, Nora," was Mrs. Colwyn's fretful response; "and if the other brother is coming here, I shall certainly not disturb myself, for I believe him to be a wild, dissipated, immoral, young man."

"Just the sort of man for Janet to receive alone," murmured Georgie, maliciously. Georgie was the member of the family who "had a tongue."

Meanwhile Wyvis had come into the house, though without Cuthbert, who had thought it better to disappear into the gathering darkness; and Janetta received him in the hall.

He laughed a little as he took her hand. "Cuthbert is a little impatient, is he not? Well, he has persuaded me into talking this matter over with you. I'm to come in here, am I?" as Janetta silently opened the sitting-room door for him. "This looks pleasant," he added after a moment's pause.

In the gathering evening gloom the shabbiness of the furniture could not be seen, and the fire-light danced playfully over the worn, comfortable-looking chairs drawn up to the hearth, on the holly and mistletoe which decorated the walls, and the great cluster of geranium and Christmas roses which the Adairs had sent to Janetta the day before. Everything looked homelike and comfortable, and perhaps it was no wonder that Wyvis—accustomed to the gloom of his own home, or the garish splendor of a Paris hotel—felt that he was entering a new sphere, or undergoing some new experience.

"Don't light the lamp," he said, in his imperious way: "let us talk in this half-light, if you don't mind? it's pleasanter."

"And easier," said Janetta, softly.

"Easier? Does it need an effort?"

"I am afraid I have something unpleasant to say."

"So have I. We are quits, then. You can begin."

"Your brother has been asking if he maybe engaged to Nora——"

"If he may marry her out of hand, you mean. That's what he wants to do."

"We know very little of him," said Janetta, rather unsteadily, "or of you. Things have been said against you in Beaminster—you have yourself told me things that I did not like—indeed, my father almost warned me against you——"

A murmur from Wyvis Brand sounded uncommonly like "the devil he did!"—but Janetta did not stop to listen.

"I never heard anything but vague generalities against *him*, but then I never heard anything particularly good. I don't like the way in which he has pursued his acquaintance with Nora. I have no authority with her—not much influence with her mother—and, therefore, I throw myself on you for help," said Janetta, her musical voice taking a pathetically earnest cadence; "and I ask you to beg your brother to wait—to let Nora grow older and know her own mind a little better—to give us the chance of knowing him before he asks to take her away."

"You have not said either of the things that I was expecting to hear," said Wyvis.

"What were those?"

"How much money he had a year!"

"Oh, he told me about that."

"Or—an allusion to his forbears: his father's character and his mother's relations—the two bugbears of Beaminster."

"I think nothing of those, if Cuthbert himself is good."

"Well, he *is* good. He is as different from me as light is from darkness. He is a little thoughtless and unpractical sometimes, but he is sweet-tempered, honest, true, clean-living, and God-fearing. Will that suit you?"

"If he is all that— —"

"He is that and more. We are not effusive, Cuthbert and I, but I think him one of the best fellows in the world. She'll be lucky who gets him, in my opinion."

"All the more reason, then, why I must say a still more unpleasant thing than ever," she replied. "Nora is in great trouble, because she has been told what I have known for some time. Her mother does not always control herself; you know what I mean? She must not marry without telling this—we cannot deceive the man who is to be her husband—he must know the possible disgrace."

"If every woman were as straightforward and honorable as you, Janetta, there would be fewer miserable marriages," said Wyvis, slowly. "You are, no doubt, right to speak; but, on the other hand, *our* family record is much worse than yours. If one of you can condescend to take one of us, I think we shall have the advantage."

Janetta drew a long breath.

"Then, will you help me in what I ask?"

"Yes, I will. I'll speak to Cuthbert and point out how reasonable you are. Then—you'll let him cultivate your sister's acquaintance, I suppose? In spite of your disclaimers, I believe you are supreme in the house. I wish there were more like you to be supreme, Janetta. I wish—to God I wish— that I had met you—a woman like you—eight years ago."

And before she could realize the meaning of what he had said to her, the man was gone.

CHAPTER XXII
WYVIS BRAND'S IDEAL

Everything was satisfactorily settled. Cuthbert was put on his probation; Nora was instructed in the prospect that lay before her, and was allowed to correspond with her "semi-betrothed," as he insisted on calling himself. Mrs. Colwyn was radiant with reflected glory, for although she despised and hated Mrs. Brand, she was not blind to the advantages that would accrue to herself through connection with a County family. She was not, however, as fully informed in the details of the little love-affair as she imagined herself to be. Janetta's share in bringing about a *dénouement* and retarding its further development was quite unknown to her. The delay, which some of Mr. Colwyn's old friends urged with great vigor, was ascribed by her chiefly to the hostile influences of Wyvis Brand, and she made a point of being openly uncivil to that gentleman when, on fine mornings, he brought his boy to Gwynne Street or fetched him away on a bright afternoon. For it had been decided that little Julian should not only come every day at ten, but on two days of the week should stay until four o'clock in the afternoon, in order to enjoy the advantages of Tiny's society. He had been living so unchild-like a life of late that Janetta begged to keep him for play as well as for lessons with other children.

Nora went back to her school somewhat sobered by the unexpected turn of events, and rather ashamed of her assumption (dispelled by Janetta) that Cuthbert Brand had given drawing lessons at Mrs. Smith's in order to be near her. Mr. Cuthbert Brand discontinued these lessons, but opened a class in Beaminster at the half-deserted Art School, and made himself popular wherever he went. Janetta was half inclined to doubt the genuineness of his affection for Nora when she heard of his innocent, but quite enthusiastic, flirtations with other girls. But he always solemnly assured her that Nora had his heart, and Nora only; and as long as he made Nora happy Janetta was content. And so the weeks passed on. She had more to do now that Julian came every day, but she got no new music pupils, and she heard nothing about the evening parties at Lady Ashley's. She concluded that Sir Philip and his mother had forgotten her, but such was not the case. There had been a death in the family, and the consequent period of mourning had prevented Lady Ashley from giving any parties—that was all.

For some little time, therefore, Janetta's life seemed likely to flow on in a very peaceful way. Mrs. Colwyn "broke out" only once between Christmas and Easter, and was more penitent and depressed after her outbreak than Janetta had ever seen her. Matters went on more quietly than ever after this event. Easter came, and brought Nora and Georgie home again, and then there was a period of comparative excitement and jollity, for the Brands began to come with much regularity to the little house in Gwynne Street, and there were merry-makings almost every day.

But when the accustomed routine began again, Janetta, in her conscientious way, took herself seriously to task. She had not been governing herself, her thoughts, her time, her temper, as she conceived that it was right for her to do. On reflection, it seemed to her that one person lately filled up the whole of her mental horizon. And this person she was genuinely shocked to find was Wyvis Brand.

Why should she concern herself so much about him? He was married; he had a child; his mother and brother lived with him, and supplied his need of society. He went out into the world about Beaminster more than he used to do, and might have been fairly popular if he had exerted himself, but this he would never do. There were fewer reports current about his bad companions, or his unsteady way of life; and Janetta gathered from various sources that he had entirely abandoned that profane and reckless method of speech for which she had rebuked him. He was improving, certainly. Well, was that any reason why she should think about him so much, or consider his character and his probable fate so earnestly? She saw no reason in it, she told herself; and perhaps she was right.

There was another reason even more potent for making her think of him. He had had an unsatisfactory, troublous sort of life; he had been unfortunate in his domestic relations, and he was most decidedly an unhappy man. Many a woman before Janetta has found reasons of this kind suffice for love of a man. Certainly, in Janetta's case, they formed the basis of a good deal of interest. She told herself that she could not help thinking of him. He came very often, on pretext of bringing or of fetching Julian—especially on the days when Julian stayed until four o'clock, for then he would stray in and sit down to chat with Janetta and her mother until it was sheer incivility not to offer him a cup of tea. Softened by the pleasures of hospitality, Mrs. Colwyn would be quite gracious to him at these times. But now and then she left him to be entertained by Janetta, saying rather sharply that she did not care to meet the man who chose to behave "so brutally to her darling Nora."

So that Janetta got into the way of sitting with him, talking with him on all subjects, of giving him her sage advice when he asked for it, and listening with interest to the stories that he told her of his past life. It was natural that she should think about him a good deal, and about his efforts to straighten the tangled coil of his life, and to make himself a worthier father for his little son than his own father had been to him. There was nothing in the world more likely than this sort of intercourse to bring these two kinsfolk upon terms of closest friendship. And as Janetta indignantly told herself—there was nothing—nothing more.

She always remembered that his wife was living; she never forgot it for a moment. He was, of course, not a man whom she ever thought of loving— she was angry with herself for the very suggestion—but he was certainly a man who interested her more than any one whom she had ever met. And he was interested in her too. He liked to talk to her, to ask her advice and listen to her pet theories. She was friend, comrade, sister, all in one. Nothing more. But the position was, whether they knew it or not, a rather dangerous one, and an innocent friendship might have glided into something closer and more harmful had not an unexpected turn been given to the events of both their lives.

For some time Janetta had seen little of the Adairs. They were very much occupied—visiting and receiving visits—and Margaret's lessons were not persevered in. But one afternoon, shortly after Easter, she called at Mrs. Colwyn's house between three and four, and asked when she might begin again. Before the day was settled, however, they drifted into talk about other things, and Margaret was soon deeply engaged in an account of her presentation at Court.

"I thought you were going to stay in town for the season?" Janetta asked.

Margaret shook her head. "It was so hot and noisy," she murmured. "Papa said the close rooms spoiled my complexion, and I am sure they spoiled my temper!" She smiled bewitchingly as she spoke.

She was charmingly dressed in cream-colored muslin, with a soft silk sash of some nondescript pink hue tied round her waist, and a bunch of roses at her throat to match the Paris flowers in her broad-brimmed, slightly tilted, picturesque straw hat. A wrap for the carriage-fawn-colored, with silk-lining of rose-pink toned by an under-tint of grey—carried out the scheme of color suggested by her dress, and suited her fair complexion admirably. She had thrown this wrap over the back of a chair and removed her hat, so that Janetta might see whether she was altered or not.

"You are just a trifle paler," Janetta confessed.

As a matter of fact there were some tired lines under Margaret's eyes, and a distinct waning of the fresh faint bloom upon her cheek—changes which made of her less the school girl than the woman of the world. And yet, to Janetta's thinking, she was more beautiful than ever, for she was acquiring a little of the dignity given by experience without losing the simple tranquillity of the exquisite child.

"I am a little tired," Margaret said. "One sees so much—one goes to so many places. I sighed for Helmsley Court, and dear mamma brought me home."

At this moment a crash, as of some falling body, resounded through the house, followed by a clatter of breaking crockery, and the cries of children. Janetta started up, with changing color, and apologized to her guest.

"Dear Margaret, will you excuse me for a moment? I am afraid that one of the children must have fallen. I will be back in a minute or two."

"Go, dear, by all means," said Margaret, placidly. "I know how necessary you are."

Janetta ran off, being desperately afraid that Mrs. Colwyn had been the cause of this commotion. But here she was mistaken. Mrs. Colwyn was safe in her room, but Ph[oe]be, the charity orphan, had been met, while ascending the kitchen stair with the tea-tray in her hands, by a raid of nursery people— Tiny and Curly and Julian Brand, to wit—had been accidentally knocked down, had broken the best tea-set and dislocated her own collar-bone; while Julian's hand was severely cut and Curly's right eye was black and blue. Tiny had fortunately escaped without injury, and it was she, therefore, who was sent to Margaret with a modified version of the disaster.

"Please, Janetta says, will you stay for a little minute or two till she comes back again? Curly's gone for the doctor because Ph[oe]be's done something to one of her bones; and Janetta's tying up Julian's thumb because it's bleeding so dreadfully."

"I have never seen you before, have I?" said Margaret, smiling at the slim little girl with the delicate face and great blue eyes. "You are Tiny; I have often heard of you. Do you know me?"

"Yes," said Tiny. "You are the beautiful lady who sends us flowers and things—Janetta's friend."

"Yes, that is right. And how long will Janetta be?"

"Oh, not long, she said; and she hoped you would not mind waiting for a little while?"

"Not at all. Is that the doctor?" as a knock resounded through the little house.

"I dare say it is," said Tiny, running to the door; and then after a moment's pause, she added, in a rather disappointed tone, "No, it's Julian's father. It's Mr. Brand."

"Mr. Brand!" said Margaret, half-astonished and half-amused. "Oh, I have heard of him." And even as she spoke, the door opened, and Wyvis Brand walked straight into the room.

He gave a very slight start as his eyes fell upon Margaret, but betrayed no other sign of surprise. Tiny flew to him at once, dragged at his hand, and effected some sort of informal introduction, mingled with an account of the accident which had happened to Julian.

"Don't you want to go and ascertain the amount of the injury?" said Margaret, with a little smile.

"Not at all," said Wyvis, emphatically, and took up his position by the mantel-piece, whence he got the best view of her graceful figure and flower-like face. Margaret felt the gaze and was not displeased by it, admiration was no new thing to her; she smiled vaguely and slightly lowered her lovely eyes. And Wyvis stood and looked.

In spite of his apparent roughness Wyvis Brand was an impressionable man. He had come into the room cold, tired, not quite in his usual health, and more than usually out of humor; and instead of the ordinary sight of Janetta—a trim, pleasant, household-fairy sort of sight, it was true, but not of the wildly exciting kind—he found a vision, as it seemed to him, of the most ethereal beauty—a woman whose every movement was full of grace, whose exquisitely modulated voice expressed refinement as clearly as her delicately moulded features; whose whole being seemed to exhale a sort of perfume of culture, as if she were in herself the most perfect product of a whole civilization.

Wyvis had been in many drawing-rooms and known many women, more or less intimately, but he had never, in all his purposeless Bohemian life, come across exactly this type of woman—a type in which refinement counts for more than beauty, culture for more than grace. With a sudden leap of memory, he recalled some scenes of which he had been witness years before, when a woman, hot, red, excited with wine and with furious jealousy, had reviled him in the coarsest terms, had struck him in the face and had spat out foul and vindictive words of abuse. That woman—ah, that woman was his wife—had been for many years to him the type of what women must always be when stripped of the veneer of society's restraints. Janetta had of late shaken his conviction on this point; it was reserved for Margaret Adair to shatter it to the winds.

She looked so fair, so dainty, so delicate—he would have been a marvel amongst men who believed that her body was anything but "an index to a most fair mind"—that Wyvis said to himself that he had never seen any woman like her. He was fascinated and enthralled. The qualities which made her so different from his timid, underbred, melancholy mother, or his coarse and self-indulgent wife, were those in which Margaret showed peculiar excellence. And before these—for the first time in his life—Wyvis Brand fell down and worshipped.

It was unfortunate; it was wrong; but it was one of those things that will happen sometimes in everyday life. Wyvis was separated from his wife, and hated as much as he despised her. Almost without knowing what he did, he laid his whole heart and soul, suddenly and unthinkingly, at Margaret's feet. And Margaret, smiling and serene, utterly ignorant of his past, and not averse to a little romance that might end more flatteringly than Sir Philip's attentions had done, was quite ready to accept the gift.

Before Janetta had bound up Julian's hand, and made some fresh tea, which she was obliged to carry upstairs herself, Mr. Brand had obtained information from Margaret as to the day and hour on which she was likely to come to Janetta for her singing-lesson, and also as to several of her habits in the matter of walks and drives. Margaret gave the information innocently enough; Wyvis had no direct purpose in extracting it; but the attraction which the two felt towards each other was sufficient to make such knowledge of her movements undesirable, and even dangerous for both.

CHAPTER XXIII
FORGET-ME-NOTS

Lady Caroline, always mindful of her daughter's moods, could not quite understand Margaret's demeanor when she returned home that afternoon. She fancied that some news about Sir Philip might have reached the girl's ear and distressed her mind. But when she skilfully led the conversation in that direction, Margaret said at once, with a complete absence of finesse that rather disconcerted her mother—

"No, mamma, I heard nothing about the Ashleys—mother or son."

"Dear Margaret," thought Lady Caroline, "is surely not learning *brusquerie* and bad manners from that tiresome Miss Colwyn. What a very unlucky friendship that has been!"

She did not seize the clue which Margaret unconsciously held out to her in the course of the same evening. The girl was sitting in a shady corner of the drawing-room holding a feather fan before her face, when she introduced what had hitherto been, at Helmsley Court, a forbidden topic—the history of the Brands.

"Papa," she said, quietly, "did you never know anything of the Red House people?"

Lady Caroline glanced at her husband. Mr. Adair seemed to find it difficult to reply.

"Yes, of course, I did—in the old days," he answered, less suavely than usual. "When the father was alive, I used to go to the house, but, of course, I was a mere lad then."

"You do not know the sons, then?" said Margaret.

"My dear child, I do not hunt. Mr. Brand's only appearance in society is on the hunting field."

"But there is another brother—one who paints, I believe."

"He teaches drawing in some of the schools of the neighborhood," Lady Caroline interposed, rather dryly. "I suppose you do not want drawing lessons, dear?"

"Oh, no," said Margaret, indifferently. "I only thought it seemed odd that we never met them anywhere."

"Not very suitable acquaintances," murmured Lady Caroline, almost below her breath. Mr. Adair was looking at an illustrated magazine and did not seem to hear, but, after a moment's pause, Margaret said,

"Why, mamma?"

Lady Caroline hesitated for a moment. Mr. Adair shrugged his shoulders. Then she said slowly:

"His father married beneath him, my love. Mrs. Brand is a quite impossible person. If the young men would pension her off and send her away, the County would very likely take them up. But we cannot receive the mother."

"That is another of what Sir Philip Ashley would call class-distinctions, is it not?" said Margaret, placidly. "The sort of thing which made Miss Polehampton so anxious to separate me from poor Janetta."

"Class-distinctions are generally founded on some inherent law of character or education, dear," said Lady Caroline, softly. "They are not so arbitrary as young people imagine. I hope the day will never come when the distinction of class will be done away with. I"—piously—"hope that I may be in my grave before that day comes."

"Oh, of course they are very necessary," said Margaret, comfortably. "And, if old Mrs. Brand were to go away, I suppose her sons would be received everywhere?"

"Oh, I suppose so. The property is fairly good, is it not, Reginald?"

"Not very," said Mr. Adair. "The father squandered a good deal, and I fancy the present owner is economizing for the sake of his boy."

"His boy?" A faint color stole into Margaret's cheeks. "Is he married, papa?"

"Oh, the wife's dead," said Mr. Adair, hastily. It was part of Lady Caroline's system that Margaret should not hear more than was absolutely necessary of what she termed "disagreeable" subjects. Elopements, separation and divorce cases all came under that head. So that when Mr. Adair, who knew more of Mr. Brand's domestic history than he chose to say, added immediately—"At least I heard so: I believe so," he did not think that he was actually departing from fact, but only that he was coloring the matter suitably for Margaret's infant understanding. He really believed that

Mrs. Wyvis Brand was divorced from her husband, and it was "the same thing as being dead, you know," he would have replied if interrogated on the subject.

Margaret did not respond, and Lady Caroline never once suspected that she had any real interest in the matter. But the very fact that Wyvis Brand was represented to her as a widower threw a halo of romance around his head in Margaret's eyes. A man who has "loved and lost" is often invested with a peculiar kind of sanctity in the eyes of a young girl. Wyvis Brand's handsome face and evident admiration of herself did not prepossess Margaret in his favor half so much as the fact that he had known loss and sorrow, and was temporarily ostracized by County society because his mother was "an impossible person." This last deprivation appealed to Margaret's imagination more than the first. It seemed to her a terrible thing to remain unvisited by the "County." What a good thing it would be, she reflected, if Mr. Brand could marry some nice girl, who would persuade him to send his mother back to France, and for whose sake the County magnates would extend to him the right hand of fellowship. To reinstate him in his proper position—the position which Margaret told herself he deserved and would adorn—seemed to her an ambition worthy of any woman in the world. For Margaret's nature was curiously mixed. From her father she had inherited a great love of the beautiful and the romantic—there was a thoroughly unworldly strain in him which had descended to her; but, then, it was counteracted by the influences which she had imbibed from Lady Caroline. Margaret used sometimes to rebel against her mother's maxims of worldly wisdom, but they gradually permeated her mind, and the gold was so mingled with alloy that it was difficult to separate one from the other. She thought herself a very unworldly person. We all have ideals of ourselves; and Margaret's ideal of herself was of a rather saint-like creature, with high aspirations and pure motives. Where her weakness really lay she had not the faintest notion.

It was strange even to herself to note the impression that Wyvis Brand had produced on her. He was certainly of the type that tends to attract impressionable girls, for he was dark and handsome, with the indefinable touch of melancholy in his eyes which lends a subtler interest to the face than mere beauty. The little that she knew of his history had touched her. She constructed a great deal from the few facts or fancies that had been given to her, and the result was sufficiently unlike the real man to be recognizable by nobody but Margaret herself.

It has already been said that the Adair property and that of Wyvis Brand lay side by side. The Adair estate was a large one: that of the Brands' comparatively small; but at one point the two properties were separated for some little distance only by a narrow fishing stream, on one side of which stretched an outlying portion of Mr. Adair's park; while on the other side lay a plantation, approached through the Beaminster woods, and not very far from the Red House itself. It was in this plantation—which was divided from the woods only by a wire fence—that Janetta had found little Julian and had afterwards encountered Wyvis Brand.

In spring the plantation was a particularly pleasant place. It was starred with primroses and anemones in the earlier months of the year, and blue with hyacinths at a later date. At a little distance the flowers looked like a veil of color spread between the trees. The brook between the park and the plantation was a merry little stream, dancing gaily over golden pebbles, and brightly responsive to the sunshine that flickered between the lightly-clothed branches of the trees bordering it on either side. It was famous in the neighborhood for the big blue forget-me-nots that grew there; but it could hardly have been in search of forget-me-nots that Margaret Adair wandered along its side one morning, for they were scarcely in season, and her dreamy eyes did not seem to be looking for them on the bank.

From amongst the trees of the plantation there appeared suddenly a man, who doffed his cap to Miss Adair with a look of mingled pleasure and surprise.

"Oh, good-morning, Mr. Brand."

"Good-morning, Miss Adair." No greeting could have been more conventional. "May I ask if you are looking for forget-me nots? There are some already out lower down the stream. I will show you where they are if you will turn to the left."

"Thank you," said Margaret.

They moved down the slight slope together, but on different sides of the stream. At last they reached the spot where a gleam of blue was visible at the water's edge.

"It is on your side," Margaret said, with a little smile.

"I will get them for you," he replied. And she stood waiting while he gathered the faintly-tinted blossoms.

"And now," she said, as he rose to his feet again, "how will you give them to me? I am afraid I cannot reach across."

"I could come over to you," said Wyvis, his dark eyes resting upon her eagerly. "Will you ask me to come?"

She paused. "Why should I ask you?" she said, with a smile, as if between jest and earnest.

"You are standing on your ground, and I on mine. I have never in my life been asked to cross the boundary."

"I ask you then," said Margaret coloring prettily. She was half-frightened at the significance of her own words, when she had spoken them. But it was too late to retract. It took Wyvis Brand a moment only to leap the brook, and to find himself at her side. Then, taking off his hat and bowing low, he presented her with the flowers that he had gathered. She thanked him with a blush.

"Will you give me one?" he asked, his eyes fixed upon her lovely face. "Just one!—--"

"Why did you not keep one?" she said, bending over her nosegay as if absorbed in its arrangement. "They are so rare that I hardly know how to spare any." Which was a bit of innocent coquetry on Margaret's part.

"Just one," he pleaded. "As a reward. As a memento."

"A memento of what?" she asked, separating one or two flowers from the bunch as she spoke.

"Of this occasion."

"It is such an important occasion, is it not?" she said, with a sweet, mocking little laugh.

"A very important occasion to me. Have I not met you?"

"That is a most charming compliment," said Margaret, who was not unused to hearing words of this kind in London drawing-rooms, and was quite in her native element. "In reward for it I will give you a flower—which of course you will throw away as soon as I am out of sight."

"No, not when you are out of sight: when you are out of mind," he said, significantly.

"The two are synonymous," said Margaret.

"Are they? Not with me. Throw it away? I will show you that it shall not be thrown away."

He produced a little pocket-book and put the forget-me-nots into it, carefully pressing them down against a blank page.

"There," he said, as he made a note in pencil at the bottom of the page, "that will be always with me now."

"The poor forget-me-not!" said Margaret, smiling. "What a sad fate for it! To be torn from its home by the brook, taken away from the sun and the air, to languish out its life in a pocket-book."

"It should feel itself honored," Said Wyvis, "because it is dying for you."

As we have said, this strain of half-jesting compliment was not unfamiliar to Margaret; but she could hardly remain unconscious of the fact that a deeper note had crept into his voice during the last few words, and that his eyes glowed with a fire more ardent than she usually saw. She drew back a little, and looked down: she was not exactly displeased, but she was embarrassed. He noticed and understood the expression of her face; and changed his tone immediately.

"This is a pretty place," he said, indicating the park and the distant woods by a wave of his hand. "I always regret that I have been away from it so long."

"You have lived a great deal in France, I believe?"

"Yes, and in Italy, too. But I tired of foreign lands at last, and persuaded my mother to come home with me. I am glad that I came."

"You like the neighborhood?" said Margaret, in a tone of conventional interest.

Wyvis laughed. "I don't see much of my neighbors," he said, rather drily. "They don't approve of my family. But I like the scenery—and I have a friend or two—Miss Colwyn, for instance, who is a kinswoman of mine, you know."

"Oh, yes!" said Margaret, eagerly. Her momentary distrust of him vanished when she remembered Janetta. Of course, Janetta's cousin *must* be "nice!"—"I am so fond of Janetta: she is so clever and so good."

"It is a great thing for her to have a friend like you," said Wyvis, looking at her wistfully. In very truth, she was a wonderment to him; she seemed so ethereal, so saint-like, so innocent! And Margaret smiled pensively in return: unlimited admiration was quite to her taste.

"Do you often walk here?" he inquired, when at last she said that she must return home.

And she said—"Sometimes."

"Sometimes" is a very indefinite and convenient word. It may mean anything or nothing. In a very short time, it meant that Margaret took a book out with her and walked down to the boundary stream about three times a week, if not oftener, and that Wyvis Brand was always there to bear her company. Before long a few stepping-stones were dropped into the brook, so that she could cross it without wetting her dainty feet. It was shadier and cooler in the closely-grown plantation than in the open park. And meetings in the plantation were less likely to be discovered than in a more public place.

CHAPTER XXIV
LADY ASHLEY'S GARDEN PARTY

It may be wondered that Margaret had so much idle time upon her hands, and was not more constantly supervised in her comings and goings by Lady Caroline. But certain occurrences in the Adair family made it easy just then for her to go her own way. Mr. Adair was obliged to stay in London on business, and while he was away very little was doing at Helmsley Court. Lady Caroline took the opportunity of his absence to "give way" a little: she suffered occasionally from neuralgia, and the doctor recommended her not to rise much before noon. Margaret's comfort and welfare were not neglected. A Miss Stone, a distant relation of Lady Caroline's, came to spend a few weeks at the Court as a companion for Margaret. Miss Stone was not at all a disagreeable person. She could play tennis, dance, and sing; she could accompany Margaret's songs: she could talk or be silent, as seemed good to her; and she was a model of tact and discretion. She was about thirty-five, but looked younger: she dressed well, and had pleasing manners, and without being absolutely handsome was sufficiently good-looking. Miss Alicia Stone was almost penniless, and did not like to work; but she generally found herself provided for as "sheep-dog" or chaperon in some house of her numerous aristocratic friends. She was an amusing talker, and Margaret liked her society well enough, but Miss Stone was too clever not to know when she was not wanted. It soon became evident to the companion that for some reason Margaret liked to walk in the park alone in a morning; and what Margaret liked was law. Alicia knew how to efface herself on such occasions, so that when Lady Caroline asked at luncheon what the two had been doing all the morning, it was easy and natural for Miss Stone to reply, "Oh, we have been out in the park," although this meant only that she had been sitting at the conservatory door with a novel, while Margaret had been wandering half a mile away. Lady Caroline used to smile, and was satisfied.

And Margaret's conscience was very little troubled. She had never been told, she sometimes said to herself, that she was not to speak to Mr. Brand. And she was possessed with the fervent desire to save his soul (and social reputation), which sometimes leads young women into follies which they afterwards regret. He told her vaguely that he had had a miserable, unsatisfactory sort of life, and that he wished to amend. He did not add that his first impulses towards amendment had come from Janetta Colwyn. Margaret thought that she was responsible for them, one and all. And she felt it incumbent upon her to foster their growth, even at the price of a small concealment—although it would, as she very well knew, be a great one in her parents' eyes.

As the days went on towards summer, it seemed to Janetta as though some interest, some brightness perhaps, had died out of her life. Her friends—her two chief friends, to whom her vow of friendship and service had been sworn—were, in some inexplicable manner, alienated from her. Margaret came regularly for her singing-lesson, but never lingered to talk as she had done at first. She seemed pensive, languid, preoccupied. Wyvis Brand had left off calling for little Julian, except on rare occasions. Perhaps his frequent loitering in the plantation left him but scant time for his daily work; he always pleaded business when his boy reproached him for his remissness, or when Janetta questioned him somewhat mournfully with her earnest eyes. Certainly he too seemed preoccupied, and when he was beguiled into the Colwyns' little drawing-room he would sit almost silent in Janetta's company, never once asking her counsel or opinion as he had done in earlier days. It was possible that in her presence he felt a sort of compunction, a sort of conscience-stricken shame. And his silence and apparent estrangement lay upon Janetta's heart like lead.

Poor Janetta was going through a time of depression and disappointment. Mrs. Colwyn had had two or three terrible relapses, and her condition could no longer be kept quite a secret from her friends. Janetta had been obliged to call in the aid of the doctor who had been her father's best friend, and he recommended various changes of diet and habits which gave the girl far more trouble than he knew. Where poverty is present in a home, it is sometimes hard to do the best either for the sinning or the suffering; and so Mrs. Colwyn's weakness was one of the heaviest burdens that Janetta had to bear. The only gleams of brightness in her lot lay in the love and gentleness of the children that she taught, and in her satisfaction with Nora's engagement to Cuthbert. In almost all other respects she began to feel aware that she was heavily handicapped.

It was nearly the end of June before she received the long-expected invitation from Lady Ashley. But it was not to an evening party. It was a sort of combination entertainment—a garden-party for the young, and music for those elder persons who did not care to watch games at tennis all the afternoon. And Janetta was asked to sing.

The day of the party was cloudlessly fine, but not too warm, as a pleasant little summer breeze was blowing. Janetta donned a thin black dress of some gauzy material, and thought that she looked very careworn and dowdy in her little bedroom looking-glass. But when she reached Lady Ashley's house, excitement had brought a vivid color to her face; and when her hostess, after an appreciative glance at her dress, quietly pinned a cluster of scarlet geranium blooms at her neck, the little songstress presented an undeniably distinguished appearance. If she was not exactly pretty, she was more than pretty—she was striking and original.

Margaret Adair looked up and smiled at her from a corner, when Janetta first came forward to sing. She was one of the very few girls who were present, for most of the young people were in the garden; but she had insisted on coming in to hear Janetta's song. She did not care about playing tennis; it made her hot, and ruffled her pretty Paris gown, which was not suitable for violent exertion of any kind; she left violent exertion to Alicia Stone, who was always ready to join in other people's amusements. Lady Caroline was not present; her neuralgia was troublesome, and she had every confidence in Alicia's chaperonage and Margaret's discretion. Poor Lady Caroline was sometimes terribly mistaken in her reading of character.

To the surprise of a good many people, the Brands were there. Not Mrs. Brand—only the two young men; but the fact was a good deal commented upon, as hitherto "the County" had taken very little notice of the owner of the Red House. It was perhaps this fact that had impelled Sir Philip to show the Brands some courtesy. He declared that he knew nothing bad of these men, and that they ought not to be blamed for their father's sins. Personally he liked them both, and he had no difficulty in persuading his mother to call on Mrs. Brand, and then to send invitations for the garden party. But Mrs. Brand, as usual, declined to go out, and was represented only by her sons.

What Sir Philip had not calculated on was the air of possession and previous acquaintance with which Wyvis Brand greeted Miss Adair. He had hardly expected that Margaret would come; and, indeed, Margaret had been loath to accept Lady Ashley's invitation, especially without the escort of her mother. On the other hand, Lady Caroline was very anxious that the world should not know the extent of the breach between the two families; and she argued that it would be very marked if Margaret stayed away from a large garden party to which "everybody" went, and where it would be very easy to do nothing more than exchange a mere passing salutation with Sir Philip. So she had rather insisted on Margaret's going; and the girl had had her own reasons for not protesting too much. She knew that Wyvis

Brand would be there; and she had a fancy for seeing him amongst other men, and observing how he bore himself in other people's society.

She was perfectly satisfied with the result. His appearance was faultless—far better than that of Sir Philip, who sometimes wore a coat until it was shiny at the shoulders, and was not very particular about his boots. Upright, handsome, well-dressed, with the air of distinction which Margaret much preferred to beauty in a man, he was a distinctly noticeable figure, and Margaret innocently thought that there was no reason why she should not show, in a well-bred and maidenly way, of course, her liking for him.

She had never had much resistant power, this "rare, pale Margaret" of Sir Philip's dreams, and it seemed quite natural to her that Wyvis should hover at her side and attend to all her wants that afternoon. She did not notice that he was keeping off other men by his air of proprietorship, and that women, old and young, were eyeing her with surprise and disapprobation as she walked up and down the lawn with him and allowed him to provide her with tea or strawberries and cream. She was under a charm, and could not bear the idea of sending him away. While Wyvis—for his excuse let it be said that his air of proprietorship was unconscious, and came simply out of his intense admiration for the girl and his headlong absorption in the interest of the moment. He did not at all know how intently and exclusively he looked at her; how reverential and yet masterful was his attitude; and the sweet consciousness that sat on her down-dropped eyelids and tenderly flushed cheeks acted as no warning to him, but only as an incentive to persevere.

The situation became patent to Janetta, when she stood up to sing. Margaret looked, nodded, and smiled at her with exquisite shy friendliness. Janetta returned the greeting; and then—as people noticed—suddenly flushed scarlet and as suddenly turned pale. Many persons set this change of color down to nervousness; but Sir Philip Ashley followed the direction of her eyes and knew what she had seen.

Miss Adair was sitting in a corner of the room, where perhaps she hoped to be unremarked; but her fair beauty and her white dress made it difficult for her to remain obscure. Wyvis Brand stood beside her, leaning against the wall, with arms folded across his breast. He was more in shadow than was she, for he was touched by the folds of a heavy velvet curtain; but his attitude was significant. He was not looking at the singer, or at the room; his whole attention was visibly concentrated upon Margaret. He was looking at her, some one remarked quite audibly, as if he never meant to look away again. The close, keen absorption of that gaze was unusual enough to shock conventional observers. There would have been nothing insolent or overbold about it were he her husband or her lover; but from a man who—as far as "the County" knew—was a comparative stranger in the land, and almost an outsider, it was positively shocking. And yet Miss Adair looked as if she were only pleasantly conscious of this rude man's stare.

Fortunately for Margaret's reputation, it was currently believed that Wyvis Brand's wife was dead. Those who had some notion that she was living thought that he had divorced her. The general impression was that he was at any rate free to marry; and that he was laying siege to the heart of the prettiest girl in the County now seemed an indisputable fact. Perhaps Janetta only, of all the persons assembled together in the room, knew the facts of Wyvis Brand's unhappy marriage. And to Janetta, as well as to other people, it became plain that afternoon that he had completely lost his heart—perhaps his head as well—to Margaret Adair.

The chatter of the crowd would have revealed as much to Janetta, even if her own observation had not told her a good deal. "How that man does stare at that girl! Is he engaged to her?" "Young Brand's utterly gone on Miss Adair; that's evident." "Is Lady Caroline not here? Do you think that she *knows*?" "Margaret Adair is certainly very pretty, but I should not like one of *my* girls to let herself be made so conspicuous!" Such were some of the remarks that fell on Janetta's ear, and made her face burn with shame and indignation. Not that she exactly believed in the reality even of the things that she had seen. That Wyvis should admire Margaret was so natural! That Margaret should accept the offered admiration in her usual serene manner was equally to be expected. But that either of them should be unwise enough to give rise to idle gossip, about so natural a state of mind was what Janetta could not understand. It was not Margaret's fault; she was very sure of that. It must be Wyvis Brand's. He was her cousin, and she might surely—perhaps—ask him what he meant by putting Margaret in such a false position! Oh, but she could not presume to do that. What would he think of her? And yet—and yet—the look with which he had regarded Margaret seemed to be stamped indelibly upon Janetta's faithful, aching heart.

CHAPTER XXV
SIR PHILIP'S DECISION

"Philip," said Lady Ashley that evening, with some hesitation in her speech; "Philip—did you—did you notice Mr. Brand—much—to-day?"

The guests had all gone; dinner was over; mother and son were sitting in wicker chairs on the terrace, resting after the fatigues of the day. Sir Philip was smoking a very mild cigarette: he was not very fond of tobacco, for, as the Adairs sometimes expressed it, he "had no small vices." Lady Ashley was wrapped in a white shawl, and her delicate, blue-veined hands were crossed upon her lap in unaccustomed idleness.

"I did notice him," said her son, quietly. "He seemed to be paying a great deal of attention to Miss Adair."

"Oh, Philip, dear, it distressed me so much!"

"Why should it distress you, mother?—it is nothing to us."

"Well, if you feel in that way about it—still, I am grieved for the Adairs' sake. After all, they are old friends of ours. And I had hoped——"

"Our hopes are not often realized, are they?" said Sir Philip, in the gentle, persuasive tones that his mother thought so winning. "Perhaps it is best. At any rate, it is best to forget the hopes that never *can* be realized."

"Do you think it is really so, Philip? Everyone was talking about his manner this afternoon."

"She was giving him every encouragement," said her son, looking away.

"Such an undesirable match! Poor Lady Caroline!"

"We do not know how things are being arranged, mother. Possibly Lady Caroline and Mr. Adair are favoring an engagement. Miss Adair is hardly likely to act against their will."

"No, she has scarcely resolution enough for that. Then you don't think that they met for the first time this afternoon?"

"Gracious heavens, no!" said Sir Philip, roused a little out of his apparent indifference. "They met quite as old acquaintants—old friends. I suppose the Adairs have renewed the friendship. The properties lie side by side. That may be a reason."

"I am very sorry we asked him here," said Lady Ashley, almost viciously. "I had no idea that he was paying attention to *her*. I hope there is nothing wrong about it—such a very undesirable match!"

"I don't really know why," said her son, with a forced smile. "Wyvis Brand is a fine, handsome fellow, and the property, though small, is a nice one. Miss Adair might do worse."

"I believe her mother thinks that she might marry a duke."

"And so she might. She is a great beauty, and an heiress." And there was a ring of bitterness in his tone which pained his mother's heart.

"Ah, Philip," she said—not very, wisely—"you need not regret her. 'A fair woman without discretion,' she would not be the wife for you."

"I beg that you will not say that again, mother." He did not turn his face towards her, and his voice was studiously gentle, but it was decided too. "She is, as you say, 'a fair woman,' but she has not shown herself as yet 'without discretion,' and it is hardly kind to condemn her before she has done any wrong."

"I do not think that she behaved well to you, Philip. But I beg your pardon, my son: we will not discuss the matter. It seems hard to me, of course, that you should have suffered for any woman's sake."

"Ah, mother, every one does not see me with your kind eyes," he said, bringing his face round with a smile, and laying his right hand over one of hers. But the smile thinly disguised the pain that lingered like a shadow in his eyes. "Let us hope, at any rate, that Margaret may be happy."

Lady Ashley sighed and pressed his hand. "If you could but meet some one else whom you cared for as much, Philip!" And then she paused, for he had—involuntarily as it seemed—shaken his head, and she did not like to proceed further.

A pause of some minutes followed; and then she determined to change the subject.

"The music went very well this afternoon, I think," she said. "Miss Colwyn was in very good voice. Do you not like her singing?"

"Yes, very much."

"The Watertons were asking me about her. And the Bevans. I fancy she will get several engagements. Poor girl, I hope she will."

Sir Philip threw away the end of his cigarette, and got up rather abruptly, Lady Ashley thought. Without a word he began to pace up and down the terrace, and finally, turning his back on her, he stared at the garden and the distant view, now faintly illumined by a rising moon, as if he had forgotten his mother's very existence. Lady Ashley was surprised. He usually treated her with such marked distinction that to appear for a moment unconscious of her presence was almost a slight. She was too dignified, however, to try to recall his attention, and she waited quietly until her son turned round again and suddenly faced her with an air of calm determination.

"Mother," he said, "I have something important to say."

"Well, Philip?"

"You have often said that you wanted me to marry."

"Yes, dearest, I do wish it."

"I also see the expediency of marriage. The woman whom I loved, who seemed to us as suitable as she is lovely, will not marry me. What shall I look for in my second choice? Character rather than fortune, health rather than beauty. This seems to me the wiser way."

"And love rather than expediency," said his mother quickly.

"Ah!" he drew a long breath. "But we can't always have love. The other requisites are perhaps more easily found."

"Have you found them, Philip?" The mother's voice quivered as she asked the question. He did not answer it immediately—he stood looking at the ground for some little time.

"My mind is made up," he said at last, slowly and quietly; "I know what I want, and I think that I have found it. Mother, I am going to ask Miss Colwyn to be my wife."

If a thunderbolt had fallen at her feet, Lady Ashley could not have been more amazed. She sat silent, rigid, incapable of a reply.

"I have seen something of her, and I have heard more," her son went on, soberly. "She is of sterling worth. She has intellect, character, affection: what can we want more? She is attractive, if not exactly beautiful, and she is good—thoroughly good and true."

"But her connections, Philip—her relations," gasped Lady Ashley.

"It will be easy enough to do something for them. Of course they will have to be provided for—away from Beaminster, if possible. She is an orphan, remember: these are only her half sisters and brothers."

"There is the dreadful stepmother!"

"I think we can manage her. These points do not concern the main issue, mother. Will you receive her as your daughter if I bring Janetta Colwyn here as my wife?"

Lady Ashley had put her handkerchief to her eyes. "I will do anything to please you, Philip," she said, almost inaudibly; "but I cannot pretend that this is anything but a disappointment."

"I have thought the matter well over. I am convinced that she will make a good wife," said the young man; and from his voice and manner Lady Ashley felt that his resolution was invulnerable. "There is absolutely *no* objection except the one concerning her relations—and that may be got over. Mother, you wish for my happiness: tell me that you will not disapprove."

Lady Ashley got up from her basket chair, and laid her arms round Philip's neck.

"My dear son," she said, "I will do my best. I wish for nothing but your happiness, and I should never think of trying to thwart your intentions. But you must give me a little time in which to accustom myself to this new idea."

And then she wept a little, and kissed and blessed him, and they parted on the most cordial of terms. Nevertheless, neither of them was very happy. Lady Ashley was, as she had said, disappointed in the choice that he had made; and Sir Philip, in spite of his brave words, was very sore at heart.

Janetta, all unconscious of the honor preparing for her, was meanwhile passing some miserable hours. She could not sleep that night—she knew not why. It was the excitement of the party, she supposed. But something beside excitement was stirring in her heart. She tried to give it a name, but she would not look the thing fairly in the face, and, therefore, she was not very successful in her nomenclature. She called it friendly interest in others, a desire for their happiness, a desire also for their good. What made the burning pain and unrest of these desires? Why should they cause her such suffering? She did not know—or, more correctly, she refused to know.

She rose in the morning feeling haggard and unrefreshed. The day was a very hot one; the breeze had died away, and there was not a cloud in the deep blue sky. Julian Brand came in the dog-cart with the groom. He had not seen his father that morning, he said, and he thought that he had gone away, but he did not know. Gone away? Janetta sat down to her work with a heavy heart. It seemed to her that she must speak either to him or to Margaret. He was compromising her friend, and for Margaret's sake she must not hold her peace. Well, it was the day for Miss Adair's singing lesson. When she came that afternoon, Janetta made up her mind that she would say a needful word.

But Margaret did not come. She sent a note, asking to be excused. She had a headache, and could not sing that afternoon.

"She is afraid to come!" said Janetta, passionately, and for almost the first time she felt a thrill of anger against her friend.

Another visitor came, if Margaret did not. About four o'clock, just as Julian was beginning to wonder when he would be fetched away, a thundering peal at the door knocker announced the appearance of Wyvis Brand. Janetta was in the drawing-room putting away some music when he came in. She saw that he glanced eagerly round the room, as if expecting to see someone else—perhaps Margaret Adair—and her heart hardened to him a little as she gave him her hand. Had he come at that hour because Margaret generally took her lesson then?

"How cold you are!" cried Wyvis, holding the little hand for the moment in his own. "On this hot day! How *can* you manage to keep so cool??"

If his heart had been throbbing and his head burning as Janetta's were just then, he might have known how to answer the question.

"You have come for Julian, I suppose?" she said, a little coldly.

"Yes—in a minute or two. Won't you let me rest for a few minutes after my walk in the broiling sun?"

"Oh, certainly; you shall have some tea, if you like. I am at liberty this afternoon," said Janetta, with a little malice, "as my pupil has just sent me word that she has a headache, and cannot come."

"Who is your pupil this afternoon?" said Wyvis, stroking his black moustache.

"Miss Adair."

He gave her a quick, keen glance, then turned away. She read vexation in his eyes.

"Don't let me trouble you," he said, in a different tone, as she moved towards the door; "I really ought not to stay—I have an engagement or two to fulfill. No tea, thanks. Is Julian ready?"

"In a minute or two I will call him. I want to ask you a question first—if you will let me?"

A True Friend | 189

"All right; go on. That's the way people begin disagreeable subjects, do you know?"

"I don't know whether you will consider this a disagreeable question. I suppose you will," said Janetta, with an effort. "I promised you once to say nothing to my friends about your affairs—about Julian's mother, and I have kept my word. But I must ask you now—does Miss Adair know that you are married?"

There was a moment's pause. They stood opposite one another, and, lifting her eyes to his face, she saw that he was frowning heavily and gnawing his moustache.

"What does that matter to *you*?" he said, angrily, at last.

She shrank a little, but answered steadily—

"Margaret is my friend."

"Well, what then?"

The color rose to Janetta's face. "I don't believe you knew what you were doing yesterday," she said; "but I knew—I heard people talking, and I knew what people thought. They said that you were paying attention to Miss Adair. They supposed you were going to marry her soon. None of them seemed to know that—that—your wife was still alive. And of course I could not tell them."

"Of course not," he assented, with curious eagerness; "I knew you would keep your word."

"You made Margaret conspicuous," Janetta continued, with some warmth. "You placed her in a very false position. If *she* thinks, as other people thought, that you want to marry her, she ought to be told the truth at once. You must tell her—yourself—that you were only amusing yourself—only playing with her, as no man has a right to play with a girl," said Janetta, with such vehemence that the tears rose to her great dark eyes and the scarlet color to her cheeks—"that you were flirting, in fact, and that Julian's mother—*your wife*, Cousin Wyvis—is still alive."

CHAPTER XXVI
"FREE!"

"And what if I refuse to tell her this?" said Wyvis Brand.

"Then I shall tell her myself."

"And break your word to me?"

"And break my word."

He stood looking at her for a minute in silence, and then an ironical smile curled his lip as he turned aside.

"Women are all alike," he said. "They cannot possibly hold their tongues. I thought *you* were superior to most of your sex. I remember that your father once spoke of you to me as 'his faithful Janet.' Is this your faithfulness?"

"Yes, it is, it is," she cried; and then, sitting down, she suddenly burst into tears. She was unnerved and agitated, and so she wept, as girls will weep—for nothing at all sometimes, and sometimes in the very crisis of their fate.

Wyvis looked on, uncomprehending, a little touched, though rather against his will, by Janetta's tears. He knew that she did not often cry. He waited for the paroxysm to pass—waited grimly, but with "compunctuous visitings." And presently he was rewarded for his patience. She dried her eyes, lifted up her head, and spoke.

"I don't know why I should make such a fool of myself," she said. "I suppose it was because you mentioned my father. Yes, he used to call me his faithful Janet very often. I have always tried—to—to *deserve* that name."

"Forgive me, Janetta," said her cousin, more moved than he liked to appear. "I did not want to hurt you; but, indeed, my dear girl, you must let me manage my affairs for myself. You are not responsible for Margaret Adair as you were for Nora; and you can't, you know, bring me to book as you did my brother, Cuthbert."

"You mean that I interfere too much in other people's business?" said poor Janetta, with quivering lips.

"I did not say so. I only say, '*Don't* interfere.'"

"It is very hard to do right," said Janetta, looking at him with wistful eyes. "One's duty seems so divided. Margaret is not my sister—that is true, but she is my friend; and I always believed that one had responsibilities and duties towards friends as well as towards relations."

"Possibly"—in a very dry tone. "But you need not meddle with what is no concern of yours."

"It is my concern, if you—my cousin—are not acting rightly to my friend."

"I say it is no concern of yours at all."

They had come to a deadlock. He faced her, with the dark, haughty, imperious look which she knew so well upon his fine features; she stood silent, angry too, and almost as imperious. But, womanlike, she yielded first.

"You asked me once to be your friend, Cousin Wyvis. I want to be yours and Margaret's too. Won't you let me see what you mean?"

Wyvis Brand's brow relaxed a little.

"I don't understand your views of friendship: it seems to mean a right to intermeddle with all the affairs of your acquaintances," he said, cuttingly; "but since you are so good as to ask my intentions——"

"If you talk like that, I'll never speak to you again!" cried Janetta, who was not remarkable for her meekness.

Wyvis actually smiled.

"Come," he said, "be friends, Janetta. I assure you I don't mean any harm. You must not be straight-laced. Your pretty friend is no doubt well able to take care of herself."

But he looked down as he said this and knitted his brows.

"She has never had occasion to do it," said Janetta, epigrammatically.

"Then don't you think it is time she learns?"

"You have no right to be her teacher."

"Right! right!" cried Wyvis, impatiently "I am tired of this cuckoo-cry about my rights! I have the right to do what I choose, to get what pleasure out of life I can, to do my best for myself. It is everybody's right, and he is only a hypocrite who denies it."

"There is one limitation," said Janetta. "Get what you can for yourself, if you like—it seems to me a somewhat selfish view—as long as you don't injure anybody else."

"Whom do I injure?" he asked, looking at her defiantly in the face.

"Margaret."

He dropped his eyes, and the defiance went suddenly out of his look and voice.

"Injure her?" he said, in a very low tone. "Surely, you know, I wouldn't do *that*—to save my life."

Janetta looked at him mutely. The words were a revelation. There was a pause, during which she heard, as in a dream, the sound of children's voices and children's feet along the passages of the house. Julian and Tiny were running riot; but she felt, for the time being, as if she had nothing to do with them: their interests did not touch her: she dwelt in a world apart. Hitherto Wyvis had stood, hat in hand, as if he were ready to go at a moment's notice; but now he changed his attitude. He seated himself determinedly, put down his hat, and looked back at her.

"Well," he said, "I see that I must explain myself if I mean to make my peace with you, Janetta. I am, perhaps, not so bad as you think me. I have not mentioned to Miss Adair that Julian's mother is alive, because I consider myself a free man. Julian's mother, once my wife, has divorced me, and is, I believe, on the point of marrying again. Surely in that case I am free to marry too."

"Divorced you?" Janetta repeated, with dilating eyes.

"Yes, divorced me. She has gone out to America and managed it there. It is easy enough in some of the States to get divorced from an absent wife or husband, as no doubt you know. Incompatibility of temper was the alleged reason. I believe she is going to marry a Chicago man—something in pork."

"And you are legally free?"

"She says so. I fancy there is a legal hitch somewhere but I have not yet consulted my lawyers. We were married by the Catholic rite in France, and the Catholic Church will probably consider us married still. But Margaret is not a Catholic—nor am I."

"And you think," said Janetta, very slowly, "of marrying Margaret?"

He looked up at her and laughed, a little uneasily.

"You think she won't have me?"

"I don't know. I think you don't know her yet, Wyvis."

"I dare say not," said her cousin. Then he broke out in quite a different tone: "No wonder I don't; she's a perpetual revelation to me. I never saw anything like her—so pure, so spotless, so exquisite. It's like looking at a work of art—a bit of delicate china, or a picture by Francia or Guido. Something holy and serene about her—something that sets her apart from the ordinary world. I can't define it: but it's there. I feel myself made of a coarse, common clay in her presence: I want to go down on my knees and serve her like a queen. That's how I feel about Margaret."

"Ah!" said Janetta, "my princess of dreams. That is what I used to call her. That is what I—used to feel."

"Don't you feel it now?" said Wyvis, sitting up and staring at her.

Janetta hesitated. "Margaret is my dear friend, and I love her. But I am older—perhaps I can't feel exactly in that way about her now."

"You talk as if you were a sexagenarian," said Wyvis, exploding into genial laughter. He looked suddenly brighter and younger, as if his outburst of emotion had wonderfully relieved him. "I am much older than you, and yet I see her in the same light. What else is there to say about her? She is perfect—there is not much to discuss in perfection."

"She is most lovely—most sweet," said Janetta, warmly. "And yet—the very things you admire may stand in your way, Wyvis. She is very innocent of the world. And if you have won her—her—affection before you have told her your history——"

"You think this wretched first marriage of mine will stand in the way?"

"I do. With Margaret and with her parents."

Wyvis frowned again. "I had better make sure of her—marry her at once, and tell her afterwards," he said. But perhaps he said it only to see what Janetta would reply.

"You would not do that, Wyvis?"

"I don't know."

"But you want to be worthy of her?"

"I shall never be that so it's no good trying."

"She would never forgive you if you married her without telling her the truth."

Wyvis laughed scornfully. "You know nothing about it. A woman will forgive anything to the man she loves."

"Not a meanness!" said the girl, sharply.

"Yes, meanness, deceit, lies, anything—so long as it was done for her sake."

"I don't believe that would be the case with Margaret. Once disgust her, and you lose her love."

"Then she can't have much to give," retorted Wyvis.

Janetta was silent. In her secret heart she did not think that Margaret *could* love very deeply—that, indeed, she had not much to give.

"Well, what's the upshot?" said her cousin, at last, in a dogged tone. "Are you satisfied at last?"

"I shall be better satisfied when you make things plain to the Adairs. You have no right to win Margaret's heart in this secret way. You blamed Cuthbert for making love to Nora. It is far worse for you to do it to Margaret Adair."

"I am so much beneath her, am I not?" said Wyvis, with a sneer. And then he once more spoke eagerly. "I *am* beneath her: I am as the dust under her feet. Don't you think I know that? I'll tell you what, Janetta, when I first saw her and spoke to her—here, in this room, if you remember—I thought that she was like a being from another world. I had never seen anyone like her. She is the fairest, sweetest of women, and I would not harm her for the world."

"I don't know whether I ought even to listen to you," said Janetta, in a troubled voice and with averted head. "You know, many people would say that you were in the wrong altogether—that you were not free——"

"Then they would say a lie! I am legally free, I believe, and morally free, I am certain. I thank God for it. I have suffered enough."

He looked so stern, so uncompromising, that Janetta hastened to take refuge in concrete facts.

"But you will tell Margaret everything?"

"In my own good time."

"Do promise me that you will not marry her without letting her know—if ever it comes, to a talk of your marriage."

"*If ever?* It will come very soon, I hope. But I'll promise nothing. And you must not make mischief."

"I am like you—I will promise nothing."

"I shall never forgive you, if you step between Margaret and me," said Wyvis.

"I shall never step between you, I hope," said Janetta, in a dispirited tone. "But it is better for me to promise nothing more."

Wyvis shrugged his shoulders, as if he thought it useless to argue with her. She was sorry for the apparently unfriendly terms on which they seemed likely to part; and it was a relief to her when, as they were saying good-bye, he looked into her face rather wistfully and said, "Wish me success, Janetta, after all."

"I wish you every happiness," she said. But whether that meant success or not it would have been hard to say.

She saw him take his departure, with little Julian clinging to his hand, and then she set about her household duties in her usual self-contained and steadfast way. But her heart ached sadly—she did not quite know why— and when she went to bed that night she lay awake for many weary hours, weeping silently, but passionately, over the sorrow that, she foresaw for her dearest friends, and, perhaps, also for herself.

CHAPTER XXVII
A BIG BRIBE

It seemed to Janetta as if she had almost expected to see Lady Caroline Adair drive up to her door about four o'clock next day, in the very victoria wherein the girl had once sat side by side with Margaret's mother, and from which she had first set eyes on Wyvis Brand. She had expected it, and yet her heart beat faster, and her color went and came, as she disposed of her pupils in the little dining-room, and met her visitor just as she crossed the hall.

"Can I speak to you for five minutes, Miss Colwyn?" said Lady Caroline, in so suave a voice that for a moment Janetta felt reassured. Only for a moment, however. When she had shut the drawing-room door, she saw that her visitor's face was for once both cold and hard. Janetta offered a chair, and Lady Caroline took it, but without a word of thanks. She had evidently put on the "fine lady" manner, which Janetta detested from her heart.

"I come to speak on a very painful subject," said Lady Caroline. Her voice was pitched a little higher than usual, but she gave no other sign of agitation. "You were at Lady Ashley's garden party the day before yesterday I believe?"

Janetta bowed assent.

"May I ask if you observed anything remarkable in my daughter's behavior? You are supposed to be Margaret's friend: you must have noticed what she was doing all the afternoon."

"I do not think that Margaret *could* behave unsuitably," said Janetta, suddenly flushing up.

"I am obliged to you for your good opinion of my daughter. But that is not the point. Did you notice whether she was talking or walking a great deal with one person, or— —"

"Excuse me, Lady Caroline," said Janetta, "but I did not spend the afternoon in watching Margaret, and I am quite unable to give you any information on the subject."

"I really do not see the use of beating about the bush," said Lady Caroline, blandly. "You must know perfectly well to what I refer. Mr. Wyvis Brand is a connection of yours, I believe. I hear on all sides that he and my daughter were inseparable all the afternoon. Greatly to my astonishment, I confess."

"Mr. Brand is a second cousin of mine, and his brother is engaged to my half-sister," said Janetta; "but I have nothing to do with his acquaintance with Margaret."

"Indeed!" exclaimed Lady Caroline. She put up her eye-glass, and carefully inspected Janetta from head to foot. "Nothing to do with their acquaintance, you say! May I ask, then, *where* my daughter met Mr. Brand? Not in *my* house, I think."

Janetta gave a slight start. She had for the moment utterly forgotten that it was in Gwynne Street that Wyvis Brand and Margaret had first met.

"I beg your pardon: I forgot," she said. "Of course—Margaret no doubt told you—she came here one day for her singing-lesson, and Mr. Brand called for his little boy. It was the first time they had seen each other."

"And how often have they met here since, may I ask?"

"Never again, Lady Caroline."

"I was of course to blame in letting my daughter go out without a chaperon," said Lady Caroline, disagreeably. "I never thought of danger in *this* quarter, certainly. I can quite appreciate your motive, Miss Colwyn. No doubt it would be very pleasant for *you* if Margaret were to marry your cousin; but we have prejudices that must be consulted."

"I hope you did not come here meaning to insult me," said Janetta, starting to her feet; "but I think you cannot know what you are saying, Lady Caroline. *I* want my cousin to marry your daughter? I never thought of such a thing—until yesterday!"

"And what made you think of it yesterday, pray? Please let us have no heroics, no hysterics: these exhibitions of temper are so unseemly. What made you think so yesterday?"

"Mr. Brand came here," said Janetta, suddenly growing very white, "and told me that he cared for Margaret. I do not know how they had met. He did not tell me. He—he—cares very much for her."

"Cares for her! What next? He came here—when? At Margaret's lesson-time, I suppose?"

She saw from Janetta's face that her guess was correct.

"I need hardly say that Margaret will not come here again," said Lady Caroline, rising and drawing her laces closely around her. "There is the amount due to you, Miss Colwyn. I calculated it before I came out, and I think you will find it all right. There is one more question I must really ask before I go: there seems some uncertainty concerning the fate of Mr. Brand's first wife; perhaps you can tell me whether she is alive or dead?"

Poor Janetta scarcely knew what to say. But she told herself that truth was always best.

"I believe he—he—is divorced from her," she stammered, knowing full well how very condemnatory her words must sound in Lady Caroline's ear. They certainly produced a considerable effect.

"*Divorced?* And you introduced him to Margaret? Of course I know that a *divorcé* is often received in society, and so on, but I always set my face against the prevalent lax views of marriage, and I hoped that I had brought up my daughter to do the same. I suppose"—satirically—"you did not think it worth while to tell Margaret this little fact?"

"I did not know it then," Janetta forced herself to say.

"Indeed?" Lady Caroline's "indeed" was very crushing. "Well, either your information or your discretion must have been very much at fault. I must say, Miss Polehampton *now* strikes me as a woman of great discrimination of character. I will say good-morning, Miss Colwyn, and I think the acquaintance between my daughter and yourself had better be discontinued. It has certainly been, from beginning to end, an unsuitable and disastrous friendship."

"Before you go, Lady Caroline, will you kindly take the envelope away that you have left upon the table?" said Janetta, as haughtily as Lady Caroline herself could have spoken. "I certainly shall not take money from you if you believe such evil things of me. I have known nothing of the acquaintance between my cousin and Miss Adair; but after what you have said I will not accept anything at your hands."

"Then I am afraid it will have to remain on the table," said Lady Caroline, as she swept out of the room, "for I cannot take it back again."

Janetta caught up the envelope. One glance showed her that it contained a cheque. She tore it across and across, and was in time to place the fragments on the seat beside Lady Caroline, just before the carriage was driven away. She went back into the house with raised head and flaming cheeks, too angry and annoyed to settle down to work, too much hurt to be anything but restless and preoccupied. The reaction did not set in for some hours; but by six o'clock, when the children were all out of doors and her stepmother had gone to visit a friend, and Janetta had the house to herself, she lay down on a couch in the drawing-room with a feeling of intense exhaustion and fatigue. She was too tired almost to cry, but a tear welled up now and then, and was allowed to trickle quietly down her pale cheek. She was utterly wretched and depressed: the world seemed a dark place to her, especially when she considered that she had already lost one friend whom she had so long and so tenderly loved, and that she was not unlikely to lose another. For Wyvis might blame her—*would* blame her, probably—for what she had said to Lady Caroline.

A knock at the front door aroused her. It was a knock that she did not know; and she wondered at first whether one of the Adairs or one of the Brands were coming to visit her. She sat up and hastily rearranged her hair and dried her eyes. The charity orphan was within hearing and had gone to the door: it was she who presently flung open the door and announced, in awe-stricken tones—

"Sir Philip Hashley."

Janetta rose in some consternation. What did this visit portend? Had *he* also come to reproach her for her conduct to Margaret and Wyvis? For she surmised—chiefly from the way in which she had seen him follow Margaret with his eyes at the garden-party—that his old love was not dead.

He greeted her with his usual gentleness of manner, and sat down—not immediately facing her, as she was glad to think, scarcely realizing that he had at once seen the trouble in her face, and did not wish to embarrass her by a straightforward gaze. He gave her a little time in which to recover herself, too; he spoke of indifferent subjects in an indifferent tone, so that when five minutes had elapsed Janetta was quite herself again, and had begun to speculate upon her chance of an engagement to sing at another musical party.

"I hope Lady Ashley is well," she said, when at last a short pause came.

"Quite well, I thank you, and hoping to see you soon."

"Oh, I am so grateful to you for saying that," said Janetta, impulsively. "I felt that I did not know whether she was satisfied with my singing or not. You know I am a beginner."

"I am sure I may say that she was perfectly satisfied," said Sir Philip, courteously. "But it was not in allusion to your singing that she spoke of wishing to see you again."

"Lady Ashley is very kind," said Janetta, feeling rather surprised.

"She would like to see more of you," Sir Philip went on in a somewhat blundering fashion. "She is very much alone: it would be a great comfort to her to have some one about her—some one whom she liked—some one who would be like a daughter to her——"

A conviction as to the cause of his visit flashed across Janetta's mind. He was going to ask her to become Lady Ashley's companion! With her usual quickness she forgot to wait for the proposition, and answered it before it was made.

"I wish I could be of some use to Lady Ashley," she said, with the warm directness that Sir Philip had always liked. "I have never seen any one like her—I admire her so much! You will forgive me for saying so, I hope? But I could not be spared from home to do anything for her regularly. If she wants a girl who can read aloud and play nicely, I think I know of one, but perhaps I had better ask Lady Ashley more particularly about the qualifications required?"

"I did not say anything about a companion, did I?" said Sir Philip, with a queer little smile. "Not in your sense of the word, at any rate."

"Oh, I beg your pardon," said Janetta, suddenly flushing scarlet: "I thought—I understood——"

"You could not possibly know what I meant: I was not at all clear," said Sir Philip, decidedly. "I had something else in my mind."

She looked at him inquiringly. He rose from his chair and moved about the room a little, with an appearance of agitation which excited her deepest wonderment. He averted his eyes from her, and there was something like a flush on his naturally pale cheek. He seemed really nervous.

"Is there anything that I can do for Lady Ashley?" said Janetta, at last, when the silence had lasted as long as she thought desirable.

"There is something you can do for me."

"For you, Sir Philip?"

Sir Philip faced her resolutely. "For me, Miss Colwyn. If I tell you in very few words, will you forgive my abruptness? I don't think it is any use beating about the bush in these matters. Will you be my wife? That is what I came to say."

Janetta sat gazing at him with wide open eyes, as if she thought that he had taken leave of his senses.

"Don't answer at once; take time," said Sir Philip, quickly. "I know that I may perhaps have startled you: but I don't want you to answer hastily. If you would like time for reflection, pray take it. I hope that reflection will lead you to say that you will at least try to like me enough to become my wife."

Janetta felt that he was very forbearing. Some men in his position would have thought it sufficient to indicate their choice, and then to expect the favored lady, especially if she were small and brown and plain, and worked for her bread, to fall at his feet in an ecstasy of joy. Janetta had never yet felt inclined to fall at anybody's feet. But Sir Philip's forbearance seemed to call for additional care and speed in answering him.

"But—I am sure Lady Ashley——" she began, and stopped.

"My mother will welcome you as a daughter," said Sir Philip, gently. "She sends her love to you to-day, and hopes that you will consent to make me happy."

Janetta sat looking at her crossed hands. "Oh, it is impossible—impossible," she murmured.

"Why so? If there is no obstacle in—in your own affections, it seems to me that it would be quite possible," said Sir Philip, standing before her in an attitude of some urgency. "But perhaps you have a dislike to me?"

"Oh, no." She could not say more—she could not look up.

"I think I could make your life a happy one. You would not find me difficult. And you need have no further anxiety about your family; we could find some way of managing that. You think as I do about so many subjects that I am sure we should be happy together."

It was a big bribe. That was how Janetta looked at it in that moment. She was certain that Sir Philip did not love her: she knew that she did not love Sir Philip; and yet—it did seem that she might have a happy, easy, honored life if she consented to marry him—a life that would make her envied by many who had previously scorned her, and which would be, she hoped, productive of good to those whom she deeply loved. It was a bribe—a temptation. She was tempted, as any girl might have been, to exchange her life of toil and anxiety for one of luxury and peace; but there was something that she would also have to lose—the clear, upright conscience, the love of truth, the conviction of well-doing. She could not keep these and become Sir Philip's wife.

CHAPTER XXVIII
"CHANGES MUST COME"

She raised her eyes at length, and looked Sir Philip in the face. What a manly, honest, intelligent face it was! One that a woman might well be proud of in her husband: the face of a man whom she might very safely trust. Janetta thought all this, as she made her answer.

"I am very sorry, Sir Philip, but I cannot be your wife."

"You are answering me too hastily. Think again—take a day, a week—a month if you like. Don't refuse without considering the matter, I beg of you."

Janetta shook her head. "No consideration will make any difference."

"I know that I am not attractive," said her suitor, after a moment's pause, in a somewhat bitter tone. "I have not known how to woo—how to make pretty speeches and protestations—but for all that, I should make, I believe, a very faithful and loving husband. I am almost certain that I could make you happy, Janetta—if you will let me call you so—may I not try?"

"I should not feel that I was doing right," said Janetta, simply.

It was the only answer that could have made Sir Philip pause. He was quite prepared for hesitation and reluctance of a sort; but a scruple of conscience was a thing that he respected. "Why not?" he said, in a surprised tone.

"I have two or three reasons. I don't think I can tell them to you, Sir Philip; but they are quite impossible for me to forget."

"Then I think you would be doing better to tell me," said he, gently. He pulled a chair forward, sat down close to Janetta, and quietly laid his hand upon hers. "Now, what are they—these reasons?" he asked.

Her seat was lower than his chair, and she was obliged to lift her eyes when she looked at him. His face compelled truthfulness. And Janetta was wise enough to know whom she might trust.

"If I speak frankly, will you forgive me?" she said.

"If you will speak frankly, I shall esteem it a great honor."

"Then," said Janetta, bravely, "one of my reasons is this. You are most kind, and I know that you would be always good to me. I might even, as you say, be very happy after a time, but you do not—care for me—you do not love me, and"—here she nearly broke down—"and—I think you love some one else."

Sir Philip made a movement as if to take away his hand; but he restrained himself and grasped hers still more closely.

"And who is it that I am supposed to care for?" he asked, in a light tone.

"Margaret," Janetta answered, almost in a whisper. Then there was a silence, and this time Sir Philip did slowly withdraw his hand. But he did not look angry.

"I see," he said, "you are a friend of hers: you doubtless heard about my proposition to her concerning the Miss Polehampton business."

Janetta looked surprised. "No, I heard nothing of that. And indeed I heard very little from Margaret. I heard a good deal from Lady Caroline."

"Ah, that woman!" cried Sir Philip, getting up and making a little gesture with his hand, expressive of contempt. "She is worldly to the core. Did she tell you why Margaret refused me?"

"I did not know—exactly—that she had. Lady Caroline said that it was a misunderstanding," said Janetta, the startled look growing in her eyes.

"Just like her. She wanted to bring me back. Forgive me for speaking so hotly, but I am indignant with Lady Caroline Adair. She has done Margaret incalculable harm."

"But Margaret herself is so sweet and generous and womanly," said Janetta, watching his face carefully, "that she would recover from all that harm if she were in other hands."

"Yes, yes; I believe she would," he answered, eagerly. "It only needs to take her from her mother, and she would be perfect." He stopped, suddenly abashed by Janetta's smile. "In her way, of course, I mean," he added, rather confusedly.

"Ah," said Janetta, "it is certain that I should never be perfect. And after Margaret!"

"I esteem you, I respect you, much more than Margaret."

"But esteem is not enough, Sir Philip. No, you do not love me; and I think—if I may say so—that you do love Margaret Adair."

Sir Philip reddened distressfully, and bit his lip.

"I am quite sure, Miss Colwyn, that I have no thoughts of her that would do you an injustice. I did love Margaret—perhaps—but I found that I was mistaken in her. And she is certainly lost to me now. She loves another."

"And you will love another one day, if you do not win her yet," said Janetta, with decision. "But you do not love *me*, and I certainly will never marry any one who does not. Besides—I should have a feeling of treachery to Margaret."

"Which would be quite absurd and unwarrantable. Think of some better reason if you want to convince me. I hope still to make you believe that I do care for you."

Janetta shook her head. "It's no use, Sir Philip. I should be doing very wrong if I consented, knowing what I do. And besides, there *is* another reason. I cannot tell it to you, but indeed there is a good reason for my not marrying you."

"Has it anything to do with position—or—or money, may I ask? Because these things are immaterial to me."

"And I'm afraid I did not think about them," said Janetta, with a frank blush, which made him like her better than ever. "I ought to have remembered how great an honor you were doing me and been grateful!— no, it was not that."

"Then you care for some one else? That is what it is."

"I suppose it is," said Janetta.

And then a very different kind of blush began—a blush of shame, which dyed her forehead and ears and neck with so vivid a crimson hue that Sir Philip averted his eyes in honest sympathy.

"I'm afraid, then," he said, ruefully, but kindly, "that there's nothing more to be said."

"Nothing," said Janetta, wishing her cheeks would cool.

Sir Philip rose from his chair, and stood for a moment as if not knowing whether to go or stay. Janetta rose too.

"If you were to change your mind——" he said.

"This is a thing about which I could not possibly change my mind, Sir Philip."

"I am sorry for it." And then he took his leave, and Janetta went to her room to bathe her hot face and to wonder at the way in which the whirligig of Time brings its revenges.

"Who would have thought it?" she said to herself, half diverted and half annoyed. "When Miss Polehampton used to lecture me on the difference of Margaret's position and mine, and when Lady Caroline patronized me, I certainly never thought that I should be asked to become Lady Ashley. To take Margaret's place! I have a feeling—and I always had—that he is the proper husband for her, and that everything will yet come right between them. If I had said 'yes'—if I only *could* have said 'yes,' for the children's sake—I should never have got over the impression that Margaret was secretly reproaching me! And as it is, she may reproach me yet. For Wyvis will not make her happy if he marries her: and she will not make Wyvis happy. And as for me, although he is, I suppose, legally divorced from his wife, I do not think that I could bear to marry him under such circumstances. But Margaret is different, perhaps, from me."

But the more she meditated upon the subject, the more was Janetta surprised at Margaret's conduct. It seemed unlike her; it was uncharacteristic. Margaret might be for a time under the charm of Wyvis Brand's strong individuality; but if she married him, a miserable awakening was almost sure to come to her at last. To exchange the smooth life, the calm and the luxury, of Helmsley Court for the gloom, the occasional tempests, and the general crookedness of existence at the Red House would be no agreeable task for Margaret. Of the two, Janetta felt that life at the Red House would be far the more acceptable to herself: she did not mind a little roughness, and she had a great longing to bring mirth and sunshine into the gloomy precincts of her cousin's house. Janetta agreed with Lady Caroline as to the inadvisability of Margaret's attachment to Wyvis far more than Lady Caroline gave her credit for.

Lady Caroline was almost angrier than she had ever been in her life. She had had some disagreeable experiences during the last few hours. She had had visitors, since Lady Ashley's garden-party, and amongst them had been numbered two or three of her intimate friends who had "warned" her, as they phrased it, against "Margaret's infatuation for that wild Mr. Brand." Lady Caroline listened with her most placid smile, but raged inwardly. That her peerless Margaret should have been indiscreet! She was sure that it was only indiscretion—nothing more—but even that was insufferable! And what had Alicia Stone been doing? Where had her eyes been? Had she been bribed or coaxed into favoring the enemy?

Miss Stone had had a very unpleasant half-hour with her patroness that morning. It had ended in her going away weeping to pack up her boxes; for Lady Caroline literally refused to condone the injury done to Margaret by any carelessness of chaperonage on Miss Stone's part. "You must be quite unfit for your post, Alicia," she said, severely. "I am sorry that I shall not be able to recommend you for Lord Benlomond's daughters. I never thought you particularly wise, but such gross carelessness I certainly never did expect." Now this was unfortunate for Alicia, who had been depending on Lady Caroline's good offices to get her a responsible position as chaperon to three motherless girls in Scotland.

Lady Caroline had as yet not said a single word to Margaret. She had not even changed her caressing manner for one of displeasure. But she had kept the girl with her all the morning, and had come out alone only because Margaret had gone for a drive with two maiden aunts who had just arrived for a week, and with whom Lady Caroline felt that she would be absolutely safe. She was glad that she had the afternoon to herself. It gave her an opportunity of seeing Janetta Colwyn, and of conducting some business of her own as well. For after seeing Janetta she ordered the coachman to drive to the office of her husband's local solicitor, and in this office she remained for more than half an hour. The lawyer, Mr. Greggs by name, accompanied her with many smiles and bows to the carriage.

"I am sure we shall be able to do all that your ladyship wishes," he said, politely. "You shall have information in a day or two." Whereat Lady Caroline looked satisfied.

It was nearly six o'clock when she reached home, and her absence had caused some astonishment in the house. Tea had been carried out as usual to the seats under the cedar-tree on the lawn, and Mr. Adair's two sisters were being waited on by Margaret, fair and innocent-looking as usual, in her pretty summer gown. Lady Caroline's white eyelids veiled a glance of sudden sharpness, as she noticed her daughter's unruffled serenity. Margaret puzzled her. For the first time in her life she wondered whether she had been mistaken in the girl, who had always seemed to reproduce so accurately the impressions that her teachers and guardians wished to make. Had it been, all seeming? and was Margaret mentally and morally an ugly duckling, hatched in a hen's nest?

"Dear mamma, how tired you look," said the girl, softly. "Some fresh tea is coming for you directly. I took Alicia a cup myself, but she would not let me in. She said she had a headache."

"I dare say," replied Lady Caroline, a little absently. "At least—I will go to see her presently: she may be better before dinner. I hope you enjoyed your drive, dear Isabel."

Isabel was the elder of Mr. Adair's two sisters.

"Oh, exceedingly. Margaret did the honors of her County so well: she seems to know the place by heart."

"She has ridden with Reginald a good deal," said the mother.

Margaret had seated herself beside the younger of the aunts—Miss Rosamond Adair—and was talking to her in a low voice.

"How lovely she is!" Miss Adair murmured to her sister-in-law. "She ought to marry well, Caroline."

"I hope so," said Lady Caroline, placidly. "But I always think that Margaret will be difficult to satisfy." It was not her *rôle* to confide in her husband's sisters, of all people in the world.

"We heard something about Sir Philip Ashley: was there anything in it?"

Lady Caroline smiled. "I should have thought him everything that was desirable," she said, "but Margaret did not seem to see it in that light. Poor dear Sir Philip was very much upset."

"Ah, well, she may do better!"

"Perhaps so. Of course we should never think of forcing the dear child's inclinations," said Lady Caroline.

And yet she was conscious that she had laid her hand on a weapon with which she meant to beat down Margaret's inclinations to the ground. But it was natural to her to talk prettily.

Wheels were heard at that moment coming up the drive. Lady Caroline, raising her eyes, saw that Margaret started as the sound fell upon her ear.

"A bad sign!" she said to herself. "Girls do not start and change color when nothing is wrong. Margaret used not to be nervous. I wonder how far that man went with her. She may be unconscious of his intentions—he may not have any; and then she will have been made conspicuous for nothing! I wish the Brands had stayed away for another year or two."

The sound of wheels had proceeded from a dog-cart in which Mr. Adair, after an absence of a fortnight, was driving from the station. In a very few minutes he had crossed the lawn, greeted his wife, sisters and daughter, and thrown himself lazily into a luxurious lounging-chair.

"Ah, this is delightful!" he said. "London is terribly smoky and grimy at this time of year. And you all look charming—and so exactly the same as ever! Nothing changes down here, does it, my Pearl?"

He was stroking Margaret's hand, which lay upon his knee, as he spoke. The girl colored and dropped her eyes.

"Changes must come to us all," she said, in a low voice.

"A very trite remark, my dear," said Lady Caroline, smiling, "but we need not anticipate changes *before* they come. We are just as we were when you went away, Reginald, and nothing at all has happened."

She thought that Margaret looked at her oddly, but she did not care to meet her daughter's eyes just then. Lady Caroline was not an unworldly woman, not a very conscientious one, or apt to set a great value on fine moral distinctions; but she did regret just then that she had not impressed on her daughter more deeply the virtue of perfect truthfulness.

"By-the-by," said Mr. Adair, "I saw some letters on the hall table and brought them out with me. Will you excuse me if I open them? Why—that's the Brands' crest."

Lady Caroline wished that he had left the words unsaid. Margaret's face went crimson and then turned very pale. Her mother saw her embarrassment and hastened to relieve it.

"Margaret, dear, will you take Alicia my smelling salts? I think they may relieve her headache. Tell her not to get up—I will come and see her soon."

And as Margaret departed, Mr. Adair with lifted eyebrows and in significant silence handed an envelope to his wife. She glanced at it with perfectly unmoved composure. It was what she had been expecting: a letter from Wyvis Brand asking for the hand of their daughter, Margaret Adair.

CHAPTER XXIX
MARGARET'S CONFESSION

Margaret heard nothing of her lover's letter that night. It was not thought desirable that the tranquillity of the evening should be disturbed. Lady Caroline would have sacrificed a good deal sooner than the harmonious influences of a well-appointed dinner and the passionless refinement of an evening spent with her musical and artistic friends. Mr. Adair's sisters were women of cultured taste, and she had asked two gentlemen to meet them, therefore it was quite impossible (from her point of view) to discuss any difficult point before the morning. Margaret, who knew pretty well what was coming, spent a rather feverish half-hour in her room before the ringing of the dinner-bell, expecting every minute that her mother would appear, or that she would be summoned to a conference with her father in the library. But when the dinner hour approached without any attempt at discussion of the matter, and she perceived that it was to be left until the morrow, it must be confessed that she drew long breath of relief. She was quite sufficiently well versed in Lady Caroline's tactics to appreciate the force and wisdom of this reserve. "It is so much better, of course," she said to herself, as her maid dressed her hair, "that we should not have any agitating scene just before dinner. I dare say I should cry—if they were all very grave and solemn I am sure I should cry!—and it would be so awkward to come down with red eyes. And, of course, I could not stay upstairs to-night Perhaps mamma will come to me to-night when every one is gone."

And armed with this anticipation, she went downstairs, looking only a little more flushed than usual, and able to bear her part in the conversation and the amusements as easily as if no question as to her future fate were hanging undecided in the air.

But Lady Caroline did not stay when she visited Margaret that night as usual in her pretty room. She caressed and kissed her with more than customary warmth, but she did not attempt to enter into conversation with her in spite of the soft appeal of Margaret's inquiring eyes. "My dear child, I cannot possibly stay with you to-night," she said. "Your Aunt Isabel has asked me to go into her room for a few minutes. Good-night, my own sweetest: you looked admirable to-night in that lace dress, and your singing was simply charming. Mr. Bevan was saying that you ought to have the best Italian masters. Good-night, my darling," and Margaret was left alone.

She was a little disturbed—a little, not very much. She was not apt to be irritable or impatient, and she had great confidence in her parents' love for her. She had never realized that she lived under a yoke. Everything was made so smooth and easy that she imagined that she had only to express her will in order to have it granted. That there might be difficulties she foresaw: her parents might hesitate and parley a good deal, but she had not the slightest fear of overcoming their reluctance in course of time. She had always been a young princess, and nobody had ever seriously combated her will.

"I am sure that if I am resolute enough I shall be allowed to do as I choose," she said to herself; and possibly this was true enough. But Margaret had never yet had occasion to measure her resolution against that of her father and mother.

She went to bed and to sleep, therefore, quite peacefully, and slept like a child until morning, while Wyvis Brand was frantically pacing up and down his old hall for the greater part of the night, and Janetta was wetting her pillow with silent tears, and Philip Ashley, sleepless like these others, vainly tried to forget his disappointment in the perusal of certain blue-books. Margaret was the cause of all this turmoil of mind, but she knew nothing of it, and most certainly did not partake in it.

She suspected that she was to be spoken to on the subject of Mr. Brand's letter, when, after breakfast, next morning, she found that her father was arranging to take his sisters and Miss Stone for a long drive, and that she was to be left alone with her mother. Lady Caroline had relented, so far as Alicia was concerned. It would not look well, she had reflected, to send away her own kinswoman in disgrace, and although she still felt exceedingly, angry with Alicia, she had formally received her back into favor, cautioning her only not to speak to Margaret about Wyvis Brand. When every one was out of the way Lady Caroline knew that she could more easily have a conversation with her daughter, and Margaret was well aware of her intent. The girl looked mild and unobservant as usual, but she was busily engaged in watching for danger-signals. Her father's manner was decidedly flurried: so much was evident to her: the very way in which he avoided her eye and glanced uneasily at her mother spoke volumes to Margaret. It did not surprise her to see that Lady Caroline's face was as calm, her smile as sweet as ever: Lady Caroline always masked her emotion well; but there was still something visible in her eyes (which, in spite of herself, *would* look anxious and preoccupied) that made Margaret uncomfortable. Was she going to have a fight with her parents? She hoped not: it would be quite too uncomfortable!

"Come here, darling," said Lady Caroline, when the carriage had driven away; "come to my morning-room and talk to me a little. I want you."

Margaret faintly resisted. "It is my practicing time, mamma."

"But if I want you, dearest— —"

"Oh, of course it does not matter," said Margaret, with her usual instinct of politeness. "I would much rather talk than practice."

The mother laid her hand lightly within her tall daughter's arm, and led her towards the morning-room, a place of which she was especially fond in summer, as it was cool, airy, and looked out upon a conservatory full of blossoming plants. Lady Caroline sank down upon a low soft couch, and motioned to the girl to seat herself beside her; then, possessing herself of one of Margaret's hands and stroking it gently, she said with a smile—

"You have another admirer, Margaret?"

This opening differed so widely from any which the girl had expected that she opened her eyes with a look of intense surprise.

"Why should you be astonished, darling?" said Lady Caroline, with some amusement in her light tones. "You have had a good many already, have you not? And, by the by, you have had one or two very good offers, Margaret, and you have refused everything. You must really begin to think a little more seriously of your eligible suitors! This last one, however, is not an eligible one at all."

"Who, mamma?" said Margaret, faintly.

"The very last man whom I should have expected to come forward," said her mother. "Indeed, I call it the greatest piece of presumption I ever heard of. Considering that we are not on visiting terms, even."

"Oh, mamma, do tell me who you mean!"

Lady Adair arched her pencilled eyebrows over this movement of impatience. "Really, Margaret, darling! But I suppose I must be lenient: a girl naturally desires to hear about her suitors; but you must not interrupt me another time, love. It is that most impossible man, Mr. Brand of the Red House."

Margaret's face flushed from brow to chin. "Why impossible, mamma?"

"Dear child! You are so unworldly! But there is a point at which unworldliness becomes folly. We must stop short of that. Poor Mr. Brand is, for one thing, quite out of society."

"Not in Paris or London, mamma. Only in this place, where people are narrow and bigoted and censorious."

"And where, unfortunately, he has to live," said Lady Caroline, with gentle firmness. "It matters to us very little what they say of him in Paris or London: it matters a great deal what the County says."

"But if the County could be induced to take him up!" said Margaret, rather breathlessly. "He was at Lady Ashley's the other day, and he seemed to know a great many people. And if you—we—received him, it would make all the difference in the world."

"Oh, no doubt we could float him if we chose," said Lady Caroline, indifferently; "but would it really be worth the trouble? Even if he went everywhere, dear, he would not be a man that I should care to cultivate; he has not a nice reputation at all."

"Nobody knows of anything wrong that he has done," Margaret averred, with burning cheeks.

"Well, I have heard of one or two things that are not to his credit. I am told that he drinks and plays a good deal, that his language to his groom is something awful, and that he makes his poor little boy drunk every night." In this version had Wyvis Brand's faults and weaknesses gone forth to the world near Beaminster! "Then he has very disagreeable people to visit him, and his mother is not in the least a lady—a publican's daughter, and not, I am afraid, quite respectable in her youth." Lady Caroline's voice sank to a whisper. "Some very unpleasant things have been said about Mrs. Brand. Nobody calls on her. I am very sorry for her, poor thing, but what could one do? I would not set foot in the house while she was in it—I really would not. Mr. Brand ought to send her away."

"But what has she done, mamma?"

"There is no necessity for you to hear, Margaret. I like your mind to be kept innocent of evil, dear. Surely it is enough if I tell you that there is something wrong."

The girl was silent for a minute or two: she was beginning to feel abashed and ashamed. It was in a very low voice that she said at last—

"Mr. Brand would probably find another home for her if he married."

"Oh, most likely. But I do not know that what he would do affects us particularly. He is quite a poor man: even his family is not very good, although it is an old one, and it has been the proverb of the country-side for dissipation and extravagance for upwards of a century."

"But if he had quite reformed," Margaret murmured.

"My darling, what difference would it make? I am sure I do not know why we discuss the matter: it is a little too ridiculous to speak of it seriously. Your father will give Mr. Wyvis Brand his answer, and in such a way that he will not care to repeat his presumptuous and insolent proposal, and there will be an end of it. I hope, dearest, you have not been annoyed by the man? I heard something of his pursuing you with his attentions at Lady Ashley's party."

"Mamma," said Margaret, in a tragic tone, "this must not go on. You must not speak to me as you are doing now. You do not understand the position of affairs at all. I——"

"I beg your pardon, darling—one moment. Will you give me that palm-leaf fan from the mantel-piece? It is really rather a hot morning. Thanks, dear. What was it you were saying?"

Lady Caroline knew the value of an adroit interruption. She had checked the flow of Margaret's indignation for the moment, and was well aware that the girl would not probably begin her speech in quite the same tone a second time. At the same time she saw that she had given her daughter a momentary advantage. Margaret did not reseat herself after handing her mother the fan—she remained standing, a pale, slender figure, somewhat impressive in the shadows of the half-darkened room, with hands clasped and head slightly lifted as if in solemn protest.

"Mamma," she began, in a somewhat subdued voice, "I must tell you. Mr. Brand spoke to me before he wrote to papa. I told him to write."

Lady Caroline put her eye-glass and looked curiously at her daughter. "You told him to write, my dear child? And how did that come about? Don't you know that it was equivalent to accepting him?"

"Yes, mamma. And I did accept him."

"My dear Margaret!" The tone was that of pitying contempt. "You must have been out of your senses! Well, we can easily rectify the matter—that is one good thing. Why, my darling, when did he find time to speak to you? At Lady Ashley's?"

"In the park, near the forget-me-not brook," murmured Margaret, with downcast eyes.

"He met you there?"

"Yes."

"More than once? And you allowed him to meet you? Oh, Margaret!"

Lady Caroline's voice was admirably managed. The gradual surprise, shocked indignation, and reproach of her tones made the tears come to Margaret's eyes.

"Indeed, mamma," she said, "I am very sorry. I did not know at first—at least I did not think—that I was doing what you would not like. He used to meet me when I went into the park, sometimes—when Alicia was reading. Alicia did not know. And he was very nice, he was always *nice* mamma. He told me a great deal about himself—how discontented he was with his life, and how I might help him to make it better. And I should like to help him, mamma: it seems to me it would be a good thing to do. And if you and papa would help him too, he might take quite a different position in the County."

"My poor child!" said Caroline. "My poor deluded child!"

She lay silent for a few moments, thinking how to frame the argument which she felt was most likely to appeal to Margaret's tenderer feelings. "Of course," she said at last, very slowly, "of course, if he told you so much about his past life, he told you about his marriage—about that little boy's mother."

"He said that he had been very unhappy. I do not think," said Margaret with simplicity, "that he loved his first wife as he loves me."

"No doubt he made you think so, dear. His first wife, indeed! Did he tell you that his first wife was alive?"

"Mamma!"

"He says he is divorced from her," said Lady Caroline, sarcastically, "and seems to think it is no drawback to have been divorced. I and your father think differently. I do not mean there is any legal obstacle; but he took a very unfair advantage of your youth and inexperience by never letting you know that fact—or, at any rate, letting us know it before he paid you any attention. That stamps him as not being a gentleman, Margaret."

"Who told you, mamma?"

"His cousin and your friend," said Lady Caroline, coldly: "Miss Janetta Colwyn."

Margaret's color had fluctuated painfully for the last few minutes; she now sat down on a chair near the open window, and turned so pale that her mother thought her about to faint. Lady Caroline was on her feet immediately, and began to fan her, and to hold smelling salts to her nostrils; but in a very short time the girl's color returned, and she declined any further remedies.

"I did not know this," she said at last, rather piteously, "but it is too late to make any difference, mamma, it really is. I love Wyvis Brand, and he loves me. Surely you won't refuse to let us love one another?"

She caught her mother's hand, and Lady Caroline put her arms around her daughter's shoulders and kissed her as fondly as ever.

"My poor dear, romantic Child!" she said. "Do you think we can let you throw yourself quite away?"

"But I have given my promise!"

"Your father must tell Mr. Brand that you cannot keep your promise, my darling. It is quite out of the question."

And Lady Caroline thought she had settled the whole matter by that statement.

CHAPTER XXX
IN REBELLION

Janetta was naturally very anxious to know something of the progress of affairs between Wyvis and Margaret, but she heard little for a rather considerable space of time. She was now entirely severed from Helmsley Court, and had no correspondence with Margaret. As the summer holidays had begun, little Julian did not come every morning to Gwynne Street, but Tiny and Curly were invited to spend a month at the Red House in charge of Nora, who was delighted to be so much with Cuthbert, and who had the power of enlivening even the persistent gloom of Mrs. Brand. Janetta was thus obliged to live a good deal at home, and Wyvis seemed to shun her society. His relations at home had heard nothing of his proposal for Margaret's hand, and Janetta, like them, did not know that it had ever been actually made. Another event drove this matter into the background for some little time—for it was evidently fated that Janetta should never be quite at peace.

Mrs. Colwyn summoned her rather mysteriously one afternoon to a conference in her bedroom.

"Of course I know that you will be surprised at what I am going to say, Janetta," began the good lady, with some tossings of the head and flourishings of a handkerchief which rather puzzled Janetta by their demonstrativeness; "and no doubt you will accuse me of want of respect of your father's memory and all that sort of thing; though I'm sure I don't know why, for *he* married a second time, and I am a young woman still and not without admirers."

"Do you mean," said Janetta, "that you think——?"

She could go no further: she stood and looked helplessly at her stepmother.

"Do I think of marrying again? Well, yes, Janetta, I do; and more for the children's good than for my own. Poor things, they need a father: and I am tired of this miserable, scraping, cheeseparing life that you are so fond of. I have been offered a comfortable home and provision for my children, and I have decided to accept it."

"So soon!"

"It will not be announced just yet, of course. Not until the end of the summer. But it is really no use to wait."

Janetta stood pale and wide-eyed: she did not dare to let herself speak just yet. Mrs. Colwyn grew fretful under what she felt to be silent condemnation.

"I should like to know what harm it can do to you?" she said. "I've waited quite as long as many widows do, and toiled and suffered more than most. Poor James was the last man to grudge me a little rest and satisfaction as a reward for all that I have undergone. My own children will not repine, I am sure, and I look to you, Janetta, to explain to them how much for their good it will be, and how advantageous for them all."

"You can hardly expect me to try to explain away an act of disrespect to my father's memory," said Janetta, coldly.

"There is no disrespect to the dead in marrying a second time."

"After a decent interval."

Mrs. Colwyn burst into tears. "It's the first time in my life that I've ever been told that I was going to do a thing that wasn't decent," she moaned. "And when it's all for his dear children's good, too! Ah, well! I'll give it up, I'll say no, and we will all starve and go down into the grave together, and then perhaps you will be satisfied."

"Mamma, please do not talk such nonsense. Who is it that has asked you to be his wife?"

"Dr. Burroughs," said Mrs. Colwyn, faintly.

Janetta uttered an involuntary exclamation. Dr. Burroughs was certainly a man of sixty-five, but he was strong and active still; he had a good position in the town, and a large private income. His sister, who kept his house, was a good and sensible woman, and Dr. Burroughs himself was reputed to be a sagacious man. His fondness for children was well known, and a little thought convinced Janetta that his choice of a wife had been partly determined by his liking for Tiny and Curly, to say nothing of the elder children. He had been a close friend of Mr. Colwyn, and it was not likely that Mrs. Colwyn's infirmity had remained a secret from him: he must have learned it from common town-talk long ago. Angry as Janetta was, and petrified with surprise, she could not but acknowledge in her heart that such a marriage was a very good one for Mrs. Colwyn, and would probably be of immense advantage to the children. And the old physician and his sister would probably be able to keep Mrs. Colwyn in check: Janetta remembered that she had heard of one or two cases of intemperance which had been cured under his roof. As soon as she could get over her intense feeling that a slur was thrown on her father's memory by this very speedy second marriage of his widow, her common-sense told her that she might be very glad. But it was difficult to rid herself all at once of her indignation of what she termed "this indecent haste."

She made an effort to calm Mrs. Colwyn's fretful sobbing, and assured her with as much grace as she had at command that the marriage would not at all displease her if it took place at a somewhat later date. And she reflected that Dr. and Miss Burroughs might be depended upon not to violate conventionalities. Her own soreness with regard to the little affection displayed by Mrs. Colwyn to her late husband must be disposed of as best it might: there was no use in exhibiting it.

And as Mrs. Colwyn had hinted, it fell to Janetta to inform the rest of the family of their mother's intention, and to quell symptoms of indignation and discontent. After all, things might have been worse. The children already liked Dr. Burroughs, and soon reconciled themselves to the notion of living in a large, comfortable house, with a big garden, and unlimited treats and pleasures provided by their future stepfather and aunt. And when Janetta had had an interview with these two good people, her mind was considerably relieved. They were kind and generous; and although she could not help feeling that Dr. Burroughs was marrying for the sake of the children rather than their mother, she saw that he would always be thoughtful and affectionate to her, and that she would probably have a fairly happy and luxurious life. One thing was also evident—that he would be master in his own house, as James Colwyn had never been.

The marriage was to take place at Christmas, and the house in Gwynne Street was then to be let. Cuthbert and Nora began to talk of marrying at the same time, for Nora was somewhat violently angry at her mother's proceeding, and did not wish to go to Dr. Burroughs' house. The younger members of the family would all, however, migrate to The Cedars, as Dr. Burroughs' house was called; and there Miss Burroughs was still to maintain her sway. On this point Dr. Burroughs had insisted, and Janetta was thankful for it, and Miss Burroughs was quite able and willing to perform the duty of guardian not only to her brother's step-children, but to her brother's wife.

"And of course you will come to us, too, dear?" Miss Burroughs said to Janetta. "This will be your home always: Andrew particularly wished me to say so."

"It is very kind of Dr. Burroughs," said Janetta, gratefully. "I have no claim on him at all: I am not Mrs. Colwyn's daughter."

"As if that made any difference! James Colwyn was one of Andrew's best friends, and for his sake, if for no other, you will be always welcome."

"I am very much obliged to you," Janetta replied, "and I shall be pleased to come to you now and then as a visitor; but I have made up my mind that now—now that my duty seems to be done, I had better go out into the world and try to make a career for myself. I shall be happier at work than leading an idle, easy life. But please do not think me ungrateful—only I *must* get away."

And Miss Burroughs, looking into the girl's worn face, and noticing the peculiar significance of her tone, refrained from pressing the point. She was sure from both that some hidden pain existed, that there was some secret reason why Janetta felt that she "*must* get away." She was anxious to help the girl, but she saw that it would be no true kindness to keep her in Beaminster against her will.

These matters took some time to arrange, and it was while some of them were still pending that Janetta was startled by a visit from Margaret Adair.

It was a sultry day towards the end of July, and Miss Adair looked for once hot and dusty. She was much thinner than she had been, and had a harassed expression which Janetta could not fail to remark. As she hurriedly explained, she had walked some little distance, leaving Alicia Stone at the Post Office, and it afterwards transpired, giving her mother the slip at a confectioner's, in order to see Janetta once again.

"It is very kind of you, dear," said Janetta, touched, rather against her will, by so unwonted a proof of affection. "But I am afraid that Lady Caroline would not be pleased."

"I know she would not," said Margaret, a little bitterly. "She did not want me to see any more of you. I told her how unjust it was to blame you, but she would not believe me."

"It does not matter, Margaret, dear, I do not much mind."

"I thought I should like to see you once again." Margaret spoke with unusual haste, and almost in a breathless manner. "I want to know if you would do something for me. You used to say you would do anything for me."

"So I will, if I can."

"We were going abroad in a few days. I don't know where, exactly: they won't tell me. They are angry with me, Janetta, and I can't bear it," cried Margaret, breaking suddenly into tears which were evidently very heartfelt, although they did not disfigure that fair and placid face of hers in the slightest degree; "they were never angry with me before, and it is terrible. They may take me away and keep me away for years, and I don't know what to do. The only thing I can think of is to ask you to help me. I want to send a message to Wyvis—I want to write to him if you will give him the letter."

"But why do you not write him through the post?"

"Oh, because I promised not to post anything to him. Mamma said she must supervise my correspondence unless I promised not to write to him. And so I keep my word—but a few lines through you, Janet, darling, would not be breaking my word at all, for it would not be a letter exactly. And I want to arrange when I can see him again."

Janetta drew back a little. "It would be breaking the spirit of your promise, Margaret. No, I cannot help you to do that."

"Oh, Janetta, you would never be so hard as to refuse me! I only want to tell Wyvis that I am true to him, and that I don't mind what the world says one bit, because I know how people tell lies about him! You know you always promised to stand by me and to be my best friend."

"Yes, but I never promised to do a dishonorable action for you," said Janetta, steadily.

Margaret started up, her face a-flame directly.

"How dare you say such a thing to me, Janetta?" she exclaimed.

"I cannot help it, Margaret, you know that I am right."

The two looked at each other for a moment, and then Margaret turned away with the mien of an insulted princess.

"I was wrong to come. I thought that you would be true to the old bond of friendship between us. I shall never come to you again."

Poor Janetta's heart was very tender, although her resolution was impregnable. She ran after Margaret, putting her hands on her arm, and imploring her with tears to forgive her for her refusal. "If it were only anything else, Margaret, dear! If only you did not want me to do what your father and mother do not wish! Don't you see that you are trying to deceive them? If you were acting openly it would be a different thing! Don't be angry with me for wanting to do right!"

"I am not at all angry," said Margaret, with stateliness. "I am very disappointed, that is all. I do not see that I am deceiving anybody by sending a message to Wyvis. But I will not ask you again."

"If only I could!" sighed Janetta, in deep distress and confusion of mind. But her anchor of truth and straightforwardness was the thing of all others that she relied on for safety, and she did not let go her hold. In spite of Margaret's cold and haughty displeasure, Janetta kissed her affectionately, and could not refrain from saying, "Dear, I would do anything for you that I thought right. But don't—don't deceive your father and mother."

"I will not, as you shall see," returned Margaret, and she left the house without again looking at her former friend. Janetta felt very bitterly, as she watched the graceful figure down the street, that the old friendship had indeed become impossible in its older sense. Her very faithfulness to the lines in which it had been laid down now made it an offence to Margaret.

Janetta's direct and straightforward dealing had the effect of driving Margaret, though chiefly out of perversity, to do likewise. Miss Adair was not accustomed to be withstood, and, during the unexpected opposition with which her wishes had been met, her mind had turned very often to Janetta with unswerving faith in her old friend's readiness to help her at an emergency.

In this faith she considered that she had been cruelly disappointed. And her mingled anger, shame, and sorrow so blinded her to the circumstances in which she stood, that she walked quietly up to Lady Caroline and Alicia Stone in Beaminster High Street, and did not think of hiding her escapade at all.

"My dearest child, where *have* you been?" cried Lady Caroline, who was always caressing, if inflexible.

"I have been to Janetta Colwyn's, mamma," said Margaret, imperturbably, "to ask her to give a message to Mr. Brand."

"Margaret! Have you quite forgotten yourself? Oh, that unsuitable friendship of yours!"

"I don't think you need call it unsuitable, mamma," Margaret rejoined, with a weary little smile. "Janetta absolutely refused to give the message, and told me to obey my parents. I really do not see that *you* can blame her."

Lady Caroline replied only by a look of despair which spoke unutterable things, and then she walked onward to the spot where she had left the carriage. The three ladies drove home in complete silence. Lady Caroline was seriously displeased, Alicia curious, Margaret in rebellion and disgrace. The state of things was becoming very grave, for the whole tenor of life at Helmsley Court was disturbed, and Margaret's father and mother wanted their daughter to be a credit and an ornament to them, not a cause of disturbance and irritation. Margaret had kept up a gallant fight: she had borne silence, cold looks, absence of caresses, with unwavering courage; but she began now to find the situation unendurable. And a little doubt had lately been creeping into her heart—was it all worth while? If Wyvis Brand were really as undesirable a *parti* as he was represented to be, Margaret was not sure that her lot would be very happy as his wife. Hitherto she had maintained that the stories told about him, his habits and his position, were falsehoods. But if—she began to think—if they were true, and if a marriage with him would exclude her from the society to which she had been accustomed, was it worth while to fight as hard as she had done? Perhaps, after all, her mother and her father were right.

Lady Caroline, not knowing of these weaknesses in Margaret's defence, was inclined for once to be more severe than caressing. She went straight to her husband when she entered the Court, and had a long conversation with him. Then she proceeded to Margaret's room.

"I have been talking to your father, Margaret," she said coldly, "and we are both very much distressed at the course which things are taking."

"So am I, mamma," said Margaret.

"Of course we cannot proceed in the mediæval fashion, and lock you up in your own room until you are reasonable," said Lady Caroline, with a faint smile. "I should have thought that your own instinct as a lady would have precluded you from doing anything that would make it necessary for us to lay any restraint upon you; but to-day's occurrence really makes me afraid. You have promised not to write to Mr. Brand, I think?"

"Yes. But I meant to send him a little note to-day."

"Indeed? Then what I have to say is all the more necessary. We do not restrict you to any part of the house, but you must understand that when you come out of your own room, Margaret, you are never to be alone. Alicia will sit with you, if I am engaged. She will walk with you, if you wish to go out into the garden. I have no doubt it will be a little unpleasant," said Lady Caroline, with a slight, agreeable smile, "to be constantly under *surveillance*, and of course it will last only until we leave home next week; but in the meantime, my dear, unless you will give up your *penchant* for Mr. Brand, you must submit to be watched. You cannot be allowed to run off with messages to this man as if you were a milliner's girl or a servant maid: *we* manage these matters differently."

And then Lady Caroline withdrew, though not too late to see the girl sink down into a large arm-chair and burst into a very unwonted passion of sobs and tears.

"So tiresome of Margaret to force one to behave in this absurd manner!" reflected Lady Caroline. "So completely out of date in modern days!"

CHAPTER XXXI
THE PLOUGHMAN'S SON

Two or three days after Margaret's visit to Gwynne Street, Janetta availed herself of Mrs. Colwyn's temporary absence in Miss Burroughs' company to pay a visit to the Red House. Her anxiety to know what was occurring between Wyvis and Margaret had become almost uncontrollable and, although she was not very likely to hear much about it from Wyvis or his mother, she vaguely hoped to gather indications at least of the state of affairs from her cousin's aspect and manners.

It was plain that Wyvis was not in a happy mood. His brow was dark, his tone sarcastic; he spoke roughly once or twice to his mother and to his little son. He evidently repented of his roughness, however, as soon as the words were out of his mouth, for he went over to Mrs. Brand's side and kissed her immediately afterwards, and gave some extra indulgence to Julian by way of making up for his previous severity. Still the irritation of feeling existed, and could not be altogether repressed when he spoke; and when he was silent he fell into a condition of gloom which was even more depressing than his sharpness. Janetta did her best to be cheerful and talkative to Mrs. Brand, and she fancied that he liked to listen; for he sat on with them in the blue room long after Nora and Cuthbert had disappeared into the garden and the children were romping in the wood. Certainly he did not say much to her, but he seemed greatly disinclined to move.

After a time, Mrs. Brand and Janetta adjourned to the hall, which was always a favorite place of resort on summer evenings. Traces of the children's presence made the rooms more cheerful than they used to be—to Janetta's thinking. Tiny's doll and Julian's ball were more enlivening to the place than even Cuthbert's sketches and Nora's bunches of wild flowers. And here, too, Wyvis followed them in an aimless, subdued sort of way; and, having asked and obtained permission to light a cigarette, he threw himself into a favorite chair, and seemed to listen dreamily, while Janetta held patient discourse with his mother on the ailments of the locality and the difficulty of getting the housework done. Janetta glanced at him from time to time; he sat so quietly that she would have thought him sleeping but for the faint blue spirals of smoke that went up from his cigarette. It was six o'clock in the evening, and the golden lights and long shadows made Janetta long to be out of doors; but Mrs. Brand had a nervous fear of rheumatism, and did not want to move.

"What is that?" said Wyvis, suddenly rousing himself.

Nobody else had heard anything. He strode suddenly to the door, and flung it open. Janetta heard the quavering tones of the old man-servant, an astonished, enraptured exclamation from Wyvis himself; and she knew—instinctively—what to expect. She turned round; it was as she had feared. Margaret was there. Wyvis was leading her into the room with the fixed look of adoration in his eyes which had been so much commented upon at Lady Ashley's party. When she was present, he evidently saw none but her. Janetta rose quickly and withdrew a little into the back ground. She wished for a moment that she had not been there—and then it occurred to her that she might be useful by and by. But it was perhaps better for Margaret not to see her too soon. Mrs. Brand, utterly unprepared for this visit, not even knowing the stranger by sight, and, as usual, quite unready for an emergency, rose nervously from her seat and stood, timid, awkward, and anxious, awaiting an explanation.

"Mother, this is Margaret Adair," said Wyvis, as quietly as if his mother knew all that was involved in that very simple formula. He was still holding the girl by the hand and gazing in his former rapt manner into her face. It was not the look of a lover, to Janetta's eye, half so much as the worship of a saint. Margaret embodied for Wyvis Brand the highest aspirations, the purest dreams of his youth.

As to Margaret, Janetta thought that she was looking exquisitely lovely. Her thinness added to the impression of ethereal beauty; there was a delicacy about her appearance which struck the imagination. Her color fluctuated; her eyes shone like stars; and her whole frame seemed a little tremulous, as if she were shaken by some strange and powerful emotion to her very soul. Her broad-brimmed straw hat, white dress, and long tan gloves belonged, as Janetta knew, only to her ordinary attire when no visitors were to be seen; but simplicity of dress always seemed to garnish Margaret's beauty, and to throw it into the strongest possible relief. She was sufficiently striking in aspect to frighten poor, timid Mrs. Brand, who was never happy when she found herself in the company of "fashionable" people. But it was with a perfectly simple and almost child-like manner that Margaret drew her finger away from Wyvis' clasp and went up to his mother, holding out both hands as if in appeal for help.

"I am Margaret," she said. "I ought not to have come; but what could I do? They are going to take me away from the Court to-morrow, and I could not go without seeing you and Wyvis first."

"Wyvis?" repeated Mrs. Brand, blankly. She had not taken Margaret's hands, but now she extended her right hand in a stiff, lifeless fashion, which looked like anything but a welcome. "I do not know—I do not understand——"

"It is surely easy enough to understand," said Wyvis, vehemently. "She loves me—she has promised to be my wife—and you must love her, too, for my sake, as well as for her own."

"Won't you love me a little?" said Margaret, letting her eyes rest pleadingly on Mrs. Brand's impassive face. She was not accustomed to being met in this exceedingly unresponsive manner. Wyvis made a slight jesture of impatience, which his mother perfectly understood. She tried, in her difficult, frozen way, to say something cordial.

"I am very pleased to see you," she faltered. "You must excuse me if I did not understand at first. Wyvis did not tell me."

Then she sank into her chair again, more out of physical weakness than from any real intention to seat herself. Her hand stole to her side, as if to still the beating of her heart; her face had turned very pale. Only Janetta noticed these signs, which betrayed the greatness of the shock; Margaret, absorbed in her own affairs, and Wyvis absorbed in Margaret, had no eyes for the poor mother's surprise and agitation. Janetta made a step forward, but she saw that she could do nothing. Mrs. Brand was recovering her composure, and the other two were not in a mood to bear interruption. So she waited, and meanwhile Margaret spoke.

"Dear Mrs. Brand," she said, kneeling at the side of the trembling woman, and laying her clasped hands on her lap, "forgive me for startling you like this." Even Janetta wondered at the marvelous sweetness of Margaret's tones. "Indeed, I would not have come if there had been any other way of letting Wyvis know. They made me promise not to write to him, not to meet him in the wood where we met before you know, and they watched me, so that I could not get out, or send a message or anything. It has been like living in prison during the last few days." And the girl sobbed a little, and laid her forehead for a moment on her clasped hands.

"It's a shame—a shame! It must not go on," exclaimed Wyvis, indignantly.

"In one way it will not go on," said Margaret, raising her head. "They are going to take me away, and we are not to come back for the whole winter—perhaps not next year at all. I don't know where we are going. I shall never be allowed to write. And I thought it would be terrible to go without letting Wyvis know that I will never, never forget him. And I am only nineteen now, and I can't do as I like; but, when I am twenty-one, nobody can prevent me——"

"Why should anybody prevent you now?" said Wyvis gloomily. He drew nearer and laid his hand upon her shoulder. "Why should you wait? You are safe: you have come to my mother, and she will take care of you. Why need you go back again?"

"Is that right, Wyvis?" said Janetta. She could not keep silence any longer. Wyvis turned on her almost fiercely. Margaret who had not seen her before started up and faced her, with a look of something like terror.

"It is no business of yours," said the man. "This matter is between Margaret and myself. Margaret must decide it. I do not ask her to compromise herself in any way. She shall be in my mother's care. All she will have to do is to trust to me——"

"I think we need hardly trouble you, Mr. Brand," said another voice. "Margaret will be better in the care of her own mother than in that of Mrs. Brand or yourself."

Lady Caroline Adair stood on the threshold. Lady Caroline addressed the little group, on which a sudden chill and silence fell for a moment, as if her appearance heralded some portentous crash of doom. The door had been left ajar when Margaret entered; it was not easy to say how much of the conversation Lady Caroline had heard. Mrs. Brand started up; Margaret turned very pale and drew back, while Wyvis came closer to her and put his arm round her with an air of protective defiance. Janetta drew a quick breath of relief. A disagreeable scene would follow she knew well; and there were probably unpleasant times in store for Margaret, but these were preferable to the course of rebellion, open or secret, to which the girl was being incited by her too ardent lover.

Janetta never admired Lady Caroline so much as she did just then. Margaret's mother was the last person to show discomposure. She sat down calmly, although no one had asked her to take a chair, and smilingly adjusted the lace shawl which she had thrown round her graceful figure. There were no signs of haste or agitation in her appearance. She wore a very elegant and becoming dress, a Paris bonnet on her head, a pair of

French gloves on her slender hands. She became at once the centre of the group, the ornamental point on which all eyes were fixed. Every one else was distressed, frightened, or angry; but Lady Caroline's pleasing smile and little air of society was not for one moment to be disturbed.

"It is really very late for a call," she said, quietly, "but as I found that my daughter was passing this way, I thought I would follow her example and take the opportunity of paying a visit to Mrs. Brand. It is not, however, the first time that we have met."

She looked graciously towards Mrs. Brand, but that poor woman was shaking in every limb. Janetta put her arms round Mrs. Brand's shoulders. What did Lady Caroline mean? She had some purpose to fulfil, or she would not sit so quietly, pretending not to notice that her daughter was holding Wyvis Brand by the hand and that one of his arms was round her waist. There was something behind that fixed, agreeable smile.

"No," said Lady Caroline, reflectively, "not the first time. The last time I saw you, Mrs. Brand— —"

"Oh, my lady, my lady!" Mrs. Brand almost shrieked, "for heaven's sake, my lady, don't go on!"

She covered her face with her hands and rocked herself convulsively to and fro. Wyvis frowned and bit his lip: Margaret started and unconsciously withdrew her hand. It crossed the minds of both that Mrs. Brand's tone was that of an inferior, that of a servant to a mistress, not that of one lady to her equal.

"Why should I not go on?" said Lady Caroline, glancing from one to another as if in utter ignorance. "Have I said anything wrong? I only meant that I was present at Mrs. Brand's *first* wedding—when she married your father, Mr. Wyvis—not your adopted father, of course, but John Wyvis, the ploughman."

There was a moment's silence. Then Wyvis took a step forward and thundered. "*What?*" while the veins stood out upon his forehead and his eyes seemed to be gathering sombre fire. Mrs. Brand, with her head bowed upon her hands, still rocked herself and sobbed.

"I hope I have not been indiscreet," said Lady Caroline, innocently. "You look a little surprised. It is surely no secret that you are the son of Mary Wyvis and her cousin, John Wyvis, and that you were brought up by Mr. Brand as his son simply out of consideration for his wife? I am sure I beg your pardon if I have said anything amiss. As Mrs. Brand seems disturbed, I had better go."

"Not until my mother has contradicted this ridiculous slander," said Wyvis, sternly. But his mother only shook her head and wailed aloud.

"I can't, my dear—I can't. It's true every word of it. My lady knows."

"Of course I know. Come, Mary, don't be foolish," said Lady Caroline, in the carelessly sharp tone in which one sometimes speaks to an erring dependant. "I took an interest in you at the time, you will remember, although I was only a child staying at Helmsley Court at the time with Mr. Adair's family. I was fourteen, I think; and you were scullery-maid or something, and told me about your sweetheart, John Wyvis. There is nothing to be ashamed of: you were married very suitably, and if Wyvis, the ploughman, had not been run over when he was intoxicated, and killed before your baby's birth, you might even now have been living down at Wych End, with half a dozen stalwart sons and daughters—of whom you, Mr. Wyvis, or Mr. Wyvis Brand, as you are generally known, would have been the eldest—probably by this time a potman or a pugilist, with a share in your grandfather's public-house at Roxby. How ridiculous it seems now, does it not?"

Astonishment had kept Wyvis silent, but his gathering passion could not longer be repressed.

"That is enough," he said. "If you desire to insult me you might have let it be in other company. Or if you will send your husband to repeat it——"

"I said a pugilist, did I not?" said Lady Caroline, smiling, and putting up her eye-glass. "Your thews and sinews justify me perfectly—and so, I must say, does your manner of speech." She let her eye run over his limbs critically, and then she dropped her glass. "You are really wonderfully like poor Wyvis; he was a very strong sort of man."

"Will you be so good as to take your leave, Lady Caroline Adair? I wish to treat you with all due courtesy, as you are Margaret's mother," said Wyvis, setting his teeth, "but you are saying unpardonable things to a man in his own house."

"My dear man, there is nothing to be ashamed of!" cried Lady Caroline, as if very much surprised. "Your father and mother were very honest people, and I always thought it greatly to Mark Brand's credit that he adopted you. The odd thing was that so few people knew that you were not his son. You were only a month or two old when he married Mary Wyvis, however; for your father died before your birth; but there was no secret made of it at the time, I believe. And it is nearly thirty years. Things get forgotten."

"Mother, can this be true?" said Wyvis, hoarsely. He was forced into asking the question by Lady Caroline's cool persistence. He was keenly conscious of the fact that Margaret, looking scared and bewildered, had shrunk away from him.

"Yes, yes, it is true," said Mrs. Brand, with a burst of despairing tears. "We did not mean any harm, and nobody made any inquiries. There was nothing wrong about it—nothing. It was better for you, Wyvis, that was all."

"Is it better for anybody to be brought up to believe a lie?" said the young man. His lips had grown white, and his brow was set in very ominous darkness. "I shall hear more of this story by and by. I have to thank you, Lady Caroline, for letting in a little light upon my mind. Your opposition to my suit is amply explained."

"I am glad you take it in that way, Mr. Brand," said Lady Caroline, for the first time giving him his adopted name, and smiling very amicably. "As I happened to be one of the very few people who knew or surmised anything about the matter, I thought it better to take affairs into my own hands—especially when I found that my daughter had come to your house. But for this freak of hers I should not, perhaps, have interfered. As you are no doubt prepared now to resign all hope of her, I am quite satisfied with the result of my afternoon's work. Come, Margaret."

CHAPTER XXXII
THE FAILURE OF MARGARET

"Then I am to understand," said Wyvis, a sudden glow breaking out over his dark face, "that you did not make this communication carelessly, as at first I thought, but out of malice prepense?"

"If you like to call it so—certainly," said Lady Caroline, with a slight shrug of her shoulders.

"This was your revenge?—when you found that Margaret had come to me!"

"You use strange words, Mr. Wyvis Brand. Revenge is out of date—a quite too ridiculous idea. I simply mean that I never wish to intermeddle with my neighbors' affairs, and should not have thought of bringing this matter forward if your pretentions could have been settled in an ordinary way. If Margaret"—glancing at her daughter, who stood white and thunderstricken at her side—"had behaved with submission and with modesty, I should not have had to inflict what seems to be considerable pain upon you. But it is her fault and yours. Young people should submit to the judgment of their elders: we do not refuse to gratify their wishes without good reason."

Lady Caroline spoke with a cold dignity, which she did not usually assume. Margaret half covered her face with one hand, and turned aside. The sight of the slow tears trickling through her fingers almost maddened Wyvis, as he stood before her, looking alternately at her and at Lady Caroline. Mrs. Brand and Janetta were left in the background of the little group. The older woman was still weeping, and Janetta was engaged in soothing and caressing her; but neither of them lost a word which passed between the man for whom they cared and the woman whom at that moment they both sincerely hated.

"But is it a good reason?" said Wyvis at last. His eye flashed beneath his dark brow, his nostril began to quiver. "If I had been Mark Brand's son, you mean, you would have given me Margaret?"

"There would then have been no disqualification of birth," said Lady Caroline, clearly. "There might then have been disqualifications of character or of fortune, but these we need hardly consider now. The other—the primary—fact is conclusive."

"Mamma, mamma!" broke out Margaret; "don't say these terrible things—please don't. It isn't Wyvis' fault."

"God bless you, my darling!" Wyvis muttered between his teeth.

"No, it is not his fault; it is his misfortune," said Lady Caroline.

"I am to understand, then, Lady Caroline," said Wyvis, to whom Margaret's expostulation seemed to have brought sudden calmness and courage, "that my lowly origin forms an insurmountable barrier to my marriage with Miss Adair?"

"Quite so, Mr. Brand."

"But that there is no other obstacle?"

"I did not say so. Your domestic relations have been unfortunate, and Mr. Adair strongly objects to giving his daughter to a man in your position. But we need not go into that matter; I don't consider it a subject suitable for discussion in my daughter's presence."

"Then I appeal to Margaret!" said Wyvis, in a deep, strong voice. "I call upon *her* to decide whether my birth is as much of an obstacle as you say it is."

"That is not fair," said Lady Caroline, quickly. "She will write to you. She can say nothing now."

"She must say something. She was on the point of giving me herself—her all—when you came in. She had promised to be my wife, and she was prepared to keep her promise almost immediately. She shall not break her word because my father was a ploughman instead of a landowner and a gentleman."

For once Lady Caroline made a quick, resistant gesture, as if some impulse prompted her to speak sharply and decisively. Then she recovered herself, leaned back in her chair, and smiled faintly.

"Is the battle to be fought out here and now?" she said. "Well, then, do your worst, Mr. Brand. But I must have a word by and by, when you have spoken."

Wyvis seemed scarcely to hear her. He was looking again, at Margaret. She was not crying now, but one hand still grasped a handkerchief wet with her tears. She had rested the other on the back of her mother's chair. Janetta marveled at her irresolute attitude. In Margaret's place she would have flung her arms round Wyvis Brand's neck, and vowed that nothing but death should sever her from him. But Margaret was neither passionately loving nor of indomitable courage.

Wyvis stepped forward and took her by the hand. Lady Caroline's eyebrows contracted a little, but she did not interfere. She seemed to hold herself resolutely aloof—for a time—and listened, Janetta thought, as if she were present at a very interesting comedy of modern manners.

"Margaret, look at me!" said the man.

His deep, vibrating voice compelled the girl to raise her eyes. She looked up piteously, and seemed half afraid to withdraw her gaze from Wyvis' dark earnestness of aspect.

"Margaret—my darling—you said you loved me."

"Yes—I do love you," she murmured; but she looked afraid.

"I am not altered, Margaret: I am the same Wyvis that you loved—the Wyvis that you kissed down by the brook, when you promised to be my wife. Have you forgotten? Ah no—not so soon. You would not have come here to-day if you had forgotten."

"I have not forgotten," she said, in a whisper.

"Then, darling, what difference does it make? There is no stain upon my birth. I would not ask you to share a dishonored name. But my parents were honest if they were poor, and what they were does not affect me. Margaret, speak, tell me, dear, that you will not give me up!"

Margaret tried to withdraw her hand. "I do not know what to say," she whispered.

"Say that you love me."

"I—have said it."

"Then, that you will not give me up?"

"Mamma!" said Margaret, entreatingly. "You hear what Wyvis says. It is not his fault. Why—why—won't you let us be happy?"

"Don't appeal to your mother," said Wyvis, the workings of whose features showed that he was becoming frightfully agitated. "You know that she is against me. Listen to your own heart—what does it say? It speaks to you of my love for you, of your own love for me. Darling, you know how miserable my life has been. Are you going to scatter all my hopes again and plunge me down in the depths of gloom? And all for what? To satisfy a worldly scruple. It is not even as if I had been brought up in my early years in the station to which my father belonged. I have never known him—never known any relations but the Brands; and they are not so very much beneath you. Don't fail me, Margaret! I shall lose all faith in goodness if I lose faith in you!"

"I think," said Lady Caroline, in the rather disheartening pause which followed upon Wyvis' words—disheartening to him, at least, and also to Janetta, who had counted much upon Margaret's innate nobility of soul!—"I think that I may now be permitted to say a word to my daughter before she replies. What Mr. Wyvis Brand asks you to do, Margaret, is to marry him at once. Well, the time for coercion has gone by. Of course, we cannot prevent you from marrying him if you choose to do so, but on the other hand we shall never speak to you again."

Wyvis uttered a short laugh, as if he were scornfully ready to meet that contingency, but Margaret's look of startled horror recalled him to decorum.

"You would be no longer any child of ours," said Lady Caroline, calmly. "Your father concurs with me in this. You have known our views so long and so well that we feel it almost necessary to explain this to you. Mr. Brand wishes you to choose, as a matter of fact, between his house and ours. Make your choice—make it now, if you like; but understand—and I am very sorry to be obliged to say a thing which may perhaps hurt the feelings of some persons present—that if you marry the son of a ploughman and a scullery-maid—I do not mean to be more offensive than I can help—you cannot possibly expect to be received at Helmsley Court."

"But, mamma! he ranks as one of the Brands of the Red House. Nobody knows."

"But everybody *will* know," said Lady Caroline, calmly. "I shall take care of that. I don't know how it is that Mr. Brand has got possession of the family estate—to which he has, of course, no right; but it has an ugly look of fraud about it, to which public attention had better be drawn at once. Mr. Brand may have been a party to the deception all along, for aught I know."

"That statement needs no refutation," said Wyvis, calmly, though with a dangerous glitter in his eyes. "I shall prove my integrity by handing over the Red House to my bro——to Cuthbert Brand, who is of course the rightful owner of the place."

"You hear. Margaret?" said Lady Caroline. "You will not even have the Red House in your portion. You have to choose between your mother and father and friends, position, wealth, refinement, luxury—and Wyvis Brand.

That is your alternative. He will have no position of his own, no house to offer you; I am amazed at his selfishness, I must own, at making such a proposition."

"No, madam," said Mrs. Brand, breaking into the conversation for the first time, and seeming to forget her timidity in the defence of her beloved son Wyvis; "we are not so selfish as you think. The estate was left to Wyvis by my husband's will. He preferred that Wyvis should be master here; and we thought that no one knew the truth."

"But I shall not be master here any longer," said her son. "I will hand over the place to Cuthbert at once. I will take nothing on false pretences. So, Margaret, choose between me and the advantages your mother offers you. It is for you to decide."

"Oh, I can't, I can't! Why need I decide now?" said Margaret, clasping her hands. "Let me have time to think!"

"No, you must decide now, Margaret," said Lady Caroline. "You have done a very unjustifiable thing in coming here to-day, and you must take the consequences. If you still wish to marry Mr. Wyvis Brand, you had better accept the offer of his mother's protection and remain here. If you come away with me, it must be understood that you give up any thought of such a marriage. You must renounce Mr. Wyvis Brand from this time forth and for ever. Pray, don't answer hastily. The question is this—do you mean to stay here or to come away with me?"

She rose as she spoke, and began to arrange the details of her dress, as though preparing to take her departure. Margaret stood pale, irresolute, miserable between her mother and her lover. Wyvis threw out his hands to her with an imploring gesture and an almost frenzied cry—"Margaret—love—come to me!" Janetta held her breath.

But in that moment of indecision, Margaret's wavering eye fell upon Mrs. Brand. The mother was an unlovely object in her abject sorrow and despair. Her previous coldness and awkwardness told against her at that moment. It suddenly darted through Margaret's mind that she would have to accept this woman, with her common associations, her obscure origin, her doubtful antecedents, in a mother's place. The soul of the girl who had been brought up by Lady Caroline Adair revolted at the thought. Wyvis she loved, or thought she loved; Wyvis she could accept; but Wyvis' mother for her own, coupled with exclusion from the home where she had lived so many smooth and tranquil years, exclusion also from the society in which she had been taught that it was her right to take a distinguished place—this was too much. Her dreams fell from her like a garment. Plain, unvarnished reality unfolded itself instead. To be poor and obscure and unfriended, to be looked down upon and pitied, to be snubbed and passed by on the other side—this was what seemed to be the reality of things to Margaret's mind. It was too much for her to accept. She looked at it and passed by it.

She stretched out her hand timidly and touched her mother's arm. "Mamma," she said falteringly, "I—I will come with you." And then she burst into tears and fell upon her mother's neck, and over her shoulder Lady Caroline turned and smiled at Wyvis Brand. She had won her game.

"Of course you will, darling," she said, caressingly. "I did not think you could have been so wicked as to give us up. Come with me! this is nor the place for us."

And in the heart-struck silence which fell upon the little group that she left behind, Lady Caroline gravely bowed and led her weeping daughter from the room.

"Oh, Margaret, Margaret!" Janetta suddenly cried out; but Margaret never once looked back. Perhaps if she had seen Wyvis Brand's face just then, she might have given way. It was a terrible face; hard, bitter, despairing; with lines of anguish about the mouth, and a lurid light in the deep-set, haggard-looking eyes. Janetta, in the pity of her heart, went up to her cousin, and took his clenched hand between her own.

"Wyvis, dear Wyvis," she said, "do not look so. Do not grieve. Indeed, she could not have been worthy of you, or she would not have done like this. All women are not like her, Wyvis. Some would have loved you for yourself."

And there she stopped, crimson and ashamed. For surely she had almost told him that she loved him!—that secret of which she had long been so much ashamed, and which had given her so much of grief and pain. But she attached too much importance to her own vague words. They did not betray her, and Wyvis scarcely listened to what she said. He broke into a short, harsh laugh, more hideous than a sob.

"Are not all women like her?" he said. "Then they are worse. She was innocent, at any rate, if she was weak. But she has sold her soul now, if she ever had one, to the devil; and, as I would rather be with her in life and death than anywhere else, I shall make haste to go to the devil too."

He shook off her detaining hand, and strode to the door. There he turned, and looked fixedly at his mother.

"It is almost worse to be weak than wicked, I think," he said. "If you had told me the truth long ago, mother, I should have kept out of this complication. It's been your fault—my misery and my failure have always been your fault. It would have been better for me if you had left me to plough the fields like my father before me. As it is, life's over for me in this part of the world, and I may as well bid it good-bye."

Before they could stop him, he was gone. And Janetta could not follow, for Mrs. Brand sank fainting from her chair, and it was long before she could be recovered from the deathlike swoon into which she fell.

And throughout that evening, and for days to come, Margaret Adair, although petted and caressed and praised on every hand, and persuaded into feeling that she had not only done the thing that was expected of her, but a very worthy and noble thing, was haunted by an uneasy consciousness, that the argument which had prevailed with her was not the love of home or of her parents, which, indeed, might have been a very creditable motive for her decision, but a shrinking from trouble, a dislike to effort of any kind, and an utter distaste for obscurity and humility. Janetta's reproachful call rang in her ears for days. She knew that she had chosen the baser part. True, as she argued with herself, it was right to obey one's parents, to be submissive and straightforward, to shrink from the idea of ingratitude and rebellion; and, if she had yielded on these grounds, she might have been somewhat consoled for the loss of her lover by the conviction that she had done her duty. But for some little time she was distressfully aware that she had never considered her parents in the matter at all. She had thought of worldly disadvantage only. She had not felt any desire to stand by Wyvis Brand in his trouble. She had felt only repugnance and disgust; and, having some elements of good in her, she was troubled and ashamed by her failure; for, even if she had done right in the main, she knew that she had done it in the wrong way.

But, of course, time changed her estimate of herself. She was so much caressed and flattered by her family for her "exquisite dutifulness," as they phrased it, that she ended by believing that she had behaved beautifully. And this belief was a great support to her during the winter that she subsequently spent with her parents in Italy.

CHAPTER XXXIII
RETROSPECT

For my part, I am inclined to think that Margaret was more right than she knew. There was really no inherent fitness between her temperament and that of Wyvis Brand; and his position in the County was one which would have fretted her inexpressibly. She, who had been the petted favorite of a brilliant circle in town and country, to take rank as the wife of a ploughman's son! It would not have suited her at all; and her discontent would have ended in making Wyvis miserable.

He was, he considered, miserable enough already. He was sore all over—sore and injured and angry. He had been deceived in a manner which seemed to him unjustifiable from beginning to end. The disclosure of his parentage explained many little things which had been puzzling to him in his previous life, but it brought with it a baffling, passionate sense of having been fooled and duped—not a condition of things which was easy for him to support. Little by little the whole story became clear to him. For, when he flung out of the Red House after Margaret's departure, in a tumult of rage and shame, announcing his determination to go to the devil, he did not immediately seek out the Prince of Darkness: he only went to his lawyer. His lawyer told him a good deal, and Mrs. Brand, in a letter dictated to Janetta, told him more.

Mary Wyvis, the daughter of the village inn-keeper at Roxby, was brought up to act as his barmaid, and early became engaged to marry her cousin, John Wyvis, ploughman. Everything seemed to be going smoothly, when Mark Brand appeared upon the scene, and fell desperately in love with the handsome barmaid. She returned his love, but was too conscientious to elope with him and forget her cousin, as he wished her to do. Her father supported John's claim, and threatened to horsewhip the fine gentleman if he visited the Roxby Arms again. By way of change, Mary then went into domestic service for a few weeks at Helmsley Manor. It was not expected that she would remain there, and it was thought by her friends that she distinctly "lowered herself" by accepting this position, for her father was a well-to-do man in his way; but Mary Wyvis made the break with Mark Brand by this new departure which she considered it essential for her to make; and she was thereby delivered from his attentions for a time. At Helmsley Manor she was treated with much consideration, being considered a superior young person for her class; and although only a scullery maid in name, she was allowed a good deal of liberty, and promoted to attend on Lady Caroline Bertie, who, as a girl of fourteen, was then visiting Mrs. Adair, the mother of the man whom she afterward married. Mary Wyvis was lured into confiding one or two of her little secrets to Lady Caroline; and when she left Helmsley Court to marry John Wyvis, that young lady took so much interest in the affair that she attended the wedding and gave the bride a wedding-present. And as she often visited the Adairs, she seldom failed to asked after Mary, until that consummation of Mary's fate which effectually destroyed Lady Caroline's interest in her.

Wyvis the ploughman was accidentally killed, and Mary's child, named John after his father, was born shortly after the ploughman's death. It was then that Mark Brand sought out his old love, and to better purpose than before. His passion for her had been strengthened by what he was pleased to call her desertion of him. He proposed marriage, and offered to adopt the boy. Mary Wyvis accepted both propositions, and left England with him almost immediately, in order to escape mocking and slanderous tongues.

It was inevitable that evil should be said of her. Mark Brand's pursuit of her before her marriage to Wyvis had been well known. That she should marry him so soon after her first husband's death seemed to point to some continued understanding between the two, and caused much gossip in the neighborhood. Such gossip was really unfounded, for Mary was a good woman in her way, though not a very wise one; but the charges against her were believed in many places, and never disproved. It was even whispered that the little boy was Mark Brand's own son, and that John Wyvis had met his death through some foul play. Rumors of this kind died down in course of time. But they were certainly sufficient to account for the disfavor with which the County eyed the Brands in general, and Mrs. Brand in particular. Mark Brand lived very little at the Red House after his marriage. He knew what a storm of indignation had been spent upon his conduct, and he was well aware of the aspersions on his wife's character. He was too reckless by nature to try to set things straight: he considered that he did his best for his family when he left England behind him, and trained the boys, Wyvis and Cuthbert, to love a foreign land better than their own.

He grew very fond of Mary's boy during the first few years of his married life. This fondness led him to wish that the boy were his own, and the appearance of Cuthbert did not alter this odd liking for another man's son. He never cared very much for Cuthbert, who was delicate and lame from babyhood; but Wyvis was the apple of his eye. The boy was called John Wyvis: it was easy enough in a foreign country to let him slip into the position of the eldest of the family as Wyvis Brand. A baby son was born before Cuthbert, and dying a month old, gave Mark all the opportunity that he needed. He sent word to old Wyvis at Roxby that John's boy was dead; and he then quietly substituted Wyvis in place of his own son. Every year, he argued, would make the real difference of age between John's boy and the dead child less apparent: it would save trouble to speak of Wyvis as his own, and troublesome inquiries were not likely to be made. Time and use made him almost forget that Wyvis did not really belong to him; and but for his wife's insistence he would not even have made the will which secured the Red House to his adopted son. Cuthbert was of course treated with scandalous injustice by this will; but the secret had been well kept, and the story was fully known to nobody save the Brands' lawyer and Mary Brand herself.

The way in which Lady Caroline had ferreted out the secret remained a mystery to the Brands. But they never gave her half enough credit for her remarkable cleverness. When she saw Wyvis Brand, she had been struck almost at once by his likeness to John Wyvis, the man who married her old favorite, Mary. She leaped quickly to the conviction that he was not Mark Brand's son. And when Margaret's infatuation for him declared itself, she went straight to her husband's man of business, and commissioned him to find out all that could be found out about the Brands during the period of their early married life in Italy. The task was surprisingly easy. Mark Brand had taken few precautions, for he had drifted rather than deliberately steered towards the substitution of Wyvis for his own eldest son. A very few inquiries elicited all that Lady Caroline wanted to know. But she had not been quite sure of her facts when she entered the Red House, and, if Mrs. Brand had been a little cooler and a little braver, she might have defeated her enemy's ends, and carried her secret inviolate to her grave.

But courage and coolness were the last things that could be expected from Mrs. Brand. She had never possessed a strong mind and the various chances and changes of her life had enfeebled instead of strengthening it. Mark Brand had proved by no means a loving or faithful husband, and did not scruple to taunt her with her inferiority of position, and to threaten that he would mortify Wyvis' pride some day by a revelation of his true name and descent. He was too fond of Wyvis to carry his threat into effect but he made the poor woman, his wife, suffer an infinity of torture, the greater part of which might have been avoided if she had chanced to be gifted with a higher spirit and a firmer will.

Wyvis Brand went immediately to London after the interview with his lawyer in Beaminster, and from London, in a few days, he wrote to Cuthbert. The letter was curt, but not unfriendly. He wished, he said, to repair the injustice that had been done, and to restore to Cuthbert the inheritance that was his by right. He had already instructed his lawyers to take the necessary steps, and he was glad to think that Cuthbert and Nora would now be able to make the Red House what it ought to be. He hoped that they would be very happy. For himself, he thought of immigrating: he was heartily sick of modern civilization, and believed that he would more easily find friends and fellow-workers amongst the Red Skins of the Choctaw Indians than in "County" drawing-rooms. And only by this touch did Wyvis betray the bitterness that filled his heart.

Cuthbert rushed up to town at once in a white heat of indignation. He was only just in time to find Wyvis at his hotel, for he had taken his passage to America, and was going to start almost immediately. But there was time at least for a very energetic discussion between the two young men.

"If you think," said Cuthbert, hotly, "that I'm going to take your place, you are very much mistaken."

"It is not my place. It has been mine only by fraud."

"Not a bit of it. It is yours by my father's will. He knew the truth, and chose to take this course."

"Very unfair to you, Cuth," said Wyvis, a faint smile showing itself for the first time on his haggard face.

Cuthbert shrugged his shoulders. "My dear fellow, do you suppose it's any news to me that my father cared more for your little finger than for my whole body? He chose—practically—to disinherit me in your favor; and a very good thing it's been for me too. I should never have taken to Art if I had been a landed proprietor."

"I don't understand it," said Wyvis, meditatively. "One would have expected him to be jealous of his wife's family—and then you're a much better fellow than I am."

"That was the reason," said Cuthbert, sitting down and nursing his lame leg, after a characteristic fashion of his own "I was a meek child—a sickly lad who didn't get into mischief. I was afraid of horses, you may remember, and hated manly exercises of every kind. Now you were never so happy as when you were on a horse's back— —"

"A strain inherited from my ploughman father, I suppose," said Wyvis, rather grimly.

"And you got into scrapes innumerable; for which he liked you all the better. And you—well you know, old boy, you were never a reproach to him, as the sight of me was!"

Cuthbert's voice dropped. He had never spoken of it before, but he and Wyvis knew well enough that his lameness was the result of his father's brutal treatment of Mary Brand shortly before the birth of her second son.

"He ought to have been more bent on making amends than on sacrificing you to me," said Wyvis, bitterly.

"Oh, don't look at it in that way," Cuthbert answered. The natural sweetness of his disposition made it painful to him to hear his father blamed, although that father had done his best to make his life miserable. "He never meant to hurt me, the poor old man; and when he had done it, the sight of my infirmity became exquisitely painful to him. I can forgive him that; I can forgive him everything. There are others whom it is more difficult to forgive."

"You mean— —"

"I mean women who have not the courage to be true," said Cuthbert, in a low voice. He did not look at his brother, but he felt certain that a thrill of pain passed through him. For a minute or two Wyvis did not speak.

"Well," he said at last, forcing an uneasy laugh, "I think that she was perhaps right. She might not have been very happy. And I doubt, after all, whether I ought to have asked her. Janetta thought not, at any rate."

"Janetta is generally very wise."

"So she is very wise. I am legally quite free, but she thinks me— morally—bound."

"Well, so do I," said Cuthbert, frankly. "On all moral and religious grounds, I think you are as much bound as ever you were. And if Miss Adair refused you on those grounds, she has more right on her side than I thought."

"Ah, but she did not," answered Wyvis, dryly. "She refused me because I was not rich, not 'in society,' and a ploughman's son."

"That's bad," said his brother. And then the two sat for a little time in silence, which is the way of Englishmen when one wishes to show sympathy for another.

"But we are not approaching what I want to say at all," said Cuthbert, presently. "We must not let our feelings run away with us. We are both in a very awkward position, old boy, but we shan't make it better by publishing it to the world. If you throw up the place in this absurd fashion—excuse the term—you *will* publish it to the world at large."

"Do you think that matters to me?" asked Wyvis, sternly.

"Perhaps not to you. But it matters to mother, and to me. And it affects our father's character."

"Your father's, not mine."

"He was the only father you ever knew, and you have no reason to find fault with him."

Wyvis groaned impatiently. "One has duties to the living, not to the dead."

"One has duties to the dead, too. You can't give up the Red House to me—even if I would take it, which I won't—without having the whole story made public. My father hasn't a very good reputation in the County: people will think no better of him for having lamed me, disinherited me, and practiced a fraud on them. That's what they will say about the affair, you know. We can't let the world know."

"Then I'd better go and shoot myself. It seems to me the only thing I can do."

"And what about Julian? The estate would pass to him, of course," said Cuthbert, coolly. He saw that Wyvis' face changed a little at the mention of Julian's name.

"No, I could will it to you—make it over to you, with the condition that it should go to the Foundling Hospital if you wouldn't accept it."

"I think that a will of that kind could be easily set aside on the ground of insanity," said Cuthbert, with a slight smile.

"I could find a way out of the difficulty, if I tried, I have no doubt," said Wyvis, frowning gloomily and pulling at his moustache.

"*Don't* try," said his brother, leaning forward and speaking persuasively. "Let things continue much as they are. I am content: Nora is content. Why should you not be so, too?" Then, as Wyvis shook his head: "Make your mind easy then if you must do something, by giving me a sum down, or a slice of your income, old man. Upon my word I wouldn't live in the old place if you gave it to me. It is picturesque—but damp. Come let's compromise matters."

"I love every stick and stone in the place," said Wyvis grimly.

"I know you do. I don't. I want to live in Paris or Vienna with Nora, and enjoy myself I don't want to paint pot-boilers. I say like the man in the parable, 'Give me the portion that belongeth to me,' and I'll go my way, promising, however, not to spend it in riotous living. Won't that arrangement suit you?"

Wyvis demurred at first, but was finally persuaded into making an arrangement of the kind that Cuthbert desired. He retained the Red House, but he bestowed on his brother enough to give him an ample income for the life that Cuthbert and Nora wished to lead. During his absence from England, Mrs. Brand and Julian were still to inhabit the Red House. And Wyvis announced his intention of going to South America to shoot big game, from which Cuthbert inferred that his heart, although bruised, was not broken yet.

CHAPTER XXXIV
FROM DISTANT LANDS

More than a year had passed away since the events recorded in the last chapter. Early autumn was beginning to touch the leaves with gold and crimson; the later flowers were coming into bloom, and the fruit hung purple and russet-red upon the boughs. The woods about Beaminster had put on a gorgeous mantle, and the gardens were gay with color, and yet over all there hung the indefinable brooding melancholy that comes of the first touch of decay. It was of this that Janetta Colwyn was chiefly conscious, as she walked in the Red House grounds and looked at the yellowing leaves that eddied through the still air to the gravelled walks and unshorn lawns below. Janetta was thinner and paler than in days of yore, and yet there was a peaceful expression upon her face which gave it an added charm. She had discarded her black gowns and wore a pretty dark red dress which suited her admirably. There was a look of thought and feeling in her dark eyes, a sweetness in her smile, which would always redeem her appearance from the old charge of insignificance that used to be brought against it. Small and slight she might be, but never a woman to be overlooked.

The past few months had seen several changes in her family. Mrs. Colwyn was now Mrs. Burroughs, and filled her place with more dignity than had been expected. She was kept in strict order by her husband and his sister, and, like many weak persons, was all the better and happier for feeling a strong hand over her. The children had accommodated themselves very well to the new life, and were very fond of their stepfather. Nora and Cuthbert had quitted the Red House almost immediately after their marriage, and gone to Paris, whence Nora wrote glowing accounts to her sister of the happiness of her life. And Janetta had taken up her abode at the Red House, nominally as governess to little Julian, and companion to Mrs. Brand, but practically ruler of the household, adviser-in-chief to every one on the estate; teacher, comforter, and confidante in turn, or all at once. She could not remain long in any place without winning trust and affection, and there was not a servant in Wyvis Brand's employ who did not soon learn that the best way of gaining help in need or redress for any grievance was to address himself or herself to little Miss Colwyn. To Mrs. Brand, now more weak and ailing than ever, Janetta was like a daughter. And secure in her love, little Julian never knew what it was to miss a mother's care.

Janetta might have her own private cares and worries, but in public, at any rate, she was seldom anything but cheerful. It was a duty that she owed the world, she thought, to look bright in it, and especially a duty to Mrs. Brand and little Julian, who would sorely have missed her ready playfulness and her tender little jokes if ever she had forgotten herself so far as to put on a gloomy countenance. And yet she sometimes felt very much dispirited. She had no prospects of prosperity; she could not expect to live at the Red House for ever; and yet, when Wyvis came home and she had to go—which, of course, must happen some time, since Mrs. Brand was growing old and infirm, and Julian would have to go to school—what would she do? She asked herself this question many times, and could never find a very satisfactory answer. She might advertise for a situation: she might take lodgings in London, and give lessons: she might go to the house of her stepfather. Each of these attempts to solve the problem of her future gave her a cold shudder and a sudden sickness of heart. And yet, as she often severely told herself, what else was there for her to do?

She had heard nothing of the Adairs, save through common town gossip, for many months. The house was shut up, and they were still travelling abroad. Margaret had evidently quite given up her old friend, Janetta, and this desertion made Janetta's heart a little sore. Wyvis also was in foreign lands. He had been to many places, and killed a great many wild beasts—so much all the world knew, and few people knew anything more. To his mother he wrote seldom, though kindly. An occasional note to Julian, or a post card to Cuthbert or his agent, would give a new address from time to time, but it was to Janetta only that he sometimes wrote a really long and interesting epistle, detailing some of his adventures in the friendly and intimate way which his acquaintance with her seemed to warrant. He did not mention any of his private affairs: he never spoke of that painful last scene at the Red House, of Margaret, of his mother, of his wife; but he wrote of the scenes through which he passed, and the persons whom he met, with an unreserve which Janetta knew to be the sincerest compliment.

But on this autumnal day she had received a letter in which another note was struck. And it was for this reason that she had brought it out into the garden, so that she might think over it, and read it again in the shadow of the great beech trees, away from the anxious eyes of Mrs. Brand and the eager childish questions of Wyvis' boy.

For three pages Wyvis had written in his usual strain. He was not perhaps an ideally good letter-writer, but he had a terse, forcible style of his own, and could describe a scene with some amount of graphic power. In the midst of an account of certain brigands with whom he had met in Sicily, however, he had, in this letter, broken off quite suddenly and struck into a new subject in a new and unexpected way.

"I had written thus far when I was interrupted: the date of the letter, you will see, is three weeks ago. I put down my pen and went out: I found that fever had made its appearance, so I packed up my traps that afternoon and started for Norway. A sudden change, you will say? Heaven knows why I went there, but I am glad I did.

"It was early in July when I reached the hotel at V— —. There was *table d'hote* and many another sign of civilization, which bored me not a little. However, I made the best of a bad job, and went down to dinner with the rest, took my seat without noticing my companions until I was seated, and then found myself next to—can you guess who, Janetta?—I am sure you never will.

"*Lady Caroline Adair!!!*

"Her daughter was just beyond her, and Mr. Adair beyond the daughter, so the fair Margaret was well guarded. Of course I betrayed no sign of recognition, but I wished myself at Jericho very heartily. For, between ourselves, Janetta, I made such an ass of myself last summer that my ears burn to think of it, and it was not a particularly honorable or gentlemanly ass, I believe, so that I deserve to be drowned in the deep sea for my folly. I can only hope that I did not show what I felt.

"Miss Adair was blooming: fair, serene, self-possessed as ever. *She* did not show any sign of embarrassment, I can tell you. She did not even blush. She looked at me once or twice with the faint, well-bred indifference with which the well-brought-up young lady usually eyes a perfect stranger. It was Mr. Adair who did all the embarrassment for us. He turned purple when he saw me, and wanted his daughter to come away from the table. My ears are quick, and I heard what he said to her, and I heard also her reply. 'Why should I go away, dear papa! I don't mind in the least.' Kind of her not to mind, wasn't it? And do you think I was going to 'mind,' after that? I lifted up my head, which I had hitherto bent studiously over my soup, and began to talk to my neighbor on the other side, a stalwart English clergyman with a blue ribbon at his button-hole.

"But presently, to my surprise, Lady Caroline addressed me. 'I hope you have not forgotten me, Mr. Brand,' she said, quite graciously. I must confess, Janetta, that I stared at her. The calm audacity of the woman took me by surprise. She looked as amiable as if we were close friends meeting after a long absence. I hope you won't be very angry with me when I tell you how I answered her. 'Pardon me,' I said, 'my name is Wyvis—not Brand.' And then I went on talking to my muscular Christian on the left.

"She looked just a little bit disconcerted. Not much, you know. It would take a great deal to disconcert Lady Caroline very much. But she did not try to talk to me again! I choked her off that time, anyhow.

"And, now, let me make a confession. I don't admire Margaret Adair in the very least. I did, I know: and I made a fool of myself, and worse, perhaps, about her: but she does, not move one fibre of my heart now, she does not make it beat a bit faster, and she does not give my eye more pleasure than a wax doll would give me. She is fair and sweet and tranquil, I know: but what has she done with her heart and her brain? I suppose her mother has them in her keeping, and will make them over to her husband when she marries?... I know a woman who is worth a dozen Margarets....

"But I have made up my mind to live single, so long as Julian's mother is alive. Legally, I am not bound; morally, I can scarcely feel myself free. And I know that you feel with me, Janet. The world may call us over-scrupulous; but I set your judgment higher than that of the world. And all I can say about Margaret is that I fell into a passing fit of madness, and cared for nothing but what my fancy dictated; and that now I am sane—clothed in my right mind, so to speak—I am disgusted with myself for my folly. Lady Caroline and her daughter should have taken higher ground. They were right to send me away—but not right to act on unworthy motives. In the long nights that I have spent camping out under the quiet stars, far away from the dwellings of men, I have argued the thing out with myself, and I say unreservedly that they were right and I was wrong—wrong from beginning to end, wrong to my mother, wrong to my wife (as she once was), wrong to Margaret, wrong to myself. Your influence has always been on the side of right and truth, Janetta, and you more than once told me that I was wrong.

"So I make my confession. I do not think that I shall come back to England just yet. I am going to America next week. You will not leave the Red House, will you? While you are there I can feel at ease about my mother and my boy. I trust you with them entirely, Janetta; and I want you to trust me. Wherever I may go, and whatever I may do, I will henceforward be worthy of your trust and of your friendship."

This was the letter that Janetta read under the beech trees; and as she read it tears gathered in her eyes and fell upon the pages. But they were not tears of sadness—rather tears of joy and thankfulness. For Wyvis Brand's aberration of mind—so it had always appeared to her—had given her much pain and sorrow. And he seemed now to have placed his foot upon the road to better things.

She was still holding the letter in her hand when she reached the end of the beech-tree shaded walk along which she had been slowly walking. The tears were wet upon her cheeks, but a smile played on her lips. She did not notice for some time that she was watched from the gate that led into the pasture-land, at the end of the beech-tree walk, by a woman, who seemed uncertain whether to speak, to enter, or to go away.

Janetta saw her at last, and wondered what she was doing there. She put the letter into her pocket, dashed the tears from her eyes, and advanced towards the gate.

"Can I do anything for you?" she said.

The woman looked about thirty-five years old, and possessed the remains of great beauty. She was haggard and worn: her cheeks were sunken, though brilliantly red, and her large, velvety-brown eyes were strangely bright. Her dark, waving hair had probably once been curled over her brow: it now hung almost straight, and had a rough, dishevelled look, which corresponded with the soiled and untidy appearance of her dress. Her gown and mantle were of rich stuff, but torn and stained in many places; and her gloves and boots were shabby to the very last degree, while her bonnet, of cheap and tawdry materials, had at any rate the one merit of being fresh and new. Altogether she was an odd figure to be seen in a country place; and Janetta wondered greatly whence she came, and what her errand was at the Red House.

"Can I do anything for you?" she asked.

"This is the Red House, I suppose?" the woman asked, hoarsely.

"Yes, it is."

"Wyvis Brand's house?"

Janetta hesitated in surprise, and then said, "Yes," in a rather distant tone.

"Who are *you*?" said the woman, looking at her sharply.

"I am governess to Mr. Brand's little boy."

"Oh, indeed. And he's at home, I suppose?"

"No," said Janetta, gravely, "he has been away for more than a year, and is now, I believe, on his way to America."

"You lie!" said the woman, furiously; "and you know that you lie!"

Janetta recoiled a step. Was this person mad?

"He is at home, and you want to keep me out," the woman went on, wildly. "You don't want me to set foot in the place, or to see my child again! He is at home, and I'll see him if I have to trample on your body first."

"Nobody wants to keep you out," said Janetta, forcing herself to speak and look calmly, but tingling with anger from head to foot. "But I assure you Mr. Brand is away from home. His mother lives here; she is not very strong, and ought not to be disturbed. If you will give me your name— —"

"My name?" repeated the other in a tone of mockery. "Oh yes, I'll give you my name. I don't see why I should hide it; do you? I've been away a good long time; but I mean to have my rights now. My name is Mrs. Wyvis Brand: what do you think of that, young lady?"

She drew herself up as she spoke, looking gaunt and defiant. Her eyes flamed and her cheeks grew hotter and deeper in tint until they were poppy-red. She showed her teeth—short, square, white teeth—as if she wanted to snarl like an angry dog. But Janetta, after the first moment of repulsion and astonishment, was not dismayed.

"I did not know," she said, gravely, "that you had any right to call yourself by that name. I thought that you were divorced from Mr. Wyvis Brand."

"Separated for incompatibility of temper; that was all," said Mrs. Brand coolly. "I told him I'd got a divorce, but it wasn't true. I wanted to be free from him—that's the truth. I didn't mean him to marry again. I heard that he was going to be married—is that so! Perhaps he was going to marry *you*?"

"No," Janetta answered, very coldly.

"I'm not going to put up with it if he is," was her visitor's sullen reply. "I've borne enough from him in my day, I can tell you. So I've come for the boy. I'm going to have him back; and when I've got him I've no doubt but what I can make Wyvis do what I choose. I hear he's fond of the boy."

"But what—what—do you want him to do?" said Janetta, startled out of her reserve. "Do you want—*money* from him?"

Mrs. Wyvis Brand laughed hoarsely. Janetta noticed that her breath was very short, and that she leaned against the gate-post for support.

"No, not precisely," she said. "I want more than that. I see that he's got a nice, comfortable, respectable house; and I'm tired of wandering. I'm ill, too, I believe. I want a place in which to be quiet and rest, or die, as it may turn out. I mean Wyvis to take me back."

She opened the gate as she spoke, and tried to pass Janetta. But the girl stood in her way.

"Take you back after you have left him and ill-treated him and deceived him, you wicked woman!" she broke out, in her old impetuous way. And for answer, Mrs. Wyvis Brand raised her hand and struck her sharply across the face.

A shrill, childish cry rang out upon the air. Janetta stood mute and trembling, unable for the moment to move or speak, as little Julian suddenly flung himself into her arms and tried to drag her towards the house.

"Oh, come away, come away, dear Janetta!" he cried. "It's mamma, and she'll take me back to Paris, I know she will! I won't go away from you, I won't, I won't!" His mother sprung towards him, as if to tear him from Janetta's arm, and then her strength seemed suddenly to pass from her. She stopped, turned ghastly white, and then as suddenly very red. Then she flung up her arms with a gasping, gurgling cry, and, to Janetta's horror, she saw a crimson tide break from her quivering lips. She was just in time to catch her in her arms before she sank senseless to the ground.

CHAPTER XXXV
JULIET

There was no help for it. Into Wyvis Brand's house Wyvis Brand's wife must go. Old Mrs. Brand came feebly into the garden, and identified the woman as the mother of Julian, and the wife of her eldest son. She could not be allowed to die at their door. She could not be taken to any other dwelling. There were laborers' cottages only in the immediate vicinity. She must be brought to the Red House and nursed by Janetta and Mrs. Brand. A woman with a broken blood-vessel, how unworthy soever she might be, could not be sent to the Beaminster Hospital three miles away. Common humanity forbade it. She must, for a time at least, be nursed in the place where she was taken ill.

So she was carried indoors and laid in the best bedroom, which was a gloomy-looking place until Janetta began to make reforms in it. When she had put fresh curtains to the windows, and set flowers on the window-sill, and banished some of the old black furniture, the room looked a trifle more agreeable, and there was nothing on which poor Juliet Brand's eye could dwell with positive dislike or dissatisfaction when she came to herself. But for some time she lay at the very point of death, and it seemed to Janetta and to all the watchers at the bedside that Mrs. Wyvis Brand could not long continue in the present world.

Mrs. Brand the elder seldom came into the room. She showed a singular horror of her daughter-in-law: she would not even willingly speak of her. She pleaded her ill-health as an excuse for not taking her share of the nursing; and when it seemed likely that Janetta would be worn out by it, she insisted that a nurse from the Beaminster Hospital should be procured. "It will not be for long," she said gloomily, when Janetta spoke regretfully of the expense. For Janetta was chief cashier and financier in the household.

But it appeared as if she were mistaken. Mrs. Brand did not die, as everybody expected. She lay for a time in a very weak state, and then began gradually to recover strength. Before long, she was able to converse, and then she showed a preference for Janetta's society which puzzled the girl not a little. For Julian she also showed some fondness, but he sometimes wearied, sometimes vexed her, and a visit of a very few minutes sufficed for both mother and son. Julian himself exhibited not only dislike but terror of her. He tried to run away and hide when the hour came for his daily visit to his mother's room; and when Janetta spoke to him on the subject rather anxiously, he burst into tears and avowed he was afraid.

"Afraid of what?" said Janetta.

But he only sobbed and would not tell.

"She can't hurt you, Julian, dear. She is ill and weak and lonely; and she loves you. It's not kind and loving of you to run away."

"I don't want to be unkind."

"Or unloving?" said Janetta.

"I don't love her," the boy answered, and bit his lip. His eye flashed for a moment, and then he looked down as if he were ashamed of the confession.

"Julian, dear? Your mother?"

"I can't help it. She hasn't been very much like a mother to me."

"You should not say that, dear. She loves you very much; and all people do not love in the same way."

"Oh, it isn't that," said the boy, as if in desperation. "I know she loves me, but—but——" And there he broke down in a passion of tears and sobs, amidst which Janetta could distinguish only a few words, such as "Suzanne said"—"father"—"make me wicked too."

"Do you mean," said Janetta, more shocked than she liked to show, "that you think your father wicked?"

"Oh, no, no! Suzanne said mother was not good. Not father."

"But, my dear boy, you must not say that your mother is not good. You have no reason to say so, and it is a terrible thing to say."

"She was unkind to father—and to me, too," Julian burst forth. "And she struck you; she is wicked and unkind, and I don't love her. And Suzanne said she would make me wicked, too, and that I was just like her; and I don't want—to—be—wicked."

"Nobody can make you wicked if you are certain that you want to be good," said Janetta, gravely; "and it was very wrong of Suzanne to say anything that could make you think evil of your mother."

"Isn't she naughty, then?" Julian asked in a bewildered tone.

"I do not know," Janetta answered, very seriously. "Only God knows that. We cannot tell. It is the last thing we ought say."

"But—but—you call me naughty sometimes?" the child said, fixing a pair of innocent, inquiring eyes upon her.

"Ah, but, my dear, I do not love you the less," said Janetta, out of the fullness of her heart, and she took him in her arms and kissed him.

"You are more like what I always think a mother ought to be," said Julian. What stabs children inflict on us sometimes by their artless words! Janetta shuddered a little as he spoke. "Then ought I to love her, whether she is good or bad?"

Janetta paused. She was very anxious to say only what was right.

"Yes, my darling," she said at last. "Love her always, through everything. She is your mother, and she has a right to your love."

And then, in simple words, she talked to him about right and wrong, about love and duty and life, until, with brimming eyes, he flung his arms about her, and said——

"Yes, I understand now. And I will love her and take care of her always, because God sent me to her to do that."

And he objected no more to the daily visit to his mother's room.

The sick woman's restless eyes, sharpened by illness, soon discerned the change in his demeanor.

"You've been talking to that boy about me," she said one day to Janetta, in a quick, sensitive voice.

"Nothing that would hurt you," Janetta replied, smiling.

"Oh, indeed, I'm not so sure of that. He used to run away from me, and now he sits beside me like a lamb. I know what you've been saying."

"What?" said Janetta.

"You've been saying that I'm going to die, and that he won't be bothered with me long. Eh?"

"No; nothing of that kind."

"What did you say, then?"

"I told him," said Janetta, slowly, "that God sent him to you as a little baby to be a help and comfort to you; and that it was a son's duty to protect and sustain his mother, as she had once protected and sustained him."

"And you think he understood that sort of nonsense?"

"You see for yourself whether he does or not," said Janetta, gently. "He likes to come and see you and sit beside you now."

Mrs. Wyvis Brand was silent for a minute or two. A tear gathered in each of her defiant black eyes, but she did not allow either of them to fall.

"You're a queer one," she said, with a hard laugh. "I never met anybody like you before. You're religious, aren't you?"

"I don't know: I should like to be," said Janetta, soberly.

"That's the queerest thing you've said yet. And all you religious people look down on folks like me."

"Then I'm not religious, for I don't look down on folks like you at all," said Janetta, calmly adopting Mrs. Brand's vocabulary.

"Well, you ought to. I'm not a very good sort myself."

Janetta smiled, but made no other answer: And presently Juliet Brand remarked—

"I dare say I'm not so bad as some people, but I've never been a saint, you know. And the day I came here I was in an awful temper. I struck you, didn't I?"

"Oh, never mind that," said Janetta, hastily. "You were tired: you hardly knew what you were doing."

"Yes, I did," said Mrs. Brand. "I knew perfectly well. But I hated you, because you lived here and had care of Julian. I had heard all about you at Beaminster, you see. And people said that you would probably marry Wyvis when he came home again. Oh, I've made you blush, have I? It was true then?"

"Not at all; and you have no right to say so."

"Don't be angry, my dear. I don't want to vex you. But it looks to me rather as though——Well, we won't say any more about it since it vexes you. I shan't trouble you long, most likely, and then Wyvis can do as he pleases. But you see it was that thought that maddened me when I came here, and I felt as if I'd like to fall upon you and tear you limb from limb. So I struck you on the face when you tried to thwart me."

"But—I don't understand," said Janetta, tremulously. "I thought you did not—love—Wyvis."

Mrs. Brand laughed. "Not in your way," she said in an enigmatic tone. "But a woman can hate a man and be jealous of him too. And I was jealous of you, and struck you. And in return for that you've nursed me night and day, and waited on me, until you're nearly worn out, and the doctor says

I owe my life to you. Don't you think I'm right when I say you're a queer one?"

"It would be very odd if I neglected you when you were ill just because of a moment of passion on your part," said Janetta, rather stiffly. It was difficult to her to be perfectly natural just then.

"Would it? Some people wouldn't say so. But come—you say I don't love Wyvis?"

"I thought so—certainly."

"Well, look here," said Wyvis' wife. "I'll tell you something. Wyvis was tired of me before ever he married me. I soon found that out. And you think I should be caring for him then? Not I. But there *was* a time when I would have kissed the very ground he walked on. But he never cared for me like that."

"Then—why——".

"Why did he marry me? Chiefly because his old fool of a mother egged him on. She should have let us alone."

"Did she want him to marry you?" said Janetta, in some amaze.

"It doesn't seem likely, does it?" said Mrs. Brand, with a sharp, heartless little laugh. "But she sets up for having a conscience now and then. I was a girl in a shop, I may tell you, and Wyvis made love to me without the slightest idea of marrying me. Then Mrs. Brand comes on the scene: 'Oh, my dear boy, you mustn't make that young woman unhappy. I was made unhappy by a gentleman when I was a girl, and I don't want you to behave as he did."

"And that was very good of Mrs. Brand!" said Janetta, courageously.

Juliet made a grimace. "After a fashion. She had better have let us alone. She put Wyvis into a fume about his honor; and so he asked me to marry him. And I cared for him—though I cared more about his position—and I said yes. So we were married, and a nice cat and dog life we had of it together."

"And then you left him?"

"Yes, I did. I got tired of it all at last. But I always lived respectably, except for taking a little too much stimulant now and then; and I never brought any dishonor on his name. And at last I thought the best thing for us both would be to set him free. And I wrote to him that he *was* free. But there was some hitch—I don't know what exactly. Any way, we're bound to each other as fast as ever we were, so we needn't think to get rid of each other just yet."

Janetta felt a throb of thankfulness, for Margaret's sake. Suppose she had yielded to Wyvis' solicitations and become his wife, to be proved only no wife at all? Her want of love for Wyvis had at least saved her from terrible misery. Mrs. Brand went on, reflectively—

"When I'm gone, he can marry whom he likes. I only hope it'll be anybody as good as you. You'd make a capital mother to Julian. And I don't suppose I shall trouble anybody very long."

"You are getting better—you will soon be perfectly well."

"Nonsense: nothing of the kind. But if I am, I know one thing," said Mrs. Brand, in a petulant tone; "I won't be kept out of my rights any longer. This house seems to be nice and comfortable: I shall stay here. I am tired of wandering about the world."

Janetta was silent and went on with some needle-work.

"You don't like that, do you?" said Mrs. Brand, peering into her face. "You think I'd be better away."

"No," said Janetta. But she could not say more.

"Do you know where he is?"

"He? Wyvis?"

"Yes, my husband."

"I have an address. I do not know whether he is there or not, but he would no doubt get a letter if sent to the place. Do you wish to write to him?"

"No. But I want you to write. Write and say that I am here. Ask him to come back."

"You had better write yourself."

"No. He would not read it. Write for me."

Janetta could not refuse. But she felt it one of the hardest tasks that she had ever had to perform in life. She was sorry for Juliet Brand, but she shrank with all her heart and soul from writing to Wyvis to return to her. Yet what else could she do?

CHAPTER XXXVI
THE FRUITS OF A LIE

When she told old Mrs. Brand what she had done, she was amazed to mark the change which came over that sad and troubled countenance. Mrs. Brand's face flushed violently, her eyes gleamed with a look as near akin to wrath as any which Janetta had ever seen upon it.

"You have promised to write to Wyvis?" she cried. "Why? What is it to you? Why should you write?"

"Why should I not?" asked Janetta, in surprise.

"He will never come back to her—never. And it is better so. She spoiled his life with her violence, her extravagance, her flirtations. He could not bear it; and why should he be brought back to suffer all again?"

"She is his wife still," said the girl, in a low tone.

"They are separated. She tried to get a divorce, even if she did not succeed. I do not call her his wife."

Janetta shook her head. "I cannot think of it as you do, then," she said, quietly. "She and Wyvis are married; and as they separated only for faults of temper, not for unfaithfulness, I do not believe that they have any right to divorce each other. Some people may think differently—I cannot see it in that way."

"You mean," said Mrs. Brand, with curious agitation of manner; "you mean that even if she had divorced him in America, you would not think him free—free to marry again?"

"No," Janetta answered, "I would not."

She felt a singular reluctance to answering the question, and she hoped that Mrs. Brand would ask her nothing more. She was relieved when Wyvis' mother moved away, after standing perfectly still for a moment, with her hands clasped before her, a strange ashen shade of color disfiguring her handsome old face. Janetta thought the face had grown wonderfully tragic of late; but she hoped that when Juliet had left the house the poor mother would again recover the serenity of mind which she had gained during the past few months of Janetta's gentle companionship.

She wrote her letter to Wyvis, making it as brief and business-like as possible. She dwelt a good deal on Juliet's weakness, on her love for the boy, and her desire to see him once again. At the same time she added her own conviction that Mrs. Wyvis Brand was on the high road to recovery, and would soon be fairly strong and well. She dared not give any hint as to a possible reconciliation, but she felt, even as she penned her letter, that it was to this end that she was working. "And it is right," she said steadily to herself; "there is nothing to gain in disunion: everything to lose by unfaithfulness. It will be better for Julian—for all three—that father and mother should no longer be divided."

But although she argued thus, she had a somewhat different and entirely instinctive feeling in her heart. To begin with, she could not imagine persons more utterly unsuited to one another than Wyvis and his wife. Juliet had no principles, no judgment, to guide her: she was impulsive and passionate; she did not speak the truth, and she seemed in her wilder moments to care little what she did. Wyvis had faults—who knew them better than Janetta, who had studied his character with great and loving care?—but they were nor of the same kind. His mood was habitually sombre; Juliet loved pleasure and variety: his nature was a loving one, strong and deep, although undisciplined; but Juliet's light and fickle temperament made her shrink from and almost dislike characteristics so different from her own. And Janetta soon saw that in spite of her open defiance of her husband she was a little afraid of him; and she could well imagine that when Wyvis was angry he was a man of whom a woman might very easily be afraid.

Yet, when the letter was despatched, Janetta felt a sense of relief. She had at least done her duty, as she conceived of it. She did not know what the upshot might be; but at any rate, she had done her best to put matters in train towards the solving of the problem of Wyvis' married life.

She was puzzled during the next few days by some curious, indefinable change in Mrs. Brand's demeanor. The poor woman had of late seemed almost distraught; she had lost all care, apparently, for appearances, and went along the corridors moaning Wyvis' name sadly to herself, and wringing her hands as if in bitter woe. Her dress was neglected, and her hair unbrushed: indeed, when Janetta was too busy to give her a daughter's loving care, as it was her custom and her pleasure to do, poor Mrs. Brand roamed about the house looking like a madwoman. Her madness was, however, of a gentle kind: it took the form of melancholia, and manifested itself chiefly by continual restlessness and occasional bursts of weeping and lament.

In one of these outbreaks Janetta found her shortly after she had sent her letter to Wyvis, and tried by all means in her power to soothe and pacify her.

"Dear grandmother," she began—for she had caught the word from Julian, and Mrs. Brand liked her to use it—"why should you be so sad? Wyvis is coming home, Juliet is better, little Julian is well, and we are all happy."

"*You* are not happy," said Mrs. Brand, throwing up her hands with a curiously tragic gesture. "You are miserable—miserable; and I am the most unhappy woman living!"

"No," I said Janetta, gently. "I am not miserable at all. And there are many women more unhappy than you are. You have a home, sons who love you, a grandson, friends—see how many things you have that other people want! Is it right to speak of yourself as unhappy?"

"Child," said the older woman, impressively, "you are young, and do not know what you say. Does happiness consist in houses and clothes, or even in children and friends? I have been happier in a cottage than in the grandest house. As for friends—what friends have I? None; my husband would never let me make friends lest I should expose my ignorance, and disgrace him by my low birth and bringing up. I have never had a woman friend."

"But your children," said Janetta, putting her arms tenderly round the desolate woman's neck.

"Ah, my children! When they were babies, they were a pleasure to me. But they have never been a pleasure since. They have been a toil and a pain and a bondage. That began when Wyvis was a little child, and Mr. Brand took a fancy to him and wanted to make every one believe that he was *his* child, not John's. I foresaw that there would be trouble, but he would never listen to me. It was just a whim of the moment at first, and then, when he saw that the deceit troubled me, it became a craze with him. And whatever he said, I had to seem to agree with. I dared not contradict him. I hated the deceit, and the more I hated it, the more he loved it and practiced it in my hearing, until I used to be sick with misery. Oh, my dear, it is the worst of miseries to be forced into wrong-doing against your will."

"But why did you give way?" said Janetta, who could not fancy herself in similar circumstances being forced into anything at all.

"My dear, he made me, I dared not cross him. He made me suffer, and he made the children suffer if ever I opposed him. What could I do?" said the poor woman, twisting and untwisting her thin hands, and looking piteously into Janetta's face. "I was obliged to obey him—he was my husband, and so much above me, so much more of a gentleman than I ever was a lady. You know that I never could say him nay. He ruled me, as he used to say, with a rod of iron—for he made a boast of it, my dear—and he was never so happy, I think, as when he was torturing me and making me wince with pain."

"He must have been——" when Janetta stopped short: she could not say exactly what she thought of Mrs. Brand's second husband.

"He was cruel, my dear: cruel, that is, to women. Not cruel amongst his own set—among his equals, as he would have said—not cruel to boys. But always cruel to women. Some woman must have done him a grievous wrong one day—I never knew who she was; but I am certain that it was so; and that soured and embittered him. He was revenging himself on that other woman, I used to think, when he was cruel to me."

Janetta dared not speak.

"I did not mind his cruelty when it meant nothing but bodily pain, you know, my dear," Mrs. Brand continued patiently. "But it was harder for me to bear when it came to what might be called moral things. You see I loved him, and I could not say him nay. If he told me to lie, I had to do it. I never forgave myself for the lies I told at his bidding. And if he were here to tell me to do the same things I should do them still. If he had turned Mohammedan, and told me to trample on the Bible or the Cross, as I have read in missionary books that Christians have sometimes been bribed to do, I should have obeyed him. I was his body and soul, and all my misery has come out of that."

"How?" Janetta asked.

"I brought Wyvis up on a lie," the mother answered, her face growing woefully stern and rigid as she mentioned his name, "and it has been my punishment that he has always hated lies. I have trembled to hear him speak against falsehood—to catch his look of scorn when he began to see that his father did not speak truth. Very early he made me understand that he would never be likely to forgive us for the deception we practiced on him. For his good, you will say; but ah, my dear, deception is never for anybody's good.

I never forgave myself, and Wyvis will never forgive me. And yet he is my child. Now you see the happiness that lies in having children."

Janetta tried to dissipate the morbid terror of the past, the morbid dread of Wyvis' condemnation, which hung like a shadow over the poor woman's mind, but she was far from being successful.

"You do not know," was all that Mrs. Brand would say. "You do not understand." And then she broke out more passionately—

"I have done him harm all his life. His misery has been my fault. You heard him tell me so. It is true: there is no use denying it. And he knows it."

"He spoke in a moment of anger: he did not know what he said."

"Oh, yes, he did, and he meant it too. I have heard him say a similar thing before. You see it was I that brought about this wretched marriage of his—because I pitied this woman, and thought her case was like my own— that she loved Wyvis as I loved Mark Brand. I brought that marriage about, and Wyvis has cursed me ever since."

"No, no," said Janetta, kissing her troubled face, "Wyvis would never curse his mother for doing what she thought right. Wyvis loves you. Surely you know that—you believe that? Wyvis is not a bad son."

"No, my dear, not a bad son, but a cruelly injured one," said Mrs. Brand. "And he blames me. I cannot blame him: it was all my fault for not opposing Mark when he wanted me to help him to carry out his wicked scheme."

"I think," said Janetta, tentatively, "that Cuthbert has more right to feel himself injured than Wyvis."

"Cuthbert?" Mrs. Brand repeated, in an indifferent tone. "Oh, Cuthbert is of no consequence: his father always said so. A lame, sickly, cowardly child! If we had had a strong, healthy lad of our own, Mark would not have put Wyvis in Cuthbert's place, but with a boy like Cuthbert, what would you expect him to do?"

It seemed to Janetta almost as if her mind were beginning to wander: the references to Cuthbert's boyish days appeared to be so extraordinarily clear and defined—almost as though she were living again through the time when Cuthbert was supplanted by her boy Wyvis. But when she spoke again, Mrs. Brand's words were perfectly clear, and apparently reasonable in tone.

"I often think that if I could do my poor boy some great service, he would forgive me in heart as well as in deed. I would do anything in the world for him, Janetta, if only I could give him back the happiness of which I robbed him."

Janetta could not exactly see that the poor mother's sins had been so great against Wyvis as against Cuthbert, but it was evident that Mrs. Brand could never be brought to look at matters in this light. The thought that she had injured her first-born son had taken possession of her completely, and seriously disturbed the balance of her faculties. The desire to make amends to Wyvis for her wrong-doing had already reached almost a maniacal point: how much further it might be carried Janetta never thought of guessing.

She was anxious about Mrs. Brand, but more so for her physical than for her mental strength. For her powers were evidently failing in every direction, and the doctor spoke warningly to Janetta of the weakness of her heart's action, and the desirability of shielding her from every kind of agitation. It was impossible to provide against every kind of shock, but Janetta promised to do her best.

The winter was approaching before Janetta's letter to Wyvis received an answer. She was beginning to feel very anxious about it, for his silence alarmed and also surprised her. She could hardly imagine a man of Wyvis' disposition remaining unmoved when he read the letter that she had sent him. His wife's health was, moreover, giving her serious concern. She had caught cold on one of the foggy autumnal days, and the doctor assured her that her life would be endangered if she did not at once seek a warmer climate. But she steadily refused to leave the Red House.

"I won't go," she said to Janetta, with a red spot of anger on either cheek, "until I know whether he means to do the proper thing by me or not."

"He is sure to do that; you need have no fear," said Janetta, bluntly.

An angry gleam shot from the sick woman's eyes. "You defend him through thick and thin, don't you? Wyvis has a knack of getting women to stick up for him. They say the worst men are often the most beloved."

Janetta left the room, feeling both sick and sorry, and wondering how much longer she could bear this kind of life. It was telling upon her nerves and on her strength in every possible way. And yet she could not abandon her post—unless, indeed, Wyvis himself relieved her. And from him for many weary days there came no word.

But at last a telegram arrived—dated from Liverpool. "I shall be with you to-morrow. Your letter was delayed, and reached me only by accident," Wyvis said. And then his silence was explained.

Janetta carried the news of his approaching arrival to wife and mother in turn. Mrs. Wyvis took it calmly. "I told you so," she said, with a triumphant little nod. But Mrs. Brand was terribly agitated, and even, as it seemed to Janetta, amazed. "I never thought that he would come," she said, in a loud whisper, with a troubled face and various nervous movements of her hands. "I never thought that he would come back to her. I must be quick. I must be quick, indeed." And when Janetta tried to soothe her, and said that she must now make haste to be well and strong when Wyvis was returning, she answered only in about the self-same words—"never thought it, my dear, indeed, I never did. But if he is coming back, so soon, I must be quick—I must be very quick."

And Janetta could not persuade her to say why.

CHAPTER XXXVII
NIGHT

It was the night before Wyvis' return. The whole household seemed somewhat disorganized by the prospect. There was an air of subdued excitement visible in the oldest and staidest of the servants, for in spite of Wyvis' many shortcomings and his equivocal position, he was universally liked by his inferiors, if not by those who esteemed themselves his superiors, in social station. Mrs. Brand had gone to bed early, and Janetta hoped that she was asleep; Mrs. Wyvis had kept Janetta at her bedside until after eleven o'clock, regaling her with an account of her early experience in Paris. When at last she seemed sleepy, Janetta said good-night and went to her own room. She was tired but wakeful. The prospect of Wyvis' return excited her; she felt that it would be impossible to sleep that night, and she resolved therefore to establish herself before the fire in her own room, with a book, and to see, by carefully abstracting her mind from actual fact, whether she could induce the shy goddess, sleep, to visit her.

She read for some time, but she had great difficulty in fixing her mind upon her book. She found herself conning the same words over and over again, without understanding their meaning in the least; her thoughts flew continually to Wyvis and his affairs, and to the mother and wife and son with whom her fate had linked her with such curious closeness. At last she relinquished the attempt to read, and sat for some time gazing into the fire. She heard the clock strike one; the quarter and half-hour followed at intervals, but still she sat on. Anyone who had seen her at that hour would hardly have recognized her for the vivacious, sparkling, ever cheerful woman who made the brightness of the Red House; the sunshine had left her face, her eyes were wistful, almost sad; the lines of her mouth drooped, and her cheeks had grown very pale. She felt very keenly that the period of happy, peaceful work and rest which she had enjoyed for the last few months was coming to an end. She was trying to picture to herself what her future life would be, and it was difficult to imagine it when her old ties had all been severed. "It seems as if I had to give up everybody that I ever cared for," she said to herself, not complainingly, but as one recognizing the fact that some persons are always more or less lonely in the world, and that she belonged to a lonely class. "My father has gone—my brother and sisters do not need me; Margaret abandoned me; Wyvis and his mother and Julian are lost to me from henceforth. God forgive me," said Janetta to herself, burying her face in her hands and shedding some very heartfelt tears, "if I seem to be repining at my friends' good fortune; I do not mean it; I wish them every joy. But what I fear is, lest it should not be for their good—that Wyvis and his mother and Julian should be unhappy."

She was roused from her reflection by a sound in the corridor. It was a creaking board, she knew that well enough; but the board never creaked unless some one trod upon it. Who could be walking about the house at this time of night? Mrs. Brand, perhaps; she was terribly restless at night, and often went about the house, seeking to tire herself so completely that sleep would be inevitable on her return to bed. On a cold night, such expeditions were not, however, unattended by danger, as she was not careful to protect herself against draughts, and it was with the desire to care for her that Janetta at last rose and took up a soft warm shawl with which she thought that she might cover Mrs. Brand's shoulders.

With the shawl over her arm and a candle in one hand she opened her door and looked out into the passage. It was unlighted, and the air seemed very chilly. Janetta stole along the corridor like a thief, and peeped into Mrs. Brand's bedroom; as was expected, it was empty. Then she looked into Julian's room, for she had several times found the grandmother praying by his bed, at dead of night; but Julian slumbered peacefully, and nobody else was there. Janetta rather wonderingly turned her attention to the lower rooms of the house. But Mrs. Brand was not to be found in any of the sitting rooms; and the hall door was securely locked and bolted, so that she could not have gone out into the garden.

"She must be upstairs," said Janetta to herself. "But what can she be doing in that upper storey, where there are only empty garrets and servants rooms! I did not look into the spare room, however; perhaps she has gone to see if it is ready for Wyvis, and I did not go to Juliet. She cannot have gone to *her*, surely; she never enters the room unless she is obliged."

Nevertheless, her heart began to beat faster, and she involuntarily quickened her steps. She did not believe that Mrs. Brand would seek Juliet's room with any good intent, and as she reached the top of the stairs her eyes dilated and her face grew suddenly pale with fear. For a strange whiff of something—was it smoke?—came into her eyes, and an odd smell of burning assailed her nostrils. Fire, was it fire? She remembered that Wyvis had once said that the Red House would burn like tinder if it was ever set alight. The old woodwork was very combustible, and there was a great deal of it, especially in the upper rooms.

Juliet's door was open. Janetta stood before it for the space of one half second, stupefied and aghast. Smoke was rapidly filling the room and circling into the corridor; the curtains near the window were in a blaze, and Mrs. Brand, with a lighted candle in her hand, was deliberately setting fire to the upholstery of the bed where the unconscious Juliet lay. Janetta never forgot the moment's vision that she obtained of Mrs. Brand's pale, worn, wildly despairing face—the face of a madwoman as she now perceived, who was not responsible for the deed she did.

Janetta sprang to the window curtains, dragged them down and trampled upon them. Her thick dressing gown, and the woollen shawl that she carried all helped in extinguishing the flame. Her appearance had arrested Mrs. Brand in her terrible work; she paused and began to tremble, as if she knew in some vague way that she was doing what was wrong. The flame had already caught the curtains, which were of a light material, and was creeping up to the woodwork of the old-fashioned bed, singeing and blackening as it went. These, also, Janetta tore down, burning her hands as she did so, and then with her shawl she pressed out the sparks that were beginning to fly dangerously near the sleeping woman. A heavy ewer of water over the mouldering mass of torn muslin and lace completed her task; and by that time Juliet had started from her sleep, and was asking in hysterical accents what was wrong.

Her screams startled the whole household, and the servants came in various stages of dress and undress to know what was the matter. Mrs. Brand had set down her candle and was standing near the door, trembling from head to foot, and apparently so much overcome by the shock as to be unable to answer any question. That was thought very natural. "Poor lady! what a narrow escape! No wonder she was upset," said one of the maids sympathetically, and tried to lead her back to her own room. But Mrs. Brand refused to stir.

Meanwhile Juliet was screaming that she was burning, that the whole house was on fire, that she should die of the shock, and that Wyvis was alone to blame—after her usual fashion of expressing herself wildly when she was suffering from any sort of excitement of mind.

"You are quite safe now," Janetta said at last, rather sharply. "The fire is out: it was never very much. Come into my room: the bed may be cold and damp now, and the smoke will make you cough."

She was right; the lingering clouds of smoke were producing unpleasant effects on the throat and lungs of Mrs. Wyvis Brand; and she was glad to be half led, half carried, by two of the servants into Janetta's room. And no sooner was she laid in Janetta's bed than a little white figure rushed out of another room and flew towards her, crying out:

"Mother! Mother! You are not hurt?"

She was not hurt, but she was shaken and out of breath, and Julian's caresses were not altogether opportune. Still she did not seem to be vexed by them. Perhaps they were too rare to be unwelcome. She let him creep into bed beside her, and lay with her arm round him as if he were still a baby at her breast, and then for a time they slept together, mother and child, as they had not slept since the days of Julian's babyhood. For both it may have been a blessed hour. Julian scarcely knew what it was to feel a mother's love; and with Juliet, the softer side of her nature had long been hidden beneath a crust of coldness and selfishness. But those moments of tenderness which a common danger had brought to light would live for ever in Julian's memory.

While these two were sleeping, however, others in the house were busy. As soon as Juliet was out of the room, Janetta turned anxiously to Mrs. Brand. "Come with me, dear," she said. "Come back to your room. You will catch cold."

She felt no repulsion, nothing but a great pity for the hapless woman whose nature was not strong enough to bear the strain to which it had been subjected, and she wished, above all things, to keep secret the origin of the fire. If Mrs. Brand would but be silent, she did not think that Juliet could fathom the secret, but she was not sure that poor Mrs. Brand would not betray herself. At present, she showed no signs of understanding what had been said to her.

"She is quite upset by the shock," said the maid who had previously spoken. "And no wonder. And oh! Miss Colwyn, don't you know how burnt your hands are! You must have them seen to, I'm sure."

"Never mind my hands, I don't feel them," said Janetta brusquely. "Help me to get Mrs. Brand to her room, and then send for a doctor. Go to Dr. Burroughs, he will know what to do. I want him here as quickly as possible. And bring me some oil and cotton wool."

The servants looked at one another, astonished at the strangeness of her tone. But they were fond of her and always did her bidding gladly, so they performed her behest, and helped her to lead Mrs. Brand, who was now perfectly passive in their hands, into her own room.

But when she was there, the old butler returned to knock at the door and ask to speak to Miss Colwyn alone. Janetta came out, with a feeling of curious fear. She held the handle of the door as he spoke to her.

"I beg pardon, m'm," he said deferentially, "but hadn't I better keep them gossiping maids out of the room over there?"

Janetta looked into his face, and saw that he more than suspected the truth.

"What do you mean?" she asked.

"The window curtains are burned, m'm, and the bed-curtains; also the bed clothes in different places, and one or two other light articles about the room. It is easy to see that it was not exactly an accident, m'm."

Then, seeing Janetta's color change, he added kindly, "But there's no call for you to feel afraid, m'm. We've all known as the poor lady's been going off her head for a good long time, and this is only perhaps what might have been expected, seeing what her feelings are. You leave it all to me, and just keep her quiet, m'm; I'll see to the room, and nobody else shall put their foot into it. The master will be home this morning, I hope and trust."

He hobbled away, and Janetta went back to Mrs. Brand. The reaction was setting in; her own hurts had not been attended to, and were beginning to give her a good deal of pain; and she was conscious of sickness and faintness as well as fatigue. A great dread of Mrs. Brand's next words and actions was also coming over her.

But for the present, at least, she need not have been afraid! Mrs. Brand was lying on the bed in a kind of stupor: her eyes were only half-open; her hands were very cold.

Janetta did her best to warm and comfort her physically; and then, finding that she seemed to sleep more naturally, she got her hands bound up and sat down to await the coming of the doctor.

But she was not destined to wait in idleness very long. She was summoned to Mrs. Wyvis Brand, who had awakened suddenly from her sleep and was coughing violently. Little Julian had to be hastily sent back to his own room, for his mother's cough was dangerous as well as distressing to her, and Janetta was anxious that he should not witness what might prove to be a painful sight.

And she was not far wrong. For the violent cough produced on this occasion one of its most serious results. The shock, the exposure, the exertion, had proved almost too much for Mrs. Wyvis Brand's strength. She ruptured a blood-vessel just as the doctor entered the house; and all that he could do was to check the bleeding with ice, and enjoin perfect quiet and repose. And when he had seen her, he had to hear from Janetta the story of that terrible night. She felt that it was wise to trust Dr. Burroughs entirely, and she told him, in outline, the whole story of Mrs. Brand's depression of spirits, and of her evident half-mad notion that she might gain Wyvis' forgiveness for her past mistakes by some deed that would set him free from his unloved wife, and enable him to lead a happier life in the future.

The doctor shook his head when he saw his patient. "It is just as well for her, perhaps," he said afterwards, "but it is sad for her son and for those who love her—if any one does! She will probably not recover. She is in a state of complete prostration; and she will most likely slip away in sleep."

"Oh, I am sorry," said Janetta, with tears in her eyes.

The doctor looked at her kindly. "You need not be sorry for her, my dear. She is best out of a world which she was not fitted to cope with. You should not wish her to stay."

"It will be so sad for Wyvis, when he comes home to-day," murmured Janetta, her lip trembling.

"He is coming to-day, is he? Early this morning? I will stay with you, if you like."

Janetta was glad of the offer, although it gave her an uneasy feeling that the end was nearer than she thought.

CHAPTER XXXVIII
THE LAST SCENE

"She does not know you," Dr. Burroughs said, when, a few hours later, Wyvis bent over his mother's pillow and looked into her quiet, care-lined face.

"Will she never know me?" asked the young man in a tone of deep distress. "My poor mother! I must tell her how sorry I am for the pain that I have often given her."

"She may be conscious for a few minutes by-and-bye," the doctor said. "But consciousness will only show that the end is near."

There was a silence in the room. Mrs. Brand had now lain in a stupor for many hours. Wyvis had been greeted on his arrival with sad news indeed: his mother and wife were seriously ill, and the doctor acknowledged that he did not think Mrs. Brand likely to live for many hours.

Wyvis had not been allowed to enter his wife's room, Juliet had to be kept very quiet, lest the hæmorrhage should return. He was almost glad of the respite; he dreaded the meeting, and he was anxious to bestow all his time upon his mother. Janetta had told him something about what had passed; he had heard an outline, but only an outline, of the sad story, and it must be confessed that as yet he could not understand it. It was perhaps difficult for a man to fathom the depths of a woman's morbid misery, or of a doating mother's passionate and unreasonable love. He grieved, however, over what was somewhat incomprehensible to him, and he thought once or twice with a sudden sense of comfort that Janetta would explain, Janetta would make him understand. He looked round for her when this idea occurred to him; but she was not in the room. She did not like to intrude upon what might be the last interview between mother and son, for she was firmly persuaded that Mrs. Brand would recover consciousness, and would tell Wyvis in her own way something of what she had thought and felt; but she was not far off, and when Wyvis sent her a peremptory message to the effect that she was wanted, she came at once and took up her position with him as watcher beside his mother's bed.

Janetta was right. Mrs. Brand's eyes opened at last, and rested on Wyvis' face with a look of recognition. She smiled a little, and seemed pleased that he was there. It was plain that for the moment she had quite forgotten the events of the last few hours, and the first words that she spoke proved that the immediate past had completely faded from her mind.

"Wyvis!" she faltered. "Are you back again, dear? And is—is your father with you?"

"I am here, mother," Wyvis answered. He could say nothing more.

"But your father——"

Then something—a gleam of reawakening memory—seemed to trouble her; she looked round the room, knitted her brows anxiously, and murmured a few words that Wyvis could not hear.

"I remember now," she said, in a stronger voice. "I wanted something—I thought it was your father, but it was something quite different—I wanted your forgiveness, Wyvis."

"Mother, mother, don't speak in that way," cried her son. "Have you not suffered enough to expiate *any* mistake?"

"Any mistake, perhaps, not any sin," said his mother feebly. "Now that I am old and dying, I call things by their right names. I did you a wrong, and I did Cuthbert a wrong, and I am sorry now."

"It is all past," said Wyvis softly. "It does not matter now."

"You forgive me for my part in it? You do not hate me?"

"Mother! Have I been cold to you then? I have loved you all the time, and never blamed you in my heart."

"You said that I was to blame."

"But I did not mean it. I never thought that you would take an idle word of mine so seriously, mother. Forgive me, and believe me that I would not have given you pain for the world if I had thought, if I had only thought that it would hurt you so much!"

His mother smiled faintly, and closed her eyes for a moment, as if the exertion of speaking had been too much for her; but, after a short pause, she started suddenly, and opened her eyes with a look of extreme terror.

"What is it," she said. "What have I done? Where is she?"

"Who, mother?"

"Your wife, Juliet. What did I do? Is she dead? The fire—the fire——"

A True Friend | 273

Wyvis looked helplessly round for Janetta. He could not answer: he did not know how to calm his mother's rapidly increasing excitement. Janetta came forward and bent over the pillow.

"No, Juliet is not dead. She is in her room; you must not trouble yourself about her," she said.

Mrs. Brand's eyes were fixed apprehensively on Janetta's face.

"Tell me what I did," she said in a loud whisper.

It was difficult to answer. Wyvis hid his face in a sort of desperation. He wondered what Janetta was going to say, and listened in amazement to her first words.

"You were ill," said Janetta clearly. "You did not know what you were doing, and you set fire to the curtains in her room. Nobody was hurt, and we all understand that you would have been very sorry to harm anybody. It is all right, dear grandmother, and you must remember that you were not responsible for what you were doing then."

The boldness of her answer filed Wyvis with admiration. He knew that he—manlike—would have temporized and tried in vain to deny the truth, it was far wiser for Janetta to acknowledge and explain the facts. Mrs. Brand pressed the girl's hand and looked fearfully in her face.

"She—she was not burned?"

"Not at all."

"Stoop down," said Mrs. Brand. "Lower. Close to my face. There—listen to me. I meant to kill her. Do you understand? I meant to set the place on fire and let her burn. I thought she deserved it for making my boy miserable."

Wyvis started up, and turned his back to the bed. It was impossible for him to hear the confession with equanimity. But Janetta still hung over the pillow, caressing the dying woman, and looking tenderly into her face.

"Yes, you thought so then—I understand," she said. "But that was because of your illness. You do not think so now."

"Yes," said Mrs. Brand, in the same loud, hoarse whisper. "I think so now."

Then Janetta was silent for a minute or two. The black, ghastly look in Mrs. Brand's wide-open eyes disconcerted her. She scarcely knew what to say.

"I have always hated her. I hate her now," said Wyvis' mother. "She has done me no harm; no. But she has injured my boy; she made his life miserable, and I cannot forgive her for that."

"If Wyvis forgives her," said Janetta gently, "can you not forgive her too?"

"Wyvis does not forgive her for making him unhappy," said Mrs. Brand.

"Wyvis,"—Janetta looked round at him. She could not see his face. He was standing with his face to the window and his back to the bed. "Wyvis, you have come back to your wife: does not that show that you are willing to forget the past and to make a fresh beginning. Tell your mother so, Cousin Wyvis."

He turned round slowly, and looked at her, not at his mother, as he replied:

"Yes, I am willing to begin again," he said. "I never wished her any harm."

"Then, you will forgive her—for Wyvis' sake? For Julian's sake?" said Janetta.

A strange contraction of the features altered Mrs. Brand's face for a moment: her breath came with difficulty and her lips turned white.

"I forgive," she said at last, in broken tones. "I cannot quite forget. But I do not want—now—to harm her. It was but for a time—when my head was bad."

"We know, we know," said Janetta eagerly. "We understand. Wyvis, tell her that *you* understand too."

She looked at him insistently, and he returned the look. Their eyes said a good deal to each other in a second's space of time. In hers there was tenderness, expostulation, entreaty; in his some shade of mingled horror and regret. But he yielded his will to hers, thinking it nobler than his own; and, turning to his mother, he stooped and kissed her on the forehead.

"I understand, mother. Janetta has made me understand."

"Janetta—it is always Janetta we have to thank," his mother murmured feebly. "It was for Janetta as well as for you that I did it. Wyvis—but it is no use now. And, God forgive me, I did not know what I did."

She sank into silence and spoke no more for the next few hours. Her life was quietly ebbing away. Towards midnight, she opened her eyes and spoke again.

"Janetta—Wyvis," she said softly, and then the last moment came. Her eyelids drooped, her head fell aside upon the pillow. There was no more for her to say or do. Poor Mary Brand's long trial had come to an end at last.

Juliet was not told of Mrs. Brand's death until after the funeral, as it was feared that the news might unduly excite her. As it was, she gave a hoarse little scream when she heard it, and asked, with every appearance of horror, whether there was really "a body" in the house. On being informed by Janetta that "the body" had been removed, she became immediately tranquil, and remarked confidentially that she was "not sorry, after all, for the old lady's death: it was such a bore to have one's husband's mother in the house." Then she became silent and thoughtful, and Janetta wondered whether some kindlier feeling were not mixing itself with her self-gratulation. But presently Mrs. Wyvis Brand broke forth:

"Look here, I must say this, if I die for it. You know the night when my room was on fire. Well, now tell me true: wasn't my mother-in-law to blame for it?"

Janetta looked at her in speechless dismay. She had no trust in Juliet's disposition: she did not know whether she might revile Mrs. Brand bitterly, or be touched by an account of her mental suffering. Wyvis, however, had recommended her to tell his wife as much of the truth as seemed necessary; "because, if you don't," he said, "she is quite sharp enough to find it out for herself. So if she has any suspicion, tell her something. Anything is better than nothing in such a case."

And Janetta, taking her courage in both hands, so to speak, answered courageously:

"May I speak frankly to you, Juliet?" For Mrs. Wyvis Brand had insisted that Janetta should always call her by her Christian name.

"Of course you may. What is it?"

"It is about Mrs. Brand. You must have known that for some time she had been very weak and feeble. Her mind was giving way. Indeed, she was far worse than we ever imagined, and she was not sufficiently watched. On that night, it was she whom you saw, and it was she who set fire to the curtains; but you must remember, Juliet, that she was not in her right mind."

"Why, I might have been burned alive in my bed," cried Juliet—an exclamation so thoroughly characteristic that Janetta could hardly forbear to smile. Mrs. Wyvis Brand looked terribly shocked and disconcerted, and it was after a pause that she collected herself sufficiently to say in her usual rapid manner:

"You may say what you like about her being mad; but Mrs. Brand knew very well what she was doing. She always hated me, and she wanted to get me out of the way."

"Oh, Juliet, don't say so," entreated Janetta.

"But I do say so, and I will say so, and I have reason on my side. She hated me like poison, and she loved you dearly. Don't you see what she wanted? She would have liked you to take my place."

"If you say such things, Juliet——"

"You'll go out of the room, won't you, my dear? Why," said Juliet, with a hard laugh in which there was very little mirth, "you don't suppose I mind? I have known long enough that she thought bad things of me. Don't you remember the name you called me when you thought I wanted Julian? You had learnt every one of them from her, you know you had. Oh, you needn't apologize. I understand the matter perfectly. I bear no malice either against her or you, though I don't know that I am quite the black sheep that you both took me to be."

"I am sorry if I was unjust," said Janetta slowly. "But all that I meant amounts to one thing—that you did not make my Cousin Wyvis very happy."

"Ah, and that's the chief thing, isn't it?" said Juliet, with a keen look. "Well, don't be frightened, I'm going to change my ways. I've had a warning if anybody ever had; and I'm not going to get myself turned out of house and home. If Wyvis will stick to me, I'll stick to him; and I can't say more than that. I should like to see him now."

"Now, Juliet?" said Janetta, rather aghast at the idea. The meeting between husband and wife had not yet taken place, and Janetta shrank sensitively from the notion that Juliet might inflict fresh pain on Wyvis on the very day of his mother's funeral. But Mrs. Wyvis Brand insisted, and her husband was summoned to the room.

"You needn't go away, Janetta," said Juliet imperatively. "I want you as a witness. Well, Wyvis, here I am, and I hope you are glad to see me."

She lifted herself a little from the couch on which she lay, and looked at him defiantly. Janetta could see that he was shocked at the sight of her wasted outlines, her hectic color, the unhealthy brilliance of her eyes; and it was this sight, perhaps, that caused him to say gently:

"I am sorry not to see you looking better."

"The politest speech he has made me for years," she said, laughing. "Well, half a loaf is better than no bread. We didn't hit it off exactly the last time we saw each other, did we? Suppose we try again: should we get on any better, do you think?"

"We might try," said Wyvis slowly.

He was pale and grave, but, as she saw, not unwilling to make peace.

"All right," she said, holding out her hand to him with easy, audacious grace, "let us try then. I own I was aggravating—own in your turn that you were tyrannical now and then! You witness that he owns up, Janetta—why, the girl's gone! Never mind: give me a kiss now we are alone, Wyvis, and take me to the Riviera to-morrow if you want to save my life."

Wyvis kissed his wife and promised to do what she asked him, but he did not look as if he expected to have an easy task.

CHAPTER XXXIX
MAKING AMENDS

"It is pleasant to be home again," said Margaret.

For two years she had not seen the Court. For two year's she and her parents had roamed over the world, spending a winter in Egypt or Italy, a summer in Norway, a spring or autumn at Biarritz, or Pau, or some other resort of wealthy and idle Englishmen. These wanderings had been begun with the laudable object of weaning Margaret's heart away from Wyvis Brand, but they had been continued long after Margaret's errant fancy had been chided back to its wonted resting place. The habit of wandering easily grows, and the two years had slipped away so pleasantly that it was with a feeling almost of surprise that the Adairs reckoned up the time that had elapsed since they left England. Then Margaret had a touch of fever, and began to pine for her home; and, as her will was still law (in all minor points, at least), her parents at once turned homeward, and arrived at Helmsley Court in the month of May, when the woods and gardens were at their loveliest, bright with flowers, and verdant with the exquisite green of the spring foliage, before it becomes dusty and faded in the summer-heat.

"It is pleasant to be at home again," said Margaret, standing at the door of the conservatory one fair May morning and looking at the great sweep of green sward before her, where elm and beech trees made a charming shade, and beds of brightly-tinted flowers dotted the grass at intervals. "I was so tired of foreign towns."

"Were you, dear? You did not say so until lately," said Lady Caroline.

"I did not want to bring you and papa home until you were ready to come," said Margaret gently.

"Dear child. And you have lost your roses. English country air will soon bring them back."

"I never had much color, mama," said Margaret gravely. It was almost as though she were not quite well pleased by the remark.

She moved away from the door, and Lady Caroline's eyes followed her with a solicitude which had more anxiety and less pride than they used to show. For Margaret had altered during the last few months. She had grown more slender, more pale than ever, and a certain languor was perceptible in her movements and the expression of her beautiful eyes. She was not less fair, perhaps, than she had been before; and the ethereal character of her beauty had only been increased by time. Lady Caroline had been seriously distressed lately by the comments made by her acquaintances upon Margaret's appearance. "Very delicate, surely," said one. "Do you think that your daughter is consumptive?" said another. "She would be so very pretty if she looked stronger," remarked a third. Now these were not precisely the remarks that Lady Caroline liked her friends to make.

She could not quite understand her daughter. Margaret had of late become more and more reticent. She was always gentle, always caressing, but she was not expansive. Something was amiss with her spirits or her health: nobody could exactly say what it was. Even her father discovered at last that she did not seem well; but, although he grumbled and fidgeted about it, he did not know how to suggest a remedy. Lady Caroline hoped that the return to England would prove efficacious in restoring the girl's health and spirits, and she was encouraged by hearing Margaret express her pleasure in her English home. But she felt uneasily that she was not quite sure as to what was wrong.

"People are beginning to call very quickly," she said, looking at some cards that lay in a little silver tray. "The Bevans have been here, Margaret."

"Have they? When we were out yesterday, I suppose?"

"Yes. And the Accringtons, and—oh, ah, yes—two or three other people."

"Who, mamma?" said Margaret, her attention immediately attracted by her mother's hesitation. She turned away from the door and entered the morning-room as she spoke.

"Oh, only Lady Ashley, dear," said Lady Caroline smoothly. She had quite recovered her self-possession by this time.

"And Sir Philip Ashley," said Margaret, with equal calmness, as she glanced at the cards in the little silver dish. But the lovely color flushed up into her cheeks, and as she stood with her eyes cast down, still fingering the cards, her face assumed the tint of the deepest rose-carnation.

"Is that the reason?" thought Lady Caroline, with a sudden little thrill of fear and astonishment. "Surely not! After all this time—and after dismissing him so summarily! Well, there is no accounting for girls' tastes."

She said aloud:

"We ought to return these calls pretty soon, I think. With such old friends it would be nice to go within the week. Do you not agree with me, love?"

"Yes, mamma," said, Margaret dutifully.

"Shall we go to-morrow then? To the Bevans first, and then to the Ashleys?"

Margaret hesitated. "The Accringtons live nearer the Bevans than Lady Ashley," she said. "You might call on Lady Ashley next day, mamma."

"Yes, darling," said Lady Caroline. She was reassured. She certainly did not want Margaret to show any alacrity in seeking out the Ashleys, and she hoped that that tell-tale blush had been due to mere maiden modesty and not to any warmer feeling, which would probably be completely thrown away upon Philip Ashley, who was not the man to offer himself a second time to a woman who had once refused him.

She noticed, however, that Margaret showed no other sign of interest in Sir Philip and his mother; that she did not ask for any account of the call paid, without her, by Lady Caroline a day or two later. Indeed, she turned away and talked to Alicia Stone while Lady Caroline was telling Mr. Adair of the visits that she had made. So the mother was once more reassured.

She was made uneasy again by an item of news that reached her ear soon after her return home. "Mr. Brand is coming back," said Mrs. Accrington to her, with a meaning smile. "I hear that there are great preparations at the Red House. His wife is dead, you know."

"Indeed," said Lady Caroline, stiffly.

"Yes, died at Nice last spring or summer, I forget which; I suppose he means to settle at home now. They say he's quite a changed character."

"I am glad to hear it," said Lady Caroline.

She felt annoyed as well as anxious. Was it possible that Margaret knew that Wyvis Brand was coming home? In spite of the inveterate habit of caressing Margaret and making soft speeches, in spite also of the very real love that she had for her daughter, Lady Caroline did not altogether trust her. Margaret had once or twice disappointed her too much.

"His little boy," continued Mrs. Accrington in a conversational tone, "has been spending the time with Mr. Brand's younger brother and his wife, one of the Colwyn girls, wasn't she? And the eldest Colwyn girl, the one who sang, has been acting as his governess. She used to be companion to old Mrs. Brand you know."

"I remember," said Lady Caroline, and managed to change the subject.

She would have liked to question Margaret, but she did not dare. She watched her carefully for the next few days, and she was not satisfied. Margaret was nervous and uneasy, as she had been about the time when Wyvis Brand made his indiscreet proposal for her hand; it seemed to Lady Caroline that she was watching for some person to arrive—some person who never came. Who was the person for whom she watched? so Lady Caroline asked herself. But she dared not question Margaret.

She noticed, too, that Mr. Adair looked once or twice at his daughter in a curiously doubtful way, as if he were puzzled or distressed. And one day he said musingly:

"It is surely time for Margaret to be getting married, is it not?"

"Somebody has been saying so to you," said Lady Caroline, with less urbanity than usual.

"No, no, only Isabel; she wrote this morning expressing some surprise at not having heard that Margaret was engaged before now. I suppose," Mr. Adair hesitated a little, "I suppose she *will* marry?"

"Reginald, what an idea! Of course Margaret will marry, and marry brilliantly."

"I am not so sure of that," said Mr. Adair, who seemed to be in low spirits. "Look at my two sisters, and lots of other girls. How many men has Margaret refused? She will take up with some crooked stick at last."

He went out without waiting for his wife's reply. Lady Caroline, harassed in mind and considerably weakened of late in body, sat still and shed a few silent tears. She was angry with him, and yet she shared his apprehensions. Was it possible that their lovely Margaret was turning out a social failure? To have Margaret at home, fading, ageing, growing into an old maid like the sisters of Reginald Adair, that was not to be thought of for a moment.

Meanwhile Margaret was taking her fate in her own hands.

She was at that very moment standing in the conservatory opposite a tall, dark man, who, hat in hand, looked at her expectantly as if he wished her to open the conversation. She had never made a fairer picture than she did just then. She was dressed in white, and the exquisite fairness of her head and face was thrown into strong relief by the dark background of fronded fern and thickly matted creeper with which the wall behind her was overgrown. Her face was slightly bent, and her hands hung clasped before her. To her visitor, who was indeed Sir Philip Ashley, she appeared more beautiful than ever. But his eye, as it rested upon her, though attentive, was indifferent and cold.

"You sent for me, I think?" he said politely, finding that she did not speak.

"Yes." Margaret's voice was very low. "I hope you did not mind my writing that little note?"

"Mind? Not at all. If there is anything I can do for you— —?"

"It is not that I want you to do anything," said Margaret, whose self-possession, not easily disturbed, was now returning to her. "It was simply that I had something to say."

Sir Philip bowed. His role was that of a listener, it appeared.

"When I was in England before," Margaret went on, this time with some effort, "you found fault with me— —"

"Presumption on my part, I am sure," said Sir Philip, smiling a little. "Such a thing will certainly not occur again."

"Oh please hear me," said Margaret, rather hurriedly. "Please listen seriously—I am very serious, and I want you to hear what I have to say."

"I will listen," said Sir Philip, gravely; he turned aside a little, and looked at the flowers as she spoke.

"I want to tell you that you were right about Janetta Colwyn. The more I have thought of it, the more sure I have been that you were right. I ought not to have been angry when you asked me to prevent people from misjudging her. I ought to have written to Miss Polehampton and set things straight."

Sir Philip made an inarticulate sound of assent. She paused for a moment, and then went on pleadingly.

"It's such a long time ago now that I do not know what to do. I cannot ask mamma. She never liked Janetta—she never was just to her. I do not even know where Janetta is, nor whether I can do anything to help her. Do you know?"

"I know where she is. At the Red House just now, with Mr. and Mrs. Cuthbert Brand."

"Then—what shall I do?" said Margaret, more urgently. "Would it be of any use if I wrote to Miss Polehampton or anyone about her now? I will do anything I can to help her—anything you advise."

Sir Philip changed his position, as if he were slightly impatient.

"I do not know that there is anything to be done for Miss Colwyn at present," he replied. "She is in a very good position, and I do not think she wants material help. Of course, if you were to see her and tell her that you regret the manifest injustice with which she was treated on more than one occasion, I dare say she would be glad, and that such an acknowledgment from you would draw out the sting from much that is past and gone. I think that this is all you can do."

"I will do it," said Margaret submissively. "I will tell her that I am sorry."

"You will do well," replied Sir Philip in a kinder tone. "I am only sorry that you did not see things differently when we spoke of the matter before."

"I am older now, I have thought more. I have reflected on what you said," murmured Margaret.

"You have done my poor words much honor," said he, with a slight cold smile. "And I am glad to think that the breach in your friendship is healed. Miss Colwyn is a true and loyal friend—I could not wish you a better. I shall feel some pleasure in the thought, when I am far from England, that you have her for your friend once more."

"Far from England"—Margaret repeated the words with paling lips.

"Did you not know? I have accepted a post in Victoria. I shall be out for five years at least. So great a field of usefulness seems open to me there that I did not know how to refuse it."

Margaret was mute for a time. Then, with a tremendous effort, she put another question. "You go—alone?" she said.

Sir Philip did not look at her.

"No," he said, kicking a small pebble off the tesselated pavement with the toe of his boot, and apparently taking the greatest interest in its ultimate fate, "no, I don't go quite alone. I am taking with me my secretary—and—my wife. I suppose you know that next week I am going to marry Miss Adela Smithies, daughter of Smithies the great brewer? We sail ten days later."

CHAPTER XL
MY FAITHFUL JANET

"Good blood," they say, "does not lie." Margaret was true to her traditions. She did not faint, she did not weep, over what was complete ruin to her expectations, if not of her hopes. She held her head a little more erect than usual, and looked Sir Philip quietly in the face.

"I am very glad to hear it," she said—it was a very excusable lie, perhaps. "I hope you will be happy."

Strange to say, her calmness robbed Sir Philip of his self-possession. He flushed hotly and looked away, thinking of some words that he had spoken many months ago to Margaret's mother—a sort of promise to be "always ready" if Margaret should ever change her mind. Had she changed it now? But she was not going to leave him in doubt upon this point.

"You have only just forestalled a similar announcement on my part," she said, smiling bravely. "I dare say you will hear all about it soon—and I hope that you will wish me joy."

He looked up with evident relief.

"I am exceedingly glad. I may congratulate you then?"

"Thank you. Yes, we may congratulate each other."

She still smiled—rather strangely, as he thought. He wondered who the "happy man" could be? But of that, to tell the truth, Margaret was as ignorant as he. She had invented her little tale of an engagement in self-defence.

"Ah, Margaret," he said, with a sudden impulse of affection, "if only you could have seen as I saw—two years ago!"

"But that was impossible," she answered quietly. "And I think it would be undesirable also. I wanted you to know, however, that I agree with you about Janetta—I think that you were right."

"And you have nothing more to tell me?"

For the moment he was willing to throw up his appointment in Australia, to fly from the wealthy and sensible Miss Adela Smithies and incur any odium, any disappointment, and any shame, if only Margaret Adair would own that she loved him and consent to be his wife. For, although he liked and esteemed Miss Smithies, who was a rather plain-faced girl with a large fortune, he was perfectly conscious that Margaret had been the one love of his life. But Margaret was on her guard.

"To tell you?" she echoed, as if in mild surprise. "Why no, I think not, Sir Philip. Except, perhaps, to ask you not to speak—for the present, at least—of my own prospects, they are not yet generally known, and I do not want them mentioned just now."

"Certainly. I will respect your confidence," said Sir Philip. He felt ashamed of that momentary aberration. Adela was a very suitable wife for him, and he could not think without remorse that he had ever proposed to himself to be untrue to her. How fortunate, he reflected, that Margaret did not seem to care!

"Will you come in?" she said graciously. "Mamma will be so pleased to see you, and she will be glad to congratulate you on your good fortune."

"Thank you very much, but I fear I must be off. I am very busy, and I really have scarcely any time to spare."

"I must thank you all the more for giving me some of your valuable time," said Margaret sweetly. "Must you go?"

"I really must. And—" as he held out his hand—"we are friends, then, from henceforth?"

"Oh, of course we are," she answered. But her eyes were strangely cold, and the smile upon her lips was conventional and frosty. The hand that he held in his own was cold, too, and somewhat limp and flabby.

"I am so glad," he said, growing warmer as she grew cold, "that you have resolved to renew your acquaintance with Miss Colwyn. It is what I should have expected from your generous nature, and it shows that what I always—always thought of you was true."

"Please do not say so," said Margaret. She came very near being natural in that moment. She had a choking sensation in her throat, and her eyes smarted with unshed tears. But her training stood her in good stead. "It is very kind of you to be so complimentary," she went on with a light little laugh. "And I hope that I shall find Janetta as nice as she used to be. Good-bye. *Bon voyage.*"

"I wish you every happiness," he said with a warm clasp of her hand and a long grave look into her beautiful face; and then he went away and Margaret was left alone.

She stole up to her room almost stealthily, and locked the door. She hoped that no one had seen Sir Philip come and go—that her mother would not question her, or remark on the length of his visit. She was thoroughly frightened and ashamed to think of what she had done. She had been as near as possible to making Sir Philip what would virtually have been an offer of marriage. What an awful thought! And what a narrow escape! For of course he would have had to refuse her, and she—what could she have done then? She would never have borne the mortification. As it was, she hoped that Sir Philip would accept the explanation of the little note of summons which she had despatched to him that morning, and would never inquire what her secret motive had been in writing it.

She set herself to consider the situation. She did not love Sir Philip. She was not capable of a great deal of love, and all that she had been capable of she had given to Wyvis Brand. But the years of girlhood in her father's house were beginning to pall upon her. She was conscious of a slight waning of her beauty, of a perceptible diminution in the attentions which she received, and the admiration that she excited. It had occurred to her lately, as it had occurred to her parents, that she ought to think seriously of getting married. The notion of spinsterhood was odious to Margaret Adair. And Sir Philip Ashley would have been, as her mother used to say, so *suitable* a man for her to marry! Margaret saw it now.

She wept a few quiet tears for her lost hopes, and then she arrayed herself becomingly, and, with a look of purpose on her face, went down to tea.

"Do you know, mamma," she said, "that Sir Philip Ashley is going to marry Miss Smithies, the great brewer's daughter, and that he has accepted a post in Victoria?"

"Margaret!"

"It is quite true, mamma, he told me so himself. Why need you look surprised? We could hardly expect," said Margaret, with a pretty smile, "that Sir Philip should always remain unmarried for my sake."

"It is rather sudden, surely!"

"Oh, I don't think so. By the bye, mamma, shall we not soon feel a little dull if we are here all alone? It would be very nice to fill the house with guests and have a little gaiety. Perhaps—" with a faint but charming blush—"Lord Southbourne would come if he were asked."

Lord Southbourne was an exceptionable viscount with weak brains and a large rent-roll whom Margaret had refused six months before.

"I am sure he would, my darling; I will ask him," said Lady Caroline, with great satisfaction. And she noticed that Margaret's watch for an unknown visitor had now come to its natural end.

It was not more than a month later in the year when Janetta Colwyn, walking in the plantation near the Red House, came face to face with a man who was leaning against the trunk of a fir-tree, and had been waiting for her to approach. She looked astonished; but he was calm, though he smiled with pleasure, and held out his hands.

"Well, Janetta!"

"Wyvis! You have come home at last!"

"At last."

"You have not been up to the house yet?"

"No, I was standing here wishing that I could see you first of all; and, just as I wished it, you came in sight. I take it as a good omen."

"I am glad you are back," said Janetta earnestly.

"Are you? Really? And why?"

"Oh, for many reasons. The estate wants you, for one thing," said Janetta, coloring a little, "and Julian wants you——"

"Don't you want me at all, Janetta?"

"Everybody wants you, so I do, too."

"Tell me more about everybody and everybody's wants. How is Julian?"

"Very well, indeed, and longing to see you before he goes to school."

"Ah yes, poor little man. How does he like the idea of school?"

"Pretty well."

"And how do you like the idea of his going?"

Janetta's face fell. "I am sure it is good for him," she said rather wistfully.

"But not so good for you. What are you going to do? Shall you live with Mrs. Burroughs, Janet?"

"No, indeed; I think I shall take lodgings in London, and give lessons. I have saved money during the last few months," said Janetta with something between a tear in the eye and a smile on the lip, "so that I shall be able to live even if I get no pupils at first."

"And shall you like that?"

She looked at him for a moment without replying, and then said cheerfully:

"I shall not like it if I get no pupils."

"And how are Cuthbert and Nora?"

"Absorbed in baby-worship," said Janetta. "You will be expected to fall down and worship also. And your little niece is really very pretty."

Wyvis shook his head. "Babies are all exactly alike to me, so you had better instruct me beforehand in what I ought to say. And what about our neighbors, Janet? Are the Adairs at home?"

"Yes," said Janetta, with some reserve of tone.

"And the Ashleys?"

"Old Lady Ashley. Sir Philip has married and gone to the Antipodes."

"Married Margaret? I always thought that would be the end of it."

"You are quite wrong. He married a Miss Smithies, a very rich girl, I believe. And Margaret is engaged to a certain Lord Southbourne—who is also very rich, I believe."

"Little Southbourne!" exclaimed Wyvis, with a sudden burst of laughter. "You don't say so! I used to know him at Monaco. Oh, there's no harm in little South; only he isn't very bright."

"I am sorry for Margaret," said Janetta.

"Oh she will be perfectly happy. She will always move in her own circle of society, and that is paradise for Margaret."

"You are very hard on her, Wyvis," Janetta said, reprovingly. "She is capable of higher things than you believe."

"Capable! Oh, she may be *capable* of anything," said Wyvis, "but she does not do the things that she is capable of doing."

"At any rate she is very kind to me now. She wrote to me a few days ago, and told me that she was sorry for our past misunderstanding. And she asked me to go and stay with her when she was married to Lord Southbourne and had a house of her own."

"Are you sure that she did not add that it would be such an advantage to you?"

"Of course she did not." But Janetta blushed guiltily, nevertheless.

"And did you promise to accept the invitation?"

She smiled and shook her head.

"I thought you were such a devoted friend of hers!"

"I always tried to be a true friend to her. But you know I think, Wyvis, that some people have not got it in their nature to be true friends to anyone. And perhaps it was not—quite—in Margaret's nature."

"I agree with you," said Wyvis, more gravely than he had spoken hitherto. "She has not your depth of affection, Janetta—your strength of will. You have been a very true and loyal friend to those you have loved."

Janetta turned away her face. Something in his words touched her very keenly. After a pause, Wyvis spoke again.

"I have had reason since I saw you last to know the value of your friendship," he said seriously. "I want to speak to you for a moment, Janetta, before we join the others, about my poor Juliet. I had not, as you know, very many months with her after we left England. But during those few months I became aware that she was a different creature from the woman I had known in earlier days. She showed me that she had a heart—that she loved me and our boy after all—and died craving my forgiveness, poor soul (though God knows that I needed hers more than she needed mine), for the coldness she had often shown me. And she said, Janetta, that *you* had taught her what love meant, and she charged me to tell you that your lessons had not been in vain."

Janetta looked up with swimming eyes. "Poor Juliet! I am glad that she said that."

"She is at peace now," said Wyvis, in a lower voice, "and the happiness of her later days is due to you. But how much is not due to you, Janetta! Your magic power seemed to change my poor wife's very nature: it has made my child happy: it gave all possible comfort to my mother on her dying bed—and what it has done for me no words can ever tell! No one has been to me what you have been, Janetta; the good angel of my life, always inspiring and encouraging, always ready to give me hope and strength and courage in my hours of despair."

"You must not say so: I have done nothing," she said, but she let her hand lie unresistingly between his own, as he took it and pressed it tenderly.

"Have you not? Then I have been woefully mistaken. And it has come across me strangely, Janetta, of late, that of all the losses I have had, one of the greatest is the loss of my kinship with you. No doubt you have thought of that: John Wyvis, the ploughman's son, is not your cousin, Wyvis Brand."

"I never remembered it," said Janetta.

"Then I must remind you of it now. I cannot call you Cousin Janet any longer. May I call you something else, dear, so that I may not lose you out of my life? I want you to be something infinitely closer and dearer and sweeter than a cousin, Janetta; will you forgive me all my errors and be my wife?"

And when she had whispered her reply, he took her in his arms and called her, as her father used to call her—

"My faithful Janet!"

And she thought that she had never borne a sweeter name.